CW00518484

VERNON I

RUBIES IN THE DUST

ISBN number 9781521727218

Authors note. This is a work of fiction and while real events are related here it is not a historically accurate work. The mentioned places do exist but the people are fictitious. Rubies are still mined in Mogok, there are still inter-ethnic tensions and poverty in Myanmar as Burma is now called, and the Nats still make their mysterious presence felt in jungle and mountain.

Dedication

Thanks to my wife Catherine for putting up with my seven month mental absence in the jungles of S.E. Asia, and Paul Roy and Gina Gailiunas for their comments on and corrections to the manuscript.

Part One

CHAPTER ONE

Mogok, Central Burma 1960

The girl stood on the veranda over-looking the neglected garden and the front drive that was besieged on
either side by a rampant and untamed vegetation. Her
hands rested listlessly on the rail as she stared out into
the gathering darkness as if seeking something in the
shadows and the mist that rose from the ground like a
ghostly grey tide. She was of mixed race, tall having
inherited her height from her English father, but with the
feminine characteristics of her Burmese mother. Her
face was oval with high cheekbones, large almond
eyes, and a shapely full mouth with the suggestion of a
slight pout. The soft sensuality of her mouth contrasted
with the slight frown and a certain sharp gleam in her
strange blue-green eyes that could on occasions give
her the impression of impatience, or even anger although she felt none of those emotions at the moment.

Her head was uncovered, allowing a cascade of
black hair to fall casually about her shoulders and back,

framing and accentuating the pale amber of her face that seemed to glow in the failing light, for the sun had set a full fifteen minutes ago and in another fifteen it would be dark.

Beyond the concrete drive, cracked and stained from years of hopeless battle with the forces of nature, the gates to the property lay jammed half open, immobile and rusting, crusted with the remains of paint applied years before the girl was born. And beyond the gates was the narrow track that led to the main road and then the town, disappearing into the dark and noisome jungle that lapped against the walls of the garden. The girl's eyes rested on the towers and wheels of the ruined mine a mile or so away in the town, silhouetted against the darkening sky, immobile and unchanging, as they had been for as long as she remembered, an ever present reminder of the mystery and enigma that had dominated her life and her thoughts.

There were days when she grew tired of it all. When the house in the jungle at the end of the track seemed a prison, with her mother the gentle jailer. Tired of days when she hardly spoke, when she saw no one but her mother, when the silence of the daytime seemed to fill her head with voices, questioning, demanding, protesting, and the house and garden bathed in the hard brittle light of a merciless sun, part of a separate and incomprehensible reality.

The nights seemed unending. For when cloud covered moon and stars a total claustrophobic blackness smothered the valley unbroken by light from any artificial source, for there was no electricity after six pm.

As soon as the last daylight faded the jungle awoke. A manic chorus from a multitude of crawling, creeping, jumping, flying things that filled the night with croaks, whistles, buzzing, hissing, chirping; an unearthly cacophony that defied analysis and continued unbroken until the first lightening of the sky over the mountains to the east.

She heard her mother's voice from inside the house calling.

'Sandar, the candles, light the candles.'

She turned away from the veranda, a faint sigh escaping her.

'Yes mother. I come.'

They spoke English together most of the time, only reverting to Burmese on the occasions when their modest vocabulary seemed insufficient. It had always been thus, her mother insisting that as a child and later as she grew older she should be able to converse in the language of her father. Part of the strange story that seemed to Sandar to belong to a past not her own, neither fact not fiction, something in between, for she had never seen her father except in a few fading and yellowing photographs in small wooden frames dotted about the house. There were times, many times where she doubted his continued existence, and even more the possibility of his return to the house, his partner, and the daughter he had never seen and whose existence was unknown to him.

Myitsu, her mother would accept no doubts. Her man would return some day, for had not he promised that when he left, and was he not a man of honour, a man who would never break a promise?

'I'll be back. I swear.' He had whispered to her that night long ago when the sky flickered over the mountains and the sounds of distant gunfire rose and fell. 'Wait for me Myitsu, wait for me.' And then he was gone, the sound of the car engine fading into the distance. And she waited.

His words had a profound effect on Myitsu, the girl of eighteen who had watched her lover disappear into that night so full of sound and terror, leaving her

alone in the big house, newly aware of the life beginning to grow inside her. She clung to her belief as a
priest clings to his creed, defying logic, ignoring what
the world told her...that he was dead, or perhaps worse,
not wanting to return to her. He would return, of that
she was certain, and she would wait, just as long as
she lived and breathed.

Sandar entered the room behind the veranda
where the sparse dark wood furniture stood barely visible in the gloom. She had no need of light to find the
matches and light the four candles of a brass candelabra that was placed in the bay window looking out
over the drive. Every night she would do that, every
night the candles would burn until nearly dawn when
they were finished, guttering briefly before extinction.
Often in the night she would hear her mother's steps as
she entered the room, just below where Sandar slept,
checking the light was still burning, the signal, the hope.
She would stand for a moment in the doorway, a small
slight figure in her long white night-dress looking at the
light, then at the window, black, with the ghost-like reflection of the room and the figure by the door. Then
turning she would make her way back up the stairs to
her room and her bed.

Sandar joined her mother who held a large oil
lamp in her hand in the darkened hallway by the front
door. Wordlessly they went out, down the steps and
along the drive to the useless gates. Just outside the
gates stood the Spirit House, painted a white and gold
that shone and gleamed in the lamplight. The two women removed the small offerings of food and drink left
the previous day, and replaced them with fresh. A half
mango, a peeled orange, a tiny bowl of rice, a glass of
water. Two small red candles were lit and placed on
either side of the offerings and the women made obeisance, with hands together and bowed heads, before

returning to the house that loomed huge and dark, one light burning in the window over the veranda.

The two women shared the task of preparing the evening meal, often a papaya salad made from the fruit of one of the trees in the garden, a little sticky rice with roast chicken, and whatever fruit was in season and available from the garden or the nearby jungle.

After they had eaten Myitzu would retire to her room to lie on her bed and listen to the sounds of the jungle outside her window. Her eyes would close, a smile forming on her lips, and she would dream again. She heard his voice, his laughter, felt his arms about her and the touch of his hands on her body. It was bitter sweet, a salve, a drug, like the opium she smoked from time to time when sleep evaded her and the pain of his absence was too much to bear.

Sandar would go and sit on the veranda, taking an oil lamp and a book with her, but often the book remained unread, and she would pass the hours dreaming her solitary dreams before tiredness drove her to her bed. Then later, when the house was darkened save for the one light in the downstairs window, Jianyu, their old Chinese neighbour would appear noiselessly on the veranda. He would move silently, slowly, to his chair overlooking the front drive, his special chair, where he would spend the night, watching and listening, his old combat knife resting across his knees, until the first hint of dawn over the mountains to the east.

In earlier times, when he first took up his nightly vigil, he would sit on the floor, his legs crossed, his back against the wall, but as he aged, and Myitsu had one night discovered him there, a chair appeared, his chair.

When Sandar was young she had believed, and found a happiness in the sharing of the belief with her mother, but as the years passed and she grew to be a woman, the doubts also grew. She would try to push them aside, loving her mother, her sole family and friend, too much to wish to destroy her life with the impossible and insupportable conclusion that they would never see her father again.

But in spite of her doubts she could not help imagining him. How he looked, what he might think of her, what was the sound of his voice. Would he be rich like westerners she had heard of and seen in pictures in magazines, drive a big car, live in a modern house with servants, a western wife, two children with blonde hair, a well fed dog? No, in her mind she wanted him to return as in the photos, young, clean shaven, unfashionably long shorts, always smiling, and loving her and her mother. To return here, to this his home.

CHAPTER TWO

Mandalay, Burma 1939.

The young man stepped down from the train onto a platform crowded with a fluid, noisy, and colourful mixture of people. There were the Burmese in their longis, Shan villagers in baggy trousers, Karen natives down from the hills and mountains in purple and blue, dark and stately beauties from the Raj, their proud and erect figures swathed in brilliantly coloured flowing silk and chiffon saris showing a glimpse of bare brown flesh about the waist, with velvet eyes, white teeth smiling and the flash of a small diamond set in flaring nostrils. Mon tribesman with elaborate brightly coloured turbans jostled doe-eyed Moslem girls, beautiful and chaste in black hijabs. Boy monks in their dark red robes and brass begging bowls waited patiently for offerings, and dainty Burmese girls with bright sarongs drawn tightly over virginal breasts, the sheerest of silken jackets covering their small brown shoulders.

Mountains of luggage lay about platform often unattended; bamboo cages containing chickens or piglets, Hessian sacks of rice and grain, sheets of raw rubber rolled and tied with raffia and wrapped in banana leaves. Further away he could make out the grey massive form of an elephant moving sedately and carefully, while next to it an old man was driving an emaciated ass loaded with mangoes through the crowd, encouraging it by the frequent application of a bamboo cane to its scarred and skinny backside. Near to the young man a lone Sikh immaculate in the uniform of the British Army of India, bearded and fierce and towering head and shoulders over the throng, moved slowly and imperiously through the crowds, magnificently indifferent to the lesser mortals around him. The air was heavy with the scent of spices, jasmine, sewage and wood smoke. It was furnace hot. It was the end of the line. It was Mandalay.

Julian Drake had his new brown suitcase in one hand and an old black violin case in the other as he struggled though the crowd towards where he imagined the exit from the station might be. He had been told he would be met and driven to his final destination, Mogok, apparently located somewhere far to the north, by an employee of the mine. He was a young man of above medium height wearing a lightweight tropical suit that appeared rather rumpled from the long train journey from Rangoon. His hair, a dusty blonde, and his clear and intense blue eyes made him immediately conspicuous, soliciting smiles, stares, and admiring glances from the women who had never seen such a thing before. He too had a ready smile, with an open face that inspired immediate confidence that nothing was hidden; one would trust such a face without knowing anything about the man.

The agent back in London had been vague about the geography of the place, knowing simply the barest details of his job, Julian's first, such as remuneration, contract, travel itinerary, and medical necessaries. He had handed Julian a list of these latter items such as quinine, Scotts Emulsion, Dr Jenner's Cure, Smedlies Chillie Past, and Camphor, that were, he assured him, essential to maintain health in that distant and unknown part of the world. The pay was poor, but the agent explained that because of the cheapness of living in the place it was the equivalent of a much higher salary in Europe. Julian in any case had little choice, he was nearly out of money, and this was the only employment open to an inexperienced and newly graduated mining engineer. The name of the company was given on his contract as being Burma Mines Inc., registered office in Singapore, and his employer's name, typed under an illegible signature read as Jock MacGreggor (Manager). It was a ruby mine, the richest in Burma, that was Julian's destination.

Julian knew little about rubies or their mining, vaguely remembering pictures of open caste workings in South Africa in one of his textbooks, and the word Burma had conjured up few associations in his mind beyond elephants, jungle, and Buddhists.

'Please sir! Please sir.' Julian felt a tugging on his sleeve and turned to find a portly Indian man of about fifty in a rather grubby white tropical suit trying to attract his attention. Julian stared at him for a moment before replying.

'Yes? Are you meeting me? The name's Drake, Julian Drake, for the mine.'

The mans head bobbed several times in quick succession.

'Yes indeed sir, I am taking you there. Please, please to follow me, I have a car awaiting exteriorwise. Ah! Excuse sir. I must be relieving you of your case, I can be carrying for you.'

And he seized Julian's case, turned and began pushing his way roughly towards the entrance.

There was an old Morris 12/4 parked in the shade of a tamarind tree outside the station. The original paintwork had been bleached to a patchy grey and there were numerous rust holes, dents, and scratches in its bodywork. Julian wondered just how long they would be traveling in the vehicle, and if it could possibly carry them any great distance. He had imagined that a vehicle belonging to the mining company would have been rather more modern and in better condition. But, he told himself, this was Burma, and he couldn't expect it to be the same as England, or even Europe.

Julian was about to take the seat next to the driver when the latter held up his hand, stopping him.

'Please sir, this is very old tired car, can I ask you to rotate the handle while I myself control the acceleration?' And he produced a rusty starting handle from under his seat and offered it to Julian.

After several tries the engine burst into life emitting clouds of oily black smoke, rapidly dispersing the crowd of curious spectators who had gathered closely around to observe the attempt. Julian climbed gratefully into the front seat, sweating and with oily hands and brown stains on his new tropical suit, purchased from Crokers of Piccadilly before he left. The driver turned and smiled at him.

'Next stop Mogok!' He proclaimed, 'That is hoping this vehicle is not breaking down, but then you are engineer, easy fix it I think.' And he crashed it into gear and they set off, the car jerking and backfiring for the first half mile.

Julian had been hoping to see something of Mandalay, imagining somewhere exotic and mysterious, but his view from the car through the dust caked window revealed a rather dirty and run-down city with temples and stupas on every corner but little other architecture of interest.

'How far is it to Mogok?' He asked the driver, already feeling cramped and hot in the stifling interior of the little car.

'How far?' Echoed the driver giggling nervously, 'Oh sir that is not easy to tell, in miles it is exactly one hundred and thirty eight, but in time one cannot be estimating due to variable conditions. If this vehicle does not break down, if the road remains open, if the Dacoits do not ambush us, I am believing we will be in Mogok by seven or eight this evening...but maybe it will be ten or midnight. And maybe tomorrow if the lights on this vehicle are not working.'

'Dacoits?' Said Julian suddenly nervous, 'What are they? Why should they ambush us?'

The driver turned towards Julian laughing.

'Dacoits sir are bad people. Not work, not live in house, move everywhere all around all time. Like bandits sir, robbers. Many in jungle in mountains. But not to worry sir, I do not believe we are in danger. Many months now since they bother people here.'

Julian glanced behind to where his luggage lay on the back seat. There was nothing much of value in the case he decided, but the violin, paid for by most of his inheritance following the death of his father five years ago was a costly instrument, and meant a great deal to him.

He had learnt to play at an early age, taught by his mother, and after she died when he was eight years old his father had paid for further tuition until he left school to attend the Camborne School of Mines in Exeter. His choice of subject had somewhat surprised his father, but he was at that time already too ill to object or even interest himself. The fact was that Julian had nurtured a passion for mines ever since he was a child, and after his three years at Camborne he had passed out with the highest grades to begin his search for employment.

The imminent threat of war, the prospect of conscription, and the death of his father, his sole relative, combined to make the prospect of working in another country, far away from the European cauldron, an enticing proposition.

'It's not like I've anything to keep me here,' He told his best friend in a letter a few days before leaving, 'And it might be the only chance I'll get if this thing with Germany blows up and I have to sign up. It's a big world out there, and I want to see a bit of it at least before I settle down.' He was in fact a serious minded young man, but like most young men the thirst for adventure was fresh and keen after the completion of his education. Armoured with the confidence and optimism of youth he felt he could do anything, go anywhere, and the world awaited him.

For the first two hours the road north from Mandalay was reasonably straight and level, following the valley of the river Ayeyarwadi until branching off and leaving the main highway to turn vaguely east and began climbing into the mountains. On this stretch there was little traffic, just the occasional bullock cart going from village to village, or an even more infrequent lorry. The road, now unsurfaced, potholed, and narrow, rose in a seemingly interminable series of hairpin bends, a cliff on one side and a vertical drop on the other. Everywhere there was evidence of landslides, huge blocks and slabs rocks fallen from above, even the occasional wrecked and abandoned car or lorry pushed off the road.

Darkness fell quickly, the feeble headlights reducing their progress to a crawl, but Mr. Patel, as Julian learned the driver was called, seemed familiar with the road and knew when to slow down and where he could safely speed up. They rumbled across narrow bridges spanning rushing torrents in unknown depths, sometimes made from rough teak planks that shook and rattled as they crossed. The old Morris made hard work of the ascent, necessitating a number of halts to allow the engine to cool down, but finally the road leveled out somewhat, although continuing to twist and turn.

'We will arrive this day!' Announced Mr. Patel at one of the stops where he was filling the petrol tank of the car from a rusty can. 'Mr. MacGreggor is expecting you for dinner. Maybe he wait a little, but I think Mrs. MacGreggor not like waiting. Very punctuos lady.'

It was in fact that evening when they reached Mogok. Julian could make out little of the place, as few lights were showing in the main street that seemed to consist mainly of single story wooden buildings.

'Electricity not work nighttime.' Giggled Mr. Patel, seeming to find something amusing in that situation, 'Mr. MacGreggor not allow.'

'You mean Mr. MacGreggor controls the electricity here?' Said Julian, rather surprised.

'Of course, sir. Everything here controlled by mine; electricity, water, school, everything. Every family have person work for mine, sometimes two, three...father, son, grandfather...Mr. MacGreggor pay good, everyone want come here, work here, very safe, very good for life.'

'So why no electricity at night? I would have thought that was when it is most needed.'

'Ah! Indeed you are correct sir. It would be most convenient, but electricity come from big generators at mine, take much fuel. Mr. MacGreggor say too expensive to keep running nighttime. Mine not work at night so no need electricity!'

Julian was beginning to wonder just what sort of man his boss could be, benevolent in providing for the local population, but evidently taking care about what he considered unnecessary expense, a true Scotsman.

Mr. Patel pulled up in front of a bungalow in the centre of the town. Next to it he could make out the darkened forms of the mine buildings, a single light in the watchman's hut by the gates.

'We are here!' He announced in a triumphal voice that sounded as if there had been some doubts as to whether they would have arrived at all.

CHAPTER THREE

The 'punctuos' Mrs. MacGreggor had in fact held back dinner for the new arrival. It was a rare and exciting event when a new westerner arrived, whether on government or private business. The last person invited to dine with the couple had been a missionary traveling further into the mountains with the aim of converting the indigenous Kachins to Christianity, a pointless endeavour Mr. MacGreggor thought to himself, he had been long enough in the country to appreciate that the locals saw no reason to abandon their multitude of deities for one single god, and what's more one who was patently white, foreign, cruel, and incomprehensible.

Mr. MacGreggor was himself a Scott, but although he had spent all his life in Burma after moving from India with his parents as a child, he never lost his Scottish brogue. His father had been District Officer for Mogok and around, responsible for an area of several hundred square miles of forest and mountain as well as several thousands of people. He was not just the local governor, but the head of a five man police force, magistrate, judge and jury, and on a couple of occasions executioner.

Jock had grown up to love the place, and when his parents returned home to Scotland when he was eighteen, he stayed on, finding a job as overseer in the Mogok Ruby Mine.

In nineteen fifteen feeling the need of a change and adventure he signed up as an engineer in the Army of India and was sent to the Western Front. On arrival the Division was thrown immediately into the Battle of Neuve Chapelle, where with antiquated Lee-Enfields they faced the German war machine. The youthful Jock found himself promoted rapidly due simply to the losses of his seniors, and was a captain by the end of the year.

A slight wound later that year sustained during a German night raid necessitated a short period of treatment in the field hospital at Montreuil, and it was there he met Stella, a nurse fresh from training school. It was no ordinary courtship. Jock was serious about life, love, and responsibility, and he was at first reluctant to enter into a relationship of any sort, above all with a young inexperienced girl from the Highlands. They were both aware of the very strong possibility that he would not survive the war, and he had tried his best to keep her as simply a friend. As his condition improved and he was able to take exercise outside they would sometimes go together to the fishing village at Etapes, walk along the quays watching the boats returning with their catch in the morning. Once or twice they took the bus to Le Touquet, to walk the promenade, staring at the rich people who still, in spite of the war a few miles away, came to gamble in the casino or lie on the beach if the day was warm.

When the day came for him to return to his regiment and she accompanied him to the train station, for the first time in his life he gave way to an irrational impulse, and as the train moved slowly away from the platform he leant from the window, planted a brief first kiss on her cheek, and asked her to marry him. The girl stopped dead, and stood staring after the receding carriage, an expression of sheer disbelief and delight upon her face. As it reached the end of the platform she began to run, and when she could finally go no further she cried out, waving furiously at the man returning to war.

'Yes! Yes! Yes!'

They were married on his next leave, and took a brief two day honeymoon in Paris. At the end of the war, when Jock was de-mobbed, he took his new wife straight back to Burma, and from that time they were never separated for more than a couple of nights, and both never regretted Jock's impulse.

Over the delayed dinner Julian had the impression of a kind and competent man, blunt and maybe a little gruff, but friendly. His wife was obviously delighted to have a young man to entertain, fussing around him, her hands fluttering like birds and chattering none stop, asking questions about home, his voyage out, his family, or lack of one.

'And do you have a young lady back home Julian?' She asked coyly, winking at him as if she was thirty years younger.

'Afraid not.' Admitted Julian, 'Never seemed to have the time for that sort of thing. It's my first job here you know, and the college kept me pretty busy.'

'Aye, by all accounts ye did mighty well there.' Jock said, 'I studied your reports. I'll be thinking you'll know more than me about the mining business. But ye'll be finding out that mining for the ruby in Burma is not like any other sort of mining anywhere else. There's no laws about safety here, and we rely on muscle and sweat rather than machines. The men are mainly honest, but they have to be watched, that'll be part of your job, but the thing is that the wages aren't high, and an uncut ruby that can be slipped...well, I'll not say where...and smuggled out of the mine, can be worth more than they'll earn in a lifetime. Aye! A huge temptation. Tomorrow I'll be showing you around, we'll go down the main shaft and see the working face, wear yer oldest clothes, it's a mite muddy down there.'

'I'm looking forward to that sir, and really I know I'm a beginner here, all theory and little practice.'

'Well I hope you'll be liking it here Julian, for a young man there's not a lot to do when you finish work. The only westerners here are Mrs. MacGreggor, myself, and the minister and his wife, so you'll have to learn Burmese pretty quickly if you need a person to talk to. Oh, you can do a spot of shooting if you're that way inclined...do you hunt Julian? There's wild pig, deer, plenty of birds, might even get a chance of a tiger though I wouldn't recommend it, that's where your predecessor went wrong.'

'I don't hunt...no, but what happened to him, my predecessor I mean.' Asked Julian, having heard nothing about a predecessor from the agent in London.

'Oh he thought he could wander around the jungle like it was Hyde Park you know, went after a pig in a thicket of bamboo, spooked a tiger having a wee kip there, his barer ran for it but he tried for a shot, missed of course, next to impossible to hit a charging tiger. When the barer took us back to where it happened there was just his head left. Funny how they always leave the head you know.'

'Oh I'll not be hunting anything Mr. MacGreggor, I guess I'll be busy for a good while learning the language, perhaps you could recommend a teacher? And I've always got the old fiddle to keep me amused, I try to practice a couple of hours every day if I can.'

'Well, your driver, Mr. Patel, could give you a start on basic Burmese maybe, knows that as well as three or four other local dialects. It's a hotchpotch this country you know as far as languages, twenty or thirty on top of Burmese, I don't know how they get along themselves, and always fighting each other if they're not fighting us.'

'Julian must be tired Jock, you should let him get off to his bed, you can talk as much as you like tomorrow.' Interrupted Mrs. MacGreggor. 'Julian you'll be staying here with us tonight, tomorrow Jock will show you your house. I hope you'll be happy there, it's the old government lodge, a bit out of the town but very spacious, and cooler than here. We used to live there but Jock prefers to be near to the mine, working the hours as he does.'

Julian slept well that night, exhausted from the journey, the heat, and the strangeness of it all. His head, just before he slept, was full of dacoits, tigers, broken cars and lorries, avalanches, and fistfuls of rubies, all revolving in a kaleidoscope of multi colours, strange tongues, oriental faces. He realised for the first time he was really very far from home and the world he knew.

After a breakfast of toast and coffee, Julian and Jock set off in the Morris for the house that was to be the new assistant managers home. In the daylight Julian could see the small town was situated in a narrow valley surrounded by steep hills growing to misty mountains in the distance. There was a long shallow lake dividing the town that Jock said was man-made, albeit by accident when a drainage tunnel dug at around the beginning of the century had collapsed. The hills all around the town were scarred and pitted with workings that had removed the vegetation and top soil to reveal the underlying yellow earth, and Julian could make out groups of the men swarming like ants over an upturned anthill.

'The locals are allowed to look for whatever they can find on the slopes.' Jock informed him, 'They used to have to pay a percentage of what they got for their finds, but it was unworkable, too many loopholes, so now they just pay a fee to allow them to work the hills.'

'And do they find much?'

'They can, from time to time. Some of them co-operate together to buy equipment like for washing the ore, but we might have to move 'em off, if the mines here in the town give out.'

Jock swung the car off the main road and onto a narrow rutted track that led into the jungle, climbing slightly. The track became a gloomy green tunnel passing through the dense vegetation that reached out to caress the sides of the car as it passed. Then suddenly a clearing appeared, with a large white house standing incongruously in a walled garden with lawns, flower beds, and fruit trees. It could almost have been transported straight from the English countryside. The iron gates painted white and gold were open and Jock drove straight up the short drive and stopped in front of the stairs that led to the front door.

Jock turned to Julian, smiling at the others expression.

'Well here y'are laddie. Not too small or poky I hope.'

Julian just stared for a moment, his mouth half open.

'Good god! It's huge. It's for me? Just me?'

'Aye, it is. Was meant to be for me and Mrs. MacGreggor, but it was a bit far out of town for me, and to be honest she didn't like to be so cut off from everything, didn't like the nights alone when I was working, scared of beasties and dacoits maybe. It was built to be the local governor's place in the last century, but I think they couldn't find anyone willing to come here, too isolated, so they let it to the Company at the turn of the century.'

As they left the car and mounted the steps the front door opened by unseen hands and a young Burmese boy of about fifteen stepped out to greet them with a deep bow, his hands clasped prayer like before him. Julian noticed the boy limped, one leg seeming shorter than the other and an ugly birthmark marred one side of his otherwise pleasant and open face.

'Morning Boy.' Jock said, and turning to Julian continued, 'This is Boy, and that's actually his name not description, he looks after the place, he sleeps in the annex round the back, he'll look after you, like clean and cook and anything else. Speaks a bit of English too, don't you Boy.'

Boy nodded vigorously.

'Boy speak English yes Papa. Papa teach Boy.' And he grinned at Julian exposing many gaps in his brown stained teeth.

'Ye'll get used to the Papa nonsense, they call anyone older than themselves and in a bit of authority Papa, sort of mark of respect. I'll give them that, they look up to their old folks. I took him on after his father died in a cave-in at the mine, and as his mother had died at birth he had no one to look after him. And with his leg he couldno' work much. A good lad really if a bit of a scatter brain sometimes.'

Boy stood to one side as they entered the house. It had the scent of warm wood Julian noticed, not un-pleasant but welcoming, the floors walls and ceilings being either exposed and varnished, or painted. The first room Jock led them into on the right of the hallway was a large lounge; windows all along one wall led out onto a veranda overlooking the front garden and drive.

'Now if you come out here you'll see why it was built so far out of town.' Jock said leading them out through the French doors. Newly drenched orchids hung from the eaves, filling the air with strange and exotic scents, and a rattan lounger, table, and chairs seemed to be waiting for someone to occupy them. Looking almost due south the whole of the valley and town lay before them, the surrounding hills and mountains providing a fantastical backdrop of jungle covered peaks and slopes partially covered by shifting morning mists. The very forms of the mountains seemed eccentric, unworldly, steep sided, pinnacled, the ranges rising higher and higher towards the far far distance veiled in a blue and purple haze. They spoke of mystery and enigma, strange tribes, hidden valleys, the heart of wild and unexplored Burma. On one peak overlooking the town a white temple with stupas was perched precariously, accessed by a single twisting path that wound serpent like up an apparently sheer cliff face. Jock, seeing Julian's gaze nodded towards it.

'It's worth a trip up there some day, if you've got a head for heights and a strong constitution, watch out on the path though, it's not in good repair and nobody seems to worry too much. It's the culture you know, Buddhist, fatalistic. They recon if it's their time to go then that's it. No point in worrying or trying to escape fate, if the path gives way and they fall to their deaths then that's how it was meant to be. And as they were on their way to the monastery that gives 'em a bit of extra credit for their next life, you see?'

Julian nodded.

'It's just amazing, I've never seen a view like it.'

'Aye, but it was a bit of a waste on me when we lived here, it was dark when I left in the morning and when I got back at night, never got a chance to enjoy it much. Mrs. MacGreggor used to come and read or do her knitting here of an afternoon, it's much cooler you'll find than in the valley.'

Over the next few minutes Jock showed Julian the rest of the house. Only a few of the rooms were furnished, but it was more than Julian would ever need on his own, indeed he was starting to wonder just how he would spend his free time there, alone except for the grinning Boy.

Leaving his case for the youth to unpack they drove back to the town and pulled up outside the mine. A bamboo fence enclosed a group of timber buildings surrounding the main shaft, distinguished by a tower and winding wheel that was rotating slowly. Everything was coated with yellow dust, including the men working there, who stared curiously at Julian as they passed.

'It's not much to look at but don't ye be fooled. There's more rubies been torn from the earth here than any other ten acres anywhere in the world. And there's still more to come god willing. But the earth doesn't give up its treasure easily, and it's not machines that find and harvest the gems, no Julian, it's human muscle. The labour of arm and the sharpness of eye, that's what we use here; a pick, a shovel, a hammer, those are the tools of our trade.

Rubies have been mined in Burma for centuries, they've caused wars, deposed kings, driven men mad with longing, and women crazy for their beauty. And it's no coincidence they're the colour of blood, it's what is in them I think, their birthright.'

They entered the main building at the head of the shaft.

'It's the dry season so we work double shifts.' Jock told Julian 'In the rainy season we spend most of the time pumping out the water, might manage only a couple of hours a day actually working the seam.'

'But it's still profitable? Even working so little time'

'Aye, it is, just so long as we keep pulling out the good stuff. But you never can tell when it'll run out, it's a day-to-day existence. I'll show you this end of the business before we go underground.'

At one end of the building was a wide table over which a tall young mixed race man was standing, two other men stood one on either side of him. A pile of what looked like gravel was at one end of the table and as they watched the man with a sweep of his hand spread the gravel across the width of the table.

'That's Zeya. He's in charge of inspecting the tailings, what's left after the washing, picking out the good stuff, and that's not just rubies ye ken. We can get all manner of stones here but mainly ruby, sapphire, and spinel. Spinel's not worth a lot as a gem, but ground up its the best abrasive you'll find, nearly as hard as diamond. It takes a keen eye to pick them out and Zeya has got one. Isn't that a fact Zeya?' Jock called out to the man.

The man lifted his eyes from the table before him and looked up at Julian, a gaze intense and unnerving, unfriendly even.

'That is so, sir.' He said after a moment, 'My eyes can see many things, the good stones and the bad. The treasures of the earth need a true eye to see them, lest they be wasted and lost. Look...' And here he reached down and plucked a small piece of rock from the table before him and held it up between two fingers for the two men to observe.

'Not an impressive thing one might think, a piece of dross, worthless. And yet...'

Here he turned the stone in his fingers, squeezing and rubbing it between thumb and forefinger.

'See now Sirs, what is revealed to the knowledgeable man.'

The two men looked closely at the small piece of rock in his hand, and saw the gleam of something red. He passed it to Jock who gave it on to Julian. 'Look and learn Julian. This is what it's all about.'

Julian studied the rock, the size of a thumbnail, and saw for the first time the deep red transparency of one side partially obscure by dust and dirt, he pressed hard with his thumb and bit by bit the rock fell away to finally reveal a pure transparent ruby, irregular in shape, but seeming to glow deep red against the white of his skin. A feeling of wonder came over him, the perfection, the beauty, the mystical attraction of the jewel torn from the darkness of the earth where it had lain for uncountable ages and now lying in his hand luminescent, intense, and red like living blood.

'Its amazing.' He murmured eventually. 'I never knew it could be like this, just so perfect.'

Zeya reached out and took the stone from Julian, dropping it into a wooden box to one side.

'Sometimes there are stones that are so perfect they can be mounted directly from the ground, without the need for the hand of man to polish or grind.' He said, and again looked up at Julian, the same stare, his eyes black and unreadable.

'Come now Julian, I'll show you the previous stage, washing, and then we'll pop down to the face and see what's going on there.'

They went outside, Zeya returning to his work without another word, and Jock led them to one of the other buildings.

'Ye'll get used to Zeya Julian, don't worry about him, I trust him absolutely. His father was an American missionary, got mixed up with a local girl, scarpered off to Sumatra as soon as he found out she was expecting his child. Stella knew the girl well, and when she died giving birth she found Zeya a foster family. They have hard time the mixed bloods here, not accepted by either the locals or the Brits. Bloody silly if you ask me. Zeya's got a bit of a chip on his shoulder, but who wouldn't in his place?

Anyway, we paid for his education, sent him to college in Rangoon, did well there. But he did get mixed up in student politics, you know the sort of thing, independence movement, workers rights, and so on, but he came back and got stuck into his work here, so no complaints.'

'Is there much pressure for home rule here?' Asked Julian, 'I heard it's very strong now in India.'

Jock sighed and scratched his head.

'Oh! It'll come in the end I guess, bound to, give it another ten years and we'll be booted out. Though who'll be able to govern this place I can't imagine, with so many different tribes. One hundred and thirty five distinct ethnic groups to be exact, sixty five languages, and a handful of religions; there'll be a bit of blood letting I'll be bound before you'll get them to accept a central government. When it comes I'll have to take Mrs. MacGreggor back to Scotland I think, and I've never been there myself, can't say I'm looking forward to it. But look now....' Jock indicated a complex system shallow tanks containing what looked like muddy water. 'This is the pulsator jig, where the gravel is washed, the lighter stuff floats away, the interesting part stays, then the whole process is repeated several times until all that's left is the heavy pay dirt. That's then dried and it's over to Zeya and his men to sift through it.'

'I'm guessing there must be a percentage of wastage, washed away in the water, no?'

'You're right there Julian, maybe five or ten percent. But that's not the biggest wastage, not by a long chalk.'

'And that would be?'

'Theft Julian, theft. It's huge and unstoppable. We let the town women go through the tailings from the jig for free, and the miners on the hillside only pay a small annual fee, but still we loose I estimate thirty percent of the stones mineable in our area, and that's all the town and the hills around for ten miles. We pay twenty thousand a year to the government for the license, plus thirty percent of the turnover, yes, turnover I said, the pen pushers in Whitehall want more than a pound of flesh. Then add in the running costs like wages, diesel for the gennies, wear and tear on the equipment, and you can see we have to keep the gems coming in and theft down. And Mrs. MacGreggor wonders why I work an eighteen hour day.'

After they had watched the ore being washed Jock led them to the top of the main shaft.

'Ye'll observe Julian we're in a hollow here, already a good thirty feet below ground level, that's because we started five years ago here with an open cast pit, using high pressure water to uncover the rock. After a while we weren't finding enough near the surface so we did a test bore and found a likely seam at about ninety feet. So we sank the main shaft here and followed the seam out from there, must be about three hundred feet now going down gradually towards the lake, its a good seam, nearly six feet wide in places, and no sign yet of it diminishing.'

At the end of an exhausting morning for Julian scrambling along narrow tunnels deep underground, and then climbing the hillside to view the other workings, they took a light lunch with Mrs MacGreggor on the shaded and relative cool veranda of her house. It was the heat he found draining as much as the physical exercise, and he found himself wondering how the workers could keep working through the hottest part of the day.

'Ye'll tek a while to get used to the heat.' Jock told him, 'in a way you're lucky it's not the rainy season, the humidity is much more difficult to support, for us westerners at least.'

'Oh I just hate it when it rains for days on end.' Said Mrs. MacGreggor,' You can't go out without getting soaked, everything's damp, you get mildew everywhere, clothing rots, make the most of this season Julian, it's as good as it gets.'

CHAPTER FOUR

It was another couple of months before Julian experienced the southwest monsoon with its stifling humidity and torrential rain. By then he had settled into a comfortable routine; woken by Boy at five thirty for breakfast and shower, driving the old Morris down to the mine for the mornings work, lunch with the Mac-Greggors, work until around dusk when if he had finished what he was doing he could stop for the day. Before driving home he liked to visit the local market, perhaps stopping to buy some fruit or a simple delicacy for Boy who loved a sweet of any description. Twice a week there was the Gem Market, when the local miners, often represented by their wives, would try to sell whatever they had managed to find or steal. Dealers from out of town would be driving hard bargains for a single stone or a handful of red chippings. In small makeshift workshops stones could be cut and ground, some would be heated to enhance the colour, and several of the workshops specialised in mounting the stones in rings, bracelets, necklaces.

Sometimes Julian would stop to buy a tepid beer from a food stall, a low shack also selling cheap liquor and cigarettes and with a kitchen to the rear. He would sit on one of the tiny chairs that seemed to him made really for children and watch the procession of different races pass by, and it was at one of these places when he took refuge from a sudden downpour that he met Zeya one evening, sitting alone and drinking tea from a small cup.

He had sat down and ordered his beer before he realised Zeya was also seated at a table a few feet away, an oil lamp burning on the table before him. He was watching Julian but made no move to greet or recognise him.

Julian picked up his beer and went over to his table.

'Evening Zeya, mind if I join you?'

Zeya silently inclined his head slightly by way of acceptance.

'Waiting for the rain to pass eh?' Said Julian, feeling slightly unwelcome.

Zeya nodded noncommittally.

'Waiting yes, but as a matter of fact I am waiting for a friend, the rain you understand, for us Burmese at least, is merely a slight inconvenience.'

What was it Julian wondered that everything Zeya said to him seemed a veiled accusation, of what he had no idea.

'Quite.' Replied Julian, 'At least it's not cold like at home.'

'Home,' Repeated Zeya, turning away from Julian and staring morosely into the distance, '*Your* home you mean, England.'

For a while they sat in silence, Julian sipping his beer and Zeya playing with his cup. From behind the counter came the sounds and smells of cooking; a woman throwing handfuls of vegetables and spices into a wok that for an instant ignited, sending grey smoke into the rafters where a large gecko hung, frozen in motion. Julian stared at the outdated calendars with pictures of Chinese deities in gaudy and improbable colours decorating the wooden walls and tried to think of a topic of conversation.

'I believe you're interested in politics, or so Jock said.'

Zeya looked at Julian sharply, as if wondering what else Jock had told him. He took a moment to reply, as if gathering his thoughts.

'Interested you say. Well, for an Englishman one might truthfully say that. But for me, for a Burmese, a Burmese patriot, it is not a word I would use.' And he lent forward towards Julian, his dark eyes fixed intently on the Englishman.

'You see sir, here, here in one of King George's colonies, politics is not a pastime like collecting stamps, or playing bridge, or racing horses. Politics is a much more serious affair, an affair that touches the soul of the people, their hopes, their fears, their needs.'

He picked up his cup suddenly as if he had just noticed it, draining it in one swift swallow.

'You must realise Sir that this country is not England, its people are not English, its language is not English, and yet...'

He left the phrase hanging for a moment, as if afraid he had gone too far, but then he passed a hand over his face, looking at Julian for the first time as if he wanted him to understand something before continuing in low horse whisper.

'And yet we are ruled by Englishmen, according to English laws. Our judges are English, our police chiefs are English, our Universities teach in English.' He waved a hand vaguely in the direction of the mine. 'And tell me sir, where do the profits from the mine end up? Why, in the pockets of English shareholders. The treasures of our land torn from our earth and stolen from us to line the pockets of gentlemen thousands of miles away who could not give a damn about Burma and its people.' He stopped, sitting back in his chair as if the subject was closed.

Julian could think of nothing to dispute the words. In truth he had never thought deeply about the situation. He accepted that Burma was not a country able to rule itself, as Jock had intimated, but had never thought further about the politics of colonialism. Everything seemed to be under control, a few dacoits causing problems maybe, a bit of scrapping between tribes or races, but apart from that it all seemed peaceful, calm, and the people generally seemed happy with their lives.

Zeya extracted a cigarette from a packet on the table and lit it, blowing smoke up towards the thatched ceiling where thousands of moths and other insects danced to their death around the oil lamps.

'And yet we are a subject people who must obey at all times our colonisers.' He murmured eventually as an afterthought. 'And there, sir, you have the core of what is politics in Burma, the people versus the colonisers.'

At that moment a man sheltering under a broad umbrella stepped out of the rain and shadows that surrounded the little establishment and greeted Zeya with a handshake.

He was strangely dressed for a monsoon night in Mogok with dark suit, now mottled with rain, patent leather shoes, shinny but now mud stained, and a black brief case. He peered short sightedly at Julian through thick framed glasses as he folded his umbrella, and Zeya murmured something to him in Burmese whereupon he bowed slightly and extended his hand.

'I am pleased to meet you sir, my name is Mr. Kaw. I trust you are settling in well here in Mogok, and that business is satisfactory.'

There was, Julian thought, something not right about the man. His handshake was weak, damp, and brief, almost snatching it away from Julian's touch, and he found he had no desire to talk with the man, feeling as if he were unwholesome or diseased.

'I'm settling in fine thank you.' He said briefly, turning to Zeya and finding him looking uncomfortable.

Julian stood up, he had the feeling he was interrupting something, something private between the two men.

'I guess I will have to leave you two gentlemen, the rain seems to be abating and dinner awaits.'

The new arrival bowed, smiling.

'It was most agreeable meeting you sir, I hope we will have the chance to meet again sometime, I would be most interested to talk with you, and who knows what the future will bring.'

Julian nodded to Zeya who was looking elsewhere feigning disinterest, and turned to leave. As he stepped out into the rain he realised that the man's English had been exceptionally good, almost perfect in fact, and he wondered if he had been educated in Europe. Julian could not have guessed that when they would meet again, three years into the future, it would be under very different and quite unimaginable circumstances.

'There's a bit of local culture coming to the town over the next few days.' Jock announced one lunchtime some months after Julian's arrival as they sat on the veranda of his home finishing their coffee. 'A dance troop, traditional stuff, very picturesque, you should take a look. Starts late and finishes in the early hours, usually in the space in front of the market, you'll need to get there early if you want to get near enough to see properly, people will be coming from miles around.

How's your Burmese coming along by the way? Understand anything yet?'

'Ah! Wish you hadn't asked that,' replied Julian, 'it's hard, very hard, and so different. I learnt French and Latin at school and those were easy compared to Burmese. Mr. Patel does his best, but I'm a slow learner I'm afraid.'

Jock looked around to check that Mrs. MacGreggor wasn't around before leaning towards Julian and whispering.

'Of course in India, in the old days, they had a solution. The young men who came out to be agents or district officers whatever were encouraged to take a Bibi.' And he winked at Julian before swallowing his coffee and sitting back in his chair, a slight smile on his face.

'A Bibi? Not sure I understand.' Julian said, having heard the word but not aware of its meaning. Jock leant forward towards him, taking a quick look around to make sure he wasn't overheard.

'A Bibi, or as they were known sometimes, a sleeping dictionary.'

Julian remained nonplussed, still looking at Jock with a blank expression. Jock sighed deeply.

'Och! Laddie, where've you been all your life?' And he looked around again to where Stella had disappeared into the other room.

'The old India hands knew the best way for a young man to learn the lingo was for him to have a girlfriend, a local who spoke the language. Best way to learn by far. In the old East India Company they actually used to encourage it in the beginning. But then when travel got quicker and easier to get out here, and the memsahibs started arriving, they didn't like it and got it discouraged. Of course it continued, can't stop nature when you get young men far from home living among attractive and available young women, but it's more discrete now, the girls are kept out of the way. Now don't get the wrong idea Julian, I'm not advising you to get a Burmese girlfriend, just giving you a bit of information like.'

Julian felt his face colouring with embarrassment. He had of course noticed the many beautiful girls around, girls whose ready smiles and bold looks seemed so different from the reserved and distant girls back home. And sometimes he had wondered what they would be like to know. Once or twice when he was with Boy shopping in the market for food, he had received a hard nudge in the ribs as a particular girl took the lads fancy, and he would half-whisper laughingly to Julian while pointing unashamedly towards the girl in question.

'Look look Papa, pretty girl for you.'

Julian would quickly turn away to hide his blush.

'Shut up Boy, don't be silly.' And Boy would laughingly follow him looking over his shoulder to where the girl was watching them, laughing too, her mouth covered with her hand.

'I think I'll stick with Mr. Patel.' Said Julian, 'Not really interested in girlfriends yet...too much to do.'

However after a moments pause he couldn't help asking...

'Did you ever have one Jock, a Bibi I mean, before Mrs. MacGreggor of course?'

Jock leant toward Julian, whispering conspiratorially.

'Now that would be telling', A gentleman never reveals his private arrangements of that sort, but I'll say this, I'm only human like everyone else, and when my folks went back home I was a mite lonely, and well, there were lots of pretty local gals around to help a young man forget his pain.' And he winked. 'Now, time to get back to work now. Enough of dreaming...back to reality!'

CHAPTER FIVE

Two days later Julian accompanied by an excited Boy drove back into town after their evening meal at the house. The streets were packed with people necessitating them leaving the old Morris some way away from the market. Boy was tugging on Julian's arm as soon as they left the car.

'More fast Papa, more fast. Maybe late, maybe miss dancing ladies.'

And Julian had an idea that it was the prospect of seeing the girl dancers that excited him rather than any appreciation of the aesthetics and the culture.

A space had been cleared in the market by removing a number of the tables upon which the stallholders normally displayed their wares. Around this space the crowd was already settled, sitting expectantly on the ground, eating food they had brought or purchased, chatting with neighbours, smoking foul smelling cheroots. Boy towed Julian through the seated spectators, stepping over bodies where necessary and all the time calling out in Burmese for them to make way for the Englishman. Eventually he secured a narrow spot on one of the tables right on the edge of what would be the stage. No sooner had he seen Julian safely installed than he disappeared back into the crowd, only to re-emerge minutes later with a bottle of beer for Julian and a paper bag of a sticky sweet for himself.

'Good good, not late, soon start now. I think they wait for you come!'

As if he was correct in his assumption group of about ten musicians appeared from one side and made their way onto the stage. They formed a circle of nine large drums around which several smaller ones were placed, and around them in turn a bell and clapper, an oboe like instrument, and a bamboo xylophone were positioned.

For several minutes the musicians chatted amongst themselves playing the odd note or tapping lightly on a drum. The audience seemed to pay little attention, continuing to chatter loudly.

Then suddenly as if on an invisible signal the musicians took up their instruments and a single loud drumbeat began the music. It was the first time Julian had heard Burmese music, and for a moment he was lost, unable to relate the sounds to what he understood music to be. Years of playing the violin had accustomed him to certain qualities of harmony, rhythm, and melody, and he could discover little of these in what the musicians were playing. But after a minute or two, gradually, he began to detect something. Something different from what he knew, but interesting, exciting even. He could find no harmony, just something rhythmic and percussive, a single melody line enveloped in flourishes and swirls of sounds on drums, gongs, and xylophone. He closed his eyes and let the sounds wash over him. Somehow it seemed just right, no other music would have fitted so well the place, the time...it was exotic to his ears, full of the mysteries of the east he had yet to understand or experience; the intoxicating fragrance of the flowers, the unremitting heat and humidity, the bold eyes and bare arms, the covert sensuality of bodies clothed lightly and moving with a slow sinuous grace through deep shadow and intense light. A sharp nudge awoke Julian from his reverie.

'Look Papa! Dancers come.'

Four male and four female dancers filed into the space in front of the musicians. The women wore tight skirts that flared at their feet, embroidered tops, and gold headpieces. They began a slow intricate dance that seemed to Julian more like a series of stylised poses than a dance. To begin with their movements were slow, one pose followed the other, the men and women never touching but seeming to create a dialogue between their bodies. The women's faces, heavily made up, wore fixed smiles, directed at neither their partners nor the audience, their eyes looking always dead ahead.

'Bilu dance.' Boy shouted in Julian's ear, for not only was the music loud, but the audience were still talking amongst themselves, applauding at regular intervals, and periodically shouting what Julian took to be encouragement to the dancers.

The dance went on for quite some time until reaching some sort of conclusion where the girl dancers left the stage and the remaining men adopted poses of dejection as a final crash of drums signaled the end.

There was a general shifting of position amongst the audience, people getting up to go and buy food, others crossing the stage to greet friends on the other side.

'There's more to come I take it?' Julian said.

'Oh yes Papa! Many dance, long time. Soon we see more lady dance, Papa like lady dance I think.'

There were indeed many more dances, some with just women, and some with both women and men. Julian began to feel tired, not understanding the background to each dance they seemed to him to be very much the same. The music loud, wailing, with crashing drums and gongs, the stylised posing with twisted limbs, hands and arms outstretched as if repelling invisible forces. The gorgeous multicoloured costumes enclosing the slim fine bodies of both male and female.

A dance ended and Julian turned to Boy.

'Time for bed for us Boy. Work tomorrow remember, for you too.'

Boy put a restraining hand on his arm, an expression of alarm on his normally smiling face.

'No Papa! Cannot! Must wait. Next dance very good. Lady dance. Papa like.' And he forced Julian to sit back down. 'Never mind Papa, wait for last dance.'

In fact an air of expectancy seemed to have suddenly descended upon the audience, bit by bit conversations ceased and all faces turned towards the stage area. The musicians who had disappeared for a moment to slake their thirst on locally brewed beer filed back and took up their positions. In the far distance over the mountains thunder rumbled, and the first drops of rain began to fall on the unfortunate few who had not managed to squeeze under the market roof. Julian turned to look behind him towards where he had left the car. Then as he turned back there was a brilliant flash of lightning over the town, for an instant turning everything a stark electric blue, and as his eyes adjusted and he looked back towards the stage she was there. The dancer, appearing as if from nowhere, suddenly in front of him not ten feet away. No one had seen her arrive, and there was an awed sigh from the crowd. Boy's hand gripped tightly Julian's arm.

'Lady dancer called Myitsu. Very good. Every person know.' He whispered.

The girl, for she seemed little more than a girl, stood completely motionless, her knees slightly bent, her head on one side, her arms lifted and bent at the elbow and wrist, the fingers splayed. Her face was pure white, her eyes outlined in black seemed huge, but there was no smile this time. Rather a serious expression, that could have been thought fierce had it been on another larger and less beautiful person. For beautiful she was, and the crowd knew it. Even motionless she seemed to exude an aura of authority, something very special, not worldly, a figure from another age perhaps, another world, a Nat, or a forest spirit.

For perhaps a whole minute she remained still. Around the town the thunder rumbled while the lightning danced over the hills, until a soft steady beat of a drum introduced the music, and she began to dance.

A rhythmic nodding posturing and twisting of the elbows and hands...like a jointed doll, but smooth and incredibly sinuous. Her knees would bend and she would lean forward, apparently defying gravity, her hands describing figures in the air, her head turning but her eyes remaining fixed upon one point. She hardly seem to move from the spot she had first appeared from, but Julian realised she was now only a few feet away from him. So near he could hear the soft rustle of her garments over the sound of the music as she moved, and he fancied he could catch the scent of her, something wild, exotic, strange.

Very slowly the tempo of the music increased, one drum in particular beating a steady hypnotic rhythm, from which the other instruments seemed to take their timing. The girl's movements kept pace, never hurried, but intricate, complex and perfect. They told a story, but not a story that could be put in words, a mystical story that had entranced the watchers as they stared at the human doll that danced before them.

She danced faster and faster, one instant the train of her dress flicking Julian she passed so close. For a brief second their eyes met as her head turned away, and then a few seconds later her large black almond eyes turned again towards him, as if seeing him for the first time. A white face like hers amongst the brown.

Julian felt something, he couldn't analyse what exactly, but a feeling as if the earth had slipped away from under his feet, the market, the town, the hills and mountains, becoming an unreality, transparent, ephemeral. And replaced by something bigger, more solid, and utterly strange. He found himself following her face with his eyes, watching, trying to see if she would look towards him again, but she did not. After a crescendo of wild drums and gongs, the music abruptly stopped. The girl was once more frozen immobile in the centre of the stage, only the slight rise and fall of her breast indicating the physical demands of her performance. And then she was gone, not even acknowledging the explosion of cheering and clapping from the crowd. She simply turned, her face impassive, and disappeared behind the stage.

Julian was conscious of Boy poking him playfully in the ribs, and heard his voice as if from far away.

'Good Papa! Good! Boy say Papa must stay, OK! OK? Papa like lady dancer I think. Boy like lady too. Everyone like lady. Best dancer in Burma. Ok Papa?'

Julian rubbed his eyes as if to dispel an illusion.

'Right Boy. Yes, she was good. Thank you for making me stay, it was worth it.'

'Yes! Boy know, Boy know this lady, see her many times. Best dancer in Burma. Everyone know.'

They left the market and made their way through the rain to where the Morris was parked without noticing that among the people remarking their exit, standing discretely by the edge of the stage at the rear, stood Zeya. He had been watching the girl dance, and watching Julian as well. As they disappeared he turned and made his way behind the stage to where the dancers were preparing out of sight of the crowd. The girl Myitsu was seated before a mirror, removing make up with a damp cloth, he went and stood behind her placing his hands on her narrow shoulders, she looked up at his reflection in the mirror, impassive. Zeya nodded to her approvingly, then turned and left. He had work at the mine that awaited him. Myitsu finished cleaning off her make up but remained staring at her reflection in the mirror. Her face was still pale even without make up, much paler than the average Burmese woman, she avoided exposing herself to the sun wherever possible, and if she was obliged to she would apply thanaka paste in the fashion of the country. Now she thought about the white man in the crowd, how her face was white like his, it was a face that had instantly effected her. A foreigner, English probably, she had never known an Englishman, and she wondered what they could be like to know, to love maybe. Zeya had told her what her duty was, and had ignored her objections, she would have to try, after all he was a man like any other it could not be difficult, and having seen him she now thought it would not be too unpleasant for her.

It was two years earlier that Zeya had first seen Myitsu. He had just returned from University and started work at the mine, his mind busy with dreams of independence and frustrated by his seeming inability to do anything in the sleepy backwater town. He had watched her dance, and like others had been entranced. But what fascinated him, what stimulated his imagination, was not her performance or her appearance, but the effect she had on the watchers. Here, he thought was power. Innocent for the moment, the girl being only just fourteen, but with the potential to be a tool, perhaps in the struggle for freedom.

He approached her cautiously. Visiting her after the show to congratulate her. Buying her little presents, walking with her in the afternoons when the town was quiet and her time was her own. And when the show moved on he would take a day off work, feigning illness, to travel to where she was. They would sit sometimes in the shade of a tree or the grounds of a temple and he would talk to her, tell her his dreams of another life, another country where men were free to govern themselves. And the girl was entranced by his words.

Nobody had ever shared thoughts like this with her. She knew nothing of politics or the great world outside, and his words revealed something new. She discovered her place in his world, who and what she was. How things could and must change. She shared with him his secret, and in sharing it made her feel changed, grown, an adult. Of course he was right, now he had explained it to her she could understand. The injustice, the tyranny, the oppression, became wonderfully and tragically clear to her. In her innocence she embraced the one sided arguments, the flawed logic, the devious promises. She was in a way intellectually deflowered by the young graduate.

He explained how she might play her part in the struggle, how she might use her talent to further the aims of the party. It might not be immediate he told her, but she should prepare herself and be ready when the time came.

Another young man might have thought of her in terms of a lover even a wife, been attracted by her pale soft skin, her large expressive eyes, her youth and innocence, but in Zeya's world there was no room for such feelings; the party and the cause were omnipotent, excluding all else.

The following day Julian found his thoughts often straying to the previous evening and the young girl dancer, and after work he made his way as usual towards the market hoping to find out if the dancer troop were performing again.

His basic Burmese was just sufficient to make the question understood when he put it to a stall holder from whom he had just purchased some Rambutan, and he gathered that only some of the troop would perform, the stall holder being unable to tell him if the girl would be there or not.

Rather discouraged and depressed he went and sat down in his usual place and ordered a beer. For the first time since he had arrived in Burma he felt lonely. He missed friends he realised. Jock and his wife were agreeable and kind, but Jock was still his boss, and they were after all another generation. He wished he could be back in England, perhaps seated in country pub where the temperature was not thirty degrees and the humidity not one hundred percent, where he could have an intelligent conversation in English, real English, not pidgin English.

Exceptionally for him he took a second beer without it seeming to have any effect on his humour, Jock's words of warning coming back to him; 'There's two main dangers living here that most men succumb to sooner or later, the drink and the women. That's why Mrs. MacGreggor is here and I'll only have scotch in the house.'

Julian began to understand a bit about both, but when the stall owner removed his empty second bottle and with raised eyebrows tempted him with a third he nodded with only a moment's hesitation.

But it was not the owner who brought his drink to him, but a young girl. Julian didn't look up as she placed the bottle on the table in front of him, just remarking in his peripheral vision the coloured longi with small bare feet emerging from underneath. He was suddenly conscious of a scent, a half remembered scent, overlaying the usual town smells of rotting food, smoking fires, cooking spices, and bad sewage, and he turned and looked up at the girl. It was her, the dancer, he recognised immediately in spite of the fact she was wearing normal Burmese clothes and had no make up except two swirls of white thanaka paste on her cheeks.

He could not mistake the face, the huge dark eyes, almond shaped, liquid, an open window to the unknown beyond. She was regarding him calmly, without expression, as if waiting. He had no idea what she wanted, what he should say.

'My name is Myitsu, you watch me dance last night.'

She spoke in English, with a strong accent that betrayed an unfamiliarity with using the language.

There was a long silence, Julian totally unable to find a reply, unable to connect the girl, or young woman he saw next to him, with the apparition of the night before. At last she continued.

'I want to speak you.'

Julian could only nod towards the vacant chair opposite to him.

The girl sat down, moving with the smooth grace of a dancer, seeming to flow rather than move.

Julian indicated his untouched bottle in front of him.

'Would you like a drink? A juice? Something else?'

The girl ignored his question as if irrelevant.

'You are English man, work at mine.' It was more a statement than question.

'I'm the engineer there, yes. At the mine.'

There was a long silence before she spoke again.

'Many peoples work at mine, many I think. How many you say?'

Julian began to wonder just where the questions could be leading.

'We have about seventy-five permanent employees, plus about fifty seasonal workers. Why do you want to know?'

Again the girl ignored his question, her eyes steady on his, deep, unreadable.

'What is your name please?' She asked eventually.

'My name is Drake, Julian Drake. Now, please miss, what can I do for you?'

The girl leant forward toward him, bowing her head slightly, and Julian realised she was not the child he had taken her for the previous night when she danced. Without the makeup emphasising her large eyes against the white skin of her face, her tint was more of a pale amber. There were faint laughter lines at the corners of her mouth, and even wearing the tight longi and bodice she had on he could detect the concealed curves of a woman's body, not a child's. Again he caught the scent of her, and felt his heart beating and a sudden heat in his body. He slipped a finger under the collar of his shirt to loosen it.

'Mr. Drake I want to ask you if you give me work at your mine.'

Of all the things the girl might have asked of him Julian could not have been more surprised.

'The mine? You want to work at the mine? But you're a dancer, you can't be a miner! It's impossible.'

The girl said nothing but continued staring at Julian expectantly.

'And why would you? It's hard dirty dangerous work, not for a young lady like yourself. There are women who work on the hillsides, but they're not paid by the mine, they just find what they can to sell. You can't do that. It's impossible.' To Julian what she had asked was unimaginable. The slight, she could not have been more than five feet tall, doll like figure seated opposite him would never survive the heat, dirt, and physical labour of the mine, in any capacity. He found he was profoundly shocked by the idea.

She tilted her head to one side, a very feminine and expressive gesture.

'But perhaps some other work I can do? Please, I can work hard, not need much money. Please Mr. Drake, please find me work for you.'

For a moment Julian forgot her request.

'But I don't understand why you want a job. You're a dancer, a very good one, well known I believe. Why can't you stay a dancer?'

She sat back in her chair, closing her eyes and bringing her hands together before her face, touching her lips, Julian stared at her, mesmerised.

'Maybe I tell my story, maybe you understand. My family very poor Shan people, live in mountain. When I little girl, about six year, they sell me to traveling dance troop, 300 rupees. They need money you understand, three other children boys, girl no good, cost money for nothing. The troupe teach me dance, I learn quickly, soon best dancer. Then they sell me to another troupe when I thirteen, same troupe as now. But now I tired, not want dance any more. Everyday same same, go new place, dance two or three day, go new place again. And when I too old, not young girl any more they find new girl, send me away. Then I no home, no money, nothing. Mr. Drake I want have home, maybe family, not be dancer anymore. Please help me.'

Julian couldn't think. Before him was this strange totally foreign girl, beautiful beyond words, telling a story potentially tragic and disturbing, and expecting his help. He realised that he wanted very much to help her escape from the life she was rejecting, but could not think of any possible way.

Certainly if he went to Jock and asked him to find employment for an ex-dancer he'd met at the market, he would think him mad, it was simply not on, and he would probably think the worst. He could never embarrass both his employer and himself like that.

But then he suddenly thought of Jock's story about the Bibis. He had no intention of asking the girl to be his sleeping dictionary, but maybe he could offer her a job as a domestic for him, cook, housekeeper whatever. It was not as if Boy would mind, being paid in any case by the mine, and Julian knew he was a great admirer of the girl. Julian pushed to the back of his mind his own feelings, the impression the girl had made on him, and the novel attraction he was feeling towards her. He was simply helping her out as well as getting a housekeeper he told himself.

The girl interpreted his long silence as a refusal, and without a word rose gracefully to her feet, bowed deeply making obeisance, and turned to go.

'Hey, wait a minute, let's talk about it. Maybe I can do something. If you want, if you're interested.'

When Julian explained his proposal to her she made only one stipulation before accepting. Without a hint of embarrassment she wanted to stress that she was a 'good girl', would not share his bed, and would expect respect and privacy in his house. She was, she insisted honest, a good cook, could mend and make clothes, and promised to work very hard to look after him. The modest payment Julian offered her seemed to please, and for the first time he saw a smile break out on her face.

CHAPTER SIX

When Julian arrived back at his house later that night, feeling much happier than when he had left, he found to his surprise Jock's car parked in front.

His boss was in the front room sipping a scotch and talking to Boy. He greeted Julian, his expression serious, worried.

'Sorry to interrupt your evening Julian, but I've got some news you should hear straight away.'

Boy had already poured Julian a drink, but he stood irresolute, holding the glass as if unsure what to do with it.

Julian sat down opposite Jock, wondering what could have brought Jock out in the night to find him.

'What's the matter Jock? What news?'

Jock paused and took a sip from his drink before replying.

'The balloons gone up. Heard it on the radio earlier. It's war with Germany.'

Julian's drink materialised before him and he took the glass, swallowing half of it.

'I know it's only Europe now.' Jock continued, 'But it'll spread I'll be bound. It'll be a world war for sure.'

'But here, here in Burma, do you think it'll effect us?' Julian knew the answer even as he asked the question.

'Aye, it will. Although how much and when is anyone's guess. There are already problems here, our own problems, and they'll get worse. The nationalists will think it's time to put on the pressure, maybe even an armed struggle. There's not much of an army here and I guess they'll be needing all the men they can get in Europe, it'll change things here, make everything more insecure. And Laddie...' He leant forward over the table tapping it with his finger to emphasise his point, 'When you're sitting on top of one of the most product-ive gem mines in the far east, insecurity is the last thing you want.'

For a while the two men sat in silence, nursing half empty glasses while Boy watched from the door-way, serious and uncomprehending.

'What do you suggest Jock? What's to do?'

Jock stood up, finished his glass in one swallow, and picked up his hat from where it lay on the table.

'Tonight nothing, think about it. We'll have a meeting tomorrow morning, with the senior employees maybe, they'll have to know, and better from us than by the jungle telegraph. We'll have to review security for a start. All aspects. There's a delivery due to be shipped out next week, I'd like to set up some new arrange-ments by then.'

Once every month the gems produced by the mine were shipped down to Mandalay to the companies secure depot. They were escorted by a company of Sikhs from the army base there, as well as a dozen of the mine's employees armed with ancient Lee Enfields. From there, after sorting and valuation they were sent to Singapore, again with an army escort. So far none of the local armed factions had attempted to seize the treasure, but in a war situation it might be an irresistible temptation for a determined and well-armed group if the guard was weakened.

The two men walked out to Jocks car together as distant thunder over the mountains announced another rainstorm.

'I'll see you tomorrow Julian, first thing mark you, before the others get wind of it.' Jock said, climbing stiffly into the narrow seat. 'I just hope to god this one's not as bad as the last.'

That night Julian had the impression he didn't sleep until the lightening sky brought Boy into his room with his morning coffee at five thirty. His waking dreams had been of war, change, pain, death, going back. But everywhere, in all the noise-sum images drifted the image of the girl, her eyes looking into his, the sudden smile that came again and again like a flickering movie, captivating and entrancing. And when he finally awoke it was with the image of her here, in his house, his room, his bed.

'We'll have to look at security right from here to Mandalay Julian.' Announced Jock the next morning as they sat in his office half and hour before the workers began the morning shift. 'After Mandalay it'll be up to the army. It's here and on delivery we have to look at. Tighten it all up.'

'What do you suggest Jock? I always thought it's pretty secure now. What more can we do?'

'Well, there's not much more we can do here, everyone knows there are gems stored here in my safe before they're shipped out, we just have to be extra vigilant, and I'll put a couple of the men I can trust to watch at night, they'll stay outside my office until I arrive in the morning.

They both looked towards the massive dark green object in a corner of the room.

'I'll agree it's next to impossible to break into it, but it's still a temptation. But there's one question I've got to ask you before we do anything.'

'What is it Jock?'

"I have to know if you'll be staying like, now the country's at war, I thought you might want to go back, sign up, take the Kings shilling?'

Julian had asked the same question of himself most of the night. Before, he had always thought if war came he would go back home and join up. But now, after several months in the country he was starting to feel at home. He enjoyed the many challenges of his work, the town so different to English towns, the exotic peoples with their ready smiles and simple curiosity, his house with laughing Boy, and now, intruding on his every thought came the girl. The child woman who had entered his life, and now the thought of leaving her, never seeing her again, seemed impossible, not to be contemplated.

'I don't know Jock, it's so sudden. I think I'll stay, at least until we see what's going to happen. After all it might blow over,' he said with a shrug, 'and in any case I'm not going to leave you in the lurch after the chance you've given me.'

Jock slapped him playfully on the back, very relieved as he had invested many hopes for his and the mine's future in his new engineer.

'That's settled then, I'm probably worrying too much, but you never know.'

'So what about the transport to Mandalay, what can we do about that?'

"All we can do I think is to change the dates when we ship it out, and not tell anyone but the soldier boys escort. We'll have to let them know in advance, but nobody else, just our fellows on the night before.'

The two men talked until the first of the workers began arriving.

'That's about all we can do for now I think.' Jock said finally. 'I'll get the men together and give them the news, tell 'em there's nothing to worry about, business as usual. Any questions Julian?'

Julian had already thought of one that he had been hesitant about broaching.

'Jock, about Zeya, he's a Nationalist isn't he, maybe even a communist. I know you trust him, but...well with those sort of conflicting loyalties I'm a bit uneasy.'

Jock stood still for a moment, his hand on the door.

'Ach! It's the hothead student stuff he was exposed to. I still think he's loyal to us, but you're right to bring it up. We'll just have to keep a close eye on him, make sure he's not getting mixed up with the wrong sort of people.'

One of those wrong sort of people was in fact talking to Zeya at that very moment, seated under a beribboned Tamarind tree near the market. Mr. Kaw was seated with a small suitcase at his feet and his briefcase upon his knees. He was waiting for a lorry that would convey him to Mandalay in time to catch the night train to Rangoon. Zeya stood close by his side, close enough so any passer by could not hear their whispered conversation.

'It's our time now,' the black suited man was saying, 'The British cannot hold their possessions east of Suez. The Germans will probably defeat them in Europe, and if not occupied they will be emasculated, a spent force. Our comrades in China and Russia will help us take back our country. Already we are receiving arms from across the border by Muse.'

'But Japan? They are making gains in north and east China are they not?'

'For us Zeya, here in Burma, Japan is not our problem. One thing at a time. First kick out the British, worry about Japan later. Chairman Mao has their measure.'

The rattle of a badly tuned diesel grew in volume as an ancient lorry emitting prodigious amounts of black smoke turned the corner of the market and stopped next to the two men. Mr. Kaw climbed into the cab next to the driver and Zeya handed him his case.

'Remember comrade your duty, the party and the country are calling you now.' The bespectacled man in the lorry murmured to Zeya through the open window, ' The time has come!' And he banged the side of the door with his fist as the lorry lurched into motion with much crashing of gears and clouds of smoke.

CHAPTER SEVEN

Julian was anxious to return home that same evening. Instead of his usual wander around the town centre, stopping here and there for a halting conversation with a local, he drove rather faster than usual back to his house at the end of the track in the jungle.

When he arrived and parked the car it was already growing dark and he noticed that someone had put a lamp in the window giving onto the veranda, there were other lights inside the room. Boy was frugal in his use of oil, lighting the absolute minimum amount of lamps. As he approached the steps to the front door he saw the small figure on the veranda, leaning over the rail, silhouetted against the light. A voice came to him.

'Good evening Mr. Drake.' And Julian knew it was the girl.

When he stepped through the front door she was waiting for him, and he was aware of Boy hovering in the shadows behind her. She reached out and took his rucksack from him while he stood silent and baffled, but with his heart suddenly seeming to beat very fast in his chest.

'I very sorry but not know what time you come home sir, food ready maybe very soon. You take drink first? Maybe whiskey, please come.' And turning she led him into the front room where several lights were burning. He noticed the furniture had been rearranged, several items he didn't even recognise like a brass Indian coffee table and an old but respectable leather arm chair, dotted about.

'Miss Myitsu, excuse me I didn't know you wanted to start so soon. I should have been here, you know, to show you the ropes.'

She stood looking at him, her head on one side, unsure.

'Ropes? Sorry I not understand. You show me ropes? For what please?'

Julian couldn't help grinning.

'Excuse me, it's Myitsu your name isn't it, it's bad English, I meant show you the house, where everything is, what to do....' He trailed off, unable to concentrate under the disturbing gaze of the girl.

From behind him Boy's voice, strangely subdued.

'Papa, Boy not understand. Lady come this morning, say she live here now, look after Papa. But lady dancer, Boy not understand.'

Julian turned, Boys face in the lamplight was a picture of misery and Julian immediately guess the reason.

'It's all right Boy, don't worry. That's right, miss Myitsu is going to live here and look after the house. But it doesn't change anything for you.'

'Can stay Papa? Boy not send away?' He stepped forward, eager, hopeful.

'Of course Boy, this is your home. You can look after the garden and the things a man should do, Miss Myitsu will do the housework and cooking. Alright?'

Boy almost jumped with pleasure, seizing both Julian's hands, bowing over them.

'Oh! Thank you Papa thank you. Boy very happy now, make beautiful garden, many flower, many fruit. Boy take care everything.'

Julian extricated his hands from Boy's and turned to where Myitsu was watching, a wide smile making her seem even younger than before.

'Now if it's alright I'll have that drink you promised, and maybe you can tell me what's on the menu tonight.'

Myitsu had made her way to the house in the late morning after accepting Julian's offer and telling Mr. Pat, the troop leader that she would no longer be working for him. He accepted the news philosophically having noted the close interest Zeya had been taking in the girl for several months, and assumed a romantic attachment between the two young people. He was a kind man and knowing of Zeya's position in the mine assumed the girl would be well taken care of. When he learnt upon his next visit to Mogok that she was employed by the English engineer he assumed that the romance had not flourished, and she had taken this other opportunity, and the English engineer was definitely a better catch than the Burmese graduate.

Boy had been astonished to open the front door to her a few hours after Julian had left. He could not imagine what she was doing there, what could possibly have made her walk a half hour in the mid morning heat carrying a large bag to his home. For a moment he just stood and stared at her, his mouth open, before, and without invitation, she had brushed past him and entered the house.

'I'm here to work for Mr. Drake. ' She said as she passed by him, in a tone that brooked no discussion or argument, and Boy, stuttering with nervousness and anxiety had replied.

'I...I...don't know...Papa never told me. I work here for Papa, we d...don't need anyone else.'

The girl simply turned and smiled at him.

'It was agreed yesterday.'

And with that she began an exploration of the house with Boy following morosely at her heels.

His feelings towards her remained mixed until Julian's return. On the one hand he was excited and amazed at her presence in his home, but then he wondered why she was there, the real reason, for he could see no point in a second servant when there was so little work looking after the sole occupant. And she was a dancer, a wonderful dancer, what could she want here. But they were very nearly the same age, and although Myitsu was more experienced and worldly, he thought that eventually he could be friends with her.

In spite of the news of the war that evening, the first evening the three of them spent together, was for Julian the happiest of his life. He insisted they eat together, in spite of Myitsu's insistence that she couldn't sit with them and serve the food. In the end they all sat around the table in the kitchen, the dining room deemed to large and gloomy. Boy was in his idea of heaven, his idol, suddenly appearing like magic to live in the same house as himself, to work along side him everyday. He could hardly believe it, chattering incessantly in both Burmese and English, trying to show off in front of the girl, inflating his importance in the household.

Julian questioned Myitsu on her leaving the troop, and she assured him it had all passed of amicably, which Julian found a little hard to believe in view of her popularity.

'But they not give me much money ever.' She told them, 'I make money for them, but they not give me. No problem, I go.'

Julian suddenly thought about the money aspect.

'Myitsu, I pay Boy every week on Friday. Would it be ok if I pay you then too?'

'No problem sir, I not need money now except shopping for you.'

'Well you and Boy can decide how much you need each week for shopping and anything else, and I'll give it to you on Friday too.'

Julian couldn't get over how little money was needed to live in Burma, what he would pay Boy and Myitsu plus the weekly shopping was almost what a child would get as pocket money in England. One could live like a prince on next to nothing.

When Boy started dozing off in his chair, Julian realised he had not told Myitsu where she could sleep. He woke Boy and sent him to his room in the chalet with instructions to wake him at his usual time of six. There were four bedrooms on the first floor, plus an enormous attic room with windows, and Julian took the girl upstairs, each of them holding a lamp, to choose her room. To his surprise she had already explored there and had installed her meager possessions in the room directly opposite his own. There was just a double bed, a table with two chairs, and a heavy Chinese wardrobe. A worn and frayed carpet covered part of the floor.

'Are you alright here?' He inquired, noticing how neatly she had made up the bed, 'Is there anything else I can get you?'

She turned to look at him, her face half lit by the lamp she held, her big eyes dark and unreadable.

'Thank you sir. I am very happy here. Never have room for me alone before, always share.'

Julian felt suddenly awkward, not knowing quite how to take his leave and end the conversation.

'Err...well...I hope you'll be alright. If you need anything just bang on my door, my room is opposite. And Myitsu, can you please call me Julian, we've no need to be formal here, at least among ourselves.'

'Yulian,' She said to herself, 'Difficult for me. Please, what it mean?'

'It's just a name, I don't think it means anything.' He noticed his voice, tight, almost hoarse. He could detect the scent of her again as she stood close to him in the pool of light, surrounded by darkness where only the vague grey forms of the furniture stood witness. He wanted suddenly so much to reach out and touch her, to feel the warmth of her body under his fingers, the life within her. His past, his culture, education, nationality seemed to have faded away, there was only him and her in a dark place, a place without moral judgments; strange, exotic, like the sounds of drums in the jungle at night. They were simply a man and a woman on the edge of a precipice.

'Goodnight Yulian.' She said simply, and turned away to place her lamp on the table. Julian left the room, quietly closing the door behind him.

When he entered his own room he knew immediately she had been there. The bed was made much better than Boy would normally have done, his night clothes were folded neatly on his pillow, and a small vase he had never seen before was on the table, filled with a mixture of orchids and jasmine, filling the room with delicate sweet scent.

Not feeling tired he went back downstairs and went and sat on the balcony, taking a glass of scotch with him. The sky was clear, unusual for the monsoon season, the air fresh and heavy with the scents of the jungle. A carpet of stars stretched across the whole sky from horizon to horizon, from the dark outline of the distant mountains to the valley where the town lay sleeping. The war in Europe seemed very far away, another planet even, and he knew he could not go back, for was not the girl now sleeping in his house, not twelve feet away from his own bed. After a while he went back into the room and took up his violin. It had been a week at least since he had touched it, and he spent a few minutes carefully tuning it, and then began to play.

Upstairs the girl sat up in her bed, hearing the sounds of the foreign music, faint, distant, and strange to her, drifting though her open window, overlaying the night sounds of the jungle in an eerie and mystical duet. After a while she lay down again, her eyes open, listening, until sleep stole over her.

CHAPTER EIGHT

Two days later, four hundred miles to the south in a small room in Yar Street, Rangoon, seven men were holding a secret meeting. They were the committee of a new political party, the BCP, the Burmese Communist Party. Among the seven was one Dr. Nath, a medical doctor qualified in Calcutta and the proposed leader of the group. He was in his late thirties, slightly built with very straight black longish hair parted in the middle and thick horn rimmed glasses. Outside that room, to the world at large he was known as Mr. Kaw.

'The problem is the failure of our comrades in China to defeat the Japanese.' He was saying, 'As long as Chang Kai Chek's army holds the border lands along our frontier it will be difficult to obtain arms. And now this is the critical time, with Britain facing war and possible invasion this part of the world will be forgotten, why would they worry about Burma when they are facing defeat at home? '

There was a nodding of heads around the room, his argument seemed persuasive.

'We must expand our contacts in Thailand, there we can buy arms secretly, and the border presents no difficulties whatsoever. We must be ready to strike as soon as the British army and their Indian slaves are reduced in numbers. I am sending an agent to Bangkok with specific instructions to prepare for a massive purchase of arms.'

Thakin Aung San, another of the seven raised a hand.

'The money Mr. Kaw, where will we find the money for this massive purchase?'

Mr. Kaw smiled, showing two rows of yellowish teeth.

'Never forget comrades we are not alone. The struggle against the powers of capitalism and colonialism is worldwide. I have received information, reliable information, that our Soviet friends will provide some funds. The rest, will be sourced here, here in Burma.'

The other six delegates looked at each other doubtfully, and it was Thakin Aung San again who asked the question.

'Forgive me comrade, but where will we find such a quantity of money in our country.'

Mr. Kaw began putting away his notes and papers back in his battered brief case, not acknowledging the question at first. He snapped the lock and looked up at the men around him.

'That must remain my secret for the moment comrades, security is paramount to the operation, but believe me, the money will be found, Burma is not the poor country the British would make us believe. There is wealth here, and we must take it.'

For Julian the arrival of the girl in his house changed everything. No longer did he loiter in town after work, but hurried home to where he would find lamps lit on the veranda, a glass of scotch regrettably without ice on the table, and Boy and Myitsu waiting to welcome him. The two youngsters spoke Burmese together, seeming to laugh a lot, often looking towards Julian as they spoke. He would feign anger, demanding to know the joke and insisting on a translation.

The months passed happily for Julian. Slowly his Burmese began to improve, much to Jock's satisfaction.

'It's that lassie you have with you now. I told you so, never fails.'

Julian would protest that she was simply a housekeeper, not a 'sleeping dictionary'.

"Aye well, that's as maybe. But by all accounts she's a bonnie wee lassie. The word is out you know, not much secret in this place. Just don't let Mrs. Mac-Greggor get wind of it, ye'll never hear the last, or the minister too, he'll be in town next week to meet the District Officer, we'll have to have 'em to stay I expect.'

The annual visit of the District Officer, a man of sweeping powers, was a great event for the mine. As agent for the government he controlled the allocation of mineral licenses as well as government spending on the town and its surrounding country. Jock was hoping to obtain a promise of more money for the roads in the town, especially the road out to Mandalay which was being frequently closed due to subsidence and land slides.

'He'll be bringing the Memsahib of course, and the minister will bring his too. I don't know where Mrs. MacGreggor will put them all, might have to send a pair of them up to you for the night, we'll see about that later.'

Julian was not keen on the idea of having either a Churchman or a government official and their respective wives to stay in his home. It seemed like an intrusion into his private world, a world he wanted to keep inviolate, carefree, and happy, and when a couple of days before the visit Jock informed him that the District Officer had expressed a wish to see the old Government Lodge, and it would be necessary for them to pass the night with him, he was dismayed.

'I've not enough stuff,' He complained to Jock, 'Sheets, pillows, mosquito nets, not to mention cups and saucers and all the breakfast paraphernalia, and I can't imagine Boy making an English breakfast, he can just about manage an attempt at a decent cup of tea. You're sure you can't have them?'

Jock laughed.

'Don't worry, ye can get what you need from Mrs. MacGreggor, she'll pop over this afternoon and see what's needed.'

'This afternoon?' Exploded Julian, 'That's in a couple of hours, what'll I do about the girl?'

Jock stopped what he was doing, peering at un-cut stones on a polished brass sheet placed in the sun by the window.

'Weel, you'll have to either find a good reason for her to be there, or get rid of her for a couple of days 'till the coast's clear.'

Julian grabbed his hat and jacket and ran out of the office. Ten minutes later he pulled up outside his house relieved to see there were no other cars in the drive, but when he opened the front door he heard immediately the sound of a woman's voice, Mrs. Mac-Greggor had already arrived. He rushed into the front room his mind buzzing with possible excuses, to find Mrs. MacGreggor seated and with a cup of tea in one hand, Myitsu was standing a few feet away from her, hands meekly folded, attentive and demure.

'Ah Julian, you needn't have come home, your...now what was your name dear...yes...Myitsu. Myitsu here has been most useful, she seems to know just where everything is, so now I know what you need for the Frobishers. Mrs. Frobisher...' and here she dropped her voice as if the lady in question was listening behind the door, 'is difficult. Accustomed to the comforts of Mandalay or Rangoon you know, doesn't like the country much, but don't worry. It's just for one night.'

Julian had kept making discrete glances towards Myitsu, trying to guess what she had told the other woman about her place in his household.

'Oh! I'm sure we'll manage, try to make her at home. Can I get you anything? More tea perhaps? We might rustle up a bit of lunch if you'd like to stay. You could manage that couldn't you Myitsu?'

The girl turned towards him.

'Oh yes sir, I can make lunch easy.' And she grinned mischievously at him before turning back to Mrs. MacGreggor.

'What would you like Madam?'

Mrs. MacGreggor put down her tea and stood up.

'What I'd like Julian is for you to run me back home, you'll be going back yourself won't you?'

'Indeed, if everything is satisfactory to you we can leave straight away.'

Julian couldn't wait to get her out of the house, afraid of an indiscretion on the part of the girl as she seemed to be taking the situation as a joke.

'Julian,' Mrs. MacGreggor began as soon as they had passed the gates of the lodge, 'I hope you don't mind me saying this, and don't think of me as an interfering old lady, but that girl...well, she's very young and quite frankly shouldn't be staying alone with you in the government lodge. These things get out, tongues wag, and although we're a day away from Mandalay, news travels.'

'I am aware Mrs. MacGreggor, but she is simply a housekeeper, asked me for a job in the mine at first, obviously not possible, so I thought she could look after the house. Boy is not exactly very domesticated. And I can assure you that nothing improper has occurred or will occur.'

Mrs. MacGreggor turned to look at Julian as he drove down the narrow trail to the main road. He was slightly flushed she noticed, a fine sheen of sweat on his forehead.

'Julian, I'm not stupid, or inexperienced in the ways of the world. You might have the best of intentions, morals etcetera, but you're still a young man far away from home and civilisation. And I have to say she is an exceptionally lovely young creature. The women of this country are not like English girls, quite different in fact. They're clever, they know how to use men to get what they want, and Julian their morals are not the same as our morals.' And with that she turned once more to the front and said nothing more until they arrived at the house next to the mine.

It was an unwelcome event Julian thought later, he had hoped nobody would remark the girl, an obvious mistake. And now the District Officer and his wife were coming, it seemed the only course open to him was to keep her out of the way until they left.

That evening on his return to the lodge he sat down with Myitsu and tried to explain the situation. She either pretended not to understand deliberately in order to embarrass him or she genuinely didn't see what the problem was, he couldn't decide.

'Why Myitsu must go away? You need I look after guests, cook, all things. No problem.'

'Sorry Myitsu, you don't understand, you're not supposed to live here with me. It's a government lodge, the government won't have it. And these people who are coming are government people.'

Myitsu turned away, pouting. A sulky expression making her face even more childlike.

'Don't be angry Myitsu.' He said, feeling a sudden and unexpected pang of regret, hating the idea that he had hurt her feelings. Before he could realise what happened his hand had gone out to rest gently on her small shoulder. At his touch she started, turning slowly her head to face him, her big dark eyes brimming with tears.

Around the house during the day she wore a simple length of material wrapped around her and leaving her shoulders bare, the touch of his hand on her bare skin seemed to send a tremor of electricity through him, but he couldn't take it away, but gently squeezed and caressed her shoulder. She dropped her eyes to look down at his hand, watching without moving, then reaching up she placed her own hand over Julian's.

The sudden appearance of Boy in the doorway made him snatch his hand away. The lad looked curiously at them both, a slight knowing smile appearing on his face.

'Papa, come eat now?' He enquired innocently.

The Frobishers arrived mid afternoon two days later and were welcomed by Jock and his wife to their home. He was a tall thin man with white hair and a white moustache carrying himself very erect as if on a parade ground, a legacy of his days in the Guards. His piercing blue eyes seemed to be constantly in movement, searching, evaluating, and although in his sixties he moved quickly, as a much younger man might. He strode from the car ignoring his wife exiting from the opposite door, and greeted his hosts with a firm handshake and a quick nod. His wife, Hetty, following behind more sedately greeting them with a short embrace.

'That journey,' She proclaimed, 'gets worse every time I come here. Freddy, can't you do something about that road, it's a disgrace, I'm absolutely shattered. Stella my dear how are you? You never come and see us in Mandalay these days but now I understand why. Jock you should be ashamed to keep your wife locked up in this backwater, I insist she comes to visit soon, Christmas perhaps.'

The minister, the reverend Jacob Sprout and his wife Maureen arrived an hour later. They had traveled two days by bullock cart from the area east of Mogok where they were trying to convert the Palaung to their particular branch of Christianity. The reverend wore a crumpled and sweat stained tropical suit complete with his 'dog collar,' that he insisted on wearing in spite of the stifling heat and humidity. His wife, who seemed similarly impervious to the climate, was clothed in a long grey dress reaching her ankles and with tight long sleeves. They had made the arduous journey in the hope of extracting funds from the government for their struggling and frankly hopeless mission.

It was obvious that the Frobishers thought the Sprouts beneath them socially, and worse than that, slightly eccentric, something that was really not acceptable in the ex-patriot community of Mandalay. Freddy was concerned that their preaching and missionary work would disturb the status quo, give the natives modern ideas about their position in the world, perhaps even feed the desire for independence. But the couple seemed unaware of the chill atmosphere between them, enthusing about their recent converts, the medical service that Maureen had been able to provide on several occasions, the kindly character of the people.

'Mind you,' Jacob said at the end of a long eulogy to life amongst the tribes, 'It's going to take a while to break some of their more unsavoury customs.'

'And what might those be Jacob?' Enquired Hetti, 'They don't still eat people I hope.'

'Oh cannibalism has never existed in these parts of the world.' Jacob continued blithely, unaware of the joke. 'Too much food readily available in the forests. No, what we have to stamp out are the lax moral attitudes. Nat worship in particular, and they're far too free and easy with their...what can I say...private relationships. You know, we get girls having babies and they've no idea who the father might be...'

'Jacob!' Interrupted Hetty, 'I don't think we really need to discus that sort of thing. Please keep it for your jungly friends. Stella, did you know the New Year Dance has been cancelled? This stupid war they say, can't think why a dance should be stopped just because of a war on the other side of the world.'

It had been decided that they would all eat at the lodge that evening, and both couples were to spend the night there. Julian had told Myitsu she could stay in the house as long as she kept out of sight. She would sleep in the annex with Boy.

A smartly dressed Boy was serving drinks when Julian arrived home from the mine wearing his best tropical outfit newly washed and pressed by Myitsu. He had the impression of being studied carefully by the guests, so carefully that he wondered if the news of the girl had filtered through to Mandalay.

'You've heard the latest from home I take it?' Freddy said during a lull in the conversation.

'Not much,' Replied Jock, 'Reception's been bad the last few days. Anything new?'

'Nothing good. Very bad in fact.' Freddy replied helping himself to a second scotch, having turned down the offer of soda or water. 'We've been kicked out of France, whole bloody army, managed to save a lot of men from Dunkirk apparently, but lost most of the gear, guns, tanks, supplies, what-have-you. Absolute disaster in fact. Of course Churchill's trying to make out it's some sort of victory, but even he can't disguise the fact that we've been soundly beaten. France can't last much longer now, bound to throw in the towel.'

'Good god! So soon, I thought we'd make a fight of it at least, like in fourteen. So Hitler's boss of the continent now, where'll he go next I wonder.' Both Jock and Freddy had served in the First World War, and the memories were still fresh in their minds.

Freddy turned to Julian, who had had little to say in the conversations so far.

'How about you young man, thought of going back to sign on?'

Julian paused to gather his thoughts before replying.

'I have considered it sir. And still am. But I don't want to leave Jock in the lurch if I can avoid it.'

Hetti suddenly spoke up, addressing Julian directly.

'Oh Jock won't mind, will you Jock, what's more important, doing your duty or digging around in the dirt for a few coloured gems.'

Julian heard Jock clearing his throat noisily.

'I can assure you...' Began Julian, ready to defend himself.

'Now both our boys are serving the king aren't they Freddy,' She continued shrilly.

'John's at the war office, working all hours the poor dear, and Damian is in the home guard, tried to get a commission but his eyes let him down, didn't they Freddy.'

Freddy made sort of humph sound, and stared out of the window.

'I will probably go back.' Julian said at last. 'Just a question of when.'

'Aye, well don't be in too much of a hurry laddie, ' Said Jock, 'they said the last one would be over by

Christmas...it lasted four years. These things are easy to start but the very devil to stop. If it's anything like the last one there'll be a lot of blood spilt before somebody sees sense.'

'Do your duty Julian, do your duty.' Hetti persisted, 'Get yourself off home and take the shilling.'

The other side of the half open door Myitsu was standing, listening intently.

The remainder of the Frobisher's visit passed off uneventfully. Myitsu had disappeared, probably to the annex, Jock and Stella returned to their house after dinner and the guests took an early night pleading tiredness from the day's journey.

The following morning Julian found the table already laid for breakfast when he arose. He was relieved that Myitsu was nowhere to be seen, and Boy competently served a modest meal when the guests appeared downstairs.

They were to join Jock for a tour of the mine, town and surrounding countryside before leaving for their respective homes after lunch. Freddie and wife by the official Humber, Jacob and wife by bullock cart.

Before they left Jacob insisted on making a photo of them all in front of the house. He was a keen photographer, and took every opportunity to practice his hobby, sending his exposed films to a place in Mandalay to be developed and printed. He set up his large Ensign camera on a tripod on the drive and arranged the group on the stairs leading up to the front door. The two women in the centre with their husbands on either side, and Julian standing behind on the steps. He worked slowly and meticulously, trying everyone's patience, to make sure his exposure would be successful, and when satisfied he showed Boy how to press the rubber bulb that tripped the shutter. He took his place next to his wife before calling out.

'Now, smile everyone. Ready Boy? One two three ...press!'

The picture taken, he removed the roll of film and added it to the package of films he already had to be developed, giving it to Freddie to take with him.

As soon as their car had disappeared through the gates Julian went in search of Myitsu. Breakfast was on the table when he arose, and Boy was making coffee, so he imagined she had made herself scarce after preparing the meal. However she was not in the annex, and he wondered where she could be.

Julian left for the mine directly after the Sprouts, returning for lunch, and finding Myitsu still absent.

'Myitsu go town.' Boy informed him when he enquired after her whereabouts later that morning.

'Go after Papa.' And he looked uncomfortable, unable to meet Julian's eyes.

'When? How long ago?' Demanded Julian, feeling a sudden and deep anxiety.

Boy's appreciation of time was at best a vague concept, and he wrinkled his face and scratched his head before answering.

'Maybe...oh...maybe one hour.... maybe two.'

Julian ran to the old Morris and set off down the trail to town. Once on the main road he pushed the accelerator to the floor, managing to reach an unaccustomed thirty miles an hour. Luckily the road remained empty until he reached the town, where he slowed, peering through the dusty windscreen, looking intently for the girl. He could see her nowhere, not in the few streets that were now thronged by morning crowds, not in the market, not in the temple where he parked for a moment to rush inside like a madman, interrupting the morning chant, and leaving the handful of monks silent and open-mouthed.

He was about to start another circuit of the town when he saw her. She was coming out of the main gate to the mine, the gate where the workers were just leaving for their lunch break. He drew up alongside her and leant over to open the passenger door. She continued walking, not turning her head or acknowledging his presence. He drove slowly alongside her, calling her name, but it was as if she was deaf and blind to him.

He stopped the car and jumped out, placing himself directly in front of her, taking her shoulders in his hands as if a it the shake her.

'Myitsu! What are you doing? What's the matter? Where are you going?'

She remained still under his grip, staring directly ahead as if he was transparent, not replying.

He looked down and saw she was holding her large bag, the same she had brought with her to the lodge months ago. Gently he disengaged her fingers took it from her.

'Why my darling?' The word came out without his knowing how. He was suddenly afraid.

Eventually she raised her eyes to look at him, their difference in height making it difficult for her to make out his face against the sky.

'I know you go back your home. I hear lady say you go to be soldier. Leave Burma, leave Mogok, leave Myitsu leave Boy, leave everything.'

For a moment Julian couldn't think what she was alluding to, then he remembered the conversation at dinner the night before.

'Myitsu, it's not true. I'm not going anywhere, at least not for a long time and maybe never.'

She remained staring at him, unsure of what he was saying.

'Come now darling...' The word came naturally to him now, 'Come back home.'

Silently, obediently, she allowed him to lead her to the car where she took her seat while he placed her bag in the back.

They spoke not a word on the way home, and she followed him meekly as he carried her bag back up the stairs to her room. He placed it on the floor next to the bed and turned to her.

'It's hard to explain, it's like something I'm expected to do, but don't want to. It's like a custom, a tradition, if you're a man you have to do certain things otherwise people look down on you.'

He sat down on the bed and motioned her to sit next to him.

'Myitsu, I don't want to leave, not ever. But if I have to one day, I promise I'll come back and I'll make sure you are alright while I'm away.'

She swayed slightly, leaning her shoulder against him so he feels the warmth of her body. Then very softly began to speak.

She told him of Zeya and his idea for her to spy on him so that sometime in the future the treasure of the mine could be stolen by the nationalists who wanted to buy arms. She admitted her sympathies for the cause, but insisted that now she had changed, now she no longer wanted to be false, but to be honest with him. But she understood that now she would have to leave, he could not keep her. It was normal, she said, she had betrayed him from the start, and he must hate her now.

Julian said nothing for several long minutes. He was deeply shocked and amazed by her admission, but at the same time glad she had finally confessed freely. He tried to see her as some sort of fanatical activist, ready to do anything for the cause, but could only see a young woman, desperately unhappy, running away from her shame.

With a deep sigh he turned to face her, taking both her hands in his, looking straight into those lovely treacherous dark eyes.

'I should send you away, of course. It was very wrong what you did.' He began, his voice low, hardly a whisper, so that he had to lean towards her, his mouth close to hers, as if he were to impart a great secret.

'But I understand why you did it, and Zeya can be a very persuasive talker. But now you've told me it will be alright. I think we can forget it ever happened...'

'No!' She interrupted him pulling her hands away from his grasp. 'No. I know you must hate me now. I can see. I know what is in your heart.'

'Myitsu, my darling,' The word came out again uninvited, 'It's not true. I don't hate you, or anyone else for that matter. I don't want you to leave, you can't, I won't allow it.'

'Darlin'.' She said dreamily, tipping her head to one side, staring into the far distance, 'Darlin', why you call Myitsu your darlin'.'

Julian reached out and took her face between his hands, turning her to look directly into his eyes.

'Because Myitsu...because you are very precious to me.'

'Precious...what mean precious?'

'Precious means ...well...very sought after, valuable, expensive, like...like a ruby.'

Like the slow approach of dawn, a smile gradually came over her face.

'Myitsu your ruby? Mean Myitsu your darlin?' The smile became a grin.

'Yes.' Replied Julian, and gently brushed her smooth forehead with his lips. 'So you see you have to stay. Now you understand.'

Zeya had been very surprised to see Myitsu waiting by the gate to the mine when he arrived that morning. She was seated on the ground with her back to the wooden fence that ringed the mine and its out-buildings.

He frowned at her as he took her bag and helped her to her feet.

'Why are you here? We must not be seen to-gether. You know that. What is it?'

He unlocked the gate and led her quickly into one of the sheds where they were concealed from any passers by or workers who might be arriving at any moment.

'Well, what do you have to report? Progress I hope.'

'He's leaving. He's going to go away.' she said bleakly.

'Leaving? Why? When?' he demanded roughly.

'I don't know, I just heard them talking last night. The British people from Mandalay and the others. There's a war and he has to go and fight. It's their custom.'

Zeya took a while to digest this information. He assumed that the girl's obvious depression was due to the fact that her mission could not be accomplished if Julian left.

'What can you do to retain him? Can you find out anything before he goes?' He asked eventually.

The girl stared back at Zeya, her beautiful eyes red and enflamed.

'I can't do anything anymore. I don't want to do anything. It's not good what I said I would do.'

Shocked, he leant towards her taking her by her slight shoulders and shook her roughly.

'What do you mean? You must, you have your task, you must accomplish it, for Burma, for the people.'

'I don't care anymore.' She replied, not looking up at him. 'He is good to me, a good man for everyone. All the workers like him, he's fair and treats them like men and not slaves. I'm not going to spy on him anymore.'

Zeya jerked his hands away from her, and turned quickly away. He blamed himself, he should never have trusted a women, no, not even a woman, a girl with an important task. He stood blocking the doorway of the shed, staring out over the mine workings where men were beginning the morning's shift. It was the treasure of the mine that he had hoped to take. Not for himself, but for the party, to buy arms from the Chinese or the Thais, and he dreamed of the status that would have brought him in the party, the influence he would wield if he was successful. Myitsu should have give him secrets, secrets wormed out of the young Englishman, secrets he could have used to steal the gems, but now it had come to nothing.

The man was leaving for the war, which changed everything. Perhaps for the better, perhaps more British would leave; perhaps the goal of independence could be achieved peacefully, quickly even.

He turned back towards the girl.

'So you're leaving too? Did you tell him anything?

She shook her head, despairingly, her shoulders drooping, the her hands hanging lethargically at her sides.

'You had better go then, hurry, go anywhere he can't find you if he comes looking. Do you need money?'

Myitsu shook her head again, and picking up her bag waited for him to let her pass. At last he stepped away from the door and she walked out into the harsh morning light, turning briefly towards him as she passed.

'I'm sorry.' She said quietly.

Zeya knew now that the girl was lost to him, that she could certainly not be trusted to keep silent about the task she had abandoned. And if she talked, he himself was in danger. One day, he thought, one day she would have to pay for her actions.

He had to leave himself he knew now, and quickly. Maybe she had talked already, or would decide to stay until the Englishman left and tell him some other time. You could never guess with women he thought, they were prey to the most incomprehensible feelings and influences. His actual experience or contact with members of the opposite sex was minimal, he had never felt the need for a girl or woman in his life. He had the struggle, the cause, and he was married and faithful to that to the exclusion of everything else in life.

But before he left there was one thing he had to do. A small thing perhaps compared to the great plan he had just abandoned. But still necessary for the future of himself as well as the movement.

'Zeya's gone.' Were the first words Jock spoke to Julian when he arrived for work the next day.

'Found the guys waiting by the gate, unable to get in. Sent down to his place thinking maybe he's ill or something, but his stuff was gone. The guy he rented from said he'd left early, thought he took a lorry out of town.'

'He never said anything? Gave no indication of something amiss?' Julian asked, knowing full well the reason for his departure but unwilling to tell Jock because of Myitsu.

'Not a thing. And that's not all I'm afraid. The week's spinels that we don't lock in the safe are gone too. Not worth a fortune you know, but a tidy sum for a Burmese, enough to last him a couple of years at least.'

'That's terrible.' Julian said. 'Very ungrateful of him after all....'

'Aye, well let's not dwell on it.' Interrupted Jock, 'Nay use crying over spilt milk.'

Julian could see he was upset at the deceit, he had trusted the young man implicitly because of his father and had been let down.

'We did wonder, didn't we, about his political leanings, do you think it's connected?' Said Julian.

'Maybe, maybe it is, but now we'll just have to get on with things. I'll have to take over his work, you're not experienced enough yet, you'll fill in for me where you can. I'll make Mr. Patel overseer, I know I can trust him.'

Julian told Myitsu about Zeya's theft and escape when he returned home that evening. At first the atmosphere had been a little strained between them, there was a new dimension to their relationship that had not yet been defined or explored. They had both slept badly that night, she with her doubts and questions, he restless with uninvited images that peopled the world between wakefulness and sleep; her eyes on him, the pressure of her light soft body against his shoulder as they sat on the bed, the smooth pale skin of her bare shoulders that seemed to draw his hand to touch, caress. And other imagined images that he tried to push away, ashamed but enthralled, but that came back time and time again.

The young man was not a virgin, an end of term celebration with a group of his fellow students had ended up in Straw Street in Exeter, where in a well known establishment he had been briefly introduced to the basics of sex. He had not enjoyed the experience, in part due to the quantities of drink consumed before, but also because of the feelings of shame that came on both during and after the event. He was perhaps unusual for a young man in that he had an inborn and deeply held respect for the female sex. The loss of his mother at a very early age had resulted in his putting her on a pedestal, idealising what he never knew, and keeping close to his heart the image of his imagined and perfect mother.

He could therefore not place Myitsu in his world as a Bibi, a useful native to be picked up and discarded when no longer required. But in the society he had grown up in neither could he place her as a partner, a lover, or even a wife. His feelings ran deep for her. Deeper than he had ever experienced, opening up unknown needs, desires. But not just physical, that he might have understood and accepted. No, what Julian really wanted was to possess the girl in spirit. To know her completely, both her mind and her body, and in return to give himself to her, completely, irrevocably, and unrestrained by social considerations.

After dinner when the kitchen had been cleared and Boy had gone off to sleep in his annex Julian and Myitsu went out onto the veranda and sat on opposite sides of a low rattan table, there was an awkward silence between them for several minutes before Myitsu spoke.

'Myitsu sixteen year old. Never have real boy friend. Never go with man. Understand?'

Julian turned towards her. She was leaning forward in her chair, looking out over the veranda rail into the darkness beyond as if expecting a vision to appear, her expression unreadable.

'Understand? I understand your words, but what do you mean to tell me?'

'What you think Yulian?' She replied quietly after a moment.

On impulse he stretched out his hand across the table, reaching for her, after a second's hesitation her own small hand rested in his.

'What Yulian think...my darlin'?' And she turned to him with a mischievous grin.

Julian smiled too, conscious of her gentle tease.

'Sorry Myitsu, I really don't know. I'm not very good with that sort of thing, not much experience with girls I'm afraid.'

She turned in her chair directly towards him, both her hands now holding his, her head on one side.

'Oh! You lie I think! I think you many girls in England, maybe wife, maybe children.'

Julian stood up suddenly, dropping her hands and feeling awkward and stood with his back against the veranda rail looking down on her.

'No lie Myitsu, no girlfriend, no wife, and certainly no children! It's not done in my country, and I was too busy studying to mess around with girls, well, I'm only twenty two after all.'

They had never discussed ages before and his admission seemed to give her food for thought.

'Hmm! Twenty-two. Old man next me. Myitsu just sixteen. Maybe too old for me.'

'Myitsu! How dare you, twenty two is nothing, I'm still a young man.' He said laughing and reached down and took her hands again in his.

'And what do you mean too old for you? I've not asked to marry you have I?'

'You call Myitsu darlin'...ruby...mean what?'

And she grinned up at him, obviously enjoying his discomfiture.

Julian felt the heat building inside him, the desire to take her up in his arms, to stop her teasing with his mouth on hers, to forget the pretence and let go. Without him realising his hands gripped hers tighter until she cried out, pulling them away...

'Aiii! Stop! Yulian too strong.' But she was giggling as she stood up and ran into the house, turning briefly at the door to look back at him, laughing as if to invite pursuit.

CHAPTER EIGHT

Over the next few weeks the news from England, either picked up intermittently on the BBC, or brought up from Mandalay grew worse. Freddie told Jock in a note that most of the Indian troops based there had been pulled out and sent to Singapore to replace regular units that had been shipped home. There was talk of setting up a militia to keep order in the remoter parts of the country, but there was a reluctance to arm any Burmese in view of the political situation. Petrol rationing was introduced, and Julian brought Boy an old second hand bicycle to economise.

The flirtatious sparing between Julian and Myitsu continued, half serious, half in jest. But for Julian at least he could never sleep without imagining her, remembering everything she had said that day, every look, every smile. And the girl herself basked in the warmth of his regard. Happy simply to be admired, for she knew with a woman's instinct exactly how he wanted her, and was content to be the subject of his badly hidden longing and suspected sexual frustration.

Julian had adopted the habit of practicing his violin each night before bed. It served to calm and distract him he found. Myitsu, though at first disliking western music, came slowly to enjoy listening to him, at the same time being able to observe him without him being aware. She liked the look of concentration on his face as he played, the sensitive way his fingers touched the strings and held the bow, and was unable to stop herself imagining how they might touch her, gently, softly.

On the eighth of December nineteen forty one Freddie's Humber arrived unannounced, pulling up in front of the gate to the mine in a cloud of yellow dust. It carried not Freddie, but an urgent message for Jock. Luckily it found both him and Julian finishing lunch on the veranda. The Indian driver saluted them before handing over an envelope.

Jock tore it open, found his reading glasses in his shirt pocket, and quickly read the contents, then looked up at Julian.

'Bloody hell.' He said simply.

'What is it?' Asked Julian, rather shocked by Jock swearing, something he normally almost never did, especially with Stella within earshot.

'The Japs. They've sunk the American Pacific fleet at Pearl Harbour, and invaded Malaya. Without warning the bastards, no declaration of war. Happened yesterday, and Churchill's already declared, the Yanks too.'

He turned suddenly towards the house.

'Stella! Stella! Get the wireless on. We have to hear the news.'

The messenger clicked his heals and saluted again.

'Sahib Frobisher say I must wait to take you back if you had no means of transport. Will you come with me Sir?'

Jock turned to Julian, passing the note to him.

'Freddie wants me in Mandalay for a meeting, I'll go there with the driver, it'll be quicker, get Mr. Patel to come and pick me up tomorrow will you Julian.'

Stella appeared in the doorway looking worried.

'What's the matter Jock? Why are you shouting?'

'Why...it's war woman, that's why. Throw me somethings in a bag, I'm leaving for Mandalay directly. And try to get the BBC. Find out what's happening.'

Later that same day just as it was growing dark, in a small room over a jewellers shop on the corner of Maha Bandular Street and 37th avenue in one of the poorest districts of Rangoon, seven senior officials of the Burmese Communist Party met to discuss the latest news of the Japanese attack, and it's implications for the party and for Burma. As usual it was Mr. Kaw who lead the discussion.

'Comrades,' He began, 'The unforeseen attack by the Japanese on America and Britain will have consequences for us and our struggle.'

'They're mad!' Interrupted Aung San 'They can't fight the Chinese, the Americans, and the Brits, they've made a huge mistake.'

Mr. Kaw smiled his knowing smile, as if he were party to information denied to the others.

'Whether it is a mistake or not only the future will tell. Do not underestimate the Japanese war machine, already in one blow they are masters of the Pacific. They have invaded unopposed a British colony, and will probably soon destroy Chiang Ki-Shek's and Mao Zedong's remaining armies in Yunnan and Jiangsu.'

'But I still think the Brits and the Yanks will defeat them in the end, just look at the statistics. And if the two Chinese factions could co-operate instead of fighting each other the Japanese would be quickly driven back to their islands.'

Mr. Kaw shrugged his shoulders.

'Maybe, maybe, but for the moment co-operation is difficult and in the mean time they are masters of the Pacific, and will soon be masters of the whole far east.

What we must consider today is our reaction, how we can profit from the situation.'

'Well, there'll be a lot fewer troops to garrison Burma, but surely, as the Japs have been fighting Mao Zedong for so long, they are our enemies too. They are after all seeking to have their own Empire, a despotic fascist empire.' Said Bo Aung, the oldest of the group and a university professor.

'You are right to a certain extent comrade, but let me sketch out the scenario we might expect to develop, and it's consequences for Burma.' He stood up and went over to where a map of the Far East was pinned on the wall.

'The Japanese take Malaya and Singapore in the next couple of months. Then they strike south, through the islands of Indonesia, seizing the Dutch colonies. But after, or even simultaneously, they must secure their right flank from attack by the British from India. How? By taking both Thailand and Burma.' He prodded the map in the region of Thailand.

There was a murmur of dismay around the table, but he continued.

'Thailand will be occupied peacefully, they have already made a treaty. The British will fight them in Burma but do not have enough men or material to defeat them or even hold them, and here comrades is where we have our opportunity.'

'Are you suggesting an alliance with them? A fascist state at war with Mao?' Asked Bo Aung, looking astonished. 'Never! We can never betray our Chinese comrades.'

'Our objectives, comrades. Think what exactly are our objectives.' He said quietly with emphasis.

There was a moments pause before several of the men almost together replied.

'Independence. Freedom.'

Mr. Kaw continued.

'The importance of Burma to the Japanese cannot be underestimated, and not only to protect their flank, look carefully here on the map.' And be pointed to the southwest frontier of China, where it touched the far north of Burma.

'China, and next to it Burma, and next to Burma Nagaland, in India. A distance of less than one hundred miles. No road at the moment, but one is being built. And when it is completed, admittedly with great difficulty due to the mountainous terrain, the British and Americans will be able to send supplies directly to China, to be used against the Japanese. So this, the Japanese must stop, and quickly, and at the same time as they attack the road they will be in a position to threaten India, the jewel in the British crown.'

The room was silent, the men engrossed in the Mr. Kaw's explanations.

'Thus we can get an idea of just how important Burma is to the Japanese, it is for them absolutely essential that they secure Burma.'

'So you're proposing an alliance? Even though they are enemies of the people?' Asked Aung San.

'Comrades, I have been in contact with persons in Japan who have assured me that they support unequivocally an independent Burma, free from the British. And they are willing to help us do this in return for denying the country to any allied incursion or invasion, denying the allies access to the India China highway, and agreeing to sell our oil from the Yenaungyaung fields to the Japanese army. '

There was a stunned silence as the men digested this information.

'And a government? A parliament? How would that work?' Asked Aung San.

'They would take no part in internal affairs, we would have complete freedom and independence to rule ourselves.'

'And an army, we could have a Burmese army.'

'Indeed, an immediate necessity, there would of course be a certain amount of conflict with retrograde elements. Those opposed to the arrangement would have to be eliminated.'

The discussions continued for another two hours when by a show of hands it was agreed that Mr. Kaw would proceed with negotiations to allow Japanese forces free access to an independent Burma. Only two men failed to raise their hands, one of them being Aung San, and the other Zeya, newly arrived from Mandalay.

Mr. Kaw looked sharply at the two dissenters when a show of hands was taken, he had spoken only briefly to Zeya since his arrival, and was beginning to wonder about their commitment to the cause. When Zeya had told him of the failure of the plan to get hold of the rubies, he had said simply.

'There must be other ways. Please produce an alternative method, preferably one which does not rely upon the services of a girl dancer.'

But Zeya knew now that it would be difficult for him to return to Mogok, he was well known there, and with the theft of the spinels that he had handed over to Mr. Kaw, he would be arrested as soon as the police could be summoned from Mandalay.

The men left quietly, separating in front of the shop to go their different ways, not one of them noticing the black Ford car parked fifty yards up the street. Two men had sat patiently inside since before dark, watching and noting the arrivals and departures at the shop.

After the last person had left, just before midnight, one of the men, Inspector Frank Last, turned to the other. 'We'll bring 'em in, tomorrow, before dawn, don't want 'em disappearing do we.' And he started the car and drove off rapidly down Maha Bandular Street in the direction of the docks.

Un-noticed by them Mr. Kaw was also making his way to the docks, although not to the same destination, the Central Police Station in Strand Street. He was heading towards the wharves at the far end of Aung Yadana Street, where a small, rusty and ancient trading steamer was tied up. Its destination was Ranong, a minor port on the north west coast of Thailand. From there the Secretary of the Burmese Communist party would cross the isthmus to Surat Thani, taking there another ship that one week later would depose him at Nagasaki in Japan.

CHAPTER NINE.

'Myitsu,' Julian continued after briefly telling her the news on his return home that evening, 'this is serious, the war might come here, to Burma.'

They were sitting side by side on the veranda, and he had taken her hand in his own, but couldn't bare to look at her.

'I not understand, why Japanese come here? Why fight?'

Julian tried to explain, but he could see she couldn't or wouldn't understand. In the end he had to confess what he has been dreading to tell her.

'Darling, you must understand, but I might have to go away, join the army or something. I can't just sit here and do nothing. And in any case the government will probably enforce conscription...that means they'll make me join up.'

The girl's eyes opened in shock. For a moment she simply stared at him, as if unable to accept his words, that he might leave her.

'You say.' She almost screamed at him, snatching her hand from his. 'You tell Myitsu...you promise you never go away, leave me.'

'No darling, I said I didn't think I would have to. But things have changed, I can't help it. I have to do my duty.'

'She stood up, turning to face him, a small very fierce creature, hands clenched at her sides, the mixed emotions of anger, fear, misery passing across her expressive young face.

'What is duty? Duty to die? Duty to kill other men? Not a good thing I think...bad for all people.'

'I know it's difficult for you Myitsu. I don't really understand myself, but it's just something I have to do when the time comes.'

The girl remained standing in front of him, silent. The night, enormous and as impenetrable as the mind of man surrounded the two figures on the veranda of the house. What had before seemed so safe, familiar, permanent, now seemed poisoned with unseen danger. An unfamiliar dread of something coming, some dark force gathering in the jungle and mountains. She felt it more than Julian. A power greater than hers was reaching out for him from the world outside of which she knew so little and cared less.

Fear gripped her, and fear made anger, for she was not, in spite of her youth and sex, a passive creature. She would fight for him, for possession of this foreign man who had slowly and gently captured her heart. She would fight with the only weapons she had, her mind, her heart, and her body.

She turned away from the object of her love, seemingly accepting the fate that awaited them both. As she walked back into the room her hand brushed his shoulder, casually, as if in a touch of forgiveness, a blessing. But her eyes were hard and bright with determination, she would not let him go.

Julian felt her touch, reached up to take her hand but found it gone. A great lethargy came over him, a sort of undefined sadness at some undefined loss. He could sense the reality and the proximity of his leaving, the disappearance of this world that had given him so much happiness. His house in the jungle, Boy with his permanent smile, and Myitsu, beautiful as the dawn, gentle as the touch of a butterfly wing, mysterious, exotic, enticing, and forbidden.

There was a darkness in their future he knew, the smell of smoke and blood, the crying of children, pain and death. He knew nothing of war and hated violence of any kind, the idea that he might have to take another's life was profoundly abhorrent to him. And like most young people he had never considered his own mortality up to now. Seated on his veranda that night in a warm pool of lamplight with the faint sounds of Boy and Myitsu preparing the evening meal in the kitchen, he wondered what it would be like to die.

They ate as usual in the kitchen in an awkward and unaccustomed silence. Julian realised that Myitsu must have told Boy of the situation but the two young people exchanged no words over dinner. Julian tried once or twice to lighten the atmosphere with a comment about the food or a question about their day, but they answered in monosyllables, cutting him off from them as if he had already left.

After the meal Julian stayed in the kitchen while Boy cleared away and washed the dishes. Myitsu went out to the spirit house with offerings, far more than she usually took, and was gone for some time.

Boy left for his annex without a word on completion of his tasks, leaving Julian sitting alone, hurt and miserable. Myitsu came back but went straight to her room, and Julian sat listening to the muffled sounds of her moving around, wishing he could go to her, wishing she would come to him, but knowing the futility of his desires.

He finished the cigarette he was smoking, went into the front room and picked up his violin, tuning it deftly, quickly. Without thinking he began to play, the first thing that came to him, a violin transcription of *A Lark Ascending,* sad, poignant, achingly beautiful.

The music began to sooth him as it always did, especially this piece that seemed to fit so perfectly his humour, his life at that instant. The room faded, became transparent, dissolving in the sounds that became substance. Julian became lost, hearing only the slow melody, the sighing chords, the melodies changing and crossing, point and counterpoint, a web of multicoloured sound.

He stood in a pool of lamplight by the window that looked out onto the total blackness of the outside world, while all around the house the forest Nats seemed to listen to the sounds so foreign to their land.

He became conscious she had entered the room, though he had not seen her arrival. He turned slightly toward her as he played on, his eyes resting on the small figure on the edge of the lamplight. She had changed her wrap to a thin pure white silk one he had not seen before, and let down her hair so it fell in a long straight black cascade over her shoulders. For a while she stood, not looking at him, her eyes on some far distant scene, her slim body swaying slightly in harmony to the music. Then she began to dance.

This was not her music, not the rhythmic beat of the drum, the wail of the pipes, the crashing of cymbals. The music he played was continuous, a flowing melody of aching sadness, and she danced not the studied doll like poses he had seen at the market, but a flowing movement that had no end or beginning. Her body became the music, echoing the sadness and the sensuality. Her thin wrap moulded her body as she swayed, revealing and concealing at the same time, and her hair swept her shoulders in a swift caress as her head turned. Now her eyes were on him, as she moved they never left his face, as if studying, goading, seeking his reaction.

She danced closer to him, touching him at times, her arms and hands drawing shapes in the air around him. Her body undulating fluidly beneath the silk became something new for him, not the body of the young flirtatious girl he knew, but something primitive, demanding, elemental. He could see the dark outline of her nipples through the silk, he could hear her breathing as she danced, smell the scent of her, feel her desire, her need.

As the piece neared its conclusion she moved even closer to him, encircling him, her hands brushing against his chest, his back, his arms and sending electric like shocks though him. Then, at the last long note he played, drawing his bow slowly across the c string, she collapsed at his feet, her face against the floor in total and complete submission.

Julian remained still, just slowly lowering the violin and bow, to look down at small figure of the girl at his feet. He wanted to reach down, to pick her up and hold her against him. To feel that young supple body moulded to his. To feel her warmth, her soft lips against his, her breasts pressing against him. But he could not move.

He was seeing her alone after his leaving, seeing her waiting for his news, news that might never come or on coming might be bad. Seeing the face he adored wet with tears because of him, the small shoulders shaking with misery. He could not move, he could not take her, use her, deceive her and then leave her. What they had lived these past months was too good, too pure, too innocent, and he could not destroy it.

At last she lifted her head to look up at him. And seeing him unbending, immobile, her hope collapsed. She scrambled lightly to her feet, turned, and ran from the room. The slam of her door echoing through the now silent house seemed like the sound of an executioners axe to Julian as he stood alone in the room below her.

Both Julian and Myitsu slept little that night. He tormented by visions of the girl, her body moving, undulating with open eroticism before him and for him. He felt it was something he should not have witnessed, almost something private of hers, a glimpse into a part of her that should be kept secret, unrevealed, even to a partner. Julian's knowledge of female sexuality was limited to the degrading episode as a student in Exeter, he had simply no idea that a girl, and a girl as young as Myitsu, could have desires, even needs, and his feelings hovered between attraction and shock. She had told him those few months ago that she was a 'good girl', and he had no doubt she was telling the truth, now she evidently desired him as a lover, but what else?

There were times when Julian suddenly became very conscious of the alien society in which he lived. His love of the place and the people could not always cover up a profound difference between the cultures. It might come over him with the sight of an undernourished child begging in the street, a cripple parading his deformity in the market with a withered hand holding out a metal bowl for alms, a dead dog lying in the road being gnawed at by others. Perhaps even the bold and unaffected smiles of the women. This was not his country they told him, not his people, not his morals.

For Myitsu it was a similar feeling. Her idea to seduce him had failed, she had misunderstood the man. Now he would hate her she felt sure. She had offered herself to him and been rejected, and she could only surmise that it was because he was different, different to Burmese men or Indian men, or any of the men she had observed in her short lifetime. Her misery was compounded by the knowledge that he would be leaving her, possibly soon, and there would be little time to repair the damage she had wrought, if indeed it could be repaired.

Myitsu did not appear at breakfast the following morning. Julian sat silent as Boy chattered away, oblivious of the events of the night before. The lad asked if he could take his beloved bike into town to visit friends, and Julian told him to make sure Myitsu knew where and when he was going before he left.

The drive into town gave Julian time to think about his future. He could not imagine that they could keep on living together as if nothing had happened, something was changed now, brought out into the open, something he would have liked kept a secret, unaccepted and unrecognised. He shied away from the idea of Myitsu as his Bibi, the possible scandal, the jokes between men, the nudges and winks. It was demeaning both to him and her.

His train of thought was interrupted as he approached the town and he was obliged to stop the car. The road was blocked by an escaped buffalo outside a place that served as an abattoir. The huge beast stood irresolutely in the middle of the road snorting and pawing at the ground surrounded at a respectful distance by a crowd of onlookers. A short rope hung down from the creatures muzzle that from time to time a man would try to snatch. But the animal was too wary, as if knowing of the fate that awaited it inside the building. There was a great deal of shouting of advice and warnings, and Julian lent over the steering wheel to watch the outcome.

A large fat man dressed only in a shortened longi appeared from the abattoir, he carried a huge machete with a long handle, the crowd opening to allow his passage. Although still early and not yet very hot the man was sweating profusely, and as he walked towards the beast he was wiping his hands repeatedly on his filthy and blood stained longi. A respectful hush descended upon the crowd.

The man slowly approached the animal, at the same time raising his machete in both hands above his head. The buffalo remained still, watching the man from the corner of its red rimmed eye. Slowly the man advanced one foot, spreading his legs as he prepared for the strike. The watchers seemed to hold their breath as he lifted the blade the last few inches, raising himself on his toes at the same time.

Just as with a grunt he swung down the blade the beast started, moving slightly to one side. The blade struck it, but not on the base of the neck where it met the backbone, paralysing it and allowing it to bleed to death, but just into the fleshy part of the neck, severing the artery but without paralysing it.

A jet of blood shot from the open fissure as the beast swung away from its tormentor, but then sensing its attacker it turned back towards him in an instinctive desire to defend itself. The man, in spite of his size moved quickly, raising the weapon again and striking at the head of the animal as it turned towards him. The blade bounced off the thick scull and sliced off half the bulls face including one eye. But it had seen its attacker in front of it and before the man could step aside the head went down as it took two or three steps towards him, then with a vicious jerk brought up its massive pointed horns.

The left horn caught the man at the base of his stomach, lifting him off the ground as if he weighed nothing, and tearing him open. A great clot of blood and something else struck the car windscreen of the car, and screams and shouts erupted all around as men turned to distance themselves from the spectacle. The body of the man fell from the horn to lie on the ground at the animal's feet. Although eviscerated he still lived, making feeble movements with his arms and legs.

The buffalo stood over him, blood still jetting from its neck and nostrils, then as if suddenly tired, collapsed onto the man, crushing his body completely except for his head, which remained visible to one side, an expression of mild surprise on its features. After a moment the blood stopped running and with an audible sigh the creature died.

Julian remained frozen in shock, his hands clenching the wheel, unable to process what he had just witnessed. Sudden death in the morning, blood, screams, terror. One moment two lives, then gone, man and animal. The world seemed suddenly alien, this shouldn't, couldn't happen. Death had suddenly appeared before him, unfamiliar, swift, meaningless.

At that moment a line of half a dozen monks appeared, making their way from the temple to the town, red robes and with brass begging bowls in their hands. The crowd stepped back to allow them passage. They walked calmly past the two bodies, passed the blood and guts, without turning, without looking, without acknowledging anything. Their eyes straight ahead. Only the youngest one, a shaven head novice of about six allowed his eyes to turn briefly towards the bloody mess on the road.

Julian slammed the car into reverse, made careless three point turn, and raced back along the road towards his house, narrowly missing Boy at the cross roads as he shot recklessly by on his way to town.

Pulling up outside the house he saw Myitsu, broom in hand, standing on the veranda. He climbed quickly out of the car and looked up at her. For an instant their eyes locked, understanding, before she turned and disappeared inside.

He ran up the steps through the door and into the room, but she was already gone. Somehow he knew where she would be, and took the stairs two by two almost running through the open door into her room.

The shutters were drawn, leaving the room in a soft diffused light. Myitsu was standing by her bed looking at him, her eyes huge, dark, achingly beautiful. She had removed her blouse and was nude from the waist up. As he watched she folded the garment neatly and placed it on the bed. In a movement so natural she could have been alone she unfastened the longi at her waist and let it fall to the floor, her eyes never leaving his. A sound escaped his lips, her name he could hardly articulate

She stood before him, her entire body exposed to him, a small ivory figure, perfect in every detail, unashamed, even proud, for she knew of her beauty. His eyes traveled over her, drinking in the vision as a man dying of thirst might drink from a fountain of pure cold water. Her small high breasts, the nipples pointed and erect, her narrow waist and flat abdomen, the tiny shadow of hair between her thighs that failed to conceal the virginal cleft of her sex.

Then he was next to her, taking her head in his hands and bending to kiss the lips that waited. Her arms went around his neck and he felt her body pressing urgently against his. It seemed so natural, as if choreographed and practiced as he lifted her and placed her gently on the bed. For a moment he stopped and stood over her as she waited, her arms and legs akimbo and her eyes watching him. And something inside him was telling him that finally this was meant to be, this was right.

It was like waking from a long deep sleep. Slowly he became aware he was lying on her bed, her head rested on his chest, a small hand on his shoulder. He felt the soft warmth of her body where it was pressed against him, and the coolness where their sweat was still drying. He had never felt such peace.

The memories of their love-making floated through his consciousness, vague but intense. Her cry when he had first entered her, and then her arms and legs around him, holding, keeping. The unbelievable softness of her small body under him, moving, matching his own movements. His mouth on hers, wide and accepting, then the taste of her nipple as she offered her breast to him.

He had been afraid to hurt her, and at one moment had asked. Unable to speak she had shook her head, putting her hands on his buttocks and accepting him fully into her. And in the end he could think only of his own pleasure, the last few moments nothing mattering except to thrust deeper and deeper, spurred on by her little cries as her nails raked his back and he felt the spasms of her climax.

He had no idea that the act could be like that. The joining of not just their bodies but their minds. The final acceptance of their love for each other and the giving of their bodies to each other. It seemed to him as he lay in the dim light of the one lamp that burned low and yellow on the table, that he was no longer the same person as before. He had both given and received in equal measure, and could never now separate himself from the person at his side. In his heart now they were one entity, joined irrevocably by this strange and primitive ceremony of sensual pleasure.

She turned her face towards him, questioning.

'Yulian? You happy?'

He could only nod, smiling down at her anxious face.

'Sure? I not know. First time for Myitsu. Want you be happy.'

He reached around and lifted her light body onto his so that she lay full length on top of him.

'It was...I can't explain darling...it was wonderful...I just never knew...'

But her mouth stopped him talking, and then she was moving on him and her legs spreading to receive him as her hand reached down to guide him into her.

'Myitsu want Youlian.' She gasped as he entered her again.

CHAPTER ELEVEN

Jock returned to Mogok late that day in the old Morris with Mr. Patel. After dropping his driver in the town he took the car straight to Julian's house. The lodge was in darkness, no light showing in any of the windows, and it was several minutes after he knocked before Julian opened the door, naked except for a cloth wrapped around his waist in the style of the natives. Jock apologised for disturbing him, although he was somewhat surprised to see the young man had already taken to his bed at what was a fairly early hour.

Julian led him into the front room and offered him a seat and a scotch, both of which Jock was happy to accept.

'You look worn out.' Julian told him, 'How was Mandalay? And the road back, any problems?'

Jock swallowed his scotch, thinking that Julian too looked tired.

'Road was quiet, not much traffic, no major problems. Mandalay...different. Lots of coming and going around the barracks, lorries on the move south, looked like the Indians were moving out somewhere.'

'And the meeting? With Freddie? How did that go?'

'Well, there was a bloke there, from intelligence I guess, gave us a talk on local security, how the situation could develop now we're at war with Japan.'

Jock finished his glass and accepted another when Julian held out the bottle.

'Sorry. I should have asked...have you eaten this evening?'

Jock confessed he had eaten nothing since leaving Mandalay.

'I'll see what we can rustle up.' Said Julian, and went to the bottom of the stairs and called Myitsu.

The girl arrived immediately, dressed similarly to Julian in a simple sarong, leaving her shoulders and arms bare. Her feet too were bare and her hair was loose, slightly tangled as one who has just awoken. Jock had met her several times before on visits, but this time there seemed something different about her. Her eyes seldom left Julian only glancing briefly at Jock to return his brusque greeting. Although small she had a presence that through her beauty seemed to dominate the room. A sort of glow surrounded her, and Jock was reminded of the Nats, spirits of the forest, for she seemed to be not entirely of this world.

Julian gave her brief instructions to prepare a light meal for Jock and she left without a word, just a slight nod and smile.

'Humph!' Commented Jock after she left the room. 'She seems to be looking after you I can see. A pretty wee thing I'll have to admit.'

'So what else did he say?' Julian asked, anxious to change the subject.

'Well, he didn't reckon the Japs much. Didn't think they'd get very far in Malaya. Said the quality of their men was inferior to ours, short sighted, weak, stupid, etcetera. Said there were heavy naval reinforcements on the way. Wouldn't tell us what exactly. Seemed to think it would all be over for them in a few months, even though the yanks had got a bloody nose at Pearl Harbour.'

'Well that sounds good, no? Nothing much for us to worry about here?'

'That's more or less what he was trying to tell us. But Freddy and I are not so sure.'

'Oh, why's that?'

'Call it intuition, a sort of bad feeling. They said the same sort of thing about the last war. All over by Christmas they said, lasted four years.'

'And Christmas is coming soon here.' Observed Julian.

'Ach! Maybe we're wrong, Freddie and me, a couple of old fools, armchair strategists, but it just sounded too glib, to complacent. They're convinced for a start that Singapore, if the Japs ever reach there, is impregnable. Well, they said the same about the Maginot Line, and that didn't last long.'

Myitsu appeared with a tray of food, some cold barbecued chicken with rice and salad, and placed it in front of Jock, who watched her with ill concealed interest.

'Myitsu, has this man been treating you all right? Not working you too hard?' He asked her suddenly before she could leave. 'Because if he has I have a mind to get you to come and look after me.'

Myitsu looked anxiously from Jock to Julian.

'No sir. Not hard. Work easy, no problem.'

'Well, that's alright then, it's just I thought you looked a bit tired, maybe not enough sleep, wouldn't you say that's probably it Julian?'

'I really wouldn't know Jock.' said Julian, beginning to feel embarrassed, 'She's fine, just you woke us...I mean me...her...woke her up.'

'Aye, that must be it.' Jock said and winked salaciously at both Julian and Myitsu.

Myitsu left them and Jock attacked his meal.

'So anything else happen there?' Asked Julian.

Jock paused to reflect.

'Well, one good thing, they gave us a radio, short wave, send and receive. We're supposed to report in twice a day. Tell 'em if all's well. They're more worried about the communists and the new Burmese Liberation Army than the japs.'

'What do they expect us to do?'

'Us, here, not a lot. We already have good security because of the gems. I'll give the boys who ride shot-gun for us a bit of practice with the Lee Enfields, they were more danger to themselves than the enemy last time I gave 'em five rounds apiece to try and hit something.'

Jock finished his food and pushed the plate away. As if by magic Myitsu instantly appeared to clear away.

'I'd best be off, Stella will be waiting up for me.'

They stood up and made their way to the door.

'I've got the radio in the back of the car. I was going to leave it with you to have a play with.' he glanced toward Myitsu who was hovering near and offering him his hat, 'but I can see you've other things more interesting to play with. Goodnight to you.'

And he seized his hat, jammed it hard onto his head, and disappeared down the steps and into the car.

They waited by the door until the lights of the car had vanished into the night, then turned to each other, both smiling.

'He knows.' Said Julian.

'Yes, but not care I think.' Said Myitsu. 'Now you come back bed with me, ok?'

Julian felt a warmth spreading through his belly as he thought of what he now knew awaited him above. They turned, and hand in hand climbed the stairs to her room and her bed.

The days and weeks that followed seemed a surreal mixture of joy and dread for the two young lovers. The joy of getting to know each other, and the dread of the approaching tide of war. For Julian he could never have enough of his Myitsu. He spent his days at the mine longing for the moment when he could leave his work and return to the lodge in the jungle where she waited his return with equal impatience. She would be there on the veranda, sitting motionless while observing the trail from the gates, or sometimes standing, her hands clasped tightly in front of her in an effort to keep them still. She lived for the moment when leaving the car and striding up the steps to the door he would take her on his arms, lifting her light body up so he could kiss her lips, and her hands could at last touch, hold, caress. Most often, unable to control the need they had of each other, he would carry her straight upstairs to her bed, remove the single garment she wore in one swift motion, carelessly throw off his own clothes, and kneel over her for a moment as they both savoured the anticipation of what was to come. Boy had quickly and diplomatically learnt to absent himself at these times.

She was a country to explore for Julian. Not just her body that he never tired of admiring, but her mind, so strange and different to what he knew. He was infatuated by her many idiosyncrasies, the sudden pout of her lips when unsure or doubtful of something. The tilt of her head and raised eyebrows when she failed to understand him, the slight frown of concentration when they made love, her white kitten-like teeth biting down on her bottom lip as she climaxed with little animal cries of pleasure. At first she was shy when he touched her breasts, for Burmese women the ideal was a flat, formless chest, and Myitsu although small and slim was generously endowed. But eventually she would lie, a slight smile upon her face, enjoying his touch as a cat allows a gentle stroke.

Through her he learned more in those weeks of the language and culture of the country, than in the previous two and half years. She told him about the thirty seven sorts of Nats, in which she believed absolutely. The spirits of the forests, stones, trees, mountains, rivers, as well as deceased ancestors, who lived amongst the people and had to be respected and propitiated with regular offerings. With this in mind she had persuaded Julian to instal a new spirit house outside the gate, a miniature temple on a post, complete with a small ladder to enable those smaller Nats easier access to the offerings left each evening before bed, or just before dawn.

She told him how they occasionally took wives from among the human population, either women, or transvestite or homosexual men, who then became important conduits to the spirit world. The more the dangers of war approached, the more assiduous became her attention to the Nats, unable to understand or accept Julian's unvoiced but obvious skepticism.

Oh but he was different her man she knew, and in the difference she rejoiced. Not like the Burmese men she had known through her childhood and adolescence, hard brown men who had the reputation of infidelity, shallowness, and changeability. She respected his intelligence, was he not an engineer and important man at the mine when so young? Did he not show his love with kind words, generosity, and gentleness? Did he not arouse and excite her as she had never believed possible, giving her such intense pleasure that left her exhausted, spent, and perfectly satisfied? For Myitsu, although he was her first lover, she could not imagine how she could ever take another.

The Christmas Ball in Mandalay, the event of the year, had been canceled, there was no appetite among the Europeans for revelry with the somber news from both the war in Europe as well as the war a few hundred miles from them. It was the loss of the battleships Repulse and Prince of Wales earlier that month that brought home the seriousness of the situation, the Japanese, in spite of what the BBC told them, were winning.

Then on Christmas day, just as Julian, Jock, and Stella sat down for their festive lunch, came the call on the new radio from Freddie. Hong Kong had fallen to the Japanese. But it was not just the military defeat that shocked, Freddie had told Jock that the Japanese had massacred civilians as well as prisoners, had stormed the hospital killing the staff, bayoneting the patients in their beds, raping and murdering the nurses. The short wave radio transmission detailing the atrocities had been cut off abruptly in mid transmission and had not reported in since.

Stella's face had gone white as Jock related Freddie's message.

'Jock! What if they come here...what will we do?'

Jock had reached over to place a protective hand over hers.

'We'll not be here if they come, dinna fret yerself. If there's any danger of that we'll be away from here.'

Stella looked down at the roast potatoes in front of her that she had been about to serve in spite of the heat and humidity.

'But to where Jock? Where will we go? This is our home.

CHAPTER TWELVE

It was to the notorious Insien prison in Rangoon that they brought Zeya, handcuffed to a sweating British corporal, and escorted by half a dozen Sikh soldiers. He had been woken before dawn by the sound of his door being smashed down, and before he was properly awake had been pulled from his bed, had his arms wrenched behind his back, and his wrists manacled. There were two civilians with the soldiers, both men in their forties wearing what looked to Zeya like a sort of uniform of tropical suits and solar toupees. They were police he surmised, but not normal police. Not a word was spoken as they dragged him downstairs and outside to where a large black American Ford V8 was parked, engine running, lights extinguished.

He was pushed roughly into the back seat with the corporal, one of the civilians taking the seat on the opposite side of him while the other sat next to the driver.

'Where are you taking me?' Said Zeya, trying to keep the fear out of his voice. 'What is the meaning of this? My clothes, I must have my clothes.' He was still dressed only in his pants and vest.

The man on his right turned to look briefly at him, apparently indifferent.

'You'll see chummy.' He murmured, 'We'll not be going far, not far at all.' And with that he turned to look out of the window as the car moved off, followed a lorry containing the soldiers.

During the drive Zeya tried to guess who had betrayed him, for it was certain one of the group, one of the men he had considered as a friend, a comrade in the struggle, had been an agent of his enemy, the British. His inclination was to doubt Mr. Kaw, for no other reason than he disliked the man and knew nothing of his past. The other members of the group were all known to him since his student days, all young men like himself save for Bo Aung, the professor, all dedicated to the cause. He wondered how many of the group had been arrested like himself, if indeed he was arrested, for nothing had been said.

The first thing Zeya noticed about the prison when after passing through the main gates and into the interior courtyard was the smell. It hit him as soon as he was manhandled out of the car. A mixture of excrement, sweat, and fear. There were no lights in any of the barred windows overlooking the courtyard, just one over an armoured door that opened moments after one of the police had knocked hard upon it.

A half dressed warden opened the door after several minutes, his uniform jacket hastily thrown over a vest and left undone. The man accompanied Zeya and the two police along gloomy and filthy corridors, through several other doors that had to be unlocked and locked again after them, before finally opening a door to an almost empty room. Just a desk stood in the middle of the space with three chairs, one on one side and two on the other.

The two police entered behind Zeya and he heard the door slam and the sound of a lock turned. One of them unfastened his handcuffs and motioned him to sit on the chair facing the desk. Both of them removed their jackets and sat down opposite him.

For a while nobody spoke, the men just stared at Zeya, unblinking and expressionless. Zeya thought it best to say nothing and wait for the questions that were bound to come.

After a few minutes there was a knock on the door. One of the police went over and unlocked it, opening it to admit another man. He was smartly dressed, as if about to attend a fashionable race meeting at the Rangoon Turf Club, or a lunch at the Pegu Club. He went straight over to Zeya and without hesitation held out his hand to be shaken. Zeya stared at it, uncomprehending, and looked up at the man. He smiled affably, maintaining his hand outstretched.

'Good morning Zeya, welcome to Insein, sorry to get you out of bed so early but ...well...time presses.'

Reluctantly Zeya took, the offered hand and halfheartedly shook it.

'What do you want with me? They didn't even let me get dressed.'

The man smiled looking down at Zeya's state of undress as if he had not noticed it before.

'Dam! Awfully sorry, I'll send someone to get your stuff directly. In the meantime just relax, it's not the Pegu club here, no need to be formal.'

'What do you want?' Zeya repeated, disturbed by the apparent friendliness of the man.

'Want? Ah! Yes, I'll get round to that directly. But first let's just have a little chat about things.' Here he turned towards the two police, waving a hand vaguely towards the door.

'Thank you gentlemen, you can leave us now. Wait outside please, we won't be long.'

Without a word the men stood up and left the room, closing but not locking the door behind them. The other man walked behind the desk and sat down, leaning over towards Zeya, still smiling his disturbing and enigmatic smile.

'Should have introduced myself, excuse... Smith's the name, John Smith.' And he grinned at Zeya, showing very white long teeth.

'Now, first of all, let me put your mind at rest. This might be the Insien prison, but it's under our control, for the moment at least, and we aren't going to bop you off. Just not the way we do things old boy...understand?' He sat back in his chair, looking serious for the first time.

'But to be frank, and I think we should be honest with each other, don't you? You are in a bit of a pickle. Been seen with some unsavoury characters, some rather extreme literature with your name on, and we do know all about your University mates...you'll be meeting up with them soon bye the way.'

So they had the rest of the group Zeya thought.

He stood up here and came and sat on the edge of the desk next to Zeya.

'Now, what would you say my friend, if I were to tell you that Burma, *your* country, let's not beat about the bush, your country could become independent in say five or six years. And without bloodshed mind you. Or very little at least.'

'I probably wouldn't believe it.' Replied Zeya, 'A century and a half of British rule and oppression aren't going to disappear over night. It'll take an armed struggle to free our country, and it will come, and it will be soon and fierce.'

Mr Smith stood up and began to pace backwards and forwards behind Zeya.

'Your aims then Zeya can be summarised simply as the independence of your country, a country free from foreign dominance. True?'

Zeya nodded silently, wondering where the conversation was leading, and if there was a trap somewhere.

'Now shall I tell you our aims Zeya, the aims of the British Government and people? They are also simple at this time, the defeat of the fascist axis; Germany, Italy, and Japan. Burma, it's independence or otherwise does simply not figure.'

He stopped pacing and stared at Zeya, as if to guess if he had followed what he had said. Zeya, still mystified, stared back at him.

'I shall tell you something not generally known yet, and I'd appreciate it if you'd...so to speak...keep it under your hat. At least for a while.'

Zeya couldn't help the smile that appeared. The people who had apparently arrested him were now asking for his confidence!

Mr Smith sat down on the desk again, leaning towards him and lowering his voice as if afraid of being heard.

'The japs are winning the war at the moment. Singapore could fall in a week or so, and right after that or even before, Burma will be invaded, probably from the South, there's a huge Japanese build up in Thailand, around Ranong. They'll start there and move north.'

Zeya could not stop himself interrupting here.

'We are aware of this. However we will not call it an invasion, for us, when they defeat you, it will be our liberation.' He stopped, wondering if he had gone to far, revealed too much. The other man seemed not to have noticed.

'Quite, quite, and as things stand there's nothing much to stop them before they reach India. That's not being pessimistic, just realistic. The military high command and Whitehall can't seem to absorb the situation, living in a fantasy world, but the fact is we're beaten in the far-east, no two ways about it.'

He paused, as if to let his words sink in. Mr Kaw had voiced similar prognostics, but hearing it from a British man, probably an intelligence officer, made it suddenly seem real, imminent.

'Beaten for the moment that is.' Mr Smith got up from the desk and went to stand behind Zeya, putting two firms hands on his shoulders in a strangely intimate way, as if they were old friends.

'But just as I know we're loosing now, I know that in the end Japan will be destroyed, not maybe by us, but by the Americans.'

'Why am I here Mr Smith?'

'Because at the end of this war, with the defeat of Japan, Burma will be given almost immediately complete independence. It has already been decided. In the next few weeks a provisional government will be appointed, not here, but in Dhaka. A government in exile if you like.'

'The Japanese have promised self rule when they liberate us from you.'

'The Japanese will promise anything. Meaningless words.' He went and sat down behind the desk and opened a brown folder and extracted a document of three or four pages, pushing it across the table to Zeya.

'What is this.' He said, making no effort to touch it.

'We have a source, a contact, in the Japanese government, under deep cover, been there for years. This...' and he indicated the document with an elegant movement of his hand, 'is a memo concerning the promise of theirs, how it's all talk, the only government they'll give you will be controlled tightly by them, they'll appoint, set policy, everything. They'll just be a bunch of Burmese puppets to rubber stamp everything, make it look right. Burma, my dear Zeya, will become merely a vassal state of Japan. A colony, and with no prospect at all of independence, at least in your lifetime.'

Zeya reached out slowly and lifted a corner of the paper, it was in Japanese with an English translation written underneath.

'This could be fake.' He said, at the same time knowing in his heart it was real.

'Oh Zeya, it's real, very real, and I think you know it.'

'What do you want from me Mr Smith. Why did you bring me here to tell me this?'

'We want your help Zeya, to beat the Japs. The quicker we beat them the quicker you get your independence. We want you to help build up a resistance movement to them, before they come. Recruit, explain, tell the people who their real enemy is. You already have the basic infrastructure with the communist movement, turn it into an anti-Japanese movement. Work with us, not against us. We'll give you any help we can, but time's running out.'

'And if I...we refuse, what then?'

Mr Smith stood up again as if the interview was at an end.

'You'll stay here, you and your mates. And when the Japs come I don't think they'll have any use for you, and you know what that means don't you Zeya.'

At the door as he went out he turned.

'I'm sending your comrades in for you to talk to, let them know the score. I need your answer today one way or another.'

It was the next day in fact when Zeya and the other arrested communists signed the Insein Manifesto, signalling the end of resistance to British rule and the beginning of a resistance movement against the Japanese. All executive members were present except Mr Kaw, who was at that time disembarking in Nagasaki, warmly welcomed by his Japanese hosts.

Chapter Thirteen

The festive season that never really happened was passed. The news continued to be either bad or obviously selective. Jock had a call from the C/O Mandalay to tell him that unfortunately no troops could be spared to escort the mine's produce to Mandalay and beyond. Talking it over with Julian they decided that for the moment they would suspend shipments and store the gems until such time as they could find a secure way to ship them out of the country, the usual route to Singapore being definitely out of the question now.

But the depression that hung over most of the Europeans in Burma at that time had no effect on Julian and Myitsu. It was as if they lived in another world for those few months. What relevance was the advance of armies, the destruction of cities, the sinking of battleships compared to the words they spoke to each other every night, those whispers in the dark that promised ever lasting love, and so much more. They watched each other, reading every gesture, every expression, jealous of the unknown. Like children they were easily hurt, her if he perhaps arrived home a few minutes late, he if she was not waiting on the veranda when he did. But the vexation could not survive the meeting of their eyes, would melt in the warmth of their smiles, and disappear in the joy of the meeting of their lips.

They thought not of the future, their present was so huge, so all encompassing, leaving no room for anything outside the single orbit of their two planets. In fact the noise of war that filtered from time to time through to their private universe only reinforced their isolation, barriers were set up, walls built, and the dream continued inviolate.

Boy too was enjoying the warmth of the atmosphere in the house. Never having had much of a family since his mother and sister had died in the cholera outbreak of nineteen thirty five, he loved the unaccustomed companionship of the girl when Julian was away at work. Myitsu replacing the sister he could hardly remember but still strangely missed.

One day he returned from town announcing he had a present for Myitsu, and handed her a cardboard box containing a tiny black kitten, barely a few weeks old, it's pale blue eyes having just opened. Myitsu was besotted by the little creature, calling it 'Baby', and carrying it about with her most of the day. Julian like to watch her playing with it, her obvious happiness, the hands he knew so well giving the caresses he himself could later expect, and he wondered once or twice what would a real baby be like if he were to give her one.

An unusually severe heat wave in January fell upon the country around Mogok, keeping Myitsu indoors and Boy's excursions on his bike into town infrequent. Weeks of blistering heat made whirlwinds of fine dust and dry leaves scatter across the exhausted rice fields and the flimsy farmer's huts of bamboo and matting.

Production at the mine diminished as the workers, although a tough and resistant group, took long breaks through the furnace like heat of the afternoon. The metal of their tools grew too hot to touch, the ground too hard, blunting pick and spade, the men sought the shade to sit there sweating and panting until their foreman drove them back to work with kicks and curses.

One late afternoon when Julian had taken his day off, allowed every two weeks, and he and Myitsu were sitting in a shady spot on the veranda he asked her if she could swim.

'No swim.' She affirmed very definitely, 'No like, never learn.'

'Then it's about time you were taught. I've not shown you the swimming pool yet have I?'

A quarter of a mile from the lodge a stream sourced from the distant mountains ran through the jungle, descending in a series of small waterfalls and shady pools. Many years ago, the first inhabitants of the lodge had dammed the stream at one spot to form a pool deep enough to swim in. A rough track ran from the lodge to the place, overgrown now as the pool had not been used for twenty years or more. They had also built a small cabin by the pool, perhaps for the Victorian or Edwardian ladies to change in, which still stood in a reasonable state of repair.

Myitsu took a little persuading that a tramp and climb through the jungle in the heat of the afternoon could be worth the effort, but Julian was insistent, anticipating the pleasure of swimming in comparatively cool water.

The entrance to the trail leading to the pool was at the back of the garden between the annex and the water tower. Boy had made some effort to keep at least the start of the trail open, but a few feet into the jungle it all but disappeared, overgrown by the vigorous plant life. A group of banana trees had grown up a little way along the path, their broad heavy leaves and long clusters of fruit totally concealing the path. Julian asked Boy to go in front of them, clearing the way with his machete. Although not the rainy season the jungle felt damp, the air humid with the scents of flowers and decomposing vegetation, and all around them came the buzzing, humming, droning sounds of insects, and the calls of unseen and unknown birds.

Myitsu was not happy following behind Julian and Boy, muttering about the heat, mosquitoes, and

Nats, and holding on to Julian's shirttail as if afraid to be left behind. The trail climbed gently, zigzagging the hillside, until it straightened out as the jungle finally thinned, affording occasional views of the valley behind them. Soon the sound of running water was heard, and the trail dipped, leading them down to where the stream has been dammed all those years ago forming a pool of deep clear water with small cascades at each end. Low trees surrounded the pool save for where on one side a large flat slab of rock was shaded by a Tamarind tree at the end of the trail. Behind the rock, nestling half hidden in the jungle was the cabin, somewhat overgrown with creepers but still standing.

Julian was imagining the Edwardian ladies with their unsuitable clothes sitting before the cabin, perhaps drinking tea provided by Indian servants, while the men in long woollen bathing suits, moustaches, and pallid skin, splashed about in the water.

They spread their towels on the rock and Julian put the bottles of lemonade he had carried into the edge of the pool to cool down. Boy busied himself clearing out the cabin, chopping at the vines and sweeping the fallen foliage out with an improvised broom. Myitsu having regarded the water in the pool with some misgivings sat down carefully on the edge of the rock dangling her small shapely feet in the water.

'Water cold.' She pronounced, 'Not good.'

'Can't be cold!' Protested Julian, 'It just feels cold because you're hot. 'You'll feel wonderful when you get in.'

'Aiii! Myitsu not go into water, maybe die. Not good for Burmese lady.'

Julian had stripped off to his underwear and went and stood in the edge of the pool where the water just reached up to his knees.

'Myitsu, you're not going to die, it's just a little pool, hardly deep enough to drown in. Come on in, you'll love it.'

Myitsu looked around to where Boy was finishing cleaning the cabin and stood up on the edge of the rock.

'Maybe Nat live here, not like we stay. Better go back home.'

Julian thought he'd heard enough about Nats and their likes and dislikes since Myitsu had moved in with him.

'It's alright Darling, we'll leave him a bottle of lemonade when we go, should keep him happy.'

Myitsu pulled an unhappy face, and advanced one foot into the water.

'Aiii! Cold!' She murmured.

Julian turned and dived, allowing himself to sink deep under the water into a wonderful cool world where the only sound was the distant muffled noise of the cascade. When he surface Myitsu hadn't moved, but stood regarding him nervously.

'See! Not drown.' He called to her.

Nervously, slowly she moved the other foot into the water until she was standing with both feet submerged, the water barely covering her ankles.

'Enough now I think.' He heard her say quietly.

Julian waded towards her, smiling. She looked up at him, suddenly afraid.

'Now come on darling. Nothing to worry about...I'll look after you.'

'No look after.' She said and turned to retreat to the bank, but Julian caught her round the waist and lifted her effortlessly into his arms.

'Don't worry darling...you'll be alright, just a little swim, a little tiny one.' He said laughing.

'Nooo!' Wailed Myitsu clinging tightly to him with both arms and legs. 'No, not want, let go!'

'Let go? Let go? Is that what you want?'

And he lowered her quickly into the water until it covered with only her face exposed.

A scream of incomprehensible Burmese brought Boy out of the cabin and caused several birds to take wing from the tops of nearby trees.

'Bad words.' He said, shaking his head in bemusement, 'Lady say bad words.' before returning to his cleaning.

Julian lifted her out of the water, laughing while at the same time covering her face with kisses.

'I hate you mister. Not good to your darlin'. I leave you now I think... very cruel you are.'

Julian knew by now the game. He had to make up to her with kisses and words and the gentle caresses that he knew she could not resist. Slowly she relaxed in his arms, slowly returning his kisses, and when his hands sought through the wet material of her sarong those places where he knew she loved to be touched, she sighed deeply.

'Cannot darlin...Boy watch.'

At that moment Boy's voice came from the cabin.

'Papa, come and see. I find something.'

Julian waded out of the water with Myitsu clasped close to him, enjoying the novel feeling of her wet body pressed to his through the thin material that clung to her revealing the curves of her breasts and hips. He put her down on the rock, kissing her lightly on the forehead, and made his way over to the cabin where inside Boy was on hands and knees pointing at something. Julian knelt beside him to see better what he had found.

'I sweep floor Papa, and then feel floor move. And look, here is big hole.'

There was in fact a large square recess below the floor that Boy had uncovered by removing a couple of teak floorboards. It was like a wooden box, but appeared to be lined with something like silver foil, it was quite empty save for a small piece of paper that Boy extracted and handed to Julian.

'Patum Peperium. The Gentleman's relish.' He could make out the faded letters, and underneath

'Fortnum and Mason. Est 1707'

'It's a cold store.' He said, 'you know, a place to keep food cool for a few hours. The people who came here in the old days must have used it when they had picnics. Give it a wipe out and fix the floor properly again, might come in useful one day.'

When Julian emerged from the cabin he stopped and stared in disbelief. Myitsu was in the pool, only her head emerging from the water, doing a confident dog paddle through the water. She turned towards him laughing.

'Myitsu swim good, no? You think Myitsu scared water. Ha! You better know mister, Myitsu not scared anything...anyone!'

'Why you little...' Julian plunged into the water to exact a thorough but gentle revenge, as she screamed and tried to paddle away.

They returned home later that afternoon, Boy going ahead of them to start preparing the evening meal. Julian walked behind Myitsu, the track being too narrow to do otherwise, and in any case he enjoyed watching her move in front of him, smooth, sinuous, and graceful. He liked the way her hips moved, the sway of the young straight body under her damp sarong, the slim bare arms and white shoulders dappled by the late afternoon light through the trees. They had played and flirted all afternoon, enjoying the unfamiliar feelings of being out-doors, partly dressed, and free to express their feelings. But of course with Boy watching their flirting could not be consummated, leaving both of them eagerly anticip-ating their arrival home when they could be alone, and satisfy the need they had for each other.

Boy was not in the kitchen when they entered by the back door. Playfully Julian made a grab for her, in-tending to carry her upstairs in his arms, but she skipped away for him, laughing. He caught up with her in the hallway tried to grab her again, missed, but caught her sarong, dragging it from her. Naked and laughing she ran into the front room, looking over her shoulder at Julian who pursued her making growling noises. She stopped suddenly at the entrance to the room and Julian threw his arms around her cupping her small pert breasts in his hands. Her sudden silence made him look up. The Reverend Sprout and his wife were sitting at the table staring open mouthed at the spectacle of the naked young girl and the man who had materialised before them.

'G...g....g...good afternoon.' Was all Julian could think of to say.

The Sprouts did not stay long. Myitsu had fled the room leaving Julian red faced and mortified. The equally red faced minister had explained briefly that they had wanted to drop in on him to thank him for his hospitality and leave him a print of the photograph he had taken on their previous visit.

'We've decided to leave, go back home.' Jacob explained, 'don't like the look of things. The reports from our ministries in China make the Japs look like a horde of savages. Can't take the risk with Maureen.

Jock lent us the car to get up here, have to get back soon, Freddie's sending the Humber up for us, decent of him.'

'I'm sorry to hear that.' Julian said. 'It's a worrying time for us all. But I think it must be the right decision for you.'

'There's things happening too, things we don't understand, a bunch of Chinese suddenly appeared out of nowhere the other day. Uniformed, soldiers, couldn't tell if they were Commitung or Reds, but we're more than a hundred miles from the border. Didn't reply when I asked 'em. Pretended they didn't understand, but they did...tried Mandarin and Cantonese...didn't say a word. Just looked around the village, made a few notes and left. About twenty of them, platoon strength and well armed. I've told Jock and he radioed Freddie who didn't seem too surprised. Anyway, we'll be glad to get out of here. Not a minute too soon.'

He handed an envelop to Julian.

'Came out pretty well, 'cept Hetti has got her eyes closed. Had prints made for us all, Jocks got one.'

'That's very kind of you.' Said Julian, still feeling very uncomfortable under the scrutiny of Maureen who hadn't said a word so far but was staring at him with a look of imperious disgust on her face.

'Errr...sorry to barge in like that, knocked on the door but no one came, guessed you'd be back soon as it'll be dark soon and the car was in the drive. Thought to wait.'

'We'd been swimming.'

'Harrumph!' Said Maureen.

'Quite.' Said the Reverend. 'Don't blame you...terrible heat today.'

Maureen stood up.

'Jacob we must go. Can't keep the car waiting.' She took several steps towards Julian, her eyes blazing with indignation.

'And you young man, had better pull your socks up and do your duty. What d'you mean by lounging around here with that...that...that... when better men than you are dying...'

'Quite Maureen, no need to labour the point.' Interrupted Jacob, for the first time seeming sympathetic towards Julian. 'We'll leave you to...err...get on...'

Maureen swept out of the room with a toss of her head and a final 'Harrumph!', followed meekly by Jacob.

After their car had disappeared down the trail Julian opened the envelope and extracted the photograph, it smelt slightly of chemicals. The group was stiffly posed, frozen and severe, in front of the lodge, Julian slightly behind the four others, the only one with a smile on his face. He felt a hand on his shoulder as Myitsu peered around him to study the image. Then the shaking of her body with suppressed laughter.

'What's funny? Is it me? You don't think I look handsome?'

Myitsu was laughing openly now, her hand half covering her face, unable to speak and pointing to a place on the print.

'What? What is it?'

He peered closer to where her finger pointed. In an upstairs window Myitsu's pale face looked out, barely visible, but once pointed out unmistakable, it almost seemed as if one could discern a smile on her face.

'Why you little minx!' Exploded Julian, 'Lets hope the Sprouts haven't noticed, or there'll be trouble.'

'Myitsu never have photo, nobody take.' She complained theatrically, pouting and arranging her long hair about her slim shoulders.

Julian sighed and smiled indulgently at her, putting his arm around her waist.

'Tomorrow, I promise. I'll borrow Jocks camera and take a whole roll of film of you.'

CHAPTER FOURTEEN

The day that Julian made his first photos of Myitsu was the day the Japanese invaded Burma. The Japanese invasion was carried out by General Shojiro Iida's Fifteenth Army, which initially consisted of 35,000 men in the 33rd and 55th Divisions. The crossing into Burma at Kaw Thung was unopposed, and they drove rapidly north and west. Tavoy fell on 19 January, isolating the garrison of Mergui, which had to be withdrawn by sea. This gave the Japanese control of three airfields, and allowed them to launch the first air raids on Rangoon.

The British and Indian troops, largely untrained and inexperienced in jungle warfare, were pushed further and further north, and on the twentieth of February the Japanese crossed the Salween, taking Rangoon a few days later.

The taking of Rangoon, so quickly and apparently easily, was a huge shock to the Europeans in the rest of Burma. No longer could supplies be brought in by sea, and no longer was there any practical way to get out of the country except by air. Refugees crowded the roads leading north in a desperate attempt to cross the hundreds of miles of jungle and mountains to reach India with tens of thousands dying in the attempt.

Julian was surprised to find that the departure of the Sprouts had a sobering effect not just on himself, but on Jock and Stella. None of them were especially religious, but the knowledge that the Reverend and his formidable wife were not far away in his mountain and jungle fastness, enthusiastically proselytising to the gentle and unimpressed natives, gave a feeling of security, that was noticeable only now because of its absence.

Myitsu however was unmoved by the stories of conflict. Julian tried to impress upon her the seriousness of the situation without worrying her unduly, but being a Buddhist not just nominally, but through her culture, education, upbringing, and personal inclination, she was completely philosophical about their future.

'We have to make some plans.' He told her one morning at breakfast, asking Boy to join them at the table. 'What to do if the Japs come here.'

Boy, who had listened to the gossip around the town and market had formed a vague idea of the situation.

'Japanese people not like British people. Kill kill kill, always want kill. Japanese soldiers come and make British people go back home, man tell me this in market. Tell everyone British finished here now. Go home.'

'Well Boy, he may be right. I hope not, but it's possible. So what do we do.'

Boy was not finished.

'Man say Japanese soldiers no problem for Burmese people, make friend, look after people. Only make problem for British people. Kill maybe.'

Myitsu said something very quickly to Boy in Burmese, not looking too pleased. Julian looked at her.

'What do you think Myitsu?'

'I go pray temple tomorrow.'

Julian sighed. 'That's not a solution darling. We can't just wait and hope they'll be nice to us if they get here. Because from all we've heard they aren't going to be. We have to think about getting away.'

Both of them looked at him, shocked, unbelieving.

'Where go?' Myitsu demanded.

'Well, as far as I can see there's just two possibilities. North to India, or East to China. Either way is long and hard, virtually no roads, high mountains, rivers to cross, and the locals might not be too friendly.'

'But who look after house if Boy go away?' Boy said, looking suddenly tearful and distressed. 'Boy must stay, my work, look after house never mind.'

'Boy, of course you can stay. And like you say the Japs have no quarrel with the Burmese, you'll be ok.'

Julian wasn't at all sure that he would be ok, the possibility of being able to continue being paid for looking after the lodge seemed slim, but there was no point in telling the young man this.

'What about you Myitsu? What do you want to do.'

'I not know what do, but I stay with you. You go China I go too, you go India I go too.'

'But darling, it might be safer if you stayed here. The journey to either place will be very hard, dangerous, and takes a long, long time.'

'You want to leave me?' She said angrily, 'You want leave me behind and you go home England never come back? No! You go, I go! No problem.'

Later that day Julian discussed the situation with Jock in his office, finding him equally undecided about a course of action.

'I keep hoping the lads'll hold them before they get this far. Freddie says there are reinforcements on the way from Blighty, the Eighteenth Division, but they might be sent to Malaya, it's getting desperate there too, they're nearly as far as Singapore now.'

'What does Stella think?'

'Och! She's putting a brave face on it, should have sent her out ages ago but she wouldn't hear of it.

She'll stay as long as I do she says, and anyway, I don't fancy the trip to India in the Morris or the Austin, don't think they would get even half way there. Freddie said he would try to get Hetti on a plane from Mandalay, but apparently there's not much going in or out.'

'You should try Jock. Take Stella down there straight away and try to get both of you on a flight. I can manage here, you can come back when it's all blown over.'

'Blown over! You think this'll just blow over. No laddie, there's upwards of a hundred thousand Japs heading our way and we haven't even a third of that number to stop them.'

The two men sat silent for a while, listening to the monotonous thump of the diesel pumps and generators outside and the occasional shouts of the workmen.

'The Indians are disappearing.' Jock remarked eventually, 'Got the wind up some of them. Of course there's more than a few would love to see us get bloody nose here I'm afraid.'

'I knew about them drifting away, Mr. Patel had a chat with me the other day. Said he was scared too, asked me what to do, told him I had no idea.' Said Julian.

There was another long silence.

'So we do nothing for the moment...is that it?' Said Jock.

'Wait, I guess, and hope.' Replied Julian.

'And what about the wee lassie? You have plans for her?'

'I don't want to leave her, that's for sure.' Julian said quietly, 'It's known around here she's living with me...well you know...But I don't know if it might be worse to take her with me.'

'Aye, say no more, I'm not stupid. But it's to your credit you're thinking of that. The Japs or even the Burmese might make it difficult for her once we're gone. Some men would have just walked out, you don't treat a dog like that.'

Jock went over to a cupboard in the corner of his office and withdrew a bottle of Glenfiddich and two glasses.

'It's never too early for a wee dram. And to be frank I feel I need one.'

He put the glasses down on his desk and poured a generous measure in each, handing one to Julian.

'I'll not be leaving the Japs any of this stuff, that's for sure. Even if I have to pour it down the shaft. Cheers!'

They drank silently, each of them busy with their own thoughts.

'Jock, what's to do about the gems? We'll have over two months produce stored soon. That's a lot of capital waiting to be realised.'

'I've been thinking about that Julian, let me show you something.'

He went over to the massive safe at the side of the room, unlocked it and withdrew a glass jar, handing it to the other man.

'One of Stella's Kilner jars, uses them for preserving ginger and stuff.'

Through the glass Julian could see the bottle was full to the top with rubies. Not just any rubies, but large, perfect and near perfect stones, some as big as bird's eggs.

'I've picked out the very best from the last few weeks. This is small and light enough for one person to carry, you or me maybe, or Stella if she gets out on her own. There's a small fortune there, not sure what will happen if Singapore falls as the company's head office is there, but there's enough money in that lot to start up the mine again if all's lost here.'

Julian weighed the jar in his hand, not light he thought, but transportable even for a woman.

'What about the rest.'

'The other gems I've put in a locked strong box ready for transport if we get any, the spinels will just have to stay here in the safe, take their chance. It's not perfect I know, but it's the best I can think of.'

'How much are we talking about, on the open market?'

Jock thought for a moment, frowning in concentration.

'Aw...I'd say a couple of million in the jar, another three or four in the strong box, and a quarter of a million in spinels, roughly that is, depends on the market.'

Julian whistled, amazed to think he was holding two million pounds worth of gems in his hands.

'And Julian, you'd better have this in case it's you carrying it.'

Jock was holding out a heavy black pistol he had removed from his desk draw.

'I've got one, and so has Stella. D'you know how to use it?'

Julian stared at the gun, an unwanted symbol of the breakdown of the world he had grown to love. He was conscious as he took it in his hand that this was an instrument to take life, suddenly, violently. Something so alien to him could hardly force himself to touch it. It felt cold, heavy with menace, totally impersonal. Could he point it at another being, pull the trigger, extinguish a life? He doubted it very much.

'You think it's necessary Jock? I've never shot anything before, not sure I could.'

Jock rummaged around in the draw, pulling out a small heavy box that he passed to Julian.

'Twenty rounds there. Probably won't need any more than that. I'd like you to keep it on you at all times now, just to be safe, you never know.'

'But the Japs are miles away still, might not ever get here.' Protested Julian.

'It's not for the Japs. If they get here it's not that little thing that will save you. It's the locals I'm wary of, there's fellows around who know all about the gems we have stored, and they might just decide to have a go, it's a big temptation now, and it'll get worse as the Japs approach. There'll be little law and order from now on I'm thinking, it'll be every man for himself. Here, I'll show you how it works, you might practice a shot or two when you get home, but don't waste the ammo, it's all we've got.'

That evening back at the lodge Julian was thinking about the risks for Myitsu. If they left together to try to escape on foot he doubted that the girl would be up to the long and arduous journey. She was not the peasant girl she had been as a child accustomed to long hours bent double planting rice, carrying water, or any of the other tasks normal for a girl from a poor rural background. Dancing, although physically demanding, was not adequate preparation for weeks or months of trekking through jungles and over mountains.

Yet if she stayed in Mogok where she was known to have been the partner of an Englishman, and the Japanese arrived who knows what could happen to her. There had been horrific tales of the treatment of civilians in the hands of the invaders both in Malaya and southern Burma, mass executions, rape, and torture seemed to be the norm in occupied areas.

And to complicate matters Freddie had told them of the arrival with the Japanese troops of the newly formed Burmese Independence Army, trained in Japan to fight alongside the invaders as well as tasked with organising a rural uprising against the British. The mine and it's British managers had always enjoyed excellent relations with the local community, paying good wages with fair treatment, but Jock had said he felt the atmosphere changing, there were fewer smiles for them as they passed through the town, or shopped in the market. Several of the younger workers had simply disappeared like Zeya. The world as they knew it, secure, easy, pacific, was changing. The days of colonial Burma were ending, and ending probably in a bloodbath.

Julian decided the least he could do was to prepare for a possible flight, and he acquired two back packs to fill with what he imagined might be needed for a long trek through the jungle. He included basic medical supplies such as quinine, mosquito repellent, antiseptics, and bandages, as well as tins of food, a sack of rice, and water bottles. In spite of these preparations he could not believe they would ever have to set out on the journey, somehow it seemed it would never happen. And when he helped Myitsu try one of the backpacks on she nearly collapsed under the weight, it seemed obvious she wouldn't be able to carry it more than a few hundred yards.

CHAPTER FIFTEEN

Julian and Jock were working together in Jock's office one afternoon when there was a very faint and distant rumble of thunder. Both men failed to notice it at first, but after a few minutes Jock got up and walked over to the window. He looked out over the mine workings and the town towards the distant mountains, the air was dry, still, and in the furnace like heat the view shimmered and danced in the rising thermals.

'That's odd.' He said after a moment, 'The monsoon's months away, the sky's clear, but listen, there's thunder.'

Julian joined him at the window.

'Well, it certainly sounds like it. But...'

They both turned and looked at each other.

'It's coming from the south? Or the west perhaps?' Said Julian.

The sounds stopped abruptly.

'That's nay thunder. That's either heavy artillery or bombs.' Said Jock, 'Heard enough of it in the last war to recognise it.'

He had turned a little pale under his weathered complexion.

'Where?' Asked Julian, 'Mandalay's too far for us to hear anything, and there's not much to bomb between there and here.'

'There's Chauna Gyi, it's only tiny place, but there's a bridge over the river there. Destroy that and Mandalay is effectively cut off from the north of Burma, at least to motor vehicles.'

'Maybe we should tell Freddie.'

'Aye, I'll call him, see if he has anything new.'

Jock went and sat down in front of the radio they had installed in one corner of the office and called for Mandalay on the agreed frequency.

An unknown voice answered sounding flustered and when Jock asked for Freddie he was asked for his name and told to wait. After several minutes Jock heard Freddie's familiar voice.

'Jock, what's up? How's things up there?'

'Just checking, thought we heard either artillery or bombing a few minutes ago, away to the south west of us.'

'It's bombing Jock. They just hit us too. Came in low, no warning, hit the airfield and destroyed several planes I think. A few hits in the town, nothing too bad. My guess it was a test run for something bigger to come. Hetti got out yesterday on a medical flight thank god.'

'Did they shoot any Japs down?'

'Christ no! They came in low and fast, it was all over before we knew what hit us. But they'll be back I'm sure. Sorry Jock, got to go now, hell of a lot to do.'

Jock switched off the radio and turned to Julian.

'Listen laddie, it's time now. If you're going to get out you'd better go now. You can take the Morris, though I don't know how far it'll get you, not much petrol left. I'll take the Austin when Stella and I leave.'

'Jock, I'm not going anywhere if you stay here. We'll leave together or not at all.'

Jock studied the young man in front of him for a moment, a lump in his throat.

'You're a dam fool then Julian, but I'll thank you anyway, it means a lot to me, and Stella too. You've made preparations?'

'As much as I can Jock. It's Myitsu I'm worried about.'

'You're leaving her I take it?'

'I'm taking her with me. She insists. But she's such a tiny little thing I don't think she'll stand a long journey on foot.'

Jock smiled grimly.

'I can see you're well smitten there, and I can't say I blame you, but you know the girls here, they're not like English girls, they're tougher than you can imagine, even if they are small.'

The only good news in the days that followed was that a Chinese Expeditionary Force had entered Burma and was supposed to be holding the front south of Mandalay. The 17th Indian division and the 7th Armoured Brigade were to defend the Irrawaddy Valley, and the bridges at Chauna Gyi had not after all been destroyed although much of the town had been damaged and over a hundred Burmese killed.

There was no more pretence in Mogok that all was well. Nearly all the Indian population had left, heading for the north where the unhealthy Hukawang Valley and the precipitous and densely forested Patkai Range barred their way into India, resulting in the deaths of tens of thousands from starvation and disease. Their plight was worsened by the attitude of many Burmese who had resented the influx of Indians over many years, and now found the opportunity to express their hatred in the ambush and slaughter of the helpless and fleeing refugees.

The lodge in the jungle remained a refuge for Julian those days. They talked little of the war, or their future, content to live from day to day in the hope that the Japanese could be defeated before they arrived at Mogok, or at least held before Mandalay. Boy seemed to think it an exciting time, hurrying to town after his morning's work each day on his bike to hear the latest rumours, and adding various details from his own vivid imagination. In the end Julian had to forbid him reporting the stories in case they should depress or frighten Myitsu.

Not all the horrors he heard of around the market in early February were false rumours. In Kalagong the Japanese rounded up all the villagers for questioning, massacring over six hundred of them. Tales of the strafing of refugees by the Japanese air force were common, as were stories of casual beheadings by badly disciplined soldiers.

A lorry with a platoon of British soldiers appeared in Mogok in mid February, the young captain in charge telling Jock he was scouting for a road going east. He seemed disappointed when told that there was only a rough trail into the mountains in that direction, totally unsuitable for motor vehicles. Mogok was, as far as mechanised transport was concerned, a dead end.

He allowed the men a ten minute break before turning back, and they took advantage of it to buy food from the market. They were fresh out from England, laughing over the strange fruit and unknown vegetables, making pointed remarks about the women stall holders, complaining about the heat. To both Jock and Julian they seemed very young and rather innocent, difficult to imagine them fighting the Japanese. The captain, a tall young man with a public school accent and expensive binoculars around his neck, told them that the army was setting up a road block at the cross roads on the Mandalay road, but he seemed distracted, unsure, and when questioned about how far the Japanese had pushed he didn't seem to know.

'Will we hold Mandalay?' Jock had asked him, 'If we don't we'll have to get out quick.'

The man seemed confident on that at least.

'Oh, we'll hold it alright. The Japs have come too far and too fast, they can't supply quickly enough for a big offensive. And we've got armour now, they haven't.'

The big air raid on Mandalay Freddie had expected happened that night. Jock checked in before going to bed to find the reception bad and Freddie's voice hardly audible above the sounds of explosions and the banging of anti-aircraft guns. All Jock could understand was that things were very bad, it was a major air-raid. So he signed off saying he'd get back to him later when it was all over. He sat up all through the night in his office, watching the light on the radio that would indicate a call, but at four AM, so tired he could hardly keep in his chair, he decided to call back.

Freddie answered after several minutes sounding hoarse and despondent.

'They've hit us hard this time.' He replied to Jocks query, 'Looks like half the city's gone up in flames. The airfields had it, as well as all the planes that were there, including half a dozen Hurricanes I believe. The barracks are destroyed, god knows how many men killed there, fuel depots gone up, and the station just doesn't exist anymore. Never seen the like...total destruction. Efficient, damned efficient, and bloody scary.'

'You ok though Freddie? And the staff?'

'Jock, half the residence has disappeared, hit in the first wave. Didn't catch fire luckily, but several of our people killed or missing. John Cleall, you remember him, accountant chappie, lost both legs, died in me arms, loss of blood I think.'

'Freddie, I'm so sorry...are you ok?'

'Ok Jock, ok. Just bloody tired now, and I've got to meet the military in half an hour, see just how bad things are.'

'Sorry I can't help Freddie, let me know if there's anything...'

'You get some sleep yourself Jock, you might need it later.'

Jock turned off the radio, and not feeling like sleeping walked out of the office and stood outside looking up at the night sky. There was just a sliver of new moon rising over the mountains in the east, dawn was still an hour away. The mechanical silhouettes of the mine and its buildings were barely visible against the sky where the great river of the Milky Way stretched from horizon to horizon. There was total silence. He breathed deeply, suddenly aware that the heat of the previous month had gone, but leaving a pleasant warmth still radiating from the ground, and a freshness in the air. He thought how he loved the place. The years of work that had made the mine, his mine, his creation. The source of wealth for the town, feeding its people, employing its men, making it special. How would it be to leave it all behind, the mine, the people, the country, it was all he knew, his life.

He heard Stella's voice calling from the veranda of his house, and with a sigh turned, and went to her, slipping his arm through hers as he told her of the raid, and leading her to the bed she had just left.

Just over one mile away, across the sleeping town, along the deserted road, up the dark trail through the forest, Julian was woken by the cries of the girl sleeping next to him. Small sobs, whimpers, odd words mumbled and then the scream. He held her shoulder and shook it gently.

'Wake up darling, wake up, it's a dream.'

The girl sat up, searching around her for light, for anything. Great sobs shook her slim body and Julian took her in his arms, holding her tight against him, calming her with quiet words, gentle kisses. At last she grew still, and breathed deeply, her body relaxing, becoming soft, clinging closely to his.

'It was a bad dream.' She murmured eventually. 'So terrible.'

'But only a dream darling, not real.'

She turned towards his voice, his face invisible to her in the darkness of their room.

'I was so frightened.'

'Of what, darling. Tell me.'

She moved in his arms, settling herself lower with her head on his chest where he could feel her warm breath touching his skin.

'You were not there. I was alone. In the house, but different from now. Something was coming, through the jungle, a darkness, a bad thing.' He heard her swallow before she could continue.

'I run away, but all in house, one room, then next room, all time they come after me. Not men, not women, not animal...just bad thing. Then I fall, thing get me and I scream, scream for you to come, but you not there. Not there.'

Julian stroked her hair, thinking of nightmares he had been having recently, the same sort of thing, a darkness coming through the jungle, terror, and death.

'But I'm here now baby, and I always will be. I'll look after you come what may. It was just a bad dream, not real.'

'Please light lamp...cannot sleep now.'

Julian reached over and lit the lamp on the bedside table. Myitsu sat up and peered around, as if to reassure herself that all was well and normal.

'I think Nats have gone.' She said suddenly.

'What? Gone? Gone where?'

'Myitsu not know. Just feel. They are gone. Very bad for everyone if Nats not here look after us.'

Julian knew it was useless to argue logically against the existence or not of Nats. Their presence just had to be accepted if one lived in Burma, to deny their existence would be like denying the existence of God in the Vatican.

'We'll put more offerings out for them tomorrow, tempt them back.' He said in an effort to calm her.

She looked at him, doubting, head on one side and perfectly aware of his true feelings.

'No good. They gone. Tomorrow I go temple, ask holy man.'

She lay down again, patting the bed beside her.

'Come to bed darling. If you look after me can sleep.'

Julian lay down beside her as she curled up into her habitual position with her back against him. He rested a hand on her smooth flank, feeling her breathing, her warmth. Soon her breathing steadied, grew shallow, and she slipped back into sleep.

Julian remained awake until dawn, when he quietly arose, dressed, and went downstairs, being careful not to wake his sleeping partner. In the front room he retrieved the gun and ammunition Jock had given him from its hiding place on top of a bookcase. He sat down at the table and studied the dull black instrument of war in front of him, then taking the box of ammunition he loaded eight rounds into the magazine. For a moment it lay before him, untouchable, a thing of horror. Then he reached out and took it in his hand, feeling the weight of it, heavy with potential death, Shiva, the destroyer of worlds. Picking it up he pointed it at the open door, squinting along the barrel, and tried

to imagine the figure of a man coming through, his finger tightening on the trigger.

CHAPTER SIXTEEN

They stopped in the market the next day to buy offerings for the monks...fruit, vegetables, a selection of herbs and spices, and a robe. As a foreigner and official of the mine it was expected that the offerings would be generous, and Julian slipped a couple of packets of the black Burmese cheroots under the robe as a little extra. The monks were not supposed to smoke, but he knew many of them did surreptitiously and would greatly appreciate the gift.

Myitsu had not spoken much that morning but she seemed happy to be going to the temple, as if some answer to their problems could be found there.

The temple, a building of carved stonework, long tailed dragons, gilt statues, and bells that tinkled in the wind was surrounded by many golden pagodas, most of them donated by the mine owners over the years as recognition of the towns continuing cooperation. Others had been paid for by wealthy local merchants as insurance for their future lives. A great deal of spiritual merit could be acquired by their construction, and no sensible man would take the risk of being reincarnated as a rat, or frog, or even worse a woman, if it could be avoided by a little expenditure in this life.

Inside the temple, all gold and red and yellow, with huge crude paintings on the walls depicting the life of Buddha, a magenta robed monk sat on a small dais accepting gifts in return for blessings. Julian crouched down, shuffling forward on hands and knees so as not to elevate his head higher than the monks, while Myitsu waited to one side for her turn to address the holy man. He was a lean, brown man of indeterminate age with a smooth face and shaven head that shone and reflected spots of light from the many candles that burned all around.

The previous supplicant shuffled away and Myitsu approached and sat with feet pointing away from him, bowing low, touching her head to the ground several times before offering him the basket of gifts. He took it from her without acknowledgment, and placed it with other, more modest gifts by the side of the dais.

Myitsu began to speak, too quietly for Julian to hear and understand, the monk gazing over her head into the distance as if in another world. When she had finished speaking he immediately began to reply, speaking quickly and glancing towards Julian several times. When he stopped Myitsu made obeisance again, while he blessed her, sprinkling water over her bowed head.

They shuffled outside into the hard brittle light of mid morning and stood up. Julian looked down at small doll like figure at his side that he had grown to love.

'What did he tell you? Do you feel better now?'

Myitsu raised the yellow silk umbrella she had brought with her to protect her pale complexion from the sun, and stood silent for a moment.

'This man tell many things. He knows bad times will come because of English. Japanese people are Buddhist he say, like Burmese. English people not believe Buddha man, not believe spirits, not believe Nats. He say time for English to go away back to their country, then maybe Nats come back.'

She turned and looked up at him, the sun filtered by the yellow silk turning her face to gold, her expression serious, a small gilt goddess.

'What else did he say?' Asked Julian, sensing there was more.

Her eyes remained fixed on his face as she replied.

'This man say better I not stay with you. Leave house, leave Mogok quickly now. Not good for me alone, not good if with you. He say Burmese people not like girl who stay with Englishman.'

It was nationalism Julian knew, the rising tide that with the Japanese invasion would flood the whole country. The communists and the Nationalists would seize the chance now to throw off the imperial yoke. The force behind the rule was being defeated, the shackles smashed by the Japanese Fifth Army of forty five thousand small yellow men. Hatred of the British rulers would now have free reign.

'So...' Said Julian as they continued walking slowly towards the car, 'what do you want to do? Maybe he's right, maybe it's not good for you to stay with me.'

Myitsu dropped the umbrella, and it skipped away a few paces as if seeking freedom. She put her hands to cover her face, her shoulders shaking.

'Oh...not know, not know what I do. Cannot leave Yulian, cannot, never.'

She wiped her eyes, looking quickly around to where several women heading into the temple had stopped and were staring at them suspiciously.

'Take me home please darlin, take me home.'

CHAPTER SEVENTEEN

The next few days saw the air raids intensify on Mandalay and the surrounding areas. Freddie only managed to contact Jock once each day, due to the loss of the electricity station, and his news was always bad. The town was now largely destroyed and thousands of Burmese had been killed. The road to the north was jammed with fleeing civilians making it difficult for the army to move units away from the city. With no more fighters fit to fly, the Japanese Air Force controlled the sky, bombing and strafing at will with no distinction between military and non-military targets. Freddie himself was preparing to leave but couldn't say when, there being so much confusion about the position and movements of the attacking Japanese. Then there was silence, no more messages or replies to Jocks calls. Mandalay had gone off air.

Two days later, in the morning the first Japanese planes flew over Mogok. A pair of light bombers overflew the town several times, obviously reconnoitring the area, and in the afternoon they heard far away to the west the sound of heavy bombing.

Julian and Jock sat in the kitchen of his house with Stella and came to a decision.

'So that's settled then.' Jock had said, 'We'll leave the day after tomorrow and travel together, you and your young lady in the Morris, me and Stella in the Austin. And we'll take Mr. Patel of he's a mind to come with us. That'll give us tonight and tomorrow to sort everything out and shut down the mine.'

Both Julian and Stella knew what this meant to Jock, and his wife went over to him and stood stroking his head and patting his shoulders.

'We'll be back, you'll see love, it's only for a while.' She said.

'Well, only god knows that, I think,' he replied, 'and if we do come back, what will there be to come back to?'

Julian and Myitsu were woken the next morning before dawn by the sounds of artillery fire from the mountains to the west. The lightening sky with low heavy clouds flickered, and the thick, humid air shook with the regular thump thump thump of many guns.

They stood together on the veranda, holding hands and watching as the sun crept up between clouds and horizon, briefly painting the sky an ominous blood red.

'I have to go into town, darling. Finish up there, help Jock.'

She nodded.

'Understand. First breakfast... Must eat.'

And she led him back inside to the kitchen where a rather subdued Boy was preparing coffee. The kitten was playing on the floor with a dead moth it had found, picking it up, shaking it and growling quietly. Myitsu lifted it up, holding it to her face, burying her nose in its thick soft fur.

'How long Youlian?' She asked, 'How long you be gone?'

'Not too long I hope. You know what to do. Get yourself ready so we can leave as soon as possible. Maybe today even.'

An exceptionally loud explosion shook the house, making the windows rattle in their frames. The kitten stiffened in her arms, emitting a faint distressed cry.

'Today!' She whispered to herself. 'So soon.'

Julian found Jock in his office, pulling papers from draws, giving them a cursory glance before casting them aside.

'Got to find the government contract, might need it if we ever come back. Stella always said I should be more careful about my filing system, or lack of one.'

Julian took out his keys and opened the safe.

'They're in here Jock, I put them here for safe keeping a while ago.' And he handed the sheaf of papers to Jock, who seemed bad tempered, a dark frown on his face.

'You might have told me...och! Never mind now. Better get the gems out while your about it, mustn't forget.'

Julian lifted out the jar of rubies, familiar to him now, but somehow more impressive every time he saw it. Both men stared at it for a moment.

'So that's what it's all been for eh Julian. Pretty jewels to make some woman feel more beautiful than she would be without them. Funny, now it all seems a bit pointless, stupid.'

'But don't forget what the mine has done here Jock. Wages for the men, money for a school, clinic once a month, and revenue for Burma too, think of all the money the mine's paid in license fees and taxes. And it's second only to oil and rubber for Burmese exports.'

At that moment they heard the sound of an approaching lorry its horn blowing continually. Pushing the gems back into the safe they ran outside just as an army four-ton truck came to a halt by the gate to the mine. The horn continued blowing and no one descended from the cab although they could see the two occupants in the front.

'What the hell....' Murmured Jock, and they ran down to the gate and out to where the vehicle was stopped. The few people around were staring at it in wonder and Julian noticed there were bullet holes in the windscreen and around the cab.

Jock wrenched open the passengers' door and jumped back as the body of a British officer fell out. He had been shot several times, in the head and chest. The driver had also been shot but still lived, lying over the steering wheel, his hands still gripping it tightly. It was the pressure of his head that kept the horn blowing.

'Jesus Christ!' Julian gasped, seeing blood all over the interior and feeling suddenly sick, 'What the hell...'

'The driver's alive.' Said Jock curtly; 'Lets get him out of there.'

They went around to the driver's side and managed to extract him from the cabin. He moaned slightly when they moved him, but seemed to be only partly conscious as they laid him on the dusty yellow ground in the shade of the lorry.

'Have a look in the back.' Directed Jock as he knelt to examine the driver.

Julian went around to the back of the lorry and climbed onto the rear fender. About a dozen wounded men lay crammed into the space. Some had dressings on their wounds, others seemed to have just been dumped, their injuries untreated. One man sat holding his right arm that terminated at the elbow, a shocked expression on his young face as blood seeped though a piece of rag tied around the stump. Next to him another man lay, his face a burnt black mask showing white teeth and red liquid eyes.

For a moment Julian could just stare, taking great deep breaths, trying to control the mounting urge he felt to turn away from the horror, the pain, the smell. Jock's voice came to him as if from a distance, calm, reassuring.

'What is it Julian?'

Julian cleared his throat, not trusting his voice.

'Err, it's some wounded Jock. About a dozen. They're bad, really bad.'

'We'll need some help, see if you can round up a few of our men, I can't leave this fellow right now.'

Julian looked over towards the mine where a few of the employees who had turned up hoping to work stood in a group staring at them. He waved his hand, calling to them to come over.

They looked at each other before moving, as if reluctant to become involved. Then Let, an old hand of many years pushed through them and trotted down the slope to where the lorry stood. After a moment the rest of the group followed.

Julian let down the back of the lorry and tried to think. They needed stretchers, but the mine only possessed two, but it was a start. He sent two of the men off to locate them as he tried to assess the seriousness of the men's injuries. Several of them were conscious and obviously aware of what was going on, they could wait Julian decided. The one's whose wounds had not been dressed and were bleeding seemed the most urgent.

Jock suddenly appeared at his elbow, taking in the scene at a glance as if it were a daily occurrence.

'Send a man to get Stella and the first aid kit. Get those who aren't too bad over to the empty storeroom. We'll use that as a dressing station. But come over here a moment, I need a quiet word.'

Julian sent a man to get Stella, then they moved away out of earshot of the men.

'The driver filled me in a bit, he's just died. Things are bad down at the cross roads, he didn't think it could be held much longer. Apparently the japs came around through the jungle to the west, outflanked the defence, attacked last night, hand to hand fighting. They were pushed back eventually but with heavy losses. The ones here are the lucky ones, most are still stuck there. The japs have been bayoneting mercilessly the wounded they capture apparently.'

'So we can't get out then, if the cross roads are taken.'

Jock shrugged his shoulders.

'Who knows? And what the hell do we do with these boys? Can't just leave 'em to be murdered.'

Stella arrived at that moment, pale and carrying a large box marked with a red cross.

'Jock...Jock...Freddie's been on the radio. Couldn't wait for you. He's on the way north somewhere, but he had something important to tell you. Told me to write it down as it was a direct order from the government, here...look. Look what he wants.

Jock took the piece of crumpled paper from his wife's hands and read out loud.

'Under emergency powers government instructs all assets likely to fall into Japanese hands must be destroyed.

Jock, you have to destroy the mine. It's too valuable to leave it for the japs. Sorry, Freddie.'

Jock looked up at his wife, his face white under his tan.

'Is that all he said.'

She reached out to place a hand on his arm.

'He couldn't talk any more he said. He sounded strange, tired maybe.'

'So he wants my mine destroyed does he.'? He said half to himself.

Just then the two stretchers arrived and Julian turned and went back to the lorry to supervise the removal of the wounded. One of the workers had brought water that he was giving to the men in the lorry who asked for it. Several more men and a couple of women from the town had also arrived to help, and soon all the wounded had been transferred to the storage shed behind the main building.

Jock and Stella remained together, talking quietly. Julian approached and asked quietly.

'What do we do Jock?'

Jock turned to him, grim faced, determined.

'I'll nay blow the mine, that's for sure. My life's work, everything, all for a bunch of dirty nips. Never! We'll be back one day, mark my words, and I'll not abandon it now.'

'But darling, Freddie said you must...it's war...'

'And I know all about war don't I? Didn't I give four years of my life for it? And what was the use of that? A score years later we're fighting them again!' He was shouting now, people staring, shocked by the events and now by Jock's untypical outburst.

'We're leaving as planned. Take our chance, it's all we can do. But I'll never blow the mine.'

'What about them, the wounded.' Julian said quietly.

Jock looked at him, his pale blue eyes hard, uncompromising.

'There's nothing we can do for them, we'll leave them the first aid box, the Burmese won't let them die of neglect, not our people.'

There was another intense burst of firing from somewhere making everyone look up, wondering.

'Stella, look sharp now, take the car up to the house and get your stuff in it. I'll be up directly. Julian I'll need a hand here for a moment then go get your young lady and meet me at the maidan as soon you can.'

With that Stella ran to the car, calling after her.

'Hurry Jock. Hurry. I'm afraid.'

'Julian, come with me now, we've got business. Can't forget the rubies now can we?'

Just as they turned to go back the mine there came the sound of approaching aircraft. They stopped and looked towards the sound, coming from the mountains to the south. Heavy cloud concealed the planes at first, then they broke through, six Kawasaki Ki-48's flying in line astern, low and heading straight towards the town. For a second the men were frozen, unable to move, yet aware of what was about to happen, then Julian grabbed Jocks arm.

'They're going to bomb, they're going to bomb. The mine, quick, to the mine.'

And they started to run. Half way there Jock stopped.

'Stella...she won't have heard...'

Stella indeed had started the engine of the old Austin, a noise quite loud enough to drown out the sound of the approaching planes, and was driving down to the gate out of the mine when the first bombs fell.

The first fell on the market, some hundred yards from the mine, totally destroying the modest structure, but the second fell next to the fence, a few wards from the gate. Julian felt the explosion in his chest and stomach. A great pressure wave drove the air from his lungs, picked him up and flung him several feet through the air, dropping him painfully on a pile of rocks, his head hitting something sharp. For a moment he lost consciousness, but then he was on his feet, without knowing how or why. He put his hand to his head where he could feel warm wetness. The blast had deafened him, but he could feel each explosion through the ground, and the heat on his face. He saw Jock lying a little way away on his face. Both his hands covering his head.

Julian turned, by the destroyed gate to the mine the Austin was burning, yellow, red, and white flames engulfing every part of it, a black boiling column of oily smoke pouring from it, even the tires burning. Through the shattered side window he could see Stella, sitting quite upright and unmoving, her hair ablaze, her face already a blackened mask. He started to go towards her, feeling the heat mounting as he approached, his hands reaching out, trying for the door that he knew he would never reach, trying to shield himself from the inferno. He was crying out without realising, crying for the agony of the burning of his hands and face, but continuing to edge forward with tiny steps.

Then a hand gripped his shoulder, wrenching him backwards, dragging him away from the flames. It was Jock. He heard his voice.

'It's no good laddie, she's gone, she's gone.'

He pulled him backwards until they were well away from the burning car, stopping a short distance away, while they both watched in horror as Stella gradually disappeared in flame and fire.

The sound of the planes faded, leaving behind the sounds of the fires, popping and crackling. From the town came the wailing and crying of many voices. Smoke drifted across the valley, softening the destruction, cloaking the outline of the distant hills. It seemed suddenly very peaceful and far overhead in a sky where the sun was beginning to burn up the morning clouds, the carrion were beginning to gather, floating effortlessly on motionless wings, waiting.

Julian turned to face Jock, putting his hands on the older man's shoulders and wincing as the pain of his burns surprised him.

'Jock...I'm so sorry.' His voice was hoarse, irritated by the smoke. 'I tried, I couldn't get near her. I'm so sorry.'

Jock was looking at the smouldering car, his pale blue eyes swimming with tears.

'I know lad, I know, you did your best. No one could have got her out of there, she was probably already dead. At least I hope so.'

They both turned to survey the damage. Nearly all the buildings had been destroyed or badly damaged. The main shaft winding wheelhouse had miraculously survived intact, but the store located behind it where the wounded men were had disappeared almost completely, just a few blackened timbers remained. Several bodies were scattered around, some intact, some with missing limbs. The body of one soldier, missing most of his uniform hung grotesquely from the spokes of the winding wheel where it had been hurled.

Back in Jocks office Julian found the bottle of Glenfiddich in a desk draw and poured them both half a tumbler. Jock sat at his desk in deep shock, staring into space, his glass held half way towards his mouth as if forgotten.

Julian found a bottle of water and poured it over his hands, trying to relieve the pain of his burns, but it seemed to make it worse, forcing a gasp and sob from him.

Jock looked up at him, as if waking from a dream.

'I'll do as Freddie said. I'll blow the mine.' He said simply.

Julian looked at him, wondering at the change of mind.

'There's nay point now. None at all. I'd never come back, not now, not without my Stella.'

He fumbled in a pocket and extracted a key to the safe.

'Here Julian, take the gems, try to save them at least from the bastards that did this.'

'No Jock...you keep them, take them with you.'

'Julian, I'm not going. I'll stick around. I have to burry Stella when I can. I'm not leaving her.'

'Jock, the Japs could kill you...they'll want the rubies.'

Jock stood up stiffly and went and stood looking out through the smashed window at the devastation.

'It was all for nothing Julian, I understand that now. Rubies, sapphires, spinels, all worthless. The only thing that was worth anything was my Stella...and she's gone. There's dynamite still in the safe, enough to do the job...finish it all.'

'Jock...I can't leave without you, there's only the Morris now, you're stuck if I go.'

'Julian, you're not listening, I'm not going any-where, I'll take my chance here, blow the mine, burry Stella and the others, they deserve that at least.'

He turned, opened the safe, and removed the metal strongbox of rubies, thrusting it into Julian's arms.

'Take it...and go...quickly now. There's a wee lassie counting on you back at the lodge, look after her...if you can.'

Julian took the jewels reluctantly, realising immediately that it would be impossible to escape with them, they would have to stay in Mogok, he would have to hide them. He feared the power of them, the greed they engendered in the hearts of men...beauty and death embracing in a stone. He wished simply that he had not been given them and feared they could be ultimately the cause of his own death somewhere out there in the mountains and the dark jungles where there were no human witnesses and even the eye of God was blind.

He shook Jock's hand, trying to cover up the pain it caused him, neither man trusting himself to say more than a gruff goodbye, good luck. The Morris was where he had left it, fortunately intact save for the windows that were all shattered. He placed strongbox on the back seat and put the jar on the seat next to him and drove out of the shattered town towards the lodge.

The brief drive allowed him to come to a decision, he could not take Myitsu with him. Not only was he convinced she would be unable to survive the long journey through the dense and unhealthy jungles, but he knew now from the reports they'd received in the last couple of months that if the girl was found with him, she would suffer the same fate that had been the lot of many Burmese girls associated with the British; mass rape and imprisonment, at best.

Myitsu was waiting for him by the front door when he arrived back at the lodge. She cried out and rushed down the steps to him seeing the condition of him, his face and hands red and swollen, his clothes blackened, singed, and burnt.

In her back pack waiting in the hall she found a small jar of the Tiger Balm she used from time to time, and sitting him down in the front room she gently applied it to his burns, all the time murmuring words of comfort in Burmese and English.

When finished she sat back on her heals and looked up at him her head on one side, questioning, for he had not spoken a word since his return.

'Stella's dead.' He said bluntly. Unaware of the shock he gave her.

In a gesture towards the coming trek she had plastered her face so thickly with the white thanaka powder that it looked like a clowns mask, and the silent tears that suddenly filled her expressive eyes overflowed down her cheeks, leaving dark trails.

'A bomb...hit the car. She was killed instantly.'

'...Jock?' She asked, her voice faint, childlike.

'He's going to bury her, and destroy the mine...he's staying here.'

She came and pushed at him gently until he took her upon his knees, her arms around his neck.

'And we go? Now?'

He couldn't bare to look at her, but stared over her shoulder, out of the window where he could see the trails of smoke from the burning buildings in Mogok.

'Darling...I can't take you with me. It's just too dangerous.'

She jumped to her feet, moving away from him, standing very upright, her black brows knitted together.

'What? You leave me here? You promise you take me.'

'Darling I can't, it's too difficult for you, too hard. And if the japs caught us they would probably kill you.'

Her dark eyes blazed indignation and anger.

'Not care! I can come, not afraid. Not afraid jungle, not afraid mountains, not afraid Japanese soldier.'

'I know darling, I know you're not afraid, but I can't take the risk. If you died, didn't make it...well, I'd never forgive myself. I'd be responsible you see...'

Before he could stop her she had fallen, the full Shikoku of utter abasement. Her face pressed to the floor, her hands stretched out towards him.

'Stop it...stop it...' He reached down to lift her up, deeply shocked.

'Please, please, please...'She was saying, over and over again.

He lifted her, took her tear streaked face in his hands, and lent over until his lips were almost touching hers.

'Listen darling, it'll be alright, I promise, you can stay here. You'll be safe, just stay out of the way if the japs come. I'm going to leave the rubies with you. Hide them well, but keep some here in the house and use them when you need money. Jeannie will get you a fair price. Just sell one at a time. Hide the strong-box somewhere away from the house. Don't tell anyone, not even Boy. And I mustn't know either, just in case.... And remember, I'm coming back when it's all over, not long I hope...just wait here safely for me...'

'Noooo!' She screamed, pulling away from him, 'Nooo! Why you do this? Not want rubies...money...'

She fell to her knees weeping shamelessly like a child.

'Please my Youlian, please I come with you.'

And she looked at him through her tears, anxiously, searching his face for change of mind.

'Myitsu, please understand, I don't want to leave you, but it's for the best, so you are safe. Try to believe me my darling, I'll be back again one day...just wait for me.'

He stepped back, away from the small figure that knelt before him, unsure of how much more he could tolerate.

As if realising he would never change his mind Myitsu collapsed wailing, prostrating herself upon the floor, winding her slim arms around his ankles, kissing his feet.

The kitten appeared in the doorway, and tip-toed over to sniff at the girl's body that now shook with deep sobs.

Julian reached down and lifted her again, cradling her in his arms like a baby, and murmuring words of comfort as if she was a child. She clung to him fiercely, pressing against him hoping perhaps that the magic of her body would capture the man, hold him to her. Her face was buried in his soiled and singed shirt, and he could smell the familiar scents of scandal wood, jasmine, and coconut oil in her hair.

Gradually her breathing calmed as he rocked her, gently kissing her wet cheeks and eyes, tasting the salt of her tears.

He stayed with her in his arms until the sun touched the peaks of the mountains to the west, and from far away, as if in another world, came the sounds of explosions and distant gunfire. He carefully disengaged himself from her, holding her at arms length by her shoulders.

'I have to go darling. Be brave, I'm so sorry.'

Myitsu blinked her tears away and wiped her face with the back of a small soft hand. She nodded, accepting her fate, the fate of them both.

He went to the car and returned with the rubies.

'Hide them straight away darling, I don't know how much time there is before the soldiers come. Hide yourself, in the jungle maybe, they'll never find you there if they come looking.'

He passed the heavy metal box to her, and she took it without a word, just nodding her head slightly.

He took her briefly in his arms one last time, not trusting his own will power.

'I'll be back. I swear.' He whispered to her as the sounds of distant gunfire rose and fell. 'Wait for me My-itsu, wait for me.'

She watched, still like a statue, from the veranda as he drove away through the gates and disappeared into the dark track leading to the road, and she was still there when Boy, his eyes red from crying appeared next to her. He had watched discretely from the hallway, and understood that the Englishman had left.

'Sister, what shall we do now? Will Papa come back?'

Myitsu took him by the hand and led him back into the house.

'He will come back little brother, he will come back.'

Julian reached the end of the trail by the crossroads and stopped. He looked left, down the road to the town a quarter of a mile away. The sun was setting, turning the smoke that was still rising from the town blood red, and he wondered how much of the town would be left before the fires that were burning there were extinguished. Perhaps the Japanese would help to put them out when they arrived.

As he turned and looked to the right, where the road that the Sprouts took headed into the wildness. He wondered if he would ever see Mogok again, he knew the risks he was taking, the dangers that lay ahead, for he had decided to make for China. In just a couple of miles the road would be impossible for the Morris, and he would have to walk. Two hundred miles of jungle and high mountains lay ahead, rivers to cross, possibly unfriendly tribes, and always the risk of running into Japanese patrols.

He crunched the car into gear and swung the wheel, clumsily with his burnt hands, heading east, away from Mogok and Myitsu.

CHAPTER EIGHTEEN

Jock buried Stella late that afternoon in the little cemetery on a hillside overlooking the town. Mr. Patel had refused to allow him to remove her remains from the burnt out car, doing it himself with the help of two of the mine's employees. Mr. Patel himself had escaped the raid unhurt, his small bungalow on the outskirts of the town unnoticed by the bombers. His woman, a rather large and ugly Burmese with a sharp tongue, had run screaming from the house at the first explosion and disappeared into the jungle, from which she had not yet emerged.

Little remained of the wife of the mine manager, but the mine's carpenter made a rudimentary coffin for the brief ceremony. Stella had been widely liked and respected in the town, having been instrumental in setting up the infant school as well as starting the monthly clinic by the government doctor, and in spite of the bombing several people from the town attended. Jock read a passage from the bible in a hoarse and halting voice and two Karen men who had been brought up as Christians managed a barely comprehensible 'amen' at the end.

A rough plank of wood was all that could be managed as a headstone, and when the grave had been filled in and stones placed over it to prevent the wild dogs disturbing it the people drifted back to town, save for Jock who remained, staring at the yellow earth, reluctant to leave the woman he had loved through the years of struggle to make the mine a success, and who had been the source of all his happiness.

The skies cleared as he stood, the sun casting long shadows from the dozen or so grave stones of the British who had died there in other years. Forgotten by the world, unvisited by family or friend, they leant at angles, untended even by a passing priest. A great melancholy came over him, deeper than sorrow, a sense of ending, finality, the pointlessness of everything, the futility of his continuing existence.

Two hours later Jock was sitting at the bottom of the main shaft of the mine on a wooden box containing the mine's entire stock of blasting dynamite. He had been obliged to lower the box by hand before descending himself down the long ladders as there was no power for the winches and the winding wheel was in any case broken. A Davie Lamp stood on the floor beside him, glowing dimly but providing enough light for Jock's task. In any case it was something he could have done blindfolded; preparing the charges, connecting the detonator. He had done it hundreds of times over the years, and it took less than three minutes to complete his task.

With the detonator connected and ready he looked around one last time at the dim walls of the rock he had fought with to extract the precious stones year after year. Nothing was visible, no ruby gleamed in the darkness, no sapphire twinkled in the lamplight, there was just grey rock and blackness, and he pressed the detonator without a single regret.

It was three days later that the Japanese soldiers came to the lodge, whether because they had been informed of it and the occupant's existence, or simply by chance, Myitsu never knew. Boy had been on his bike down as far as the cross roads, too afraid to venture as far as the town having heard the occasional gunshot from time to time indicating all was not peaceful there when he saw the patrol approaching along the road. He ran back towards the lodge and hid after a few hundred yards, watching to see if they would continue along the road or turn up the track. As soon as he saw they had the intention of coming to the lodge he ran quickly back to warn Myitsu.

They had discussed what they would do beforehand, and without hesitation they both ran for the track that led towards the swimming pool. Since the day they had gone swimming the trail had been untouched and was even more overgrown than before. Being careful not to leave traces that could be followed, they slipped through the undergrowth and wormed passed the banana trees that had grown thicker and stouter than before, with many branches heavy with unripe fruit hanging across their path.

They had gone no more than a few paces further when Myitsu stopped.

'Baby, I forget Baby.' She whispered, remembering her adored kitten.

Boy turned and peered back towards the lodge. There was no sign yet of the soldiers.

'I'll go.' He said simply, and started back.

Myitsu put out a hand to restrain him, but it was too late, he had already slipped through the trees and was away.

'Boy! Come back! There's no time.' She whispered as loud as she dared.

Boy was away, knowing the service he could provide for the girl he worshiped. His eyes shone as he crossed the lawn, she would think him a hero, for her he would do anything. And in any case the soldiers must still be nowhere near the house yet, ample time for him to locate the animal, probably sleeping on her bed, and escape with it back to where she would be waiting. He could picture her happiness when he put the kitten in her arms, basking in her gratitude and admiration for his bravery.

He looked quickly in the downstairs rooms. In all its favourite places, before running limping but light-footed up the stairs and into her room. He stopped briefly in the doorway and smiled, the animal was curled up on the bed fast asleep.

'Come Baby, come.' He whispered as he gathered it in his arms. It was warm and sleepy, and meowed quietly as he carried it out of the room and down the stairs. At the bottom of the stairs he turned to run out through the kitchen and out of the back door.

A Japanese officer blocked his way, holding a heavy pistol pointed at Boys stomach. Boy stopped, for a second they both stared at each other, then the soldier said something. Boy spun around, thinking to escape through the front door, but there too a soldier had appeared, his rifle with its long shinning bayonet pointed at him.

From a little way up the hill on the old path Myitsu looked down a the lodge. Boy had already disappeared inside and she hoped he might be already on his way back. Then several soldiers appeared for around the side of the house. They advanced carefully, looking around, peering through the windows, the one holding a pistol the others rifles with fixed bayonets. The back door was open as Boy had left it, and the soldier with the pistol led the others inside.

No one appeared on the path, Boy was still inside the house she realised. Perhaps they would let him go, she thought, after all he was just a Boy, a servant, of no consequence.

After a few minutes four soldiers came out into the back garden and began to look around. They entered the annex, obviously searching, then they went over to the water tower, one of them climbing the ladders to look into the cistern.

Then the man with the pistol appeared, holding Boy by his hair and threw him roughly onto the ground. He was still holding the kitten, but let it go as the soldier kicked him viciously. Myitsu stifled a scream with her hand, and ducked down, scared she might have been heard. When she looked up again one of the men had caught the kitten and was holding it up by its neck, waving it over Boy who lay curled up on the ground at his feet. Frozen in horror she watched as the men threw it from one to another, laughing, kicking Boy every time he tried to stand up to recover the animal. Then the officer appeared. He stood a moment in the doorway watching the men's game, then he stepped forward, drawing his sword and shouted something. The man holding the kitten turned and tossed it towards him. There was brief flash of light from the blade as it cut it cleanly in two, the separate halves falling either side of Boy.

Myitsu heard his scream, a scream that became a wail. She bit down hard on her knuckles, trying to stifle her own cry as she turned half blinded with tears, and began to run away from the horror. She could no longer see the house and the soldiers and Boy, but she couldn't stop the distant sound of his screams until she reached the stream and the cascades and the pool where they had once played.

Afraid that the soldiers might follow the trail, that perhaps they might force Boy to tell of her, and lead them after her, she climbed the cascade, hitching up her sarong to free her legs, following the stream higher and higher, until exhausted and terrified, she collapsed among the roots at the base of a huge tree a few yards from the stream. She was far from the lodge, and the only sound was the music of water on stone, but Boy's screams still echoed in her head, fading only when the sun dipped below the mountains and night approached. She lay still, listening to the sounds of the jungle, aware that the approach of a human would be reflected in a change in the chorus of birds and insects. Looking up, she noticed for the first time the tree she had sought shelter under. The peepul tree, sister to the banyan and sacred to Buddhists as well as Animists. Its heart shaped leaves shivered constantly, even without wind, showing the presence of the gods within.

She scrambled to her feet and bowed, then knelt making deep obeisance, touching her forehead to the ground before the massive trunk. She knew of the trees power, its special connection with women, its ability to ensure fertility, fidelity, sexual attraction, and for the first time she felt that new life that was growing within her; irresistible and strong as the love that had created it.

A feeling of calm filled her as she stood in the twilight, listening to the faint rattle and chatter of the leaves above her that told her of the presence of the gods and spirits of the forest. She was accepted here they told her, protected, as a mother of life herself. And turning away she passed like a spirit herself, through the trees to the stream, down the stream and the cascades to the pool and the little hut, where she lay down, her head on her hands, and slept until the rising sun sent a single beam of light filtering through the branches to waken her the next morning.

CHAPTER NINETEEN

Julian had driven barely a half-mile along the road that led to the mountains when he rounded a corner and found a dozen Japanese soldiers blocking the road. They had obviously heard his approach for they had taken up positions anticipating action. Two men with machine guns stood in the middle of the road, while the others were spread out on either side, crouched in the ditches, weapons at the ready.

Julian thought for just an instant about putting his foot down and trying to crash through the ambush as it was nearly dark, but it was obvious that he and the old car would be riddled with bullets within seconds if he were to try. He braked hard, coming to a stop some twenty feet from the two men blocking the road.

For a moment they just stared at him, then one of them, obviously the officer and wearing a sword at his waist, lifted his gun, pointed it directly at Julian, and shouted something in Japanese. When Julian didn't immediately respond the man advanced a few paces, shouting the same phrase and sighting along the barrel of the gun as if about to shoot.

Julian began to open the door, raising his left hand to show it empty. The officer was screaming excitedly at him, edging closer and closer, still looking as if about to shoot. The door was just half open when another soldier who had approached unseen by Julian from the rear, wrenched it fully open, reached inside, and dragged him roughly out, holding him by the collar of his shirt. Julian staggered, lost his balance, and fell to his knees. Before he could rise a kick to the stomach sent him sprawling on his face, gasping for breath that would not come. Another kick to his kidneys sent bolt of pain through him, pain such as he had never felt before, making him roll into a foetal crouch, before hands were roughly grabbing him, lifting him upright on legs that seemed to be beyond his control, facing the Japanese officer.

The man handed his gun to another of the soldiers and stepped close to Julian, staring aggressively. He spoke something, obviously a question about Julian, and waited for a reply. Julian, barely able to speak managed to shake his head, meaning he didn't understand.

The slap when it came, without warning, spun Julian's head around, flashes of light sparking in the sudden darkness before his eyes. When he could see again he was looking down and the ground where his feet were just a few inches away from the officer's boots. Only the hands holding tightly under his arms prevent him from collapsing. With difficulty he raised his head.

The officer was waving something in front of him, shouting, accusing, and it was several moments before Julian could make out that it was the pistol that Jock had given him, that he had left on the seat beside him.

The officer prodded him in the face painfully with the barrel, enunciating his words carefully, as if it could help Julian understand.

'British...civilian.' Was all he could think to say.

The man stopped talking, studying Julian closely, then stepped back a pace and swung the pistol at his head. Julian felt just a faint crack inside his skull before everything disappeared into blackness.

Myitsu sat for a while in the door of the hut, looking out over the pool, and listening intently. Everything seemed normal, just the sounds of birdsong, the noises of the millions of insects, and the occasional croaking of a solitary frog from the other side of the pool.

At last, confident she was alone, she stood up and waded into the pool, splashing water over her face and arms, before drinking deeply. She looked down at her legs, scratched and bruised from her flight, her sarong, torn in several places, never in her life had she felt so ugly and disheveled. She remember when they had swum here together, how she had known how beautiful she was for him, how she had loved to feel his eyes upon her, admiring, wanting. And she had played him, every move like a dance, showing herself as if unconscious of the effect, the movement of an arm to reveal the curve of a breast, the lifting of her sarong just enough to uncover a pale slim thigh, the shy smile that was not really shy but tempting, alluring. The ache in her heart was real and physical, and she wondered how long she could support it, how long it could be before she gave up the struggle to live without him in this new nightmare. She was afraid, deeply afraid of returning to the lodge, and what she would find there, but she had no where else to go.

She found him before she entered the now deserted house. He was suspended from the water tower, hanging naked upside down   from a piece of rope attached to his feet. They had done things to him before he died, perhaps even after. She approached him slowly, tears running down her face, until she stood just a few feet away. He was barely recognisable, his face and body grotesquely mutilated, and a great stain of dark blood covered the ground below where he hung. Flies covered the body or flew closely around it in a dense busy cloud, the sound of their humming filling the garden where the sweet smell of death now replaced the scents of orchid and jasmine.

Myitsu was physically incapable of dealing with the body. Afraid to go to town to ask for help she walked down the track to the road, to the only person she could trust to help her. On the other side of road a short path through the trees led to a simple bamboo and rattan shack where Jianyu lived. He was an ancient Chinese who had lived there for longer than anyone could remember. A quiet, solitary man with sad eyes that told of old sorrows, he made a little money from the medicinal herbs he gathered in the forest and sold in the market from time to time. Most of the Chinese in Mogok held him in high esteem as a healer, and would visit from time to time, but he seemed to prefer to be left alone, meditating, watching the ever changing jungle, and praying before a modest altar in his hut where fading photographs of a handsome young Chinese couple and a young child stared into time.

The old man was sitting on the ground outside his hut, leaning back against wall and smoking a long pipe with a thimble size silver bowl. The sweet heavy smell of opium lingered in the air about the hut as he stood up, bowed politely to Myitsu, and invited her into his home with a slow gracious gesture. Without asking he prepared a herb tea for them both, then sat down opposite her in front of a low brass table upon which he placed the two tiny cups, his eyes, small, black, and melancholy, never leaving the girl's face but taking in the scratches and bruises on her limbs.

Myitsu related the events that brought her to his home, and asked for his help. The old man had known Boy, who would often stop by on his way into or returning from town, simply to chat and pass the time, and his eyes filled with tears when he heard Myitsu's story.

They buried Boy at the edge of the garden, under the shade of an oleander bush, and Jianyu spoke for several minutes over the grave in his own tongue.

Myitsu could not understand the words, but felt the sadness, the pity, and the repressed anger the old man expressed. The garden seemed silent as he spoke, as if listening, and the shadows reached out as the sun set to cover the flowers, the lawn, and the simple grave, as if ashamed of what had transpired, drawing a cloak of darkness over the inhumanity of the small yellow men.

After Jianyu had left Myitsu lit lamps around the house and tried to set in order the chaos the soldiers had left behind. The whole house had been violated; furniture overturned, cupboards emptied, their contents strewn about, even the sheets and pillows stripped from their bed to expose the mattress that had been slit open.

That the soldiers had been looking for something was obvious, but Myitsu was not sure if it was the gems they were after, or of it was simple looting that inspired their actions. Boy had obviously been tortured, and she was inclined to believe it was because they were looking for information, about Julian, about her, but above all about the rubies. She had little doubt now that since they had not attempted to follow her, the young man had died protecting her, his lips sealed until death released him from his tormentors.

She went out onto the veranda and sat looking out into the night, wondering where Julian was at that moment, when he would come back to her. She remembered how when he was returning late from the mine she would put lighted candles in the window for him, a welcome, a sign, and she did the same now, placing the three stick candelabra on the windowsill, an affirmation of his promise and her belief, the words still fresh in her mind, his voice unchanged.

'Wait for me Myitsu, wait for me.'

Part Two

CHAPTER TWENTY

Kunlong P.O.W. Camp North Burma 1944

Julian awoke from a half-sleep just before dawn. Already he could hear the sounds and movements of other men; a hacking cough, moaning from the Aussi with tropical ulcers on both legs in the bunk by the door, the muttering of Samuel, Julian's friend, delirious with Dengue fever for five days now and unlikely to see the fifth. It was a normal awakening in Kunlong, a Japanese P.O.W. Labour camp on the Myitngre River in north central Burma, and Julian had survived there for two years, two years in which he had seen three quarters of the original prisoners succumb to a variety of causes; malaria, starvation, tropical infections and ulcers, exhaustion, and the most lethal, the brutality of their captors.

Sometimes he wondered why he still lived when others, stronger, braver, fitter, had died. Often they seemed to simply give up the will to live, the light would go out of their eyes, they stopped communicating, didn't even try to eat the tiny amounts of food they were offered by their mates. Mainly they died in the early hours, as if unable to face another day of misery and brutality, but at least they died quietly, unlike others who screamed until their throats bled, begging for drugs that were non-existent, or for a friend to put them out of their lonely agony. And many a friend was ready to oblige with this last desperate request hoping perhaps that when their turn came a friend would do the same for them.

But for Julian there could be no giving up, no matter how tired he became with the constant battle to just stay alive; the ever present hunger, the unending work of trying to care with no medicines or equipment for sick men who would mostly die whatever he did, the brutality, the pointless beatings that had damaged his body beyond repair. No matter where he was and how he suffered he found he could retreat from this strange inhuman world of the camp into the gentle past where he could close his eyes and see her, shut out the screams and cries of tortured men and hear her voice, and feel her arms about him instead of the pain of cracked ribs, jungle ulcers, and bruised limbs. In the night he would whisper her name, bringing the dream of her close. Myitsu. Myitsu...the three magic syllables, the salve, the cure, the opium.

Julian got up, slowly and painfully, every joint in his body seeming to protest. It had been like this for months now, the doctor telling him it was a normal reaction to the lack of vitamins and minerals in his diet and to watch out for tingling and loss of sensation in his legs that might indicate the onset of beriberi, common amongst the prisoners. But he counted himself lucky even so, for working as he did in the sick bay, he was not forced marched each day up the line to where the other men slaved for eighteen hours each day to build and maintain the railway they had said was impossible.

When, nearly two years ago now, the Doctor had asked him to be an assistant in the camp hospital, Julian had protested that he had no medical background whatsoever.

'It makes no difference.' Douglas Bright the MO had told him. 'We've no medicines, and no equipment, so there's precious little we can do to help the poor fellows who need attention, doctor or not. But you're an engineer, a practical man, problem solver, and that's more use to me than a Harley Street specialist here. And if you can use your skills to bodge up a few instruments, it could make all the difference...life and death for some.' So Julian had accepted his new role and within a couple of weeks had managed to construct several scalpels, bed pans, retractors, and clamps, even a prosthetic limb, out of bits and pieces scavenged around the camp.

In the grey half-light he began his daily routine by checking on the patients, usually numbering between twenty and thirty. Every inch of floor space in the hut was occupied by the sick, some lying on the bare earth, some on stretchers, and every morning he would find at least one or two had died during the night. Later they would be undressed so their clothes, if they had any, could be washed in the river and recycled to others or torn into strips for bandages. After *tenko*, the assembly and counting, they would be taken by the two orderlies, both young Scottish lads, to the grave pit just outside the camp perimeter, and dropped unceremoniously on top of the other bodies already there. Once a layer had been completed it would be covered lightly with lime, and the new bodies dropped on top. When the pit was full it would be lightly covered with soil and a new one started a few yards away.

The two young men were quite philosophical about their work, relieved, like Julian to be excused the working parties, in their case because they had both lost an arm, and were thus unable to wield a pick or shovel, their remaining two arms being sufficient between them to carry the skeletal remains of their comrades.

He found just two deaths from that night, removed their green and red 'dog tags', and pulled up the worn and soiled sheets to cover them, before going over to where Samuel was lying, watching him with bright feverish eyes. Julian knelt by his side and took his wrist, the pulse was light and fast, the skin hot, dry.

'How's it going old boy? Manage to get any sleep?'

Samuel attempted a smile, ending up with more of a rictus.

'Like a babe, nurse, I feel a new man today.'

'I'll get you some water, need anything else?'

Feeling obliged to ask but knowing that there was nothing else.

'Oh...just a couple of aspirin maybe, frightful headache, must have drunk too much Champagne last night...or maybe the caviar was a bit off.'

'I'll have a word with the management directly.' Julian said, moving away to fetch a mug of tepid water from the oil drum in a corner of the room.

The water was from the river, a couple of hundred yards from the camp where two thousand British, Australian, and American prisoners were being held, and had to be carried by hand in buckets to where it was boiled over a wood fire before being used. The boiling was supposed to sterilise the water, but Julian doubted its efficacy, dysentery, both amoebic and bacillary, being rife in the camp.

He returned to Samuel, and helped him into a position where he could swallow the water without spilling it over himself. After only a sip or two he collapsed back onto his pillow, a straw packed rice bag, gasping for breath.

'Thank you nurse...' He panted eventually, 'I'll ring if I need anything.' And he waved a skeletal hand feebly, as if dismissing Julian.

Julian smiled as he turned away, he could only marvel at the phlegmatic courage of most of the sufferers he helped, often joking in the face of death, hiding their fear and agony behind an irrepressible humour.

He continued his round, offering what he had, just water, to those still conscious, helping those who needed a bed pan, and trying to give words of comfort wherever needed.

The dozen or so men suffering from acute dysentery and unable to walk, he left until last. These took up most of his time, changing their soiled dressings, washing them as best he could, and trying to get them to rehydrate by encouraging them to drink as much as they could. During the day the orderlies ran about with Julian's improvised bedpans, boats as they called them, or with pails of water, trying to clean up the men who in their helplessness had fouled themselves. Sometimes friends squatted between the stretchers, murmuring words of encouragement and brushing off the flies.

No one except those too weak to stand were excused tenko, the first ordeal of the day, where the whole camp was made to stand in long lines while being counted. The guards in charge of the counting were obviously semi-literate and would walk the lines counting like children on their fingers, and if the total did not tally would have to do the whole process again, sometimes making it last for over an hour. Anyone who fainted in the heat, whether through sickness or exhaustion, and there were always some, would provoke a fit of illogical rage in the guards. They would descend on the man, kicking him and hitting him with the flat of their swords until he either managed to stand up or they grew tired or he was beaten to death in front of the whole camp. Julian had long ago given up trying to understand the mentality of the Japanese, accepting that they were simply mad, or not really human.

Nobody really knew what was happening in the world outside the camp. Nearly all of the inmates had been taken prisoner in the first few months of the war, so there were almost no new arrivals to give any information, only a few hundred sent up from Changi Jail in Singapore had scraps of news, and most of that was bad. The only slightly encouraging clues about the progress of the war were the thinning out of the guards in the last couple of months, and a distinct reduction in the amount of food allocated to the prisoners. It was noticed that their jailers too were appearing to suffer from malnutrition, the obvious implication being that the war was not going well for them. The last outbreak of cholera that had killed over two hundred prisoners had also affected the guards, further reducing their numbers.

The men talked of deliverance with more hope now than in the previous years. The end would come, it was only a question of would they be alive to see it. Several of the senior officers discussed amongst themselves whether the Japanese might kill everyone before the advancing troops could liberate them, afraid perhaps of reprisals or prosecution for war crimes. Tentative plans were made for a mass breakout if this seemed to be imminent.

In the meantime there were rumours that the camp was going to be moved south, away from the advancing British army that had crossed the Arakan mountains from India and was now fighting its way towards the plains of central Burma. Julian had discussed this with the doctor, how they could move the many sick who could not even stand up let alone march through thick jungle for days or weeks.

'If we leave them the japs will just kill them.' Douglas observed, 'But if we try to move them they'll mostly die within hours in any case.'

'I couldn't face leaving them.' Julian said, 'If there's any chance of saving even just one of them we should take it.'

'Well, I agree to a certain extent Julian, but I think you'll find that a lot of them just don't want to be moved, more pain, more suffering, and for what?'

Julian shrugged his thin shoulders. 'I don't know Douglas, there's no easy answer, let's just hope it doesn't happen.'

A week later there were still rumours of an immanent move without anything happening when Julian was summoned to attend Major Smythe, the senior British officer. Major Smythe shared a rotting tent with the American and Australian CO's. As senior officers they were entitled to certain luxuries denied to the other prisoners, but all three refused to be treated any different to their men, assigning any extra food they were given to the hospital for distribution. Their health was generally better than the other ranks nevertheless, due to their exemption from work details. Major Smythe, a middle aged professional soldier who had served previously in the Indian Army, was sitting at what served as a desk outside the tent, writing another of his letters of protest to the camp commander.

'Ah! Drake.' He said, looking up at Julian, 'Good of you to see me.'

'Not at all Major, what can I do for you?'

The major indicated an upturned wooden crate next to the table for Julian to sit on.

'Julian, as a civilian I've no right to ask you to do anything, but I've had a request...yes a request from Saito.' Julian raised his eyebrows, it was unusual for

Colonel Jira Saito the camp commander to requested anything, unwilling to risk loss of face should the request be refused, normally he just issued orders, orders that had too be obeyed immediately and without question.

'Yes, odd isn't it.' Continued the Major, seeing Julian's reaction, 'But the gist of it is he wants me to find two or three Burmese speakers. Didn't say why, just said to send them to him, and you're the only one left here who speaks the lingo since the padre died, so do you want to go and see what it's all about?'

'It's pretty busy at the hospital Major, the doctor's hardly able to manage, it'll be hard on him if I'm not around.' Replied Julian. 'You've no idea what it might entail?'

'Not a clue I'm afraid, and I can't force you to go, it's your call. But remember once they know you can speak the lingo you won't have any say on what they ask of you.'

Julian thought about the hospital, the men he was trying to help, Samuel, who still lay dying a slow pitiful death.

'I don't think I can leave the doc Major, I know we can't do much for the patients, but we can try to make them a bit more comfortable. The doc needs all the help he can get...'

'I know that Drake, and you're all doing well there considering what you have to work with. But there is another consideration.' The Major leant across the table towards Julian, lowering his voice in case they might be overheard. 'You speak a bit of Japanese I hear.'

'Not much, just what I've picked up in the last couple of years.'

'I've heard you're pretty good, Drake, let's not have any false modesty, it's too important. Now we, that is the other officers and myself, believe the japs are on the run. Being beaten back now. But we have no definite news, no facts to go on, and it could be desperately important to find out. The endgame might be mass executions, extermination of prisoners, elimination of witnesses and destruction of evidence. If they're beaten they won't want it known what's gone on in the camps.'

'And you think I could find something out?'

'It's a long shot Drake, might come to nothing, but it might help...anything you hear, any info at all, could make all the difference.'

So it could make a difference, Julian thought, information that might save lives. Perhaps more lives than he could hope to save working in the hospital. He had to accept he realised.

'All right, I'll see what he wants. Can't do any harm I expect.'

It was later that day, just as the sun was setting that Julian was summoned to the camp commander. Two guards, Fat Boy and Squint Eye, appeared at the door of the hospital hut, shouting his name and banging on the walls with their bamboo clubs. They dared not enter, fearing they might catch something, and Julian took his time walking up to them and bowing, a tardiness that earned him a painful blow to his back.

They pushed and prodded him across the parade ground to the hut where Saito lived. In front of the hut he was forced to kneel, bending over so his head touched the ground in submission. The guards stood behind him, ready to strike if he moved even an inch, while they waited. Julian stared at the brown soil wondering how long he would wait, and how long he could tolerate the cramps that would soon come. He'd had ribs broken before from beatings, and knew how painfully long the recovery had been.

After what seemed hours but was probably a lot less he heard a door open and the sound of the guard's boots clicking as they stood to attention. There was a shout of command accompanied by an agonising blow to his kidneys as they forced him to his feet and pushed him up the steps and into Saito's office.

Julian bowed low, and remained bent over, staring at the wooden floor in front of the commander's desk, knowing that   looking up before being invited would result in a blow across his head, neck or shoulders. Jira Saito was a stickler for respect; a small man in his thirties he exuded an air of nervous insecurity, manifesting itself in violent rages over trivial details, particularly anything he thought might be construed as disrespectful. Even the most senior officers dreaded meeting him such was his unpredictability and instability.

'He'd be locked up in any civilised country.' The doctor had once remarked to Julian after treating one victim of the commander's vice. 'Paranoid schizophrenia...classic case. Don't know why they haven't spotted it.'

He was always dressed immaculately, his boots in particular always buffed to a shine that would have been a credit to the Brigade of Guards. The overall effect was however rendered almost comic by the enormous sword he always wore that trailed behind him as he walked and would have been impossible for him to draw without taking two hands to it.

There was however nothing comic about his actions, his treatment of the prisoners, his elaborate punishments that must have been dreamed up by a twisted mind totally devoid on any humanity.

'Mr. Drake.' The voice always surprised Julian, high pitched, rather refined, almost feminine, his English exceptional. 'Are you well?'

Julian cautiously raised his head, expecting a blow at any moment, but no, he was permitted to look across the neat, almost empty desk at the commander who sat very straight in a chair that had been raised to give him more height. His cap was folded on the desk before him and his small weak hands played nervously with a silver fountain pen. He peered up at Julian myopically through round wire-framed glasses that caught the light from time to time, hiding his eyes behind bright white discs.

'Very well, Major, thank you. Very well. I trust you are too.' There had lately been outbreaks of cholera amongst the Japanese guards.

The Major made a thin-lipped attempt at a smile.

'Of course.' He murmured, as if a Japanese Major was by nature impervious to disease.

'I have called you here today because I have had a request from the Kempeitai. They require as many Burmese speakers as they can find, immediately. Major Smythe informs me that you speak this language.'

'I'm hardly fluent Major, just what I've picked up through working here...

'Can you speak and understand Burmese...that is all I need to know.' He interrupted testily.

'Yes Sir, I can.' Julian added quickly, recognising the rising temper of the man opposite him.

Saito remained looking at him critically for a minute, the light from the window reflected form the lenses of his glasses, making his eyes impossible to see.

'I hope that is the case Mr. Watson, it would be a mistake on your part to pretend...to how do you say, to pull the wool over my eyes.'

'I'm sure my Burmese will be satisfactory sir. I will be happy to oblige you.'

Saito stood up, and Julian realised there was actually a raised dais behind the desk.

'It is not me you are obliging Mr. Drake, it is the Japanese people. And of course you are hardly obliging anyone in any case. As an inferior race it is your duty, your role, to serve. My request was merely a formality, a Japanese request to an inferior race is a form of order you must understand.'

Julian recognised the lecture that was to come, he had heard many, standing with the other prisoners in the heat of the parade ground for hours while Saito regaled them with his theories of national superiority.

'For years you arrogant British exploited the people of the east, even refusing to allow Japan to join your pathetic League of Nations,' He continued, and for the next fifteen minutes Julian had to stand immobile as Saito strode back and forth on his dais expanding on his themes of Japanese divinity, their superiority to other races, the place of the British now as a subject race of sub humans.

At length he stopped, removed his glasses, and began to polish the lenses furiously working himself up into a state of repressed anger and frustration.

'You might think you can defeat us...you cannot! You might think the recent reversals in the north signal a retreat...they do not! We are unbeatable Mr. Drake, because we are Devine, our Emperor is God. Our soldiers know no fear, death is an honour greater than anything in this life. We will regroup, not retreat, and then we will return to crush your pathetic little army.' He stopped his frantic polishing and replaced the glasses slightly askew on his sweating face.

'Do you know Mr. Drake how many Japanese soldiers were taken prisoner during the capture of Malaya and Singapore? Have you any idea?'

Julian shook his head warily.

'Twenty-two Mr. Drake, twenty-two. And do you know how many allied troops were made prisoners of the Japanese army during that time?'

Julian shook his head again.

'Sixty three thousand Mr. Drake. Sixty three thousand! Is there any more proof of our superiority than that Mr. Drake? Is there?'

Julian felt his life was in great danger, the man was mad, raving, and quite capable of having him beheaded on a whim. He had seen it before, often. It seemed to be the only thing that calmed him down.

'Indeed I see sir. It is a definite proof.'

Saito peered at him suspiciously, then took a deep breath and straightened his glasses.

'You will be sent to another camp Mr. Drake, where your dubious linguistic talents may be of use. If they are insufficient I expect they will have little need of you...except for bayonet practice perhaps.'

With that he shouted something at the guards who seized Julian and dragged him out of the room. Once outside they administered the regular beating using the flat of their swords. Julian, accustomed as were most of the prisoners to this treatment did his best to avoid serious damage to vital parts by curling into a foetal ball, covering his head with his hands, and hoping they would grow bored or tired before killing him.

They must have been aware that it was not a good idea to damage him too severely as they stopped quite quickly, and then half dragged half carried him across the darkened parade ground to a lightless cell in the punishment block.

So much for getting information for Smythe thought Julian sitting morosely with his back against the wall of the tiny room. He had found out little except the perhaps telling reference Saito had made to recent reverses and retreat, Julian could well imagine how hard it would be for his fragile grasp on reality and his obvious psychological problems to reconcile a defeat at the hands of an inferior race.

But the unprovoked rage he had exhibited was nothing new, just a week previously the whole camp had been forced to witness the decapitation of three Australian soldiers who were accused of not bowing low enough as Saito passed. The courage of the men as they knelt in a row to receive the executioner's sword was humbling. The youngest, a boy of no more than seventeen had raised his head at the last moment and called out to the appalled watchers.

'Mark this bastard for future attention mates. Mark him.' A second later his head hit the brown dirt of the parade ground, rolled a few feet to come to a stop staring with blind eyes at the blue dazzling sky.

Doc Bright would have to do without him now, and he had no idea whether his Burmese would be good enough to keep him away from being a static target for a Japanese soldier's bayonet. However, two years of existing under threat of a sudden, violent, and probably painful death had made Julian phlegmatic about events in his life over which he had little or no control. At any rate it would be a change from the routine of the hospital, where he had witnessed too much of death and misery without the means to do much to help. He regretted he would not be there for Samuel when his time came, but it was unlikely he would ever know, having been in a coma for the last two days.

Julian reached around to try to feel his back where the kicks and blows had fallen, but found it too painful. Nothing broken or cracked he thought, just a few more bruises that would take several weeks to disappear, just routine stuff in Kunlong Camp. He lay down on the flat earth floor and tried to find a comfortable position that would keep his back off the ground and tried to sleep. As always the moment his eyes closed she came to him, the hard floor became soft, the aches and pains all but disappeared, in the darkness her face appeared close to his, in the silence he heard her voice, and he remembered his promise.

It was shortly after dawn they came for him, dragging and frog-marching him across the parade ground where the rest of the prisoners were beginning to assemble for *tenko*. A captured American jeep was waiting with engine running by the main gate. Julian wanted to get a message to Major Smythe, but had no opportunity to speak to anyone before he was pushed into the back of the jeep next to a very young soldier who stared at him with a mixture of fear and dislike. A rope was attached around Julian's neck and attached to the roll bar of the jeep, and another guard took the seat next to the driver. As the jeep started off Julian heard a shout of 'Good Luck!' from the assembling ranks, followed by a chorus of other shouts, and he turned and saw Major Smythe stepping forward and waving. Julian raised his hand to wave back and was rewarded by a sharp dig in the ribs from the young guard's rifle as they turned out of the gate and headed down the muddy track leading south.

It took them the best part of the day to reach their destination, a village on the banks of a river Julian thought might be the Thanlyin or a tributary. It seemed as if the original village had been extended as a large number of long and low wood and bamboo huts surrounded it, separated from it by a barbed wire fence. Julian expected to see other prisoners, but there seemed to be only locals visible behind the wire, large numbers of emaciated Burmese dressed in rags who stared at the jeep and its occupants as it passed by. The jeep continued past the guarded gate to the enclosure, and entered the village, eventually stopping in front of what had probably been the general store before the war.

After a short wait Julian was pushed out of the jeep and led by the rope into the building. The front room was occupied by a number of Japanese and Burmese men seated at desks who didn't look up from their work as Julian was led through the room and into another office behind. This room was badly lit, the sole window being partly covered by an ancient tamarind tree growing against the outside wall. One electric light bulb hanging from an invisible chord glowed a feeble yellow high up in the centre of the room. A large dark wood desk littered with papers occupied a position in front of the window. Behind the desk Julian could make out the form of a seated man, bent over some papers, an indistinct figure, hunched, head and neck blending into the formless black mass of his body, two pale white hands resting on the desk top. Julian felt a shiver run through his body, instinct told him there was something about this man, something not right, not human. It was several minutes before he looked up at Julian, lifting his head slowly, his gaze traveling leisurely up Julian's body from feet to head, finally remaining fixed on his face. He appeared to study him, as a botanist might examine an unknown plant or an entomologist a rare insect.

'Well Mr. Drake, this is a most pleasant surprise. I had not thought we would meet again, but these are such...' and he waved both his arms vaguely before him, 'such turbulent times.'

Julian stared at the man in the chair. As his eyes became accustomed to the gloom he began to make out his features. The man knew him, but from where? His English was almost perfect, very unusual for a Japanese. But then he realised, he was not Japanese, in spite of the uniform that Julian identified as that of the dreaded Kempeitai, he was Burmese. And those thick-rimmed glasses, he'd seen them before he was sure, but when and where?

'Oh! You have not remembered our meeting I can see. It was several years ago I must admit. And after all, why would you, an Englishman, remember a chance meeting with one of the subject race. So little of consequence to you I am sure.'

It came to him in a sudden revelation, the myopic stare, the studied enunciation, the black thick-rimmed glasses. The friend of Zeya, the market of Mogok, before Myitsu, before the war, it was Mr. Kaw seated behind the desk, now obviously an officer in the Kempeitai, the Japanese military and secret police.

Julian swallowed, but said nothing, a sudden an unexplained feeling of danger coming over him.

'Mr. Kaw.' He said quietly.

'Indeed, but now Captain Kaw, Mr. Drake. Temporarily a member of Emperor Hirohito's armed forces. Ah! How times change do they not Mr. Drake, do they not?'

There was a silence as if he expected a reply from Julian.

'Changes for better or worse.' He continued eventually. 'Better for some, worse for others.' He stood up and walked around the desk to where Julian stood, and looked him critically, up and down.

'How are you keeping Mr. Drake? Not quite as...shall we say rounded, as I remember you. In fact I notice your bones are quite pronounced...not covered by much...flesh. I recommend that you do not neglect your appetite Mr. Drake, I fear you are not eating well.'

He walked slowly around Julian, humming quietly to himself. Julian noticed his smell, different to the Japanese and the prisoners, a sweetness, but not a fragrance, more the cloying sweet smell of death, rotting meat.

He stopped behind Julian, who stiffened, waiting for a blow, or something else. He felt a hand touching him, lifting his shirt, exposing his back. There was something like a sigh from the man behind him.

'Scar tissue... recent bruising...I fear you have incurred the displeasure of your hosts during your time as a prisoner.'

Julian felt the touch of his fingers, almost a caress, exploring his scars, then the hand removed, his shirt falling back into place. The man remained standing behind him, silent for a moment.

'As a civilised man I should abhor violence you might think.' He continued eventually. 'Yet it is, I'm afraid, unavoidable sometimes. Violence, death, pain, discomfort, these are all unavoidable at times. After all is not the roll of the soldier in war to slay his enemies, without thought, compassion, or any other qualities so esteemed in peacetime. What was it your Shakespeare said...that bit in Henry V...you must remember it Mr. Drake...begins... '*In peace there's nothing so becomes a man as modest stillness and humility.*' '

He appeared at Julian's side, moving noise-lessly, looking up at the Englishman.

'But now we must *'imitate the action of the tiger; stiffen the sinews, summon up the blood, disguise fair nature with hard-favour'd rage.'* And they do that quite well our Japanese friends do they not Mr. Drake? Have you seen them in action? An attack upon a fortified position maybe? Incredible. They know no fear. Fanatics one might say. Veritable tigers.'

He moved again, round to where he was facing Julian. Then abruptly turned and sat down behind his desk again.

'But forgive me Julian, do you mind my calling you Julian, you must be wondering why you have been brought here. What makes your knowledge of my language important enough to bring you and your escort fifty miles to this poor excuse for a village.'

He began to move papers around on the desk, as if searching for something.

'Our joint masters, the Japanese, have apparently run out of manpower. Not fighting troops you understand, although they appear to be loosing them at an alarming rate at the moment, but support. Supply, maintenance, administration, is all fields where they are lacking personnel. For this they must resort to using my countrymen, Burmese. Unfortunately very few Burmese speak any Japanese, and virtually no Japanese can be bothered to learn Burmese. Hence the need for translators. Here in this camp we have assembled a few thousand of my fellow citizens, and it will be your role, as well as a few others we have located, to interview these men and find out what qualifications they have that might be of use to us.'

Julian began to understand the presence of all the locals behind the barbed wire now.

'We wish to locate medical people, engineers like yourself, drivers...basically anyone with a knowledge or talent that might be of use. Simple enough don't you think Mr. Drake, well within your capabilities.'

'I understand Mr. Kaw. And the ones who have nothing, no qualifications?'

'Oh they will be used as labour, skilled or unskilled, there is always a need for more of them. They do seem to die off at an alarming rate once put to work I'm afraid.'

Julian could think of no reply to this. Ever since his capture he had been aware of the gangs of slave labour who worked alongside the prisoners, their pitiful state, worse even than the captives, many of them dying while at work under the clubs and boots of their guards.

'But now Mr. Drake I must press on, you will start work tomorrow perhaps. These men will take you back to your room, something more permanent will be arranged soon.'

He said something Julian didn't catch to the guards, who seized Julian by the arms to lead him out. Before they reached the door Mr. Kaw called out, stopping them.

'Ah! I quite forgot to ask you Mr. Drake. What exactly happened to the mine in the end, when the troops arrived?'

Julian froze in the doorway, not turning around to answer the question. After a moments hesitation he replied.

'Sorry, I can't say, I left before the Japs arrived. No idea what happened after.'

Julian noticed he was humming to himself quietly again.

'No matter, no matter.' He said, his voice quiet casual but not completed hiding a tension. 'I imagine we'll find out one day, don't you Mr. Drake. Good day to you.'

CHAPTER TWENTY-ONE

Julian began the work of interviewing the Burmese the next day. There were three other interviewers, two English and one Frenchman, but as they were not allowed to talk amongst themselves he could find out nothing about them. Four tables were set up on a raised platform in front of Mr. Kaw's office and about a couple of hundred natives were lined up on the opposite side of the road waiting to be called one by one for their interview. There was a set list of questions to be asked of each man with a space at the end for the interviewers recommendation or comments. Julian found his Burmese barely sufficient for the task, and on several occasions no use at all as the man being interviewed came from an ethnic group with a different language. On these occasions, Julian being mindful of Saito's warning, pretended he understood and invented answers, the subject being classed as unskilled, fit for manual labour. Julian was quite aware that in these cases he was probably sending the man to his death, but could find no alternative. Every morning lorries would leave the camp carrying the Burmese who had been interviewed, to return empty at the end of the day. He saw and heard nothing of Mr. Kaw during those days, but was still kept on his own, separate from the other Europeans who lived together in a small hut.

Several times over the next few days aircraft flew high overhead, American B17's and British Mosquitoes. The Japanese guards rushed to their anti-aircraft batteries around the perimeter of the camp but the planes were gone before they could get the covers off the guns. One day Julian heard the sound of explosions from the north, either bombs or artillery. It seemed the allies were drawing nearer.

It was one morning about ten days after his arrival in the camp Julian was woken before dawn by two Korean guards he had not seen before. They were both short, muscular men with shaved heads and hard faces that seemed even more brutal by the flickering light of the oil lamp they carried. Korean guards were viewed by the prisoners in his old camp as more cruel and sadistic than the worst of the Japanese who treated them with contempt on the same level as the prisoners.

The sky was just lightening as he was half dragged half carried through the village to a grey and stained concrete building on the outskirts. There were no windows Julian noticed, just a rusting metal door and he guessed it must have been a storage depot of some kind before the arrival of the Japanese. On the other side of the door was a single square room lit by bare bulb in the ceiling. The only furniture was a small metal table with a chair on either side, and a third chair in one corner of the room. Mr. Kaw occupied one of the chairs.

'Good morning Mr. Drake!' He called cheerily as Julian entered. 'No rain yet I see, the monsoon is rather overdue. These are strange times don't you think?' And he indicated Julian to take the chair opposite him.

'I wanted to have a little chat with you Mr. Drake, like between friends, just so that we get to know each other better.'

Julian noticed his smell again, stronger it seemed than before, sickly and sweet.

'But perhaps to start off with we should be a little less formal, may I call you Julian, Mr. Drake? And I would be quite amenable if you were to address me as simply Captain, we can dispense with other forms, those pigs...' and he gestured to where the two Koreans were standing against the wall, their faces blank, unreadable, 'understand nothing in any case, mere brutes, but useful on occasion.'

Julian stared back at the man opposite him. He had a slight smile on his face, as if savouring a private joke, one he would reveal in due course.

'It did occur to me Julian that you might be wondering about me. And as we are to be I hope good friends, you might like to know a little of what brings me to this rather despoiled village in this despoiled country.'

He looked enquiringly at Julian, waiting for a response. Julian thought for a moment.

'Your English is very good. Where did you learn it.'

'Too kind Julian, but true. I have many times been complemented on it, and indeed take pride in it. But you see I was brought up as an Englishman in a way. My dear father was one of the few Burmese who prospered under the British, selling to the army, anything they needed or wanted. From rice to oil, if he didn't have it he'd find it. And having amassed small fortune he sent me at an early age to your country for my education. First prep school at six, then public school, Harrow to be precise, at eleven, finishing up at Cambridge when I was eighteen. Later I qualified as a doctor at the Middlesex Hospital in London, before I returned home to Burma upon the death of my father.

Yes Julian, I should have stayed a doctor you might think. But on my return, experiencing the difference between the life of a Burmese in Burma and the one I had known in England, I became infected by politics. I use the term infected Julian because it best describes what happened to me. Eventually I joined the communist party of Burma, banned of course by the government and later, with the expansion of Japan into Korea and China I saw an opening for cooperation, and spent several months in Japan under instruction in techniques of interrogation and intelligence gathering. Lately, with the somewhat delicate military position, I have been a jack of all trades, sent hither and thither where my talents would be useful.'

He sat back in his chair, removed a large white handkerchief from a pocket, and mopped his brow. He was sweating heavily Julian noticed.

'Now your turn Julian, tell me about your life.'

Julian cleared his throat nervously.

'Well, I graduated from mining school...'

'Oh spare me all that Julian, I know. I know all about how and when you came to Burma. What you did here, where you went, your friends...'

Julian couldn't avoid looking up sharply at this last.

'Yes Julian, your friends. Including a certain young person who lived there with you in that rather quaint house in Mogok.'

Did he mean Boy, or Myitsu Julian thought. What else did he know, what had happened since he left them two years ago.

'My houseboy you mean? He came with the place, I told him he could stay or leave when the japs came. I doubt he's still there.'

Mr. Kaw stared at Julian, the smile gone, replaced by a hard, angry expression.

'Yes Julian, that brings us to what interests me...when you left.' He sat up straight suddenly and leant forward over the desk towards Julian.

'What happened to the rubies when you left?' He shouted, 'What did you do with them?'

Julian stared back at him, his mouth dry, realising what was probably coming. He tried to swallow, but found he couldn't.

'I don't know. Jock took care of that.'

There was a long silence, both men staring into each other's eyes.

'Oh my dear Julian.' He spoke in almost a whisper, imparting a confidence. 'My dear young man, I know that cannot be. Two men in charge of such an operation, hiding details such as the location of the fruits of their labour from each other, impossible. Unbelievable.'

'It's true.' He managed to say. 'He never told me anything like that.'

Major Kaw stood up, signaled to the Koreans without a word, who immediately took hold of Julian and began to frog march him out.

'I am sure that after a little reflection you will remember Julian. Think hard, we'll talk about it another day, you can tell me then. But I'll see you soon Julian. Very soon.'

Julian was hustled through the door with these last words, and brought back to his cell where he spent the rest of the day without being called out to work. That evening he was surprised to have a large bowl of vegetables with rice and even a few pieces of meat that might have been chicken pushed through his door. It was the best meal he had been given for as long as he remembered, but he couldn't help wondering why. He knew there would be another meeting with the Burmese, and he guessed it would not be a pleasant one for him. He tried not to think of what might be in store. The man wanted information, the whereabouts of the rubies, but only Myitsu knew that, and if he told that to Kaw he would find her and force her to tell. And he would not be gentle.

Whatever happened to him he couldn't tell about Myitsu, he had to keep her out of the equation. His story must stand anything they could do to him, and he began to hope, perhaps for the first time in his captivity, that he might find death, that final release, before he would betray her. He was deeply afraid.

His trial, his interrogation began the next day. Before dawn he was woken by the two Koreans, taken out into the space on front of the cellblock, tied by his wrists to a post, and beaten unconscious by the guards. It was not like the other beatings he had suffered. They took their time, judging each blow of their bamboo clubs carefully, inflicting the maximum pain without fatal damage. Julian stayed conscious for the first ten minutes before collapsing, to hang by his wrists, his knees bent, the blood pooling around his feet.

A bucket of water thrown over him brought him round for the process to be repeated, and repeated again until he remained unconscious in spite of several dousings. During all the time they worked on him they spoke not a word. They asked nothing of him, gave him no chance to beg or plead as most men do when in *extremis*, and in a small corner of his mind he knew this was only the start, a softening up process, the real test would come later.

He regained consciousness in a world of pain. It was daylight, hot, his mouth was dry as the brown dust he saw before his eyes, he had no idea of where he was. Bent double, his face pressing into the ground, he knelt, unable to move. Turning his eyes he could see bamboo bars and beyond the expanse of the parade ground, empty and shimmering in the heat. He tried to straighten his body, but found it impossible, a bar lying across his back and others   at his feet. He looked the other way and found a similar view of bamboo bars, and knew where he was. A pig basket.

A pig basket was what the local farmers carried their pigs in when transporting them, a bamboo cage about three feet long and two feet high and wide. A man could be made to fit into it only if bent in two, and this is how Julian found himself, forced into a space that prevented him stretching out, lying down, sitting, standing, or moving in any direction more than a few inches. The Japanese had found the device an excellent method of breaking a prisoner, both mentally and physically. After a relatively short period agonising cramps would rack the victim, they might twist and turn, trying to relieve to pain, but that would only make it worse. They would strain against the frame, often injuring themselves in the process. Only the minimum amount of water necessary to keep them alive would be given to them, and food was considered superfluous as usually they were unable to swallow solids. In Julian's old camp no one had survived more than three days in the basket, which was set up in the middle of the parade ground where the other prisoners could witness the slow agonising death of their comrade.

Julian's throat was dry and his mouth filled with half congealed blood. The heat throbbed in his head...steady rhythmic thumping blows. Every inch of his body seemed to have its own special pain demanding attention he could not give. His hands were tied behind his back making it impossible for him to lift his head from the ground. At that moment, with the knowledge of his predicament and what awaited him, he wished desperately he would die. He was certain he could never withstand interrogation. Already he felt that if they had asked him anything, anything at all, he would have immediately answered, if only they would take the pain away, allow him to stand up or lie down.

He found himself peering between the bars, looking towards the buildings where Kaw might be, hoping to see them coming for him so he could tell them. And even if they killed him after he had talked it would be preferable to this, the unremitting agony.

Time passed, whether slowly or quickly he had no idea. Time had no meaning any more, nothing had meaning. He seemed to exist in a separate world unlike anything he had experienced. A world that was composed simply of pain, its degrees, its proximity or distance, its subtle variations. Like a living thing it fought for possession of his body, sought to snuff out the spark of hope that sometime it might attenuate or disappear. He began to know it intimately, just as the pain knew him, his weaknesses, his fears, the darkness that was drawing in around him.

Sometime later he was conscious that it was night. And cooler so that he began to shiver. He thought he saw a man standing over him, and the man prodded him with a stick, making him scream, then the man went away.

Then it was light again, and the heat returned. He tried to lick his swollen lips but his tongue was stuck and he had no saliva in any case. There was a noise, movement, the buzzing of thousands of flies around him, and he felt them on him, feasting on the dried blood, crawling everywhere on his exposed flesh. Another sound, almost human, then realising it was his own sound, the sound of a man whose throat is too dry and can only make a strange animal grunting.

Then night came again, and cold, and again he saw the man standing over him, then kneeling to look closer by the light of a torch. A hand reached through the bars touching his neck, feeling for his pulse, and then withdrawn. The man went away, and later the light came back and with it the heat.

Sometime that day they came for him. A bucket of water thrown over him, the basket opened and dragged out still curled with his face in the dirt. They cut the bindings of his hands, lifted him off the ground, and carried him into the concrete room where Mr. Kaw waited.

A chair was positioned in the middle of the room, a chair with leather straps designed to attach arms and legs. A metal table stood to one side of the chair with a flat brown case on it. Beside the table another chair, with Mr. Kaw seated, his face a mask, sweating. A stethoscope hung around his neck.

Julian felt a long cool blade sliding against his skin and his threadbare clothes fell to the floor around his feet. He was thrust into the chair and his arms and legs attached tightly. A further strap was fixed around his waist to the chair back.

Mr. Kaw nodded to one of the guards, who brought over a tin mug of water. He took hold of Julian's hair to force his head back, and poured the water over his mouth. Julian tried to drink, coughing and choking at the same time.

'I wonder if you have had time to reflect Julian, have you?' Mr. Kaw spoke quietly, reasonably. 'You must have I'm sure. So now we can have our little chat and get back to normal. Because that's what you want isn't it Julian? This... ' He waved his hands to indicate the room, the guards and the metal table, 'to stop. The pain...it must be terrible...I can hardly imagine...you must want it to stop.'

Julian stared at him, unable to think, unable to speak, terror building inside him. He tried not to look towards the brown closed case on the table, tried not to think what it might hold.

'Let me refresh your memory then Julian. It was the fate of the rubies that interested me, the fate that seems to have escaped your memory. Now...have you recalled anything Julian, even a little detail might help us both.'

Without willing it he found himself shaking his head. A sound came from his mouth, not a word, more of a grunt.

Kaw raised his eyebrows, as if surprised.

'No? Nothing? How unfortunate Julian, for you that is. For now we must try to bring back those memories. I find that very often it takes only a little thing to help recall stubborn details lost in...somewhere. Only a little thing.'

He reached out very slowly, keeping his eyes on Julian, clicked open the catches on the case, and lifted the lid.

Even without looking directly at the case Julian could see it was a set of medical instruments. Shining stainless steel objects whose usage he tried not to imagine. Probes, scalpels, hooks, a saw, pliers, several hypodermic syringes, a small and a large hammer, and several long thin bamboo slivers rather like skewers.

'Not much you see Julian, no racks, iron maidens, branding irons, just a few medical tools of the trade you might say.'

The terror that gripped Julian paralysed him completely, and he felt a new sharp pain in his lower abdomen. Kaw was watching him intently, sweat running down his fleshy face, dripping from the frame of his glasses.

'Very well Julian. Let us begin...it will not take long I believe. But then sometimes I find it's good to take one's time, make the pleasure last.'

He stood up and walked around behind Julian.

'I feel I should make an admission before we start Julian, it might make you feel differently about me, but maybe not. I am one of those people who enjoy above all things bringing pain to my fellow humans. I'm not sure why, I was always like that. I discovered that when just a child, discovered I enjoyed torturing animals...our three pet dogs were my first experiments. Later of course I progressed to humans, infinitely more satisfactory and pleasurable even. Prostitutes were an easy prey to me when living in Rangoon. And I found females very different to males, not more or less satisfying, just different. They have a higher tolerance to pain you know Julian, in general that is. Much higher.

Of course my medical background was a huge advantage. Not only from my knowledge of anatomy, but in my ability to keep a subject alive through extremes of manipulation and degradation. I never had anyone die on me Julian, if that's a comfort to you, probably not I fear.'

Julian could smell him now, close behind him, a feral reek of excitement, and he knew the time had come. From behind him an arm reached out to the case on the table, touching with fingertips tenderly the various objects, before selecting one of the thin pointed bamboo skewers and the smaller of the two hammers. Strangely it was not until the end of the session before Mr. Kaw again asked the question.

He was lying on his favourite chair on the veranda with a cushion behind his head that allowed him to see the garden through half closed eyes. Boy was cutting flowers from the borders and he could hear the click of his shears and the sound of him singing tunelessly to himself some popular song picked up from Mandalay radio. Sitting comfortably cross-legged on the floor next to his chair Myitsu was brushing her long black lustrous hair, from time to time her eyes looked up at him, a smile of pure contentment covered her face. Her small shoulders were bare, amber coloured, smooth as the silk of her green and blue sarong. The lazy heat of the late afternoon hung over the house and the garden, radiating from the walls and floors, filling the still air with scents of jasmine, cut grass, warm wood. He was at peace.

He closed his eyes, the light suddenly too bright, and felt her hand on his arm, shaking it gently, trying to arouse him. But he wished she would let him sleep, just a little while. Boy was still singing, but his voice changing, becoming older, harsher. The grip on his arm was firm, hard, even painful and he tried to pull away from it but found he could not. And then it was not Boy's voice anymore, but a harsh Japanese intoning the diurnal ritual 'Itchy, ne, san, si, go, roco,' as they counted the prisoners. Despairing he opened his eyes and stared about him. They veranda and house was gone, the garden disappeared with Boy and Myitsu. In its place was the blinding expanse of the parade ground seen through bamboo bars, and the prisoners standing in long ragged lines while the guards walked the ranks. He looked down at the hand gripping his arm.

'Monsieur, monsieur... ' A strange voice, insistent. 'Monsieur, quickly please, take this, there is little time.' And a metal mug of water was pushed towards his face through the bars.

Julian tried to reach it, but found he couldn't move his arms. The man realised, and pushed the mug close to his face, tipping it up so the liquid ran over his parched and swollen lips, some even managing to run into his mouth. The mug was rapidly withdrawn, and the man put his mouth close to the bars and whispered.

'Courage mon ami, courage. There is hope, the allies are approaching, there will be an end to your suffering. Hold out...we know of your ordeal.'

Then he was gone, disappearing from Julian's view. For a moment he forgot the pain, his ruined feet, the burns over his chest and back, the aches of his twisted joints. He was not alone, a fellow prisoner, a Frenchman obviously had braved death to give him water and hope. And he was not dead yet, he had not talked as far as he could remember, perhaps there was a hope, if only he could survive.

Then he was in the room again, and tied in the chair, and Mr. Kaw was waiting for his reply. And when he shook his head the man seemed happy, and smiled as he reached out to open the case of instruments And Julian found himself screaming at the now familiar sight of them, trying to push away, the guards holding him fast as the torturer methodically made his selection before beginning his work.

What had happened to time? Julian had no idea how long he had been going backwards and forwards to the concrete room. Was it days? Weeks? Even Months? Time had disappeared from his life.

There were no more visits from the mysterious Frenchman, and Julian existed on the edge of a precipice to death or madness, Mr. Kaw always careful to stop his torment before Julian's heart gave up the struggle. He was winning Julian knew, there would come a point where he would talk, freely, even eagerly. And the point was near.

The nights seemed without end. The constant pain of his wounds vying with the agony of cramped joints, the terrible thirst that never left him, but worst of all the fear that the moment was near when he would tell everything. At the end of the last session, with Julian exhausted and sobbing, Kaw had shown what was awaiting him in the next session. It was a clever, diabolical, tactic. He had indicated the rope hanging from a pulley attached to the ceiling, and described impartially the process.

'The Strapado Julian, you must have heard of it. Invented by the Spanish during the Inquisition I believe.' He told him, lifting Julian's chin so as to force him to look up at it.

'So simple, and yet so effective. The arms attached behind the back, then to the rope end. The subject, yourself in this case, raised up until suspended with feet off the ground. The whole weight of the body taken on the shoulder joints that are twisted against their natural position. Pure agony apparently, but with no danger of fatal injury, except of course heart failure. And rest assured Julian, I will not permit that to happen in your case. I have never known it fail Julian, the pain is quite simply insupportable.'

He would try to hold out of course, but he knew he was at the end of his ability to resist, and once Kaw had broken him, he would tell him all he wanted. The image of Myitsu floated before him, her eyes on his, trusting, believing. He wished he had never met her, that she had never put her life in his hands, that there were no jewels that now seemed like a curse that had been put upon them both. Blood of the earth Jock had called them, beauty and death torn from the rock, imbued with their own power over the mind of man.

He thought of the huge safe in the office, and how when at the end of the day he or Jock would take the days produce and lock it away in the strong box. How strangely relieved he had always felt when the box was locked, and the heavy, six inch thick door, closed upon it. And then the final satisfying sound of the two locks engaging with the sound of hard steel upon steel. And he found himself wishing he could lock away his past like the rubies, lock it away and throw away the key, and he would have nothing to remember, no jewels, no mine, no past, no Myitsu.

No sleep came to him that night, but troubled waking dreams of torture and telling. And later the strange image of the big green safe, the door wide open, empty, waiting. Then before dawn they came for him.

In silence, watched by Kaw, they tied his hands behind his back, then attached them to the rope. They stood back and one of them took up the slack on the trailing end of the pulley. Julian felt his arms lifted just a little, not painfully, just slightly uncomfortably. Kaw moved close to him, so close he could smell him and see his liquid yellow iris eyes through the thick lenses, like those of a rabid dog.

He peered closely at Julian, his head on one side, the stepped back and nodded to the guards.

A white hot flash of pain exploded in Julian's back forcing a scream from him that emptied his lungs, then a deep sobbing gasp as he filled his lungs again to scream and scream again until suddenly dropped to the floor where he knelt half conscious on the concrete soiled by himself.

'Now Julian, perhaps it's time. You've been very brave, stubborn perhaps, but all for nothing. Because you're ready to talk to me now, aren't you Julian, you don't want any more do you, you've done your best, it's time.'

Julian opened his eyes and saw his two feet standing I front of him. Shinny black patent leather, polished to a shine, only the faintest smudge of dust visible upon them. Spit and polish suddenly came to him, the old expression, spit and polish. And clearing his throat he spat a bloody gobbet onto their immaculate surface.

There was a sharp intake of breath from above him, and the feet stepped away. A second passed and then another explosion of pain hit him as he was hoisted off his feet to hang freely in the air. He felt muscle and cartilage stretching and tearing as he tried to suck in air. The room was spinning around him, fading and coming back in waves. He struggled to speak, to tell them what they wanted, but could make no sound except a shrill inhuman scream.

Kaw was standing below him, asking something he could not hear, then one of the guards took hold of him by the waist and pulled down.

The room disappeared and left only the safe, Jock's safe, the door wide open, waiting, floating in front of him. He saw the jewels, blood red and shinning, slowly vanishing inside, and following them the mine with its wheel, Jock and Stella, the old Morris with Mr. Patel, the Sprouts, the Frobishers, the lodge, Boy, Myitsu...he saw them all pass through the six inch door that seemed able to swallow everything, and then at last himself, and he turned and watched as the door shut upon them all and heard the turning of the lock, and all was black and gone to nothing.

CHAPTER TWENTY-TWO

Mr. Kaw sat in his office staring at the brief typed order that had come in by motorbike messenger that morning. It simply instructed him to prepare the evacuation of the camp in five days time. He would receive further orders later as to the destination. A footnote added that as no lorries were available for the transport of either troops or material, only a limited number of the detainees should be retained and moved out. It was not specified what should happen to the others, but Kaw knew the unstated fate of those men.

It was frustrating he thought, after all the effort he had put in to make the Englishman reveal what he undoubtedly knew as to the fate of the Mogok rubies, he would be obliged to abandon the task for the moment. Notwithstanding his complete lack of response to either verbal or physical stimulation Kaw hoped still that he would in the end tell him what he wanted. He appeared to have retreated to a place where he neither heard nor saw the world around him. His eyes, and his expression were blank, and Kaw now feared that he would never be able to arouse him from this state to where he could resume his interrogation. He had seen the phenomena only once before where a captured Chinese agent had held out for weeks before mentally disappearing. He had died of hunger and thirst eventually, silent to the end.

Now he had just five days to resolve the problem, and as far as Julian was concerned Kaw was not sure it would be enough, but another idea had come to him. Mogok was only about a day's journey away, and that was surely where the gems were hidden, and there was the girl, Julian's house girl and Zeya's one time agent, if she wasn't still there someone might know where she was. And if he could find her he had no doubts she would tell him all she knew, one way or another.

He left the village later that day in a jeep with the two Koreans and headed southwest, towards the mountains and Mogok. He left instructions for Julian to be transferred to what they called the camp hospital, a simple shed just outside the village where the sick were taken to die, telling the Burmese in charge to make sure he was alive when he returned. The man, looking at Julian's ravaged and skeletal body on the stretcher, thought he would be lucky to last even one day.

It was a slow and frustrating journey to Mogok, many of the roads being clogged with retreating Japanese troops, destroyed and damaged vehicles, and columns of emaciated prisoners being marched away from the front. Twice they were obliged to drive off the road and take cover in the jungle as allied aircraft strafed the road, and it was the afternoon of the second day before they arrived in Mogok.

The town was quiet, many of the houses damaged and burnt two years earlier had not been repaired and the few shops along the main street had little to offer apart from sparse local produce. Most of the men had disappeared into the mountains, either fleeing the Japanese conscription gangs or joining the growing resistant movements.

The winding wheel of the mine still stood, and it was to there that they first drove. Stopping the jeep by what remained of the gate with Stella's burnt out car still rusting a few feet away, Kaw got out and studied the destruction. No attempt had been made to repair the mechanism and the surrounding buildings. A thick layer of dust covered everything and in odd corners vegetation was beginning to appear amongst the ruined buildings.

An examination of Jocks half destroyed house next to the mine revealed that it had been ransacked, probably by both locals and Japanese soldiers, but it did provide information in the form of an old man called Jib who had taken up residence there in the Mac-Greggor's old living room. The man, terrified by the unexpected appearance of the two Koreans and the sinister looking Kempeitai had been eager to answer any questions Kaw asked of him, elaborating whatever facts he knew with vividly imagined fiction...yes the young Englishman had many beautiful girls during his time at the mine, yes it was well known that the old Englishman had hidden a huge treasure of rubies somewhere before blowing up himself and the mine, which was now guarded by his ghost, visible to any who cared to look towards the mine once the sun had dipped below the mountains. He had just one remaining tooth in the front of his mouth, long and yellow, and while listening to him Kaw had the almost irresistible urge to take a pair of pliers to it and wrench it from his jabbering orifice.

Amongst the freely flowing fact and fiction Kaw gathered that there was still one of the young man's girls still living in his house, just outside the town. The old man hobbled outside and down the road a few yards to where he could point out the way to the lodge, and even the top of its roof, just visible over the trees. Kaw stared, and knew suddenly that he would find the answer he was looking for under that distant red-tiled roof, it was there he would find the key that Julian had hidden from him, a treasure of unimaginable wealth. He could sense its nearness, teasing, luring, and the girl would reveal it to him, of that there was absolutely no question, but he would take his time. It would be a pleasant task, he thought, and he hoped she would manage to hold out for the length of time that would give him satisfaction.

Myitsu was in the garden sitting in the shade of the tamarind tree watching Sandar sleeping in a hammock Jianyu had made for the child. One hand rested lightly on it as she rocked it gently, humming quietly to the sleeping child. Sandar was over two years old now, a pretty creature with black hair already long enough to touch her shoulders and huge serious eyes that seemed to view the world with studied suspicion. Her eyes were a source of amazement and admiration for not just her mother and Jianyu, who had come to look upon her as a daughter, but for the villagers who on rare occasions had the opportunity to see her. They were an astonishing blue-green, unknown in that country, and coupled with her very pale skin marked her already as a rather special child. The women of the town whispered amongst themselves, was it a curse or a gift? When she became a woman would she find herself unable to attract a man being too strange, too disturbing? Or would she be sought after as perhaps a great beauty, a different being, not like other women?

They remembered the child's father, the Englishman who also had the strange light eyes and blond hair, his ready smile and kindness, and wondered as to his fate. He had unsurprisingly abandoned the girl when the Japanese arrived, and such was the normal fate of girls who went with the colonial masters. But nobody knew what happened to him, and nobody expected he would ever return to Mogok, the girl, and the child he had made with her.

Myitsu herself had no such doubts. One day, maybe quite soon if one believed the rumours of fleeing Japanese troops on the road heading south towards Mandalay, he would return, she would have the double joy of being with him again and presenting his child to him, the child whose existence he knew nothing.

She tried to imagine his return, seeing him from the veranda walking up the path towards the house, and rushing to greet him in the garden, then leading him into his home with Sandar standing shyly at the top of the steps wondering who the strange man could be. His face, first astonished, then smiling as he reached down to take the child, lifting her, holding, accepting, and loving.

Then she looked up, suddenly aware of being observed. A man was standing in the gateway, staring at her and the child. A Burmese in Japanese uniform.

CHAPTER TWENTY-THREE

Pan-in camp and village resembled a disturbed ant heap. Lines of prisoners were snaking down the track leading south guarded by a score of soldiers spread thinly along the flanks. Several very badly damaged lorries interspersed the columns, belching black smoke as their bald tires spun in the thick mud. They carried the Japanese sick and wounded as well as any of the heavier weapons there was room for. Three bullock carts brought up the rear loaded with what meager food supplies were left, the camp having received nothing for over a month. The three translators without Julian were kept to the last together with a small rear guard and the two remaining senior officers.

Kaw had not been gone for more than a few hours before a dispatch rider arrived with new orders. An airborne drop of a large allied force had landed behind the Japanese lines and was expected to drive south in the next few days. The camp was to be evacuated immediately towards Kyaukme. Speed was deemed to be essential.

With Kaw gone the other officers had no time or inclination to bother with Julian or any of the other men in the hospital. They would simply be left to fend for themselves, most of them probably dying within a day or two. Without the doctor, or any help, there would be no one to bring them food or water, death was certain. None of the few remaining villagers would dare to approach the place for fear of infection or the return of the guards.

Julian was aware of change. He had been given water several times he knew, and he lay on a sort of bed made from straw filled rice sacks in a place he didn't know. Above him he could see a ceiling or roof made from bamboo and banana plant leaves from which water in drops or trickles ran in places. He could hear the sound of rain on the roof, the distant shouts of men, the clatter and rattle of an old diesel engined lorry, and from much nearer the faint moaning.

He tried to remember where he was, how he had arrived in this place, but nothing came to him, and the effort was too much for him to concentrate for long. He was weak, barely able to open his eyes and quite unable to move his limbs. He was aware of pain, most of all in his shoulders and back, but elsewhere too; his feet, his hands, his ribs. His heart beat steadily but faintly. What had happened to him? What hell had he woken to?

His mouth and tongue were dry, and the sounds of the dripping and trickling water a torture until at length he managed to turn his head to one side. Immediately he felt the splash of water on his cheek. For minutes he struggled to move his head the few inches to one side and finally when he thought he could do no more he was rewarded by a drop of cool sweet water falling directly into his open mouth. Drop followed drop with infuriating slowness, never seeming enough to slake his thirst, but eventually relief came, and with it sleep.

When he awoke, an unknown time later, it was to silence. It was either late afternoon or early morning, the roof shrouded in darkness and just the faintest gleam of sunlight creeping under the eaves. The rain had stopped, but his face, neck, and shoulders were still wet. He managed to turn his head to one side. All around him lay the bodies of other men, still, unmoving.

Clouds of flies hung over them and crawled over their inert bodies. No doctor or orderly moved amongst them, and he knew he was alone with the dead.

Then suddenly he saw a man lying near the door stir, his chest rising as he took a breath, his arm jerk. Julian tried to call out to him, but could only croak, and stare. And then the horror as the rat appeared from under the cloth covering him, gnawing, tugging at the flesh. And then Julian saw the others, here and there in the gloom, busy and feasting on the bodies around him. He turned away, closing tightly his eyes, his teeth clenched in a silent scream.

Chapter Twenty Four

In the kitchen of the lodge Kaw stood over the girl and the child. She was seated by the table, with the child still sleeping in her arms. Kaw's brown instrument case lay closed on the table in front of her. Myitsu's eyes were wide with fear, she could feel the danger coming from the man, the repressed violence, the unchecked cruelty. But it was not for herself she feared, but for the child. She had seen the way the man looked at her, coldly, without compassion, as if she was an object, inanimate and unfeeling.

She knew immediately what he had come for, even before he had spoken of the rubies.

'It was been brought to my attention that a large quantity of gems from the mine were stolen during the liberation. The man Drake, Julian Drake has confessed as much.'

Myitsu couldn't prevent herself looking sharply up at him as she heard the name.

'Yes, Mr. Drake, your employer. He brought the gems from the mine before its destruction by the mad old Englishman. Brought them here to hide them from the legitimate government of Burma and its Japanese allies.'

He began walking up and down behind Myitsu, his hands behind his back, the fingers twisting, anticipating. The girl and the child together excited him, the possibilities for pressure, manipulation, the complete power he felt over them. He would take his time, he thought, at least a day, even if she confessed at the start. It would be a memorable experience for them all.

'To be brief young lady, I need to find these gems. And I believe you are able to help me. So please, tell me what happened when Mr. Drake brought the gems here from the mine. What exactly happened?' And he reached over her shoulder, unlocked the case and left it open in front of her. Myitsu stared at the contents with dawning terror and realisation.

Jianyu had left at dawn for one of his trips into the jungle in search of plants for the medicines he sold. On the way back he decided to detour by the town, hoping for news of the Japanese retreat, his old friend Ae, the monk, would undoubtedly know if there was any new rumour or gossip in he town. But it was before he reached the temple, as he was passing by the ruins of the mine and Jocks old house that he heard a voice calling him.

Ye Min, who had taken up residence in Jock's house was standing in the doorway waving to him. Jianyu was reluctant to spend time talking to the old man who was an inveterate liar and gossip, with a limited grasp on reality, but he stopped by the gate and raised a hand in greeting.

The old man shouted something and pointed away, across the town. Jianyu shrugged his shoulders and was about to continue his way when he realised where the man was pointing...towards the lodge. He opened the gate and walked quickly up the path.

'They went there...looking...'

'Who did? Looking for what?'

'Oh I don't know, probably the British.'

'The British? They've been gone for two years...who where they.'

The old man shrugged his shoulders and sucked at his one tooth.

'A Burmese guy, and two Koreans, all dressed in Jap uniforms. They don't like the British. They'll kill them if they find them.'

Jianyu suddenly knew, they'd come at last, as he always thought they would.

'Were there any more? Any troops with them.'

Jib stared into the distance, trying to recall.

'No, just the three, in a jeep, about an hour ago.'

Without another word he turned quickly and set off in the direction of the lodge, not exactly running, but covering the ground in light rapid strides and at the same time loosening his old combat knife from its place in his belt behind his back.

Jib stared after him his head on one side, before returning to his home muttering about British, Japanese, and Koreans under his breath.

Jianyu saw the jeep parked at the side of the road by the end of the trail to the lodge. The two guards were standing by it, smoking and talking. Jianyu slowed down, hunching his shoulders and bending his knees, making him look older than his years. He shuffled closer, making as if to continue along the road, not looking at the men who stared at him as he approached. As he drew near one of them moved into the road and stood in front of him, his arms folded, smiling.

Jianyu shuffled as if to pass around him, but the man moved, blocking his way. Jianyu didn't look up, staring down at the ground and the Korean's boots just inches from his own feet. The man said something, laughing, and reached out to take Jianyu's bag. He opened it and peered inside.

The moment Jianyu wanted had arrived. The guard's two hands were holding the bag, making him an easy target. In one smooth motion Jianyu's hand appeared from behind his back holding the razor sharp combat knife and slicing horizontally above the man's shoulders almost severed his head and sending a fountain of blood jetting several feet into the air. The other man reacted quickly, wrenching his pistol from its holster at his belt, but before he could raise the muzzle Jianyu had reversed his grip upon the knife and plunged it to the hilt into the spot between the soldiers neck and collar bone, killing him instantly. The two men hit the ground within a second of each other, and lay at right angles to each other, their blood mingling on the dry yellow dust of the road. It had happened in total silence. Jianyu bent down to recover his bag and wiped clean his blade on the uniform of one of the men before replacing it in his belt and continuing his way toward the lodge. He worried about leaving the dead men and the jeep for any passer by to see, but all his instincts told him to hurry, he had a very bad feeling about what might be happening to Myitsu and the little one.

Kaw was disappointed. He had only to select one of the steel probes from his case and approach it towards the child sleeping in her arms for her to talk.

'I'll tell you. I'll tell you anything, just don't hurt her, please don't hurt her.' She was babbling, hugging the infant to her breast, sobbing in terror.

'Its here, not far, I hid it. I can take you there. You can have it. But please don't hurt her...there's no need. I can show you now, it's not far.'

Kaw played with the shinny steel probe, spinning it through his fingers, frowning. He should get the gems first common sense told him, time was running out, he had to get back to the camp as soon as possible. But when he looked down at the girl and the child at his feet, in total submission, weak, vulnerable, totally in his power, he could hardly bare to wait until she had shown him the treasure before satisfying his needs with them both. It would be new for him, a mother and child, already his fertile mind was busy with dark imaginings, the girls love for her child would be the essence of his work, he would play her with it. A game in which the life or death of the infant would depend upon her, and how could she watch if he were to work on the infant in front of her? The possibilities made him giddy with desire.

Jianyu approached the lodge from the jungle, having circled around to the back keeping well out of sight. He had no means of telling what sort of man was inside, what he was armed with, how competent he might be to defend himself against Jianyu's knife. He had thought briefly about taking a gun from one of the dead soldiers, but he was comfortable with his old knife that had served him well for many years.

Peering across the garden from where the trail to the pool began he could see the man through the kitchen window. He had his back to Jianyu and appeared to be of average height in the uniform of the Kempeitai. Jianyu slipped silently across the garden and stood listening, and very still by the door to the kitchen.

'An adorable little child I suppose.' Kaw was saying, coming close to Myitsu and bending down to look closely at the sleeping Sandar. Myitsu could smell him, a sweet sickly rancid odour flowing from his body, and she turned, twisting the baby away from him.

'As a doctor I never quite understood my colleagues who chose to specialise in paediatrics, children never held any attraction for me, they always seem so...how shall I put it...stupid? No, not that quite, but insensitive, not aware.'

He reached out with both his arms.

'Now please, be nice, let me hold the little one for a moment. Just for a moment.'

And his hands forced there way between Myitsu and Sandar, pulling her away from her mother. The child awoke, and on opening her eyes looked directly into the face of Kaw. Her scream of pure terror filled the room as Myitsu struggled to keep hold of her daughter.

'Put down the child please.' A voice from behind Kaw made him freeze. The voice was not loud, just loud enough to be heard over the crying of the baby. Slowly he turned his head and saw a small Chinese man standing a few feet away from him. The door was open behind him, and Kaw couldn't imagine how he had got there without making a sound.

The man was oldish, quite thin, and unarmed. Kaw relaxed a little, and allowed Myitsu to regain possession of her child. He turned slowly towards the man and at the same time reached down to the gun in his belt.

'Who are you...?' He started to say when out of nowhere the man kicked out at him, the foot made contact with his arm, snapping the radius and ulna above the wrist.

Kaw's scream joined that of the baby and he clutched his broken limb unable to comprehend what had happened so swiftly. Jianyu moved forward, his knife hand extended, bringing it to within an inch of Kaw's neck, at the same time kicking away the gun that had fallen to the ground.

'Myitsu, take the child away to your room, and please close the door.'

Myitsu obeyed instantly, hugging her sobbing daughter tightly other breast.

'Now I must ask you a few questions, but not here. Please make your way into the garden, we will take a little walk together.'

Kaw stared through tears of pain at the man, and realised he had no alternative but to do as he was told. The man was obviously skilled in hand-to-hand combat, something Kaw himself has always scorned as being below his status.

The two men left the lodge, crossing the lawn and entering the jungle where Jianyu had stood only moments earlier. Myitsu, watching from an upstairs window saw them disappear, and the sound of their movement through the undergrowth soon faded. It was not long before Jianyu returned to the lodge alone.

In the manner of young children Sandar had quickly forgotten her terror and was playing quietly in the upstairs room that was both Myitsu's bedroom and the child's playroom when Jianyu caller up to her from the bottom of the stairs. He was always reluctant to intrude upon her privacy, preferring to stay outside the house or at least downstairs. She stood at the top of the stairs and looked down at him, her face pale, her eyes anxious, a slight and fragile figure.

'There is nothing to fear daughter. The man will not trouble you again.'

Myitsu said nothing for a moment.

'I would have killed him too if he had touched her.'

Jianyu smiled.

'No man can withstand the fury of a mother when protecting her offspring. But such things are better left to us...women should be gentle of nature.'

'What did you do with him?'

'We talked a little. I had to know if he came here with others, or if he would be followed. His two companions are back at the cross roads feeding the carrion now.'

'And did he tell you anything old man?'

'He told me all I asked in the end, indeed more than I asked for, he was most cooperative.'

'I hope he died slowly. He would have killed Sandar I'm sure.'

Jianyu turned to go, anxious to remove the jeep and the dead soldiers from the cross roads before it drew unwelcome attention.

'Fear not Myitsu, no one will come looking for him, that is certain. But we must both be more careful in the days to come. There will be turbulence and lawlessness as the Japanese are defeated.'

On the way down the trail to the main road he thought about what the man had told him. The camp he had come from, the prisoner there, his onetime friend. He was probably dead now the man had confessed, but Jianyu would never tell that to Myitsu. Better Julian had disappeared than she knew his terrible fate at the hands of that man.

Before he reached the cross roads he saw the vultures, circling without the quiver of a wing above where the men lay in their own blood on the dry and dusty earth.

Chapter Twenty Five

Somewhere in the darkness there were voices, pitched low, talking quietly, as if afraid to be overheard. He wished he could open his eyes, but they seemed glued shut, and it was ages since he had been able to lift his hand to his face. It must be part of the dream he thought, the strange dream he was living. He could remember things he decided, he could remember when it rained and he had drunk a little water, he could remember a thunderstorm in the night with lightning that showed through his closed lids, he remembered the rats. But there was no more fear left in him. He had exhausted all his feelings and existed in a strange sensation-less limbo. Sometimes he wondered if he was already dead, if this was in fact the afterlife, a sort of hell. But mostly he was too weak to even think, existing somehow, not really living, but with something inside that refused to die, that clung to life even when that life was insupportable.

'Bloody hell...what a stink.' The voice was quite clear now, close.

'Jesus Sarge, come and look here.'

The young soldier in British Army combat fatigues stood in the door of the hospital shed, a Bren gun tucked under one arm, his other hand pressed to his face, covering his nose and mouth.

'Gawd! I'm not going to shift this lot, must be twenty or thirty of the poor bastards. Dead for days must be.'

Another soldier pushed through the door and stood next to him, tall, older, raw boned, a sergeants stripes on the sleeve of his sweat stained shirt.

'We'll have to burn it. Too risky to touch the beggars, all sorts of sicknesses around here. The japs must have just run off and left 'em to die. Get Frank with the flame thrower, it's too damp to burn on its own.'

'Shouldn't we check 'em out first...you know...just to make sure.'

The sergeant turned to go.

'Do as you think fit Dusty, just don't take too long about it, we're moving out in an hour.'

Dusty moved gingerly through the lines of bodies, looking down at the skeletal remains, fly covered and gnawed at. Although only just twenty he was, after two years of jungle warfare, quite used to the many indignities violent death visited upon human bodies. They were all natives he remarked, slave labour for the Japanese for work on the railway or the roads. Treated worse even than the military prisoners their life expectancy was measured in weeks rather than months. Just before the last row of bodies he suddenly stopped, peering down at a body by his feet.

'Jesus H Christ!' He exclaimed, then shouted...'Sarge! Come here, there's one of our guys here.'

A moment later the sergeant reappeared, stepping with long legs over the bodies to where Dusty was staring down at the body.

'Well he's a white man I guess. Been well worked over looks like. Does he have dog tags?'

Dusty reached down a little reluctantly to push aside the worn and rotten cloth that partially covered the body.

'Nothing.' He said quietly. Then suddenly pulling his hand away. 'Christ!'

'What is it? Fleas?'

'He's...I felt it...he's alive...felt his heart beat.'

'Piss off you fairy...he ain't alive, can see that from here.'

But Dusty was now on his knees, leaning over the body, his ear next to the mouth and a hand on the chest.

'Shhh! Wait...'

'Stop messing, we're pushed for time...'

'He's alive.' Said Dusty, straightening up, 'We need the medic.'

The sergeant was at the door of the shed in three long strides, and a shout that could have been heard a mile away brought a small bespectacled medic running.

Dusty was talking to the man, who seemed deeply unconscious.

'Hold on mate, you'll be alright now. Soon have you up and about again. What's yer name mate? What unit you from?'

Julian heard him as if in another world and understood. He was not dead, somewhere in the darkness and silence a voice had spoken, to him. Perhaps soon he would understand, perhaps they would tell him. The voice had asked his name and he wanted so much to tell, but there was nothing there, not only had his life disappeared, but so had the one thing that gave him his identity, his being. He couldn't remember even his name.

Part Three

CHAPTER TWENTY-SIX

Dorset, England 1946

The young woman stood alone on the terrace that faced south towards the sea that was just visible in the far blue distance between two low hills. The last rays of a pale winter sun now only covered the top story of the large and imposing building behind her. She was smoking a cigarette, her first of the day. A tall, blond, attractive woman in her early twenties, her short straight hair escaped here and there from under her nurses cap, and her very pale blue eyes were slightly lined with fatigue. Until this moment there had been too much to do to grab a quick smoke, and not even the time for a lunch break. There were four new patients arriving that afternoon from Southampton, where they had been disembarked from the hospital ship 'HMHS Talamba', newly arrived from Rangoon. There had been a new ward and bathroom to prepare for them, rooms on the top floor that had previously been an attic and storing all manner of items that had first to be moved into one of the outbuildings. Then a thorough cleaning had taken two nurses and two other volunteers the rest of the afternoon. Now the beds were being set up and made ready for the new arrivals.

Stanton Hall had once been home to a slightly aristocratic family whose money and claim to fame was founded on the manufacture and sale of patent 'Liver Pills', in the latter part of the nineteenth century. After the First World War the great depression had impoverished the family and the upkeep had become beyond their means, necessitating their removal to a semi-detached house in a suburb of Plymouth.   The hall, a square three story building with many chimneys that had not emitted smoke for a generation or two, was put up for sale but failed to find a buyer until the outbreak of war in nineteen thirty nine when the government acquired it. For two years it was the area HQ of the Civil Defence and Home Guard, before being converted to a convalescent unit for the armed forces, specialising in shock, trauma, and other mental conditions. It was Lydia's third year working there.

She finished her cigarette with one long inhalation, taking the smoke deep into her lungs, knowing it would probably be the last she would have before bed, before flicking the glowing end into to the weed infested flower bed at the base of the terrace.

'Once more into the breach...' She murmured to herself as she turned, pulling her cardigan tightly about her feeling suddenly cold, and made her way back through the French Doors into the lounge where a fire burnt, raising the temperature of the big room just a degree or two above the outside.

Several men were there, sitting in armchairs reading books or newspapers, or merely staring into space. A couple could be seen to be trembling violently, their eyes constantly searching the room, looking for something, aware, afraid. Lydia stopped by one of them, gently putting her hand on his shoulder.

'It's all right Frank, try to relax. You're safe now. Being looked after.'

The man looked sharply up at her, pushing her hand away brusquely.

'Shut up can't you, shut up! They'll hear.' He stared around him, his eyes wide, afraid.

'It's getting dark now.' He whispered, 'they'll be coming soon. They always come in the dark the bastards. Bayonet work...that's what the officer said, bayonet work...close up stuff...close so you can smell their breath when you do for 'em.'

Lydia knelt in front of him.

'They'll not come tonight Frank, the officer just told me. Don't worry, your safe now, they're not coming tonight I promise.'

The man stared at her, doubting.

'Not coming?' He said eventually. 'Sure?'

'For sure Frank, please don't worry yourself. Would you like me to take you back to your room.'

The man didn't reply but stood up and allowed Lydia to lead him from the room. Major Peters, a middle aged man in the uniform of a guards officer wearing several rows of medals and seated by the door watched them pass by, murmuring to himself...

'Hopeless. Mad as a hatter.' Before removing a large white handkerchief from his pocket, burying his face into it, and bursting into tears.

After seeing Frank safely installed in his room, drawing the curtains, and settling him a chair with a few copies of 'Picture Post' to distract him, Lydia climbed the stairs to the new ward in the attic. The volunteers had left and Janet, another nurse was finishing making the beds.

'It's bloody cold up here.' She remarked, standing up to survey her work. 'We'll have to do something about that. These poor men are coming from the tropics, they'll feel it more than us.'

'It's cold outside now, be a frost tonight I shouldn't wonder.' replied Lydia, going over to one of the mansard windows and checking it was firmly closed.

'These windows are hopeless, there's gaps everywhere, you can feel the draft. There's a couple of electric radiators in the office, I'll bring them up, it's more important to keep the patients warm than the staff.'

However picturesque the hall was to look at, and even agreeable to live in during the summer, in the winter it was a cold and cheerless place. With no money available for the smallest luxury the half dozen nurses and four administrative staff waged a constant battle to keep the patients warm and distracted. They ranged from the severely traumatised, who could barely function, needing help in every aspect of their lives, to the men who might seem normal for most of the time but who, like Major Peters, would suddenly loose control, plunged into some personal despair, fear, or even shame.

Three doctors visited the home, each patient being assigned to one, and usually seen at least once a week. Their physical conditions were supposed to have been stabilised, although some still suffered from recurring malarial fevers, and sometimes old wounds needed attention.

Lydia found the physical nursing the most satisfying, at least there was the likelihood of a cure, one could see improvements, even recovery from these wounds, but there seemed little hope for the mental conditions. The doctors themselves admitted they were mostly unable to treat what the men suffered from, and understood little of the workings of the mind. Usually it seemed all they could to was to listen sympathetically, and prescribe a sedative. During the whole time Lydia had worked there only a handful of patients had been discharged into the community, the rest staying on, or in some of the more severe cases sent to secure hospitals or asylums.

The sounds of vehicles arriving sent the women running down the three flights of stairs to the front door. Two army ambulances had pulled up outside and a MO was already climbing the steps, clipboard in hand.

'Four more for you today ladies.' He announced cheerily thrusting his clipboard into Lydia's hands when she opened the door. 'Just sign opposite the names as usual, show you've accepted them.'

Lydia took the board, unclipped her pen from her uniform pocket, and scanned the short list. Dawson, J., Philips, P., Nicholson, S., she read, ticking each name. Below Nicholson, S. was simply inscribed XX.

'What or who is XX?' She asked the MO, who was shuffling his feet and fidgeting, obviously anxious to be gone and on his way back to Southampton.

'XX... That means we have no name for the poor blighter. Call him what you like, he's an amnesiac, total, doesn't know who he is. Picked up in Burma apparently, it's all in here.' And he handed Lydia a few sheets of hand written notes.

'So what have you been calling him?' She asked, looking over to where she could see a number of men being helped out of the ambulances.

'Called him X, but it doesn't matter, he doesn't respond to that or anything else you say. Been through the mill I'd guess, severe shock, probably concussed, maybe brain damaged...and a pile of other stuff. Lots for you to work on there.'

Lydia ticked the XX, signed at the bottom, and handed the clipboard back.

Two other nurses appeared and the four of them helped the new arrivals up the steps and inside. From outside they heard the slamming of doors and the rattle of old diesel engines as the ambulances drove off. The new patients stood silent, gazing around them, while the women took their coats. Two of them had small canvas bags containing what possessions they had.

'What's your name dear?' The first question always, 'How are you feeling?'

Three of them responded, the fourth merely stared around curiously. Lydia noted his thinness, the clothes that seemed several sizes too large for the skeletal frame they dressed, the head, scull-like, shaved of hair and with dark deep set eyes.

'Let's take these men to their room girls, leave their bags here, we'll get them later.' Said Lydia, and she took the unnamed man gently by the arm and helped him up the stairs to the attic. Under the material of his sleeve she could feel his arm, stick-like and impossibly thin, and as always with a new patient she wondered what had happened, what horrors he had witnessed and suffered to bring him here. As they climbed the stairs she could hear his breathing, laboured, rasping, but it was only later, when she undressed him in the new bathroom next to the ward, that she saw the full extent of his physical injuries. Not an inch of his emaciated body did not bare the marks and scars of years of ill-treatment, the wheals of whipping on his back and buttocks, the deep scars of badly healed ulcers on his legs and small round scars on his chest and arms that looked like burns, and feet that were deformed and missing toes. She had seen much since her arrival at the hall two years ago, but never such an example of abuse inflicted on a human being. Without her realising it tears flooded her eyes as she knelt to remove his shoes and socks, and she stiffed a sob, looking down so he could not see her appalled expression.

Dr. Bright came the next day to meet and assess the new arrivals. He was old for a still-practicing doctor, having come out of retirement at the beginning of the war. Tall, slim and distinguished looking, he held himself with a posture that negated his seventy-eight years. He moved with an easy grace, talking quietly and gently, but exuded air of complete confidence. He was the sort of doctor that always made the patient feel better after his visit, even if he could only listen and say a few words. From him the words...'You're doing very well, keep it up,' invariably pronounced at the end of each consultation, seemed to take on a magical quality, the recipient leaving convinced that if he was not actually cured, he was well on the way.

Lydia, as senior nurse, was present at his consultations, and would scribble her own notes afterwards, hoping they might help in the treatment of the patient.

The patient XX was the last to see Dr Bright. Lydia had briefly told him the limited information there was in his notes; that he had been found by an advancing British patrol somewhere in North or Central Burma, severely undernourished with signs of torture, and apparently with a total loss of memory. He was the only survivor found in the remains of a POW camp, found lying comatose, barely alive, and surrounded by the corpses of scores of other prisoners.

The doctor began with a thorough physical examination, saying little except the occasional murmur of encouragement.

'Right. Help him get dressed please nurse. We'll have a little chat when he's ready.' He said on completion of the examination.

While Lydia was doing this the doctor sat at his desk, staring down at his note pad but writing nothing.

Once he was dressed and seated Dr. Bright leaned back in his chair and turned toward Lydia, who had taken up her usual position standing by the door.

'This won't do nurse.' He said quietly, 'Not at all.'

'Doctor?'

'Nurse, the man must have a name. It is a first step. He is not a cypher or a crossword clue, he is a human being and must be treated as one.'

'Of course Doctor, it's just we didn't know quite how to proceed...'

'Please nurse, I was not meaning my remark as a criticism, merely an observation, I am fully aware of the care you give to these men.'

He lent forward over the desk, looking intently at the man opposite.

'My name is Bright, Philip Bright and I am your doctor. I know you are afraid and confused, chiefly but not entirely because you cannot remember anything of your past life. With your help over the next few months, I will endeavour to help you recall things. Perhaps not all of your past, but enough so we can at least find out who you are, where you lived, and if you have family who are maybe looking for you.'

He stood up and moved around the desk, sitting down on the edge next to his patient. 'And we will start by finding your name, at least your Christian name to begin. Would this be agreeable to you?'

After a short pause the man nodded, very slightly. The Doctor drew a sheet of paper across the desk and placed it in front of the man, then taking his own pen from his pocket he offered it to him. Again there was a moment of hesitation, as if he was afraid to commit himself before he accepted it.

'Now, I will tell you a number of names, and I would like you to write them down just as quickly as you can on the paper. Do you understand? Good. Then I'll begin.'

The man rested his hand on the paper, prepared to write, and the doctor began to say names.

'   J   o   h   n   .   .   . George...Richard...Mark...Peter...Philip...' The list went on, the doctor watching him closely and giving out names as fast as the man could write them down, until after what seemed like at least fifty names he stopped abruptly.

He lent over the man, looking closely at his face, and placed a hand on his shoulder.

'Good, very good, that wasn't too hard was it. Now we know, your Christian name is Julian, and I wonder if you can remember that now. Julian, do you remember your name is Julian?'

Slowly the man raised his head. Looking straight up at the doctor, his eyes now wide with wonder.

'I...I...don't know...' And he brought both his hands up to his face, shaking his head from side to side.

'I can't tell...there's nothing there...nothing. I have no idea what my name is.'

'But now I'm telling you, your name is Julian. And you have made the first step towards recovering your past. That will be all for today Julian, I'll see you again in a couple of days.'

When he had left the room Lydia turned to the doctor.

'I don't understand...how can you tell, are you sure?'

The doctor was already putting his notes together and arranging his stethoscope in his bag.

'Have you any idea how many times the average person writes his or her name in their lifetime? No?

Well neither do I, but I can guess its quite a lot. We start writing it as soon as we can put pen to paper, and it goes on, establishing our own unique signature by the time we are twenty or so. Now, if you'd observed Julian writing all those names, you'd have quickly seen the difference between writing a random name and writing his own name. The conscious might have forgotten, but the subconscious remembered, when he wrote Julian it took over, directing his hand smoothly and quickly through the old routine without thinking. Quite different to when he wrote one of the other names where he thought about the spelling and the writing as he was doing it. Look nurse, it's really quite obvious.'

And he handed the paper to her. Lydia could straight away see the difference in the last name on the list, Julian...it was plainly the first half of a signature rather than just a single word.

Outside the room Julian had stopped, the door closed softly behind him, and in the silence of the dimly lit corridor where portraits of Victorian businessmen and their wives frozen in formal poses gathered dust, he whispered his name to the shadows. Julian. It meant nothing. No memories stirred, no voices spoke, only the faint and steady tick tock of the ancient Grandfather clock in the entrance hall at the end of the corridor could be heard.

Julian. Could it be? Could a name mean so much and yet nothing? In a way he felt more lost, more lonely than before, as if something, a part of him had gone forever. A paper man of two dimensions, a man without a history, a past, a new born in the body of an older man.

Everyday since he regained full consciousness in the hospital at Mandalay more and questions filled his mind, until he could think of nothing else. How old was he? What was his job? Was he married? Children maybe? Where did he live? It seemed to be taken for granted he was English since that was what he spoke, but what was he doing in Burma? They seemed to think he was a soldier at the hospital, but he knew nothing of soldiering. The questions revolved in his mind incessantly, blocking out the world around him, the hospital in Mandalay, the voyage to England, the house where he now lived. At night, lying in his bed, trying to reach back, groping for he knew not what, he thought he must go mad, nearly screaming in rage and frustration. It was there...somewhere, just the other side of a wall, and he felt that somehow he himself had built that wall, but could not tell why, or how it might be breached.

CHAPTER TWENTY-SEVEN

In the days and weeks that followed Julian's arrival Lydia grew more and more fascinated with not just his case, but the man himself, the reason being chiefly that he showed definite signs of improvement. Not in his recall, but in his opening to the world around him. Physically too he improved, putting on weight steadily, his face becoming less gaunt, gaining muscle and fat on his frame. After two months, when his memory recall showed no improvement, Dr. Bright told Lydia that for the moment he would cease his efforts to bring back his memory.

They were both sitting in the doctor's examination room after the last patient had left. Lydia had noticed the doctor looked tired recently, a little stooped, his movements not quite so assured, and she wondered if all was well with him.

'It's the deepest and most intransigent amnesia I've ever come across.' He told her, 'It's going to need a new approach. For the moment I want to concentrate on his physical and social development. You say he's beginning to mix with the other patients, well that's good, and the more mental and physical activity we can get him doing the better.'

'Will he ever recover his memory do you think Doctor?'

The old man shrugged his shoulders.

'According to all the books on the subject permanent loss only occurs after a traumatic brain injury, something quite radical. He's obviously had a few bad knocks to the head, but nothing indicates physical brain damage. Now that leaves dissociative amnesia, or repressed memory. It's a common event for the brain to forget things it doesn't want to remember, happens to us all from childhood onwards. But these forgotten memories are still accessible, we can bring them back, and sometimes they come back naturally. A piece of music, a scent, a taste, anything can trigger a sudden and total recall, just as if a door has opened, they simply pour out.'

'But you don't think Julian's like that?'

'I'm doubtful he is, but what exactly has gone wrong inside his mind, if indeed anything is wrong, I cannot tell yet.'

'How do you mean if anything is wrong, surely something is wrong?'

There was a long pause before the doctor looked up from his notes directly at Lydia sitting opposite him.

'I think he's protecting himself. You have seen the state of his body. All the signs are that he has endured severe torture and mistreatment over an extended period. One must ask oneself why, to what end. In my experience with these unfortunate men and women who have undergone similar treatment it is invariably because they had information that their tormentors wished to extract. There are two hypotheses, the first that he, after holding out for many months or years, finally gave them what they wanted, the information, and the loss of memory is connected with the shame felt by him. The desire to block out an unacceptable fact, his failure. The second, that during the torture he willed himself to forget, forget everything, as a way of keeping his secret. This is not as unlikely as it might at first sound. Under extreme conditions, extreme pain and fear, the mind works...well...in a similar way to which the body works when flooded with adrenalin. It does things that would normally be impossible.'

'So you think it could be permanent?'

'It could Nurse, it could. But I do feel there must be a key somewhere, a key to open the door to his past.'

He stood up, slowly, a little stiffly.

'We must persist Nurse, look to his well being, bring him back to as near to physical normality as we can, and who knows what might happen.'

Every other weekend when Lydia was not on duty, she would visit her parents in the nearby town of Wareham. It was they who looked after Charlie, her six-year-old son. The boy's father, John, had been a pilot in the RAF, posted missing presumed dead in Malaya in 1941. Lydia and John had grown up together. Childhood sweethearts they had married in 1939 just after the outbreak of war. Lydia had not actually contemplated marriage at that time, being only just twenty years old, but John had pressed her to commit before he was sent to Singapore. A quiet ceremony in Dorchester registry office with just their parents and two officers from John's squadron was followed by a long weekend honeymoon in blacked out London. The day after the honeymoon John returned to his unit and they left Southampton on the troop carrier HMS Nimrod for the Far East. Lydia never saw him again, but discovered a month later she was expecting his child.

Her feelings now about the relationship were complex. She felt in some ways she had never been married, and found it difficult to grieve over something she never really known. As much as she had loved John she wondered now if it was more than a childhood crush, and wondered if they would they have lasted together. She felt illogically that she had been cheated, that perhaps the marriage was not a real marriage. Had she really loved him was a question that recurred to her time and time again. And with that came the feeling of guilt. Surely he had deserved better than her, a total love and commitment from some woman, not the half-hearted infatuation of an immature girl.

When the telegram arrived from the war office, the dreaded brown envelope with a window exposing her name and address, delivered by a perspiring youth on a heavy black bicycle, she refused to believe he could be dead. She clung to the words 'missing...believed'. So it was not sure, he could still be alive, perhaps a prisoner of the Japanese, or hiding in the jungle with a guerrilla group. It was a seemingly unending torture, the hope, the fear, the uncertainty. When six months after his disappearance she received a letter from his wing commander, explaining how his plane had been shot down during an attack on a Japanese convoy, and had been seen to dive into the sea and explode, the hope still could not die, but lingered on, buried in the subconscious, but ever present.

It was partly John's loss that made her join the rehabilitation unit, a euphemistic term for the place where broken men whose experiences in the war had effected their mental state to a degree that made them unable to resume civilian life were brought. She felt that in that place she might be able to connect somehow with her missing husband, to assuage the guilt she still illogically felt.

One of her earliest patients, Ralph, a fighter pilot who suffered horrific burns that left him with not really a face but grotesque mask that he felt unable to reveal in public, she became particularly close to. But after a couple of months he was transferred to another hospital where he later committed suicide after an unsuccessful attempt at plastic surgery.

And now there was Julian, a casualty from the same part of the world, a man without a past, a man who needed to find himself. She wanted desperately to help him, and maybe more.

After an operation on his feet he was able to walk more comfortably, and Lydia asked the doctor if she might take him outside the grounds for longer trips. Dr. Bright, who's health seemed poorer every time he visited, readily agreed, and twice a week, weather permitting, she would lead him down the lane towards East Lulworth, through Spring Wood to where the land fell away in a smooth green and yellow patchwork of fields to the edge of the sea.

They spoke little on these excursions, Lydia not wanting to question him about a past he could not recall, and Julian content to feel the warm summer wind on his face, the soft grass under his feet, and the presence of a kind and gentle being at his side. It was without doubt a healing process, the peace of the English countryside better than any sedative or salve. He wondered often if this was or had been his home. Was it familiarity he felt when he walked down the lane under the ancient beech and oak trees. Had he grown up with the scent of the distant sea, hearing the sad cries of the gulls on the wind? He liked to think so, and he liked the woman at his side.

Then one October day when the first gale of the Autumn buffeted the house, blowing the smoke back down the chimneys and stripping the last leaves from the trees, Dr Bright arrived for his consultations and asked Lydia if he could have a word with her before they began. He looked at her across the desk in his office, his face pale and drawn, and she realised suddenly he was looking his age, or even more.

'I wanted a word before we start Lydia, because this will be my last visit here.'

Lydia stared at him, unable to believe him, for as long as she had worked there he had seemed an integral part of the home, it seemed impossible it could continue to exist without him. And never before had he addressed her by her Christian name.

'But...why?'

He smiled wanly.

'I'm afraid the years have caught up with me. I can't manage it anymore. It's time to let a younger man take over.'

Lydia looked at him closely, sensing there was more to it.

'Are you alright doctor? Is it simply your age? I can't believe it, you were always so dynamic...'

He waited a few moments before replying.

'I've never believed in hiding this sort of thing, so yes, I am ill. I have cancer. Lung cancer, but it's spread. I might be around in three months if I'm lucky, but I'm not counting on it.'

Deeply shocked Lydia reached across the desk to cover his hand with her own.

'No...oh Doctor... Please no.'

He took her offered hand, and squeezed it gently.

"Fraid so, I've known for a while now. But I can't go on working any more. Just too much.'

'But the patients, who'll look after your patients?'

'Oh I'm not irreplaceable you know, lots of good men out there. The powers that be are sending down my replacement from London, a younger chap, be good for the place.'

'We'll miss you...the staff and the patients. You've done so much here, helped so many people.'

'As have you Lydia, and the others too. Now my replacement, Dr. Draycot, will have my notes on the men, and I hope you can help him settle in and take over where I've left off. It'll be disturbing for them to start off with, so we must try to make it as smooth as possible.'

The following weekend, before the arrival of the new doctor, Lydia took Julian with her to her parents home. She had talked about her life and family to him often, and he seemed interested in what went on in the world outside the home. He had reached the stage where he could pass for a normal person unless questioned too closely, when he would clam up, and show signs of distress. She had primed her parents before hand about his situation and warned them against too much curiosity, something her mother in particular seemed to find difficult to curb, particularly if she brought home a man friend.

The visit went well, much better than she had hoped, very largely due to her son Charlie. The six year old took an immediate liking to Julian, taking him by the hand as soon as arrived to show him his toys, chattering away as if he had known him all his life.

'What's your name.' He inquired, a short while after he had persuaded Julian to join him playing marbles on the lounge floor.

'His name is Julian, Charlie.' Lydia said, smiling and watching them from the doorway.

The child thought a while, digesting the information.

'That's a funny name.' He said after a while, 'Youlian. Youlian.'

Julian stiffened suddenly, his hand stilled in mid action of rolling a marble towards Charlie.

Something seemed to click in his mind. The sound of his name, pronounced that way, somebody else had called him that way. He struggled to remember, Youlian, Youlian, what did it mean? It was like a voice, lost in a thick impenetrable mist. He kept on repeating it to himself, over and over again. Why, and who, and when. Questions without answers. But he could feel it, a voice, a voice with a feeling of warmth, love, and he reached out towards it, groping in the blackness, trying to capture it. But then it slid away, leaving nothing but a scent of something, jasmine, scandal wood, coconut oil, something strange, exotic, until that too faded and was gone.

Lydia, acutely attuned to his feelings and moods was immediately aware something had happened. She stepped forward to him, gently placing a hand on his shoulder, feeling the muscles hard under her fingers. He was away somewhere, his eyes unfocused, staring into another place, another time, searching.

'Julian, are you alright? What's the matter darling?' The last word, uttered without thought or volition shocked her. Why had she called him that?

Gradually she felt him relax, he flipped the marble over to Charlie, who appeared not to have noticed anything, and looked up at Lydia. She had never seen him weep before, but she saw now his eyes were filled with tears, then a smile came over his face, the first real smile he had shown her.

'It's fine Lydia, really. Don't worry...the way he said my name...it just seemed so right, so good. I don't know why but it's made me feel so...I don't know...so happy?'

The lunch with her parents was a relaxed and informal meal. Her father, the local vicar, sensitive and sympathetic, the perfect foil to his wife's robust humour that even Julian seems to appreciate. Lydia, watching him closely during the meal, found him apparently more happy and communicative than he had ever been before, and she resolved to bring him there more often. It would be good for both Julian and her son she told herself.

After lunch they walked around the small village, visiting her father's church and meeting several of his parishioners. Charlie kept tight hold of Julian's hand the whole time, giving him a running commentary on everything and everyone they passed.

Not for the first time Lydia felt how much the boy missed a father. His grandfather naturally doted on him, but somehow didn't fill the role of the missing parent. Seeing the two of them talking and laughing so naturally together she felt the ache in her heart that she had thought gone away, she realised how much she still missed John. The huge hole it had torn in her life when he died was still there, unfilled, dark, and empty. And the need of her son so suddenly and openly displayed filled her eyes with unwanted tears.

Chapter Twenty Eight

Dr. Bright's replacement arrived promptly at nine o clock the following Monday. A small youngish man with a pinched sallow face, thin black moustache and large horn rimmed glasses. He carried not the usual doctors bag but a new looking brief-case, and seemed to be in a great hurry.

Lydia and some of the other staff met him in the hall and introduced themselves, receiving a brief nod accompanied by a weak damp handshake.

'Perhaps you could give me a quick tour of the place?' He asked Lydia once the introductions were finished. 'Just a quick one, give me an idea of what we've got here. Up at the ministry they don't seem to know much about this place, I've to send them a report as soon as I've evaluated it.'

Lydia didn't like the idea of a report, and what was he going to evaluate she wondered.

After the tour of the house she showed him into the consultation room. He entered and stood looking critically around him.

'Small, dark, pokey.' He murmured to himself, but loud enough for Lydia to hear.

'I'll see the patients now nurse, can you send the first one in. Sooner I start sooner finished eh?'

Lydia held out the folder of Dr Bright's notes towards him.

'The patient's notes doctor, you'll be needing them I expect.'

He took them from her after a moments hesitation and immediately placed them on the side of the desk.

'Ah, yes. Dr. Bright wasn't it. Well, I won't be needing them for the moment, I like to make up my own mind about things.'

Lydia stared at him, shocked and amazed. In her experience a patients notes were sacrosanct, an essential guide to diagnosis and treatment, and this was especially true for the men under her care.

'Something wrong nurse?' He asked, seeing her make no movement.

Lydia turned away without comment and went in search of the first patient.

That first session with the new doctor stayed with Lydia for long afterwards. The first patient was Frank, whose extreme nervousness stemmed from his experiences in the long retreat through the jungles of North Burma. His company had been decimated, day and night, always surrounded and always just managing to escape. The Japanese would call out to them at night, just a few paces away, they would taunt the weary soldiers, telling them what they were doing to their comrades they had taken prisoner, what they would do to them when it was their turn. Every night it was ferocious hand-to-hand fighting, and when the Japanese finally broke off the pursuit there were only a dozen men left, all wounded. Frank had seemed normal when they finally reached safety in India, but later became tormented by nightmares to such an extent he was afraid to sleep, the insomnia in turn provoking a total mental breakdown.

Dr. Draycot made no effort to put Frank at ease when Lydia led him into the room, not even asking him to sit down. Instead he began questioning him about his fears, what exactly had happened to him, why was he hallucinating. Frank didn't answer, remaining staring into space, mumbling incoherently to himself.

Eventually the doctor sat back in his chair and looked from the man to Lydia.

'He always like this?'

'Not always, but often, if you just look at Dr Bright's notes you'll...'

'Thank you nurse, when I need your advice I'll ask for it.' He interrupted testily.

'But he has shown signs of improvement.' Said Lydia, determined not to be browbeaten.

'Really.' he replied skeptically, 'Anyway, that's enough, take him away and bring in the next case.'

The rest of the consultations followed the same pattern, no attempt to understand or help the men, just a sort of probing curiosity, almost goading in some cases, and Lydia wondered just why such a man had been sent. Major Peters simply burst into tears as soon as the doctor addressed him, unable to answer a single question.

Julian was the last patient, and Lydia introduced him as suffering total amnesia. Dr looked up at her skeptically.

'Really? That's very unusual you know. We'll have to see about that.'

He began by questioning Julian about why he had been in Burma, was he in the army, how old was he, was he married. All questions that Julian had no answer to, and inevitable becoming more and more distressed as the interrogation continued, in the end just shutting his eyes tightly, saying nothing, but with his lips making silent words.

'Take him away.' The doctor said eventually, loosing patience, 'I think I've got the picture.'

The negative effect of the doctor's visit was felt throughout the home. All of the patients suffered a setback in their recovery, and the staff were openly expressing their discontent with the doctors methods. As he was leaving he announced that his next visit would be in two weeks, when, he said ominously, he would have the results of his report to the ministry.

Chapter Twenty Nine

'Shut down!' Lydia almost screamed the words, 'You can't, you can't!'

It was two weeks later on his second visit Dr Draycot brought the news. He had assembled the staff on his arrival in his room in order to make the announcement.

'What about the patients?' Somebody else asked. 'Where will they go? And us...what about us?' There was a general muttering of protest.

'The patients will be transferred to other establishments according to their needs. Some who are well enough will be released into the community.' He replied, 'I have here a list you might want to display somewhere.'

'Released? Into the community? May we know who you consider fit for release?' Lydia was hardly able to suppress her anger, her voice tight, hard.

'Well, there are just two in fact, Major Peters ...'

'What? You can't! He's totally unfit to survive outside...' She said.

'Nonsense nurse, he'll learn how to control himself quicker out there than in here I can assure you.'

'Who's the other.' Somebody else asked.

He made a show of consulting his notes on the desk in front of him though it was obvious he knew who it was.

'The other is Mr. Julian, or whatever his name is, he has absolutely no place here or any other public funded establishment. We don't even know if he was in the services, and there's no reason the taxpayer should foot the bill for keeping him unemployed and idle. To be honest he could be pretending, wouldn't be the first to claim amnesia to get out of something. '

Lydia couldn't breath she was so angry, couldn't formulate words coherent enough to express her disgust.

'It's wrong..' She managed to gasp, 'It's all wrong. He can't, he won't manage and he was making such progress.'

'Why?' Shouted one of the volunteers from the back of the room. 'Why shut us down?'

The doctor moved his papers around on the desk, looking up at the staff, his eyebrows raised as if about to explain something to a child.

'It's simply money. There ain't any. I don't know if you lot read the papers, but you must know the country's broke. That war has ruined us, we're almost bankrupt in fact. There's no money for places like this, it's a luxury we can't afford. The others who can't be released will be sent to existing establishments where they can be looked after in safety and security for as long as necessary.'

'You mean asylums don't you.' Said Lydia, her voice hushed in horror, 'Lunatic asylums.'

'They'll be safe there, and the costs of looking after them will be a fraction of what it costs here. It's just simple economics you must understand.'

It was all quite clear to the staff now. Dr Draycot had been appointed simply to close Stanton Hall down. He had never been interested in the treatment of the patients, only finding an excuse to get rid of them, and close down the place.

'And what about us, I suppose we will be out of a job?' Asked someone.

The Doctor reached into his briefcase and withdrew a bunch of brown envelopes, fanning them out on the desk in front of him.

'These are your letters of dismissal, you will be paid for two weeks after the departure of the last patient. I regret it is not government policy to provide references.'

He stood up, fastened his brief case once more, and left the room, looking down so as not to meet the eyes that watched him in shock and disbelief.

For several days after the news Lydia could not sleep. The idea of the men under her care being imprisoned in an asylum was shocking enough, but worse was the idea that Major Peters and Julian would be cast adrift and be obliged to fend for themselves somehow.

She had broken the news to both of them herself. The major had, as anticipated broke down completely, rocking backwards and forwards in his chair, crying like a child, until in desperation she had been obliged to administer a mild sedative to calm him.

Julian had barely acknowledged the news, seeming to be unable or unwilling to understand what it entailed. After spending a whole day on the telephone Lydia had managed to find them a place in a halfway house in London where they could stay for a maximum of one week, after which they would have to find a place of their own.

The first group of patients, destined for the Long Grove Asylum near London left just ten days after the visit, and later that same day Major Guy Peters, DSC, MC, DCM was found dead, hanging from a beam in the old stable block.

The taxi provided by the home to take Julian to the station in Dorchester was to arrive at eleven thirty,

and at ten o clock Lydia was standing in his room looking down at him as he sat quietly on his bed, lost in
thought.

'Will you please keep in touch dear? Write care
of my parents, I've put the address in your case.'

He looked up at her, a rueful smile on his face.

'And remember, I've put some money in your
sponge bag, don't loose it. It should be enough for a
couple of weeks rent, even in London.'

He reached out to take her hand.

'You've been good to me, I'll never forget that at
least.'

'Oh Julian, I'm so sorry, you're not ready I know.'

'Don't worry yourself, I'll manage, maybe I'll remember London. But I've been happy here, because of
you, and I'm going to miss you terribly.'

Lydia sat down on the bed next to him, her hand
still clasped tightly in his.

'Julian, I want you to think about something. It's
a bit strange. But please listen and think about what I
want to say.'

He turned to face her, seeing the woman he had
come to know and even perhaps love. The untidy
blonde hair, the grey gentle eyes with just a few faint
lines around, the mouth, so expressive of her moods.

'There might be one solution, if you want that is.'

She paused a moment, finding it difficult to arrange her words.

'I know it's not a leap year, but... if we got married you could stay with me, in my flat in the village. I'd
have to find another job somewhere but I'm sure we
would manage.'

They stared at each other, the silence of the
house around them, a moment frozen in time for them
both.

'Lydia...I can't, just because you're sorry for me, it wouldn't be fair. You deserve more than a token marriage.'

She took his other hand and pulled them both to her, pressing them against her body.

'I don't feel sorry for you...it's not that. It's ...well...I think I love you.'

He studied her before answering, feeling her heart beat against his hands, fast, strong.

'Well, I think I've loved you for a long while now, so if you're sure, sure that you want a half man for a husband, I'll marry you.'

'You're not a half man.' She had just time to say before his mouth covered hers as he took her gently into his arms. And for Julian the fleeting thought that he might already be married lasted only for a fraction of a second before he forgot everything except the warm soft woman who wanted and accepted him.

CHAPTER THIRTY

Mogok, Burma 1946

Zeya approached the house through the jungle on the hillside until he reached a spot where both the house and garden could be seen clearly, the same place as where Myitsu had seen the taking of Boy years previously. A small child, just a toddler was playing alone in the garden watched over by a figure, almost hidden in the deep shadows, seated on the veranda. The garden had changed since he had last observed it, the flower beds overgrown, the grass long and unkept, the once white walls that surrounded it now stained and covered by vigorous climbing vegetation.

The house itself seemed unchanged from afar, but looking closely he could see several broken windows on both floors, and he wondered who had done it, the Japanese or one of the several guerrilla factions operating in the area.

For with the defeat of the Japanese and the return of the British peace itself had not returned. With independence, fighting between the various ethnic and political groups had broken out throughout the country. True it was not the pitched battles fought by mechanised armies, rather a war of ambush, fought by part time guerrillas, with people's courts, secret executions, and all the obscene bitterness of a civil war.

The communists, excluded from government went underground to continue their struggle for power, the Chinese Komitung in the north refused to accept the dominance of the southern Burmese, the Karen fought for an independent nation, promised by the

British in return for fighting against the Japanese. General lawlessness prevailed in the country areas fuelled by ethnic divisions.

That the woman, for she was now a woman and no longer a girl, had survived and remained in the house, had surprised Zeya greatly. Mogok itself had suffered in the fighting, both during the Japanese invasion and in their subsequent defeat. The mine was destroyed, as were many of the buildings, and the population was reduced to less than half. Without the mine, there were only the small workings on the hillsides to support the town, and even when gems were found, such were the risks of transporting them to Mandalay that their value was vastly reduced from its pre-war figure.

She was known by everyone in the town he found on his return, and referred to usually as the Englishman's woman. How she survived, on what, was the subject of much speculation, but most people guessed that she must have saved or stolen money or gems during her time with him until he fled before the advancing Japanese, probably dying in the jungle or as a prisoner. She was rarely seen in town, the old Chinese Jianyu buying food and other essentials for her on his frequent visits.

There was really no need for Zeya to spy on her, especially now he had been made the District Police Inspector for the area. It was supposedly in recognition of his services fighting alongside the British against the Japanese that he had been offered the position, but it was in fact a disappointment to him. There was not the recognition he felt he deserved when the fighting ended, certain factions in the new government sought to emphasise the roll he had played in collaborating with the British and he became a pawn in the power games played in Ranong. In the end he knew he had been sidelined, sent away to where he could be conveniently forgotten, and without any dramatic accusations or revelations. He didn't fit in with the new men in power, his past actions deemed dubious, even treacherous, and several of his old comrades who had also signed the Insien document had simply disappeared, and were probably dead. The new Burma could be a dangerous place to practise politics.

Nevertheless he held onto the hope of a change in his fortunes at sometime in the future. He had still one or two friends in Rangoon, and he was in effective charge of Mogok, with its derelict mine that still held promise of vast wealth waiting for its redevelopment. However, against this hope there was a seed of bitterness within him, a seed that would grow in the years that followed and the town languished in the Burmese heat, poor, and forgotten by the world.

In the back of his mind were the rubies, the lost treasure that had disappeared at the same time as the Englishman. He would look for them, quietly, without disturbing the sleepy routine of the townsfolk, the girl Myitsu might know things, things she would tell him in time.

He would call on her, soon, and find out. She was after all only a young country girl really, quite simple and innocent as he remembered. He was quite confident she would reveal all to him, remembering how easily he had moulded and influenced her before.

Zeya waited a month or more before paying a visit to Myitsu. He came in the afternoon, the hottest part of the day when most people stayed indoors, sleeping or resting. Myitsu had gone to her room and lain down on her bed while the child played with some coloured wooden bricks she had found in the attic of the lodge. She had few toys, and no small friends to keep herself amused, but seemed always a cheerful and happy child, seldom crying, close to and affectionate towards her mother.

Apart from her mother the only other person she came in frequent contact with was Jianyu. It was he who had summoned the two women from the town when Myitsu went into labour, and he had stayed a day and a night, squatting on the veranda smoking his pipe, preparing food in the kitchen, listening to the women talking and then to Myitsu's cries. And when the child was born upon the early hours, he had entered the room, taken the child from the woman's arms, and smiled down at it.

'A girl you say. No use, but a comfort for the heart and a joy for the eye.'

He walked over to the window and held the baby in the light of a brilliant full moon that hung over the silent valley and town. The child protested the white brightness falling upon its face, but then opened its grey-blue eyes for the first time. Jianyu chuckled.

'She must be named 'Sandar'...least the moon be jealous of her beauty.

And he turned and laid her gently on Myitsu's breast. The girl, exhausted, touched wonderingly the child's face with the tips of her fingers, her lips, then looked up at the old man.

'Sandar...the moon. Untouchable, beautiful, eternal.'

After the women left, rewarded each with a small but perfect red gem, he stayed behind, loathe to leave the girl alone with the newborn.

Many years before he had watched and waited on his own young wife as she gave birth to his son back in China. As a university lecturer they had enjoyed a privileged life, but when the war broke out between the

Kuomintung and the Chinese Communist Party, a conflict that was to last forty years, Jianyu was conscripted into the Kuomintung army and sent north to the winter war in Heilongjiang. He survived the winter that killed half a million men and later the interminable marches, the pointless and murderous advances and retreats, until he escaped, deserting the cause he had no sympathy with and walked the thousand miles back to his home. It took him two years, and when he arrived he found his house destroyed, his wife and son long dead, and every member of his extended family disappeared or dispersed.

He grieved for them just one day, sleeping in the ruins of the home where they had known a quiet and happy life, and now where every item of value had long since been looted or destroyed. He knew then that his old life was finished, he had to find a new one, without the people he most loved. He had to decide his future.

As a deserter he could no longer stay anywhere in China, so made his way south, through Yunnan, over the Hengduan Mountain Range, and into British Burma. After two years of wondering, living off the jungle and occasional work in the rice paddies and farms, he chanced across Mogok, a little town far from anywhere, but thriving and peaceful, where he finally felt safe enough to build himself a small hut outside the town, and settle down to a life of meditation and introspection. For he was, in spite of, or perhaps because of his soldiering experiences and practical knowledge, an academic, intellectual, and spiritual man.

The position chosen for his home was not haphazard, for he was aware of the Lodge, which was in those days still inhabited by the local British government official and his wife. Although detesting the enforced treaty ports and foreign concessions inflicted upon his native country, Jianyu was a great admirer of the British; their parliament with its laws and checks, their traditions of fair play and tolerance, but above all the literature. He spoke good English, and had once enjoyed a library of over two hundred books. He hoped, with his proximity to the lodge, he might meet and possible befriend an Englishman, although he had never actually encountered one.

He was however disappointed, the inhabitants of the lodge showed no desire to make his acquaintance, indeed quite the reverse, their servants refusing to allow him entry to the property when he first called, and the couple ignoring his greetings. He had stood by the side of the road at the end of the trail leading up to the lodge one morning, waiting for them to pass by. He waited an hour or more before the chauffeured open topped car appeared, driving slowly down towards the main road. As it turned he waved, bowing slightly, and called out a cheery 'Good morning Sir, good morning Madam.'

The passengers turned toward him, then looked quickly away without acknowledging him.

'Who is that horrid little man Richard?' The woman asked her husband when they were further down the road, 'He's dressed in rags, looks like the remains of a uniform.'

'The servants know about him,' Sir Richard replied, 'A Kuomintung deserter apparently, I could have him run out of town, but the locals swear by him, sort of medicine man. Nonsense of course, a complete fraud, praying on the stupidity of the people round here.'

Jianyu watched the departing car, disappearing in a cloud of yellow dust towards the town, with disappointment. Obviously he had committed some social error in attempting familiarity with the English. There must be many cultural traditions of which he was ignorant, he would try again, but be more circumspect in his approach. He had much to learn from them he decided as he made his way back to the cabin in the forest.

It was only with the arrival of Julian many years later that he managed to make friends with the lodge's inhabitants. Through Boy he had been introduced to Julian, who was pleased to have a neighbour who spoke English and who had evidently received a good education many years ago. Jianyu, wary now of being too familiar, kept a respectful distance, but invited Julian to his home from time to time, where he would serve him herb tea and fruit from the jungle, daring from time to time to ask discrete questions about the far off country.

It was when Myitsu came to him that terrible day when Boy was murdered that he began to feel protective, even responsible for the girl. He imagined how the Englishman would feel when he returned to find his partner safe and protected by himself. He would surely be grateful, recognising a debt toward him, a good basis for a deeper friendship. Like Myitsu he was sure the British would return, their empire was vast, their subjects without number, the Japanese would be beaten and sent back to their islands. It was just a matter of time, and waiting.

Jianyu had seen Zeya walking along the road from the town and turning up the track towards the lodge and wondered what his business was with Myitsu that afternoon. He knew vaguely the young man from before the war, and had heard that he had been made District Inspector for the region. Jianyu couldn't suppress a smile at the thought of the chief policeman of the town and a couple of hundred square miles around having to walk everywhere, evidently the independent

Burma was too poor to provide even a bicycle for its officials.

Myitsu had fallen asleep, the child at her side, when Zeya appeared silently in the doorway of her room. He stood for a while watching her before walking over to stand next to the bed. She had not changed much he thought, a little plumper, her skin a little darker, but still a child-woman clothed in a sheer silk sarong that clung to her slender form. Next to her the sleeping child, a girl of about four or five was dressed similarly in a bright red and yellow cotton sarong.

As if conscious of his eyes upon her the child stirred and awoke to gaze up at him with huge pale blue eyes that quite astonished him for a moment until he remembered Julian. So it's true he thought, the stories, she has his child.

Myitsu, sensing her daughter awake opened her eyes too, then instinctively pulled the sheet to cover her shoulders, for a moment not recognising the man who stood over her.

'Zeya...what are you doing here? What do you want?'

She sat up, pulling the child protectively into her arms.

Zeya said nothing, but turned and walked over to the window looking out over the untended garden and jungle-covered hillside.

'You're alone here?' He said softly. 'Where's he gone?'

'They killed Boy. Tortured him and killed him.'

'I heard. And the Englishman, Julian?'

'Gone.' She said the word with an intake of breath. 'Gone. But he will come back...'

'Why? You think that?'

'He told me...he promised.'

'He left you then...with a promise.' He said, turning towards her with a smile.

'He had to, he had to go. They would have killed us both...'

'So he made you a promise...an Englishman's promise, like the promise they made the Karen's, the promise of their own country.'

She looked down at the child, whose wide eyes had never left the man for an instant since she awoke.

'I know nothing of the Karens, I know he will return.'

Outside the room Jianyu had entered the house and silently mounted the stairs, to stand just outside the door, listening intently. He stood ready to move into the room, poised, his hand gripping the killing knife, the same one he had slain Mr. Kaw with just two years previously.

'You were leaving Mogok the last time we met, were you not?' Zeya asked innocently. 'What changed your mind?'

Myitsu didn't reply, shifting the child in her arms and rocking it gently.

'Why have you come here now? What do you want?'

He reached out tentatively to touch Sandar, but Myitsu moved her quickly away from his hand.

'I was curious...about you. I used to like you Myitsu, do you remember? Maybe more than like.'

'It was nothing.' The girl murmured. 'I was a child.'

'And now you are a mother, without a man.'

'He will return!' She insisted sharply, the tone of her voice causing the child to turn and look up at her, suddenly afraid, her eyes filling with tears. Myitsu covered her face with kisses of maternal reassurance, whispering words of comfort.

'He will return.' She said again, once her daughter was calmed. 'I know he will.'

Zeya sighed, as if confronted by a firm but erroneous conviction.

'And the rubies?' He said, 'What happened to them?'

There was moment's pause before she replied, her voice steady, controlled.

'What rubies?'

'Don't pretend to be stupid Myitsu, you know, the rubies that were kept here in the final months...before the Japanese came.'

Myitsu stood up, holding her daughter tightly against her breast.

'I know nothing of these things, if there were any he would have taken them with him. The mine was destroyed, the other Englishman and his wife were killed, who can of tell these things now. When he returns you may ask him yourself.'

A sudden suspicion entered Zeya's mind, something he had never considered before as being too unlikely, almost impossible. What if Julian had escaped the Japanese, and survived the jungle to find freedom, and what if he would return, perhaps to reopen the mine, retrieve the rubies that had probably been hidden. Perhaps he had even been in contact with the girl, sending her money, preparing his return.

He would inquire he decided, there was a British Embassy in Rangoon now, he would write to them in his official capacity, ask them about the man, had he survived, was he home in England? They could perhaps confirm his death, freeing Myitsu from the hold he had over her. A friendly request from the new independent country would surely be answered.

'You must know that things have changed, the gems, the rubies and the rest, belong now to the Burmese State. Trade in them is forbidden. To conceal is theft, and I am authorised to arrest and punish the thieves who seek personnel profit from the nation's wealth. Be warned and be careful Myitsu, once I may have loved you, but now...'

'Now I love another, you are nothing to me. You tried to use me when I was young and foolish. Don't speak to me of your love, you know nothing of it.'

With those words she walked out of her room, the child on her hip, very erect in her anger, descending the stairs to the hallway where she opened the front door and stood waiting for Zeya to leave.

Concealed in the entrance of another bedroom Jianyu watched the man follow Myitsu down and pass through the door without a word.

Myitsu closed the door firmly behind him and after a moment turned and looked up the stairs.

'You can come down now old man.' She called, 'I knew you were there.'

Jianyu came down, a smile on his wrinkled face. 'And I thought my step light enough, I must be old now if a mere woman can hear me, the communist soldiers never could.'

'It was not your step I heard old man, it was your scent I smelled...you smoke too much. A mere woman has more than ears you know.'

Jianyu bowed in recognition, laughing, his eyes twinkling.

'I underestimated you Myitsu, as always.'

'Come Jianu, this mere woman might make some tea for you, and it is time for Sandar to eat.'

They went into the kitchen where Myitsu prepared rice and   vegetables in fish source for Sandar, and tea for them both.

'Sandar don't like that man Mama.' The child announced between mouthfuls, 'He look at me...not like.'

'Hush Sandar, he's nothing. He won't come again.'

Jianyu looked at Myitsu skeptically.

'Oh, he will come I think.' He said quietly so the child could not hear. 'He is ambitious, greedy. And he believes you might have the rubies here. Maybe he will come with the police and search.'

'They can search, they will find nothing. But you old man, do you believe the stories of hidden rubies?'

Jianyu peered around the sparsely furnished room.

'If there were I would prefer not to know. Such knowledge would be a danger. The red gems belong in the earth and rock, exposed and exhibited they corrupt the mind of man. In the olden days wars were fought over them, kings killed, cities destroyed. If I knew of this treasure I would cast it down the mine from where it came. No good will ever come from the red stones.'

'And yet they have their own beauty.' Replied Myitsu, showing Jianyu the simple ring on her left hand that Julian had given her, a plain gold band with a perfect uncut pigeons egg ruby mounted on it.

Jianyu grinned as he studied it.

'Rubies, sapphires, diamonds...gold, silver...women, all are beautiful and all contain danger, enslaving men, and driving them mad with desire. I was not always a lonely old man Myitsu, I remember when passion burned in the time of my youth, and I too was a willing slave to a woman, and I too gave her gifts of silver and gold.'

'That was long ago old man, perhaps you forget or dream. I cannot see you as a romantic.' Myitsu teased.

Jianyu looked at her, his face serious now.

'Be careful daughter, there is danger everywhere in this country now. That man Zeya has some power now, and he will use it for himself, his own desires. The British have gone, and what is left is for the moment chaos, peril, lawlessness. Little people like us can be easily crushed under the wheels of an unscrupulous state machine. If you and your daughter were to disappear, who would search for you, who would care? No one I think, except perhaps an old Chinese man.'

Myitsu smiled at him, not wanting to worry her only friend, but secretly knowing he was right. The return of Zeya was an unwelcome event, exposing her to unknown dangers, her and the child. She took the girl on her knees, wiping her mouth with her hand and kissing her round soft cheeks.

'I know Jianyu, I can feel it. But what can I do? I can't run away.'

She stretched out a hand towards him, and he took it, holding it preciously in both of his.

'Will you look after us Jianyu? Until Julian returns?'

He lent over her hand, holding it close to his chest, his eyes cast down.

'I will try Myitsu. I will try' He murmured.

Sandar, restless now, struggled down from her mother's knees and toddled out of the kitchen and onto the veranda. She sat down abruptly by the balustrade, peering between the bars, watching the path that led to the broken gates through which the man had disappeared.

That night the little one slept badly, and awoke screaming in the small hours from a nightmare. Myitsu, sleeping next to her turned and taking her in her arms, rocked her gently until she slept again.

Jianyu stood at the bottom of the stairs and listened until all was silent again in the room above. On the veranda outside he resumed his position, seated comfortably with crossed legs, his back against the wall, where he could see the drive as far as the gate. The full moon illuminated the garden in a hard monochromatic chiaroscuro, just two small points of yellow showing where the candles still burned in the spirit house.

Part Three

CHAPTER THIRTY-ONE

London 1962

In the darkness came the voice, familiar, reassuring, instructing.

'Julian, I want you to listen very carefully, I'm going to count from one to five, and then I'll say, "Fully awake." At the count of five, your eyes are open, and you will be fully awake, feeling calm, rested, refreshed, relaxed. Do you understand?'

He had to listen carefully but he understood, and nodded.

'One: slowly, calmly, easily you're returning to your full awareness once again.

Two: each muscle and nerve in your body is loose and limp and relaxed, and you feel good, happy.

Three: from head to toe, you are feeling perfect. Physically perfect, mentally perfect, emotionally calm and relaxed.

Four: your eyes begin to feel sparkling clear. On the next number I count, eyelids open, fully aware, feeling calm, rested, refreshed, relaxed.

Number five: You're fully aware now. Eyelids open. Take a good, deep breath, fill up your lungs, and stretch.'

Julian opened his eyes and looked around. The room swam into focus, the desk, the bookshelves around the walls, the window with the curtains drawn to shut out most of the light, the man seated in the chair opposite him.

'How do you feel Julian?' The man spoke.

Julian cleared his throat, unsure about what had occurred in the minutes before.

'Err...fine. I'm fine. Just like waking up, a bit wooly.'

He felt a hand on his shoulder, and turning looked up at Charlie standing behind him, smiling, re-assuring.

'It's all right Dad, it's over now, your back with us.'

'I never knew I went away. I don't remember much, less than last time, just your voice Doctor, sort of vague, distant. But I don't remember what you were saying.'

'That's because you were in an even deeper hypnotic state than in the previous sessions Julian, perhaps the deepest I can take you.'

Julian looked at Dr Simpson, waiting, wondering.

'Well, I'm afraid we're not much further advanced. You didn't reveal anything much more than what we already knew.'

'That's disappointing.' Julian said after a pause. 'I'd thought we might get somewhere this time.'

'As I told you at the beginning Julian, hypnosis is not an exact science...yet. I had, I must admit, hopes of at least a partial recall...something we could work on, sort of foot in the door. But it hasn't happened.'

Julian and Charlie looked at each other, Julian smiled and shrugged his shoulders.

'Well...nil desperandum eh? Try again next week?'

The doctor stood up and went and sat behind the heavy mahogany desk littered with files, folders, and scraps of paper.

'I have to be frank with you both, I don't think there's any point in continuing. This will have to be our last session...'

'But why Doctor?' Charlie interrupted, 'Surely it's worth trying again...something else, taking him deeper perhaps?'

'Charlie, in twenty years of practising hypnosis I have never encountered a case where the repressed memory is so deeply and completely hidden. To attempt to put your father in a deeper hypnosis might have unforeseen effects, perhaps even resulting in further mental distress. It is a risk I am not prepared to take. What is clear to me is that he suffered a huge mental trauma during the war, far surpassing anything I have previously encountered, and I have treated scores of men from that theatre of war. What he has forgotten is perhaps best left forgotten. Perhaps it is the only way he can deal with the past.'

Julian and his stepson looked at each other in silence, before the young man turned again to the doctor.

'What else can we do Doctor? Just carry on not knowing?'

'I wish I could give you more hope, but as far as hypnosis is concerned we have reached the end of its possibilities, to take it further would be irresponsible.'

Julian stood up stiffly, and reached out his hand to the doctor.

'Well thanks anyway Doc., it's been interesting if nothing else. I appreciate your efforts.'

The Doctor shook the offered hand.

'Sorry I can't be of more help Julian, but don't give up hope. The mind's a strange thing, and we don't know very much about it yet, it could be that your memory will return in its own good time, or something might provoke a partial or complete return of memory, it can happen. In the meantime look after your physical health, try not to worry too much about the past.'

Outside the doctors consulting rooms in Harley Street Julian and Charlie paused. It was a grey winter day of mist and rain. London seemed colourless, drab, and cold. Charlie took his stepfathers arm to help him down the four or five steps onto the pavement, lately he seemed to have aged suddenly, become more remote, distracted and frail.

'I don't know about you Dad, but I could use a drink after that. There's a pub round the corner in Great Portland Street, we can get a pint and a snack before heading home.'

The Shakespeare Tavern was quiet after the lunchtime rush, just a couple of jaded business-men arguing in a corner and a handful of students from the Polytechnic in Regent Street having exchanged lectures for pints.

'Well, that all turned out to be a waste of time didn't it.' Charlie said putting two glasses of beer down on the table where Julian sat. 'I hope Mum won't be too disappointed.'

Julian reached out, taking hold of his glass, lifting it.

'Cheers Charlie.'

They both drank in silence for a minute or two, reflecting on the consultation.

'I don't think she'll mind too much.' Julian said eventually, 'She wasn't all that keen on trying hypnosis in the first place.'

Charlie said nothing, aware that there were differences between his mother and Julian on the subject of his amnesia.

'Not too disappointed yourself Dad?' he said.

Julian sipped more of his beer, staring into space, before replying.

'A bit.' He admitted eventually. 'I had hopes let us say. But it's been so long now, twenty years or more maybe, looks like I might have to accept it'll never come back.'

'I can guess how much it must mean to you Dad. Must be horrible to loose ones past like that.'

Julian looked up at him.

'Can you Charlie? Can anyone? It's not something I can ignore, put away. It's always there with me. Like mocking me, teasing me...Charlie...it's like a subtle torture that never ends.'

Charlie listened, shocked, never having heard his stepfather talk like that before.

'Dad...I can guess, I'm not stupid or insensitive. And don't forget you're my Dad in all but genetics, so it's part of my life that's missing too. I can't know my grandparents, where you were brought up, if you went to Uni. or not, if you were married before Mum...you know I think of that a lot too, maybe there's another family out there missing you too.'

Julian held up a hand.

'Please Charlie, stop. I'm sorry, didn't mean to sound sorry for myself. I know how hard it is for your Mum and you. You know she deserves a medal for what she's done for me, the sacrifices she's made over the years, married to half a man.'

'Jesus Dad! You're not half a man, don't say that. You've been a brilliant father to me, and Mum loves you like crazy, we both do.'

Julian reached out and patted his son's hand on the table.

'Thank you Charlie, thank you for reminding me how lucky I am. And after all it's your Mum and you who make my life now, the past is past, and forgotten in my case. I think I should just get on with things, stop searching for something I'll probably never find, and if I did, I might regret I ever looked. Here, let's drink to that.' He lifted his glass and tapped it to Charlie's.

'To the present and the future.' he said.

'Present and future.' Echoed Charlie.

But Charlie knew it was not so simple. He had loved and known his stepfather as long as he could re-member, and all his life he recognised the need Julian had to discover that forgotten life, to solve the mystery of a previous existence. But what could be done now, hypnotherapy had failed when they had such high hopes, and now he seemed discouraged, not willing to continue the search, ready to give up and accept. But Charlie knew he would never be happy, really happy, until the mystery was solved. And he himself felt the need to find out about those missing years, just exactly who was his father, the man he loved and admired.

It was with badly concealed relief that Lydia heard of the abortive session with the Doctor and that no more were planned when Julian, accompanied by Charlie, arrived home in Berkhamsted just outside London. He was tired from the journey and the stress of the con-sultation, from which he had hoped so much.

'Never mind dear.' Lydia told him, helping him off with his damp overcoat, 'It's not the end of the world. Best not to worry too much about it.'

She had never wanted him to undergo the hypnotherapy really, afraid of something she couldn't admit to herself. There was conflict in her feelings that had been there since the beginning of their relationship. On the one hand she wished earnestly for Julian's happiness, and it was obvious that he needed to find his past, recover his lost memories, but on the other hand she dreaded the discovery of past events that might shock or upset them both, perhaps destroying their relationship. Was he already married? Was there a family somewhere missing him, wondering what had become of him? She could vividly imagine the torture of a loving wife not knowing what had become of her partner, imagining how he might have died, for she would surely think him dead after all that time, and perhaps finding herself unable to make a new life with another man because of the uncertainty.

What would he do if another woman and perhaps children who had prior claim on his love, were to appear from the mists of his past. Would that love be rekindled? Would she find herself replaced by an older and deeper love.

She would lie awake some nights, listening to his quiet breathing next to her, her fertile imagination creating scenarios from his past, tormenting her with images of an other woman in his arms, another child in his heart.

Now perhaps, after what the doctor had told them, he would abandon his quest, accept that this life with her and Charlie was the only one. It was selfish she knew, but beyond her control.

Charlie returned to his own flat in Stoke Newington after dinner that evening. On the train to Euston, the Circle Line to the Angel, and the number seventy-three bus, he thought of little else but what he could do for his father. He had been concerned about his physical condition for some time, ever since he had announced he was giving up his job at the garden centre. Both Charlie and Lydia knew how much he enjoyed his work, the contact with other people, the quiet days amongst the plants, flowers, and shrubs, and the money was a welcome addition to Lydia's modest earnings as a district nurse.

'I'm just a bit too tired these days,' He told Lydia, 'Must be premature old age! And I can help around the house, make things easier for you.'

Lydia of course had seen it coming, so attuned she was to his every mood and feeling. She ruffled his hair playfully as they sat next to each other watching television.

'Oh! What rubbish! I'm in my prime. Never better. And you, well, just take it easy for a few months, you're just run down, you'll feel better soon I'm sure.'

In spite of her words she made a doctors appointment for him for the next week. On the day he refused to let her accompany him, saying he was perfectly able to walk the half-mile to the surgery on his own. He returned an hour later with a prescription for an iron tonic and another appointment in six months.

'Nothing to worry about.' He told her, 'Take it easy and three teaspoonfuls of this muck every day.'

Lydia wasn't convinced.

In fact Dr Bree had spent over forty minutes examining and questioning Julian, and had offered to refer him to a heart specialist in London, concerned about an irregularity in his heartbeat. Julian had refused, but said he'd consider it if he didn't feel any better by his next visit.

For Julian it was not just his physical condition that concerned him, but his mental. For a while he had had problems sleeping. Every night he dreamed strange shapeless scenarios, some dreams merging into nightmares from which he awoke sweating, trembling, terrified. Unknown people drifted through these nightmares, faces he knew but could not relate to, people without names, locations, reasons. Sometimes he heard music, strange unfamiliar music, and voices that he could not understand. Transparent red globes blossomed suddenly out of nothing and disappeared in silent explosions of blood-like droplets. But in every nightmare there was the dark menace, the thing that grew and grew, came closer and closer, a sweet smell of corruption. A thing he could not, dared not look at as it pursued him though a flickering twilight and his silent screams of terror. But sometimes came relief, a presence undefined but bringing peace; gentleness...perhaps a woman, a freedom from pain and fear, a form, feminine and youthful, drifting, transparent, unattainable. And when this happened, he awoke with the scent of a woman about him, the impression of a caressing touch on his face, whispered words in a strange tongue in his ears.

He sensed someone was there, someone forgotten, someone waiting. But a horror, an unimaginable horror lay there too, waiting for him to remember. Waiting to be released.

During the months that passed after Julian's visit to the doctor Lydia watched and worried as his health continued to decline. He seemed unable to walk much, and took longer to climb the stairs. A little help with the washing up was just about all he could manage around the house.

He spent most of his time in his chair by the window looking out onto the garden, an unread book upon his knees, lost in another world.

Lydia felt the distance growing between them, as if he were drifting slowly away from her. Yet she knew their love for each other did not seem to change, it was more as if he had been mentally called away somewhere, an enforced absence, and she was reminded of when John had been ordered to Singapore, for the days before he left she could see he had in someway already gone, his mind on what awaited him, the combat, the war, the possibility of death or injury.

Julian returned by taxi from his second doctor's visit clutching a letter addressed to a consultant at Mount Vernon Hospital.

'But what did he say?' Lydia insisted on knowing when she arrived back home from work, 'What's wrong with you?'

'He's not sure, but thinks it's my heart, just a bit tired maybe. The fellow in Mount Vernon's should find out. But I'm sure it's nothing to worry about, they'll fix me up I'm sure.'

Charlie insisted on coming home to accompany his stepfather to the consultation, Julian insisting that Lydia go to her work as usual.

Professor Staid the consultant cardiologist was just a year away from retirement. A heavily built man with longish white hair and very deep rather sleepy voice, he read Julian's notes, asking questions about his past history.

He looked up at Julian as he finished reading.

'Burma huh? So you were a prisoner of the Japs for maybe three years?' It was more a statement than a question. Julian shrugged his shoulders. 'I was in the medical corps when the war ended out there, sent to Singapore to help look after the survivors from the camps.'

He stared at Julian in silence.

'I've read these notes, but of course they're incomplete. We don't know what happened to you during those years, and it's probably related to your condition now.' He said eventually. 'Well, let's get a proper look at you and your ticker, if you'll go with the nurse she'll get you prepped for the examination.'

Two hours later Julian and Charlie were ushered once more into the professor's office. Staid waved them to sit without looking up from the paper he was studying on his desk. On the wall behind the desk a light box glowed, a couple of large x-ray films clipped to it.

At length, Charlie couldn't wait any longer.

'Well? What's your diagnosis professor? What's wrong with my father?'

The professor looked up, as if suddenly noticing their presence.

'Ah...yes. Perhaps if we look at your x-rays you might get a better idea of the problem.' And he stood up and turned to the light box. Charlie went around the desk and stood next to him, but Julian remained seated.

The professor tapped the film with a pencil he had withdrawn for his top pocket.

'The chest cavity...the lungs...and the heart.' He indicated various shadowy forms on the film.

'Now you'll observe the shape of the aorta on both these plates, taken a minute or two apart. What do we notice?'

Charlie stared, baffled, unable to make out anything definite.

'Well, we can notice quite easily two things. One that there is a distinct bulge on that side of the heart, and second the bulge has changed shape from one plate to the next.'

He turned and stared at Charlie as if awaiting a response to his information.

'What does that mean professor?' Charlie asked, feeling as if he must be stupid not to know.

The professor waved him back to his chair.

'Let's sit down, and I'll explain exactly what it means.'

When both men were seated the professor sat back in his chair, steepled his fingers in front of him and continued.

'We can safely surmise that while you were in the far east, probably a prisoner, you were subject to not only malnutrition, and tropical diseases, but to physical and psychological abuse. This has affected your heart, in effect weakened the muscles. Lack of minerals and vitamins, and prolonged periods of stress where the heart is obliged to work extra hard have caused this weakening, and the weakening has resulted in an embolism forming on the wall of the aorta.'

Here he stopped, as if that was all.

'So...what happens now...you can treat it can't you?'

Again there was a long pause while the professor seems to be assembling his thoughts.

'Unfortunately gentlemen there is no treatment possible in this case. No cure that is. An operation might have been possible but the general health of your father is such he would not survive the intervention. Its position makes any operation hazardous. The very best we can do is to give you a drug that will in effect calm the heart, reduce the blood pressure.'

'So...with this drug he'll be alright?' Charlie asked.

'It's not a cure you understand, not at all, just a way of prolonging life.'

Charlie felt the blood draining for his face. Julian was going to die, that's what the man was telling them in so many words.

Julian cleared his throat.

'Err...so, how long...how...how long do I have. What's going to happen...in the end.'

'One day, the embolism will burst, impossible to say when I'm afraid, but when it does death will result probably within seconds, or occasionally if the bleed is very small within hours. It will be quite painless, just as if you are falling asleep. You might notice a feeling of cold in your limbs, slight confusion, but I'm afraid it's usually a very quick conclusion.

Charlie stared at his stepfather, unable to grasp what the consultant had said. It couldn't be, he told himself, he was not even fifty yet, still a good looking man in spite of his past suffering.

'Do you have any questions Mr. Watson, any-thing at all. It's a lot to take in I know. I'm so sorry I can't be more positive, but if you feel you might like a second opinion I can happily put you in touch with a colleague.'

Julian stood up, slowly, stiffly, carefully.

'So I suppose you'll tell me to take it easy?'

'Naturally, the less work you ask your heart to do the longer it will last. No excesses, no excitement, oh...and of course, no sex.'

Julian smiled wanly,

'No life in other words.'

Chapter Thirty Two

A month passed, a trying month for Lydia, Charlie, and Julian. They tried to make life as normal as possible, not mentioning Julian's health, not talking about the future, attempting to keep Julian's physical activity to a minimum. Charlie came home every weekend, and even the odd day during the week. He was in the last year of his MA in history at Westminster University, working on his end of year thesis, but nevertheless he prioritised time with Julian over his work. Money was tight, and Lydia was obliged to take on more overtime to make ends meet, although it kept her away from him far more than she wanted.

Mentally Julian seemed more relaxed since the diagnosis, but still Lydia sensed a restlessness in him. A need for something she could not provide. And then one night she awoke to find his place on the bed next to her empty.

She waited, listening, for moments before getting up, slipping on her dressing gown, and making her way silently downstairs.

Julian was in the kitchen, seated at the table, a half-full glass of milk in front of him. He appeared not to notice her in the doorway until she spoke.

'Darling, what is it? Can't you sleep?'

He looked up, his expression troubled, distant.

'Not much.'

She moved over to him and kissed his forehead quickly, lightly.

'Want to talk about it?'

He looked up at her, then indicated the chair next to him.

'Better sit down, I need to tell you something.'

Lydia sat down, reaching out to take his hand.

'What is it Julian? What's the matter?' A sudden panic, was this it, was time up, was he going to die in front of her?

'I've been a bit preoccupied lately I know, I'm sorry, it must be hell for you...'

Lydia protested, interrupting him.

'No no no darling! Don't say that...'

'Well never mind then, I'm sorry... It's just I've had something on my mind, something difficult to resolve.'

He turned to face her.

'And I know you're not going to like it, but please, bare with me, listen.' He took a deep breath before continuing. 'I need to go back, back to Burma. Before it's too late.'

Lydia could not have been more shocked and amazed. Shocked that he could even consider such a trip, and amazed that he should want to return to the source of his problems, the unstated and undiscovered mistreatment, the horrors that had damaged his mind.

'But...darling...you can't, your health won't permit it. And what can you achieve out there, where would you go, what would you do?'

'Darling I don't know, I have no idea. But I know that I must go. It's there, the secret to my past, not here in London. And before I die, and that could be any time, I need to make a last effort to find out.'

She stared at him, horrified, and she realised that all the time she had known him, loved him, looked after him, she had dreaded this. That he should go back to something she knew nothing about. Another life, perhaps another woman. What lay out there in that strange unknown country could lay claim to him, taking him away from her and leaving her alone.

'You don't understand, do you?' he said quietly. It was more a statement than question, 'I know I can't expect you to, I'm so sorry.'

'I understand your need to know Julian, but...'

'But you think it's pointless don't you, that I'll waste what little time we have left to us...'

'No. Not that...I'm afraid. Afraid of what you might find.'

'And so am I darling. Terrified in fact. But it doesn't change anything...I still have to find out.'

'Do you want me to come with you?'

'Of course. I can't do this alone. But I have no idea what I will do there, not yet at least, just hope something turns up when I get there. Perhaps I'll start to remember things, just to be there. The doctor said it was always possible, a spontaneous recovery...it could happen. I'll go to where they found me first, take it from there.

Lydia telephoned Charlie with the news the following evening, unsure of what his reaction would be. But he said nothing about Julian's decision, simply telling her he would be home in a couple of hours. They waited dinner on him, and ate almost in silence, not mentioning Julian's wish.

While Lydia cleared away Charlie and Julian remained at the table, neither seeming to want to introduce the subject, until Charlie spoke.

'Dad, do you know much about Burma?'

Julian smiled.

'Not much I'm afraid, not as much as you I guess.'

'Well, we did a bit on it last year, the early colonisation, pre-independence, post independence, not deeply mind you, just an overview.'

'You're going to fill me in I hope, the more I know the better.'

'Right...let's start with Burma today,1966. It's a military dictatorship, highly repressive, highly secretive, very difficult to enter, and even more difficult to move around in except accompanied by an official minder. It's one of the poorest nations on earth in spite of having huge natural resources, and from being the largest exporter of rice in the region pre-war, has become a net importer. There's virtually no foreign investment, the infrastructure is falling apart, and it's reputed to be the most corrupt country in the world.'

He paused, allowing Julian to absorb the information.

'Dad, you have to consider that you might not even be allowed into the place, never mind being allowed to wonder around asking questions. People have disappeared there, westerners visiting have just vanished, the authorities claiming no knowledge of them. There are tens of thousands in prison, lots of them political prisoners, and there's still fighting going on. In the southeast it's the Karens, in the north the Kachins and the Shans. You can't just arrive there and wander off looking for your past, it's simply a fantasy.'

Lydia, having finished clearing away sat down again, taking Julian's hand in hers.

'Think about it love, it's not reasonable is it.'

Julian looked from one to the other, a slight smile.

'Oh, I know that, of course I know it's not sensible or reasonable. But...well...I'm going to die soon, and things that seem unreasonable to you make sense to me. I think that everyone when faced with their imminent demise must look back on their lives, draw comfort from memories, their past, their parents who might still live. But I can't do that. I have the impression that I've been robbed of half my life. I need to try one last time to find it, to find out who I am, and from that what I am. Because at the moment I'm just some bloke who's spent nearly all his life living in suburban London, and working in a garden centre. Not much to be proud of...'

'Dad, you're more than that, much more. You've been a great father to me, a devoted husband to mum...'

'But Charlie...maybe I'm more! Don't you see...it's tormenting me day and night, the idea, the possibility, that I must have done things, been someone, perhaps important things...'

'Another family perhaps...' Lydia said the words without thinking. Unable to hold them in any longer.

Julian turned to her, suddenly still, quiet.

After a moment he spoke.

'I have no means to tell, but if I'm honest, and you deserve that at least, I feel I must have...well...had other relationships, but how deep, how important, I have no idea.'

'This is what you want to look for isn't it Julian,' Lydia almost shouted, 'Not a vague idea of your past, not your job, your education, your family. You want to find a woman. The woman in your life before me. And if you insist on this ridiculous adventure I can't come with you. You'll do it alone.'

They should have talked about it earlier, from the start she knew now. It had always been there, the possibility, indeed the probability of the ghost woman. Their first lovemaking should have told her, he was no virgin, and he knew exactly how to please her, an obviously experienced lover. They should have talked it out between them, demystified it, accepted it as part of life. Now it was too late, the ghost had called him. From thousands of miles away in a strange mysterious country she had called, and he had responded.

'I'll go with you Dad.' Said Charlie, 'I understand, I'll not let you go alone.'

Chapter Thirty Three

The weeks that followed a cold stillness settled upon the house. A place that before had known just love and happiness became a mere building where two people lived and a third came to visit from time to time. Julian with a sadness about his distracted air, Lydia trying to pretend, her mouth set in a firm line, trying to make small talk when Charlie was there, spending long hours at her work and returning home late, grabbing a quick sandwich in the kitchen before heading to bed and feigning sleep when Julian joined her.

Charlie took upon himself the organisation of the trip, and began by approaching the Burmese Embassy to ask about obtaining visas for a visit of unknown duration and destination. After filling in a large number of forms asking an amazing variety of questions whose relevance he could not guess at, he was told his application would be considered, and they would let him know in due course. Charlie tried to press them for more concrete information, telling them he wished to visit the country as part of his dissertation for his MA, but without result. In actual fact he had already finished his work and was now awaiting his results.

In the meantime he decided to research as much as he could about the country, obtaining a ticket for the British Library Reading Room, and spending all his free time there.

The funding of the trip seemed at first an insurmountable obstacle to Charlie until Julian admitted he had a savings account, started originally for Charlie's University studies many years ago, and now with just over fifteen hundred pounds left. Charlie did a back of envelope calculation and decided it would probably be sufficient for a month or even two in the country if it was as cheap to live there as the books seemed to suggest.

It was the third week he had spent in the library when he came across the book that opened the door into his stepfather's past. At first he had almost not bothered with it as it seemed at first glance to be concerned with an indigenous tribe, not something Charlie thought could be useful. But on flipping through it he found it contained large numbers of excellent photographs, the author, a Reverend, evidently a keen and competent photographer. The title of the book was '*Five Years in the Burmese Jungle, Converting the Kachins.*' by the Reverend Jacob Sprout. The images were a mixture of landscapes and portraits of the Chins, their villages, houses, and daily lives, and Charlie was intrigued by the glimpse into a different world, as well as by the outstanding quality of the photographs. There was only one picture that featured the author and his wife, a group shot of five people in front of a handsome white painted house with dense jungle in the background. The caption under the picture stated: 'Author and wife (left) with Mr. F. Frobisher (District Commissioner Mandalay) and wife (right), our host Mr. J. Drake (rear). Mogok 1941.'

Charlie paused at the photo. He had suddenly the unusual feeling as if the air around him had thinned, making it difficult to catch his breath, he felt his face reddening. He stared intently at the figure of the young man standing behind the two couples, unable to accept what his eyes were telling him. The young man smiled at him from the pages of book, it was Julian, his stepfather. Certainly younger, fresher, his hair much thicker, his face unlined, but the smile was the same, the kindness about the eyes, it was Julian without a doubt.

For some time he could only stare at the picture, unable to grasp the significance of the find. This was

Julian's past, the first clue, the first step on the journey they would take together in search of the complete answer. But already this one image had answered several questions. In 1941 he was in this place called Mogok, he was host to important people there in what appeared to be an imposing home, and there was no woman next to him, suggesting he was probably a bachelor. He wanted to rush home straight away and show them the picture.

At the desk he was told that books were not for loan, and that copyright law prevented them from giving him a duplicate print of the page. But the librarian copied down all the details of the book such as author, publisher, publication date, description of image and page number, giving it to Charlie and suggesting that although it was probably out of print he might find a copy in one of the book shops in the Charing Cross Road.

It was not however in the Charing Cross Road that Charlie found a nearly new copy of the book, but in Stanfords in Covent Garden, where the venerable sales assistant located the work in less than a minute, just as if it had been the latest best seller.

In too much of a hurry to take a bus through the evening rush hour traffic, Charlie ran the half-mile to Euston to catch the train to Berkhamsted. All the journey he kept looking again and again at the picture, afraid he might be mistaken, or even dreamed. But no, it was there, his step-father's image, smiling at him from the slightly dog-eared yellowing page.

For once Lydia had returned for work at the usual time of six o clock, and she and Julian were sitting at the table in the kitchen drinking tea when Charlie burst into the room, waving the Reverend Sprout's book. They both looked up in uncomprehending amazement.

'Charlie! What is it...what's the matter.?

Charlie, who had run all the way from the station could hardly catch his breath enough to speak, but at last gasped out.

'I've found...I've found Dad! Here...in a book...a picture. Look!'

And he slammed the book open at the page of the photograph on the table in front of them.

They both moved closer to each other and the book, peering down at it.

'Look!' Charlie almost screamed in frustration, 'He's there, don't you see, behind the others. It's him, you Dad, and it says your name is J. Drake.'

'Are you sure?' Lydia said after a moment, 'It doesn't look like your Dad I think...does it?'

There was disbelief in her voice.

'It is Mum! Dad! Don't you see? It's you, in 1941, in a place called Mogok in Burma. It's all there...the names of the other people too. It is, isn't it?'

Julian was staring at the picture in silence, his lips moving but without speaking. Then his eyes filled with tears, he shook his head slowly, as if unable to accept or believe.

'I...I...I think it is Charlie, no...I don't think...I know it is. I don't know why, but I know, I just know.'

And he turned to his wife, taking her in his arms, burying his head in her hair and sobbing. Tentatively she returned his embrace, her hands patting his back, her face showing both shock, and fear.

The Reverend Sprout, retired and living in a quiet suburb of Leamington Spa, a world away from the tribes and jungles of the far east where he and his wife head passed the greater part of their lives, was both surprised and pleased to receive an envelope from the publisher of his first book, since it had been out of print for many years. The other two books he had written, detailing his experiences in Borneo and Sarawak had failed to excite the interest of a publisher, the manuscripts now languishing in the bottom draw of his desk.

The envelope, that he tore open eagerly standing in the gloomy hallway of his apartment while his Pekinese snuffled impatiently around his feet, enclosed two letters, one from the publisher informing him they were passing on a communication from a reader they had received, the other addressed to himself care of the publisher.

This letter, from a Mr. C. Watson, was a request for a meeting, apparently to discuss one of the photographs in the book. The writer did not specify either the photograph or the nature of the information he expected, but the Reverend was highly gratified to think that his book was still being read after all these years.

He wrote back the same day to the mysterious Mr. Watson, stating his willingness, indeed pleasure, in helping the gentleman with his enquiry, and in due course a meeting was arranged.

Charlie went alone to Leamington, Julian explaining that he felt too tired at the moment to undertake the two and a half hour train.

The directions the Reverend had included in his last letter were detailed and precise, and led Charlie from the station through elegant and affluent Georgian streets, to a slightly more modest area where the once gracious houses showed signs of their age and were obviously broken up into apartments, and it was to one of these the directions led Charlie. He was obliged to ring twice on the bell before the door was eventually opened by a small, very thin old man, dressed in the black of a minister of the church. He smiled at Charlie, seizing his hand and shaking it vigorously.

'Welcome dear sir, welcome!' He piped, a high, old man's voice and leading Charlie into the hall and then up three flights of stairs to the top floor, where he arrived quite out of breath

'Ah! So young...I had expected an older person...I don't quite know why. These stairs...nothing to me when I was your age...now quite a mountain to climb. Do you climb young man?'

Charlie confessed he did not.

'I have climbed, in the past of course, the long past. The Himalayas...yes indeed...the Lord's service took me to the high places of the world. Much as our Lord himself was shown and tempted by the evil one. And see...I talk of temptation and madam appears...' The front door to one of the top floor apartments opened revealing a large elderly lady in an elaborate lacy black dress that reached down to her ankles. Her face was very white, with heavy jowls that half covered her neck and shook as she spoke.

'Now what are you talking about Jacob, you do say the most ridiculous things.' She stared rather belligerently at Charlie as if expecting an argument.

'Nothing my dearest...nothing...here is Mr. Watson, come all the way from London to see us. Mr. Watson, meet my wife Maureen.'

The woman offered a limp white hand for Julian to take carefully for a moment before it was abruptly withdrawn.

'Well, come inside then, you're not a gypsy are you?'

'N...no Ma'am, not at all.' Charlie replied, totally baffled by the question, 'Certainly not.' He felt obliged to add.

The Reverend winked and grinned at Charlie as the woman preceded them inside, leading them into a small lounge cluttered with many objects obviously brought back from the east, Batique paintings, jade Buddhas, ivory sculptures, and on one wall a rather moth-eaten tigers head missing one eye stared gloomily into the distance. She turned, waving a hand vaguely towards the contents of the room.

'It's too small here, but we must manage. In Sibu we had many rooms, more than we required in fact, and servants too, many servants. One grows accustomed I find. But of course with Jacob, his calling, we must manage with what the lord provides. We will have tea now, please take a seat.'

Charlie sat uncomfortably in a corner of a sad and sagging settee and took out the book from his briefcase.

'Ah! You brought it! Excellent! Now how can I be of assistance young man?'

Charlie opened the book at the photograph and indicated it.

'It's this picture, I wonder if you can tell me more about it, the people in it mainly?'

Jacob drew the book onto his knees and looked down at it.

'Ah! Yes...yes indeed. An excellent study don't you think, very clear and sharp, the old Thornton Pickard, a wonderful apparatus, destroyed by the natives in north Borneo unfortunately, poor ignorant souls, thought it was capturing their spirits, and in a way it was one could say...ah, such happy times.' And he remained staring at the picture for several moments. From the kitchen Charlie heard the sound of a kettle whistling.

'Sorry Mr. Watson, or can I call you Charlie, no need to be formal here, I'm Jacob as you know, but I'm dreaming, and you want information.'

'It is rather important to me Jacob.'

'So I gather, so I gather, you wouldn't have come all this way otherwise would you. Now, as I remember, the other couple next to us was Freddie and Hetty Frobisher. Freddie was the District Commissioner for that area, just before the war, and we spent the night with them in the government lodge you see behind in the photo. Splendid chap Freddie, best Commissioner I've ever met. Spent his whole life in the country before the war, knew several of their languages, they have scores you know, looked after the people well, very fair to them all. Not exactly loved you know, couldn't be really, not in his position, but respected nevertheless.'

'It's the man behind I'm really interested in.' Said Charlie, unable to contain his curiosity.

'Ah! Yes...now I didn't know him well, just met him twice. He lived in the lodge, but worked for the mine, under Jock MacGreggor. Julian something...can't remember his other name...ah...Drake I think. Yes of course, says it here, Julian Drake.'

'He worked for the mine you say? Under this Jock fellow?'

'That's right, an engineer I recollect, not long in the country...Ah here's tea.'

Mrs. Sprout entered baring a tray that she placed carefully on a low table.

'Look dear, remember this picture, with Freddie and Hetti, Charlie here wants to know about that Julian whasisname...can you remember anything.'

Maureen removed a pair of small wire framed reading glasses from a pocket in her dress and peered down at the picture.

'Him. Of course I remember him, how could I forget, how could anyone forget...'

Jacob raised an eyebrow, looking questioningly at his wife, who volunteered no further information.

'I'd be very grateful for any information Mrs. Sprout.' Charlie murmured, 'Anything.'

Mrs. Sprout continued pouring the tea, her lips tight shut, not saying anything.

Jacob picked up the book again and studied the picture.

'Well...I'm a loss I'm afraid...what is it Maureen?'

She finished pouring the tea, handing a cup to Charlie and Jacob before taking one herself and sitting down opposite them.

'You really don't remember our second visit Jacob? As a man I can't imagine you forgetting it.'

'Erm...sorry...can't remember...' He said frowning.

'The woman Jacob! The girl if you will...you looked hard enough at the time, can't believe you've forgotten.'

Jacob slapped his forehead.

'Ah! Indeed! In....deed! I have it now. Yes, there was the incident with the girl.'

'Huh! Incident you call it. Darn disgrace...depraved...obscene I call it. Never been so shocked...'

'Oh come now dear, we've seen a lot worse, remember that fertility dance in Sulawasi? That was a bit over the top I'll admit.'

'I'm not going to talk about those things Jacob...and they were natives...didn't know any better. That man was white, and an Englishman to boot, talk about letting the side down.'

'Please...please...' Interrupted Charlie hoping nothing too bad about his step father was about to be revealed, 'I must know, it's really important.'

Both Jacob and his wife turned to look at him curiously. Charlie knew he had to come clean about his research.

'Perhaps I'd better fill you in, you've been kind enough to receive me and already my trip has been well worth while, I've nothing to hide after all.'

'Honestly...always the best policy.' Maureen brayed loudly, earning a withering look from her husband.

'Up to you Charlie...don't feel you have to if it's an embarrassment.' Jacob said.

'Well, I came across the picture when I was researching in the British Library, they have a copy of your book of course. I was looking for information about my stepfather. He was found in Burma in the last days of the war, evidently he'd been a prisoner of the Japanese. He was barely alive, malnourished and with injuries suggesting he had been tortured at some stage.'

'I'm sorry to hear that Charlie, I hope he has recovered from his ordeal.' Said Jacob, reaching over to place a hand on Charlie's shoulder.

'Well, thank you Jacob, but that's the problem, why I'm researching. He's lost his memory, everything up to his liberation is lost, later in fact...his oldest memory is being on the ship bringing him home. He knows absolutely nothing of his past life, didn't even know his name when he first came home.'

'Well how extraordinary!' Maureen said, 'I've never heard of such a thing, sort term memory loss, that's not uncommon. But a whole life...well, one must wonder what happened to him.'

'Quite, and I understand your desire to find out Charlie. But how is your step father, is he still alive?'

'Well, that's another thing, I'm afraid he's very ill. We might not have much time. And it's tormenting him, not knowing. Not knowing who he is really, where he came from, not knowing about his family, his friend's, his education and work, everything. He wants to make one last effort to find out before...well, before he dies.'

There was a long silence as Jacob and Maureen digested this information.

'And your mother, Charlie, you haven't mentioned her.'

'She loves him of course, as he loves her, but she's afraid I think, afraid of what might be in his past.'

'She's afraid he might be married to somebody else isn't she.' Said Maureen, as if knowing that for a fact.

'I think she is, in part at least.' Said Charlie.

'Of course she is.' Maureen continued, 'I would be I know, so would any woman.'

'Quite. Quite.' Said Jacob, his eyes shifting uneasily from Maureen to Charlie to the open book on the table.

'Well I think we can put your mind at rest on that at least, can't we Jacob?'

'Err...steady old girl.' Jacob murmured, 'softly softly...'

'Nonsense, Jacob. It'll put the poor woman's mind at rest...pass me the book Charlie.'

Charlie passed the book to Maureen who adjusted her glasses before leaning closely over the picture and pointing with a long thin index finger.

'Well come here young man, look closely and tell me what you can see.'

Charlie lent over the picture, smelling her scent, a mixture of faded flowers and mothballs.

'There!' She tapped impatiently on the photo.

Charlie looked. He had studied the image so much, hours in fact, he imagined he could recreate it perfectly in his mind, but he looked at where the Maureen's long red nail touch the page. She was pointing to a window on the first floor, just below the frame of the picture. In one corner of the window there was the faint head and shoulders of a figure. A pale oval face, possible long hair, perhaps bare shoulders. A ghost of an image.

'Who...who is that? I don't understand. A servant?'

The Sprouts looked at each other.

'That's one word for her.' Said Maureen stiffly.

'Err...Charlie...I should explain I think, a bit about things out there. The girl in the photo, she is a sort of servant...but more than that. Much more. It used to be the custom out there, in India and Burma that is, for young men living there without a wife, to take on what they called Bibi, a girl to live with them, keep them company sort of...'

'Be honest Jacob for goodness sake...they took them to sleep with them.'

'And you say this person in the window was my stepfather's Bibi? How do you know, it looks like she's hiding in the picture. Did you meet her? Did he introduce her? Maybe she was just a servant.'

'Charlie, this was taken on our first visit to the lodge.' Jacob said. 'We never saw her or suspected her presence then. It wasn't the custom for these girls to mix with other Europeans. They were kept out of the way.'

'So...how do you know about her then?'

'I'll clear away.' Said Maureen suddenly, gathering up the half empty cups and carrying them out of the room. 'I'll let you explain Jacob, as best you can.'

Jacob waited until she had closed the door behind her before continuing.

'An accident really, the second time we saw your stepfather. We were getting out. Just before the Japs invaded, didn't feel safe anymore where we were, up in the mountains east of Mogok. So we stopped off on our way to see Jock, find out what the situation was. I had had copies of the picture made in Mandalay, and I wanted to drop one off for Julian, and thank him for his hospitality for the last time. We stopped by uninvited and unannounced it has to be said, but didn't think it would be a problem..'

Jacob stopped here as if unsure how to carry on.

'And what happened then?'

'Well, we knocked on the door a few times without result. The door was unlocked of course, no point in locking doors out there, so we thought we'd wait a while, thinking he couldn't be far. Went and sat down in the lounge.'

Jacob appeared to be studying his fingernails very closely.

'Not been there more than a few minutes when we heard voices, laughter, coming from the back of the house. Then they suddenly appeared, rushing through the door, the girl and then him after her. Didn't see us at first. He was chasing her...this girl. Don't quite know who was more shocked, them or us.'

'Is that all?' Charlie said, feeling relieved there was nothing more serious.

'Well, the fact is, the girl...a pretty little thing about seventeen maybe, she was...how should I say...unclothed.'

For a moment Charlie could think of nothing to say, Jacob looked up at him, a slight sympathetic smile.

'Just so I get this clear, my step father was chasing this naked girl around the house?'

'So it seemed.'

'And he, was he unclothed, as you put it, too?'

'Oh! No. He was in shorts, they'd been for a swim apparently, somewhere nearby.'

Charlie suddenly seemed to see his step father in a new light, a young man, with all the normal feelings and emotions that he himself was aware of. But maybe something more.

'But Maureen said, and I don't understand this, my mother had nothing to worry about. But it appears there was a woman in his previous life, a woman with whom he was on intimate terms.'

'Maureen was right in the main Charlie, these relationships between European men and native women were almost never permanent. The most likely scenario would be that your step father would have left her behind on his return to England, or if he decided to make a permanent home out there he would have kept her for a while before getting rid of her, perhaps taking on another, very few became permanent relationships.'

'Good God!' Charlie could not disguise his shock. 'Did they really behave like that out there?'

'Oh I'm afraid they did, most of them anyway. It was quite accepted as long as it was kept quiet.'

Charlie was having difficulty in imagining the quiet serious and loving man he had known most of his life, with the image Jacob had drawn for him. Julian was devoted to his mother, he had no doubts about that, but could he have once been a different man, a man who would use a girl for his own pleasure and then abandon her?

'Of course there were exceptions,' Jacob was continuing, 'Some men did bring their partner back home, even marrying them, and some long term ex-patriots did form a genuine lasting relationship, but it was the exception rather than the rule.'

'Afterwards, did you ever hear anything more about him? Anything at all?'

Maureen returned as if on cue and sat down without a word.

'Not a thing, I'm afraid, did we darling?' Said Jacob, looking anxiously towards her. Maureen shook her head.

'We did hear that Jock and his wife didn't survive the war, both died in Mogok apparently. But we've never heard anything about Julian until now. Quite amazing isn't it dear?'

And he turned towards his wife for confirmation.

'Almost incredible.' She returned sharply.

'Well Charlie, I do hope this hasn't affected your opinion of your step father, it was a long time ago now, a different time.' Jacob continued, 'the little I do remember of him was that he seemed a fine young man, well liked by Jock and his wife. And if he sowed a few wild oats in foreign fields, well, that isn't an uncommon failing.'

'There's no excuse for that sort of behaviour Jacob, I'm surprised at you.' Maureen said. 'I certainly hope you never did any of that sort of 'sowing' when you were younger!'

'Of course not my dear, I was merely speaking in general, not from personal experience.'

Charlie thought it best to change the subject before the old couple began a serious argument.

'Can I ask if you know anyone else who might be able to give me information? You see my step father wants to go there, visit the place, a last effort to find his past.'

The Sprouts looked at each other.

'I can't think of anyone.' Jacob said after a pause, 'It's all changed now. First the war and the occupation, then independence, and there's still fighting going on I believe. The mine was destroyed, and most of the town too, so I don't imagine there are many people still there who remember anything, certainly no Europeans, we're not welcome there any more.'

'Freddie might have known.' Suggested Maureen. 'But he's lost it you know, not with us any more.'

'Dead?' Asked Charlie.

'Not exactly, senile, doesn't know what day of the week it is anymore. Never the same since he got out of Burma and was told his wife didn't make it. He'd put her on a plane before him you see, but it was shot down over the mountains, killed everyone on board. He thought she was safe, didn't find out until he flew out himself a few days later. Never recovered from the shock, blamed himself you know.'

'So that's all you can tell me about my step-father I suppose, I can't quite say if I'm shocked or impressed.' Said Charlie getting to his feet. 'But I must thank you both for taking the time to see me, it does look like we'll have to take a chance and make the trip out there, but it seems like a bit of a shot in the dark.'

It was at the front door as Jacob was shaking Charlie's hand that the clergyman, leaning conspiratorially towards him, had murmured.

'Don't be too hard on your step father Charlie, he was young, unattached, and alone out there, and things seem different there what with the heat, the food, the clothes they wear, the way the little minxes look at you. And although I shouldn't say it, the girl was a real cracker...shows he had good taste at least.'

And he winked at Charlie as he closed the door.

On the train back to London Charlie had much to think about. His appreciation of his stepfather had changed with the new knowledge. Not for better or for worse, simply throwing a new light on the man he had accepted as his father.

He would not tell either Julian or his mother about the girl he decided. He could see little point in upsetting her with what was an old story. After all there was practically no chance of ever finding or meeting the girl, if still alive she would probably have married a local and be a mother of her own family. The appearance of her old partner could cause un-necessary trouble for her. He would keep that information to himself, unless Julian himself remember something when they were out there, and this was seeming more and more un-likely to Charlie, there still being no sign of their visas from the Burmese Consulate.

In fact, the visas were delivered the next week. Lurid and colourful stamps in their passports allowing them entry into the country for a period of up to six months. It was time to make the arrangements for the trip.

Chapter Thirty Four

As the date for their departure approached it seemed that Julian's health improved. He seemed more active, less tired, and making an obvious effort to be attentive to Lydia. In truth he was feeling better than he had for some time, and put it down to the hope of a successful search, a search that would enable him to finally discover who he was.

'It's been like living with a stranger.' He confided in her one day, trying to explain his need for closure. 'Not you I mean, but myself. I have this feeling I don't know myself, like I have no foundation, no framework. I've been floating on top of life, not really living it, looking at it always from outside somewhere.'

'I've tried, Julian, I've really tried. I wanted above all else to make you happy. To give you your foundation, to create one between ourselves.'

They were sitting in the small back garden of their semi detached house, a warm spring Sunday afternoon with nodding daffodils dotting the lawn and the first fresh green leaves brightening the browns and blacks of the trees and hedges. There was a promise of summer in the air, a subtle rekindled memory of past years, sunshine, heat, the scents of warm wood and flowers.

But for Lydia the summer promised nothing except dread. She feared what waited for him in that distant country, the unknown. She could not grapple with it she knew, anymore than she could grapple with a ghost. It had a prior claim on him this past he sought, a stronger claim, and it left her feeling very inadequate and weak, acquiescent to a force superior to the only weapon she possessed, her love.

'We were happy weren't we?' She continued, trying to salvage whatever she could. 'We had a good life, and we still could, no matter for how short or long.'

'I know darling, I know.' He said, helpless to alleviate her misery. 'When you came into my life it literally saved me, from madness...or god knows what. But you saved me, gave me a life back, and I'll never stop loving you.'

He was unable to take her in his arms as he wanted, as he would have done before, something stopped him, some barrier had fallen between them.

'It doesn't mean much now though does it? Just words, you're leaving me. That's not loving, it's leaving. Whether or not you'll come back I don't know, and I suspect you don't either.'

Julian had dreaded this, an argument about it. Intellectualising, justifying, explaining, protesting, these were indeed words. But what he felt, what was about to happen, was beyond words, defying explanation and justification. It was huge, for both of them, a black cloud covering the whole sky, flashes of forked lightening, whirlwinds, the tolling of bells.

'It's my last chance Lydia, try to understand. My last chance to claim I've had a life before it's gone. I don't know what I've missed, what memories I should take with me. It's like half a painting, or a piece of music that has an end but no beginning, meaningless, irrelevant, pointless...'

'You were never pointless to me, or to your son! Yes! Your son, for he's your son in all but blood. You've made him what he is; a fine, decent, caring human being...so please don't feed yourself that nonsense about pointlessness. If anything is pointless it's this selfish excursion to the other end of the world...now that's really pointless!'

She hadn't meant to get angry, to show him the ugliness that had grown inside her like a cancer. Bitterness taking over from kindness, hatred from love.

She got up quickly, upsetting her chair and stood for a moment pressed against the table trying to control herself.

'I'm sorry Julian, there's really nothing else to say. Absolutely nothing.' And she turned and strode back inside the house.

The blight, the futility of words, communication, fell over the man seated in the spring garden, a sudden chill breeze ruffled the grass of the uncut lawn and sent a few white petals of the cherry tree blossom spinning earthwards, reminding him it was only April after all, summer, an English summer was still a long way off, and he wondered if he would live to see it one last time.

Part Four

CHAPTER THIRTY FOUR

Mogok 1962.

'There, what did I tell you, the colour is a perfect match for your eyes, and I've cut it not too long or too loose, it'll show off your figure nicely.' Zara stood back behind her friend, her head on one side as she studied the reflection in the cracked and spotted mirror of her best friend Sandar. Zara, Mr. Patel's only daughter, was without doubt the best seamstress in the town, an occupation that permitted the ageing Indian to spend a little less time in the family general store, and more time smoking cheroots and gossiping with the three other Indian men who were left in Mogok.

Sandar looked critically at the young woman in the mirror who stared back at her. She was never happy with her looks. In spite of what Zara and her mother told her, and in spite of the stares and turning heads of the young men of Mogok, she could never accept that she was beautiful. She was too tall she thought, taller than the average Burmese man, and her figure was too curvy, not flat chested that was the Burmese woman's idea of beauty. She was embarrassed as an adolescent to be developing breasts, although both her mother and Zara had told her they believed it was what men liked, although Zara could claim no first hand knowledge of the opposite sex being jealously guarded by her father and three brothers until a suitable respectable and prosperous Indian could be located and ensnared. There were none of these in Mogok at this time, and few had been seen since the war.

'It's lovely Zara, you've taken so much trouble with it, too much. I only wanted an everyday longi, this is too good to wear except on special occasions.'

'Nonsense!' Zara chided, 'it's meant to wear anytime. There's nothing wrong with always looking your best, who knows, you might catch a man with it.' And she giggled as she put away her needles, pins and thread. 'We'll go to the market together, you can try it out, you'll see they'll all be looking at you.'

'I don't need anything at the market, and I don't like being stared at.'

'Oh! Come on sister, you're the only way I can get out and talk to people, if my brothers take me everyone's too scared to approach...you know I've never talked to a man alone apart from my father and brothers, and   I'm now twenty three, nearly an old maid.'

Zara was physically the opposite to Sandar, short, a little plump, and with huge expressive brown eyes, and a flawless amber complexion. She was seldom without a smile or laugh, floating through life with a kind and generous disposition that saw only the best in people and situations, untouched by anything bad. She was perfectly happy with the idea of a husband being chosen for her, and seems to have no doubts that when one was found she would have a happy and fulfilled marriage. Until then she could wait, she had her friend Sandar.

It was in part her Indian background that had brought the two girls together as much as the family connection with the mine. Growing up in post war Burma, where both the British and the Indians were looked upon unfavourably by the majority of the population meant the two girls were set apart from the other young people of the town. They spent much time together, mainly in the back room of the family shop at the southern end of the main street, a gloomy establishment presided over by Zara's taciturn and severe mother. Mr. Patel, the one time employee of the mine had survived the war with his modest savings intact, and in the form of a small box of precious stones. He had acquired them over the years he spent working for Jock, believing that whereas paper money might devalue, the blood red stones would always retain their allure. With this little capital he had set up his store, selling anything he could acquire that might be needed by the townspeople.

The two girls set off towards the market arm in arm, Zara as usual chattering constantly and darting glances right and left in case any young man might be watching from the darkened interiors of the open-fronted shops. Sandar looked straight ahead, very straight and erect, always conscious of her appearance as well as her status as a mixed race and therefore an outsider.

'Oh look!' Whispered Zara as they approached the single story building that served as a clinic where a doctor and a couple of nurses from Mandalay Hospital would make their twice-monthly visit. 'The clinics open...that new doctor might be there, the Indian one, he's so handsome.'

'Don't stare.' Sandar whispered back, 'Look who's in the queue, that awful Yaza, I can't stand him...'

Zara giggled, 'I wonder what's the matter with him, why's he's seeing the doctor. Maybe he's caught something.' And she shook with badly concealed mirth, 'Serve him right in any case.'

'Hush! Walk fast, don't look.'

'Ladies! Good afternoon! How are you both?'

A slim young man wearing western jeans, a t-shirt figuring an image of a guitar, and wrap around silver framed sunglasses, called out to them as they approached. There was a queue of about twenty people awaiting entrance to the clinic that consisted of a single room with just a curtain to shield the patient being examined from the fascinated stares of the people crowding the door and the windows.

'Better than you obviously,' Quipped Zara before Sandar could stop her, 'What's the matter with you? A broken heart perhaps. The doctor can't fix that you know.'

Sandar tugged at her friend's arm, knowing that she loved to banter words with young men when she had the occasion.

'Shhh! Leave him alone.' She whispered, trying to speed up. But for Zara the temptation was too much and she stopped a few paces from the man. Heads turned towards them, smiles and laughter from the waiting crowd.

'It's true my love, it's you who broke it and only you can mend it.' He clasped both his hands to his chest in mock agony.

'Then it can stay broken as far as I care, you can ask one of your other girls to mend it, you have plenty to choose from.'

The young man shrugged his shoulders, spreading his hands as if helpless to deny it.

'That's true perhaps, but I can't help it if women can't resist me, not even you Sandar, you might not look at me but I know what you are thinking.'

'What's that?' Sandar couldn't resist replying, 'Thinking you're a foolish young man with stupid ideas?'

At that moment the sound of raised voices from inside the clinic caused heads to turn as people strained to hear the cause of the very unusual event.

'A damn foreigner.' The young man said to no one in particular after a moment. 'Can't speak Burmese, don't know what he wants here.'

Sandar listened closely, recognising words in a language familiar to her. The tongue of her father, English.

Releasing Zara's arm she stepped up to the door of the clinic and looked inside. At the desk where the nurse was stationed to receive the patients a tall western man was leaning over the desk and trying to make himself understood in an odd mixture of English and the occasional Burmese word.

'The hotel. It's not far. The Hotel Regent Mandalay. Just five minutes.' He waved a hand vaguely in the direction of the town centre.

The girl looked blankly at him, not understanding a word.

'Please, please, can I see a doctor. Speak English maybe?' He insisted, obviously frustrated at his inability to communicate.

'Perhaps I can help you.' Sandar spoke from where she stood by the door. The man turned, relief showing immediately on his face, smiling. He was young she saw, about her own age or a little older, tall and wearing a lightweight tropical suit. He walked towards her, the eyes of all in the room following him.

'Oh! You speak English, what a relief. I was going crazy trying to explain, nobody speaks English around her it seems.'

'There is no one to teach I'm afraid. Even the school teachers cannot speak it.'

He was standing in front of her, looking down, and she felt suddenly he was too close and she stepped back a pace.

'What is it you wanted to say. Do you need to see the doctor?'

'Yes! At least not me. It's for my father, he's very ill. We just arrived, staying at the Regent Mandalay, they said to come here.'

'You have to bring him here I'm afraid, the doctor won't come to you.'

The man looked troubled, frowning and reaching into the pocket of his jacket to retrieve a battered brown wallet and extracting a few Burmese bank notes.

'He can't, absolutely impossible. He was taken ill on the bus coming here, the heat I guess, had to almost carry him to the hotel. He needs attention quickly. I can pay whatever he wants for a visit.'

Sandar felt a pang of sympathy for the man.

'It has been very hot lately, the monsoon is late, very late. But I'm afraid it's pointless asking him, he's too busy to come out. Look at all those people waiting, He just can't.'

Zara suddenly appeared at Sandar's side.

'I too speak English.' She announced greeting the foreigner with a dazzling smile.

The man looked from one girl to the other.

'Your English is very good, both of you. How come?'

'My father teach us.' 'My mother teach us.' Both girls answered simultaneously.

The man smiled, 'Well they've done a good job, and I'm glad they did.'

Inexplicably Sandar felt suddenly nervous, here was the first Englishman she had met, and one of about the same age as her own father when he lived in Mogok. Shyness overcame her. Then silently turning away and stepping through the door.

'I have to go. I'm sorry I can't help.'

Zara followed reluctantly pulling a disappointed face.

'Wait, can I walk with you? I'd better get back to Dad in any case, maybe the hotel will know another doctor.' The young man called after them.

Together they stepped out into the hard light of the late afternoon, the road and town shimmering in heat waves rising from the baked brown earth, and walked slowly towards the centre.

Behind them the voice of Yaza called out.

'Quick work ladies! Off to his hotel with him?'

Sandar quickened her step, towing the reluctant Zara by the arm.

The sight of Mr. Patel walking slowly up the street towards them keeping in the shadows of the buildings and leaning on his white stick brought the girls to a sudden halt.

'It's Papa...he hasn't seen us. I have to go back.' Said Zara turning quickly and bringing the edge of her sari up to cover most of her face. 'I must be there when he gets home or I'll be in trouble. Come tomorrow Sandar, tell me what happens.' and she lowered her sari just enough to give the young man a quick and mischievous grin.

'Where do you live? Is it far?' He asked after they resumed their walk.

'Through the town and out the other side, not far.'

'You didn't tell me exactly how you manage to speak English so well.'

'It's from my Mother, she taught me.'

'She's English?'

'No, but my father was.'

Charlie said nothing for a moment, sensing it might be a sensitive subject.

'He's not here then, did he die?'

'I would not like to talk about this please.'

'I'm sorry, excuse me.'

They walked on in silence down the deserted main street where even the dogs would not stir from the dark shadows of the houses and deserted market stalls.

'What is wrong with your father may I ask.' Sandar said after a while.

'Mainly he's just exhausted from the journey. We're from England, took us four days to get here, Hong Kong, Bangkok, Rangoon, Mandalay, then the bus from Mandalay, just about all he could take. But he has another condition too.'

They reached the hotel and stopped outside. It was, in spite of its name, a rundown looking place of stained grey concrete and rusting metal windows. A large and ancient generator stood outside covered in a film of black oil and soot.

Charlie looked up at it apologetically.

'It's a bit of a dump but apparently it's the best in town. God knows what the others must be like.'

Sandar smiled. 'Here it is not Bangkok, or London. I'm sorry.'

'Oh, it's fine really, just a bit of a shock at first. Not what we're used to. But I must go and see Dad, thanks for your help.'

'I am sorry I can't help more.'

Charlie reached out to shake her hand and after a moments hesitation she offered her own. He felt it soft and cool in his and he smiled.

'I wonder if I might know your name miss, I'm Charlie.'

'My name is Sandar, Charlie, and I am very pleased to meet you.'

'I'm pleased to meet you too Sandar, and I hope we might meet again, we might be here for some time.'

'You stay here long time?' She asked.

'Depends, on Dad, and other things.' Charlie had decided it was best to be discrete about the real reason for their trip until he had found out more about his father's life there.

'Charlie, there is someone else here who might help your father.' Sandar said, suddenly feeling she didn't want to break off the conversation, anxious to know more about the strangers.

'Another doctor? Here, in Mogok?'

'He is not a western doctor, but he knows many things, natural cures, Chinese medicine. The people here believe he is very good doctor, maybe better than clinic doctor.'

Charlie wrinkled his nose skeptically.

'Really? Do you go to him? And your mother?'

Sandar smiled, 'He is like a father to me, and he has always looked after my mother and I.'

It could do no harm Charlie thought, any doctor was better then none, and it would surely comfort his father, perhaps he needn't tell him he wasn't a real doctor.

'How do I find him Sandar, it's worth a try.'

'I will bring him to you, Charlie. Soon, maybe this evening.'

Before Charlie could thank her she had turned and was walking away, a slim graceful figure, straight as an arrow, silhouetted against the low light of the sun and the baked yellow brown earth, walking alone and down the centre of the straight and narrow road into the distance that shimmered and danced in the unprecedented heat.

CHAPTER THIRTY-FIVE

Myitsu lay in a hammock on the veranda of the lodge, her eyes closed. Patterns of light and shade crossed her face back and forth as she rocked herself with the aid of a rope suspended from the ceiling that she tugged gently from time to time. She was listening to the old man mumbling half to himself a few feet away.

'She has been gone most of the day now. I should have accompanied her. She will have had nothing to eat or drink.

I have prepared food for her when she returns. Mr. Patel will send her home when he returns.'

He was seated cross-legged on the floor a few feet from Myitsu's gently swaying hammock, talking almost to himself, unsure if Myitsu was awake or asleep. The swaying hammock made no noise, and Jianyu could not see her hand on the rope. He had been blind now for five years.

Cataracts the young doctor at the clinic had told him on his one and only visit to the place. Nothing to be done at least not in Burma, and no cure he announced dryly, as if anxious to dismiss the old Chinaman who was reputed to be some sort of local witch doctor. In a way Jianyu was relieved, hating the idea of hospitals with western doctors dispensing western medicines. He had his herbs, his powders and potions, the familiar cures that had served him and the people of Mogok well for almost half a century. And he was philosophical about it, reasoning that there were worse things than being blind, remembering the men dying around him in their thousands that winter long ago. He had lived, and by his standards lived well. He had found his place, and two people to love whom he suspected looked upon himself with a certain affection. He still remembered his wife, and although no woman could ever replace her, Myitsu and Sandar were like daughters to him, and the last twenty or so years had been as happy as he had known since he had been forced into the army of Chiang Kai Chek.

'Perhaps I will walk down to the cross roads and wait there for her.' He continued in almost a whisper, but loud enough for Myitsu to hear.

'Foolish man.' She spoke quietly as well, 'what good would that do? She has probably stopped in town, the market will soon be opening and she likes to spend a little time there.'

'What good? Ayee...you are right daughter. Sometimes I forget I am a blind old man, good for nothing any more. Thank you for reminding me before I make a fool of myself.'

Myitsu reached out a placating hand towards him.

'Father forgive me, I spoke without thought. You know how much we still need you, and we can never forget we owe you our lives.'

Leaning out of the hammock and opening her eyes she managed to reach over to the old man, placing her hand upon his shoulder, gently caressing.

He turned towards her, as if he could still see her, placing his own brown wrinkled hand upon hers.

'How is it with you Myitsu, can I help? I should be concerned with you rather than the young woman who is perfectly capable of looking after herself.'

Myitsu sighed.

'It was better earlier, and last night I slept a little. But I woke before dawn and it made the night seem so long. I stood a while by the window and watched, waiting for the light and the sun.' Myitsu had recently been subject to periods of deep despondency and insomnia, the feeling of the passing of time surprising her without warning, reminding her of her fruitless wait, her empty life.

'Did you take the medicine I prepared for you? It should have helped you sleep.'

'I took it before...before the night came. It has a foul taste you know.'

'Maybe, but it must help. When you sleep you forget. But do not take more than I showed you, it can be a danger.'

'Forget? Forget what old friend? This place? The promise? That you are blind and I grow old while Julian has not returned?'

The last sentence spoken with an intensity not given to the others, for it was this that gnawed away at her desire to live, eclipsing her love for her daughter and Jianyu, the terrible recognition that she was obliged to admit she would never see him again. It had crept up upon her un-noticed, manifesting itself more and more in moments of bleak depression and lethargy. Before she had believed, completely, thoughtlessly. Then with the passing of time came the doubts, unwanted and growing like a cancer inside her. And with the doubts grew the fear.

A sudden shuddering sob made her withdraw her hand from him and press it against her mouth as if the misery became a real and physical pain

Jianyu sensed everything she felt.

'Shall I make you a pipe, daughter?' He asked quietly.

After a moment, her eyes tightly shut, her lips compressed, she whispered. 'Perhaps.'

Jianyu stood up and helped her to climb out of the hammock. He held her arm, as she guided him back into the house and up the stairs to her bedroom, where she half fell onto her bed.

Jianyu helped turn her onto her side before seating himself next to her, the low round brass table with her pipe and its accessories before him. She was calm now, controlled, with the anticipation of the peace the drug would give. Her wide dark eyes watched intently the movements of his hands, deft and methodical, following the familiar ritual as if it were a religious ceremony, a form of worship of a strange and demanding god. Jianyu worried sometimes that she might come to rely upon the opium too much, and it was because of this that he would often make her pipe for her, afraid that one day she might use too much and overdose, accidentally or otherwise.

He kneaded the tiny ball of hot paste on the edge of the decorated bowl of the pipe, polished and darkened by usage, and the sweet and heavy scent of the opium filled the room. Then plunging the needle into the cavity of the pipe followed by a flick of his wrist he reversed the bowl over the flame and held the pipe to her lips. She drew deeply, taking the whole pipe in one breath as the opium bubbled gently.

Jianyu replaced the pipe on the table and helped her to lie back on the cushions behind her. Her eyes had closed as she drew in the smoke, but she opened them as Jianyu stood up.

'Don't leave me please. I will sleep if I know you are there.'

The room was filling with shadows. Facing east it lost the light before the other rooms. Through the window the tops of the eastern mountains shone golden, their lower slopes now lost in mist and the gathering darkness and Jianyu watched as the shadows rose higher and higher until the mountains were just grey waves against the grey sky, distant, like a dream of another country.

He sat down stiffly on the floor with his back against the wall, the light from the window on his face, and his unseeing eyes fixed upon the sleeping woman. It was how Sandar found them when she returned from the town.

After Sandar and Jianyu had both eaten while Myitsu slept a deep-drugged sleep in her room, Sandar explained about her meeting with the Englishman and his sick father.

'The doctor would not visit him of course, even though he is a foreigner, but you could visit him, perhaps help him.'

Jianyu first protested his inability to diagnose anything but the simplest malady now he was blind, but secretly he was pleased to be asked, and intrigued by the idea of meeting another Englishman all the years after the other, Julian, had disappeared.

'If I go it should be now daughter, while your mother sleeps. She will not awaken now for several hours. But you must lead me, I fear I could not find the hotel so much has changed in the town.'

There was a half moon and no clouds, so the walk to the town with Jianyu's arm linked through the girls presented no difficulty for the couple. After the unlit trail to the main road they had the lights of the town to guide them, and even the occasional street lamp lit the road. They saw no one on their way, for that route out of Mogok was still unfrequented save for the hill tribes who came to Mogok on market days to sell their produce and buy essentials.

Sandar stopped in front of the hotel that appeared to be in total darkness save for a feeble light showing through the cracked glass of the front door. Beyond the door a small reception contained an empty desk behind which a man lay on the floor, asleep and snoring loudly. A single light bulb glowed feebly, it's light growing and diminishing with the erratic rattle of the big generator outside.

Charlie was waiting, seated in a small plastic chair to one side of the room.

'You've come! I wasn't sure of you would.' He stood up quickly, then stepped forward offering his hand. Sandar smiled, unused to the traditional western formalities, and shook it briefly, shyly.

'This is Mr. Jianyu. Jianyu, this is Charlie. He speaks English Charlie, better than me I think.'

Charlie held out his hand again, waiting for the old man to take it.

'Mr. Jianyu is blind Charlie.' She said quickly.

Immediate Charlie reached out and took Jianyu's hand in his.

'I'm very pleased to meet you, sir. It's kind of you to come here, I hope it wasn't too far for you.'

Jianyu grasped Charlie's hand with both of his, pumping it vigorously and smiling with the pleasure of hearing English spoken by a native speaker.

'Indeed not young man, two kilometres is nothing to a man who has walked the length of China when young. I welcome you to this poor town at the end of a road that leads nowhere.'

The noise from the snorer suddenly stopped as the sound of the voices interrupted his sleep. There was an indistinct muttering as the man struggled to his knees and peered over the desktop at the three figures standing watching him. He was a large bald fat man wearing only a soiled longi about his enormous waist. He was sweating in spite of his inactivity.

'What is it? What do you want with my guest?' He directed this last to the two faces he vaguely knew;

the Chinaman and the strange half-caste girl from the old lodge.

'Can we go somewhere quiet, I'd like to talk to you both before you see my father.' Charlie asked Sandar, ignoring the man.

'There's a table and chairs outside, we can go and sit there.' Sandar suggested.

The hotel owner, Thakin Bo, watched suspiciously as the three stepped outside. He didn't like them speaking English that he couldn't understand, and was distrustful of the declared motives of their visit that they were simply tourists. It was at least irregular and possibly illegal that they were here without a government guide, but they hadn't argued about the grossly inflated price he had quoted for their room, scrawled almost illegibly by pencil on a scrap of paper. He had taken a week's rent in advance, more than he would usually take in a month from other occasional guests who chanced by his hotel. But he worried nevertheless, and he would have to declare their presence to the police to protect himself.

Seated around the circular concrete table on the concrete benches Charlie wanted to fill in some of the background to Julian's sickness, but without revealing too much.

'He's actually only in his forties.' He began, 'But suffered a lot during his captivity in the last war. Must have weakened him, but lately he's been diagnosed with an embolism, untreatable, and it's made him easily tired.'

The others listened quietly, Sandar watching Charlie's face, Jianyu looking down at the table with unseeing eyes.

'Emotionally he's quite fragile, doesn't like to be questioned about the past, so please keep that in mind

Mr. Jianyu. We don't expect miracles, but if you can just take a look at him, give him some reassurance, it would be good for him.'

Sandar glanced across at Jianyu.

'Can you help them father?'

He sat silent for a moment before replying.

'I can promise nothing of course, but sometimes just to talk can help. I will see him alone if you can help me to his room.

Sandar nodded to Charlie, who stood up and took Jianyu's arm to guide him.

From behind his desk Thakin Bo watched them take the stairs to the room on the first floor where the other Englishman had been put. He worried more now, the man was obviously very ill to have called upon the old Chinaman's services, not just tired as he originally had been led to believe. If he died in his hotel there would be repercussions; enquiries, visits from all sorts of officials, papers to fill in, and maybe fines and fees and bribes to be paid. He shook his head and decided he would put them out at the end of their week.

In front of the door to Julian's room Charlie stopped and whispered to Jianyu

'Shall I go in to introduce you first?'

Jianyu shook his head.

'I will manage alone thank you, please wait downstairs with miss Sandar. I can find the way back alone.'

Charlie tapped lightly on the door then pushed it open and stepped away.

As if he could see, Jianyu stepped confidently in to the dimly lit room and closed the door behind him. Julian was sitting on the bed, trying to read by the light of a bedside lamp that glowed red and yellow as the current fluctuated. He looked up curiously at Jianyu, but with a slight smile.

'Can I help you?'

The sound of the voice seemed to affect Jianyu strangely, he was moved without knowing why. Something seemed to reach inside and touch him... a part happiness a part sadness. He was unable to reply for a moment.

'I'm sorry.' The voice continued, 'you must be the doctor. Charlie warned me you might look in. I hope it didn't inconvenience you too much.'

There was a warmth in that voice, a warmth he hadn't known for years in a man's voice. Gentleness, intelligence, kindness, and he thought he remembered.

'My name is Jianyu, but sir, I must inform you I am not a doctor. At least not in the sense you know the word. I did not go to medical school and I have no paper qualifications that might reassure you. But I have treated hundreds of people over the years who have found relief in my medicine and my counselling. It might perhaps comfort you to know that no one has died because of my intervention.'

There was a slight chuckle from the man on the bed.

'That's fine then. I'll put myself in your hands, did Charlie tell you much?'

Jianyu stepped towards the sound of the voice, his hands outstretched.

'I know all that I need to know. But you do not know that I am blind I believe.'

The voice was silent for a moment.

'Indeed not. I'm very sorry. Can I help you?'

'Please, no help is needed. Just relax and lie back on the bed.

Jianyu moved forward until his legs bumped against the bed. His hands sought out the body taking first the wrist, feeling the pulse, then leaning down with one ear pressed to Julian's chest, listening intently.

'Please remove your shirt and vest. Thank you.'

The hands moved over Julian's body, first the surface, feeling the scars, the damaged joints of the shoulders, the missing toes. Then pressing gently but firmly his stomach and abdomen, under the rib cage, the kidneys, the liver.

Julian felt the knowledge and the power in the hands, he thought of the words 'healing hands', and knew that was what he was experiencing, a total relaxation, the aches and pains of his injured limbs that he had lived with for a score or more years, fading and then disappearing.

The examination finished Jianyu helped him dress again.

'Well? What's the verdict Jianyu.' He spoke the name without thinking of using the 'Mr.', it seemed more natural, more familiar.

'Please, I wish to ask you some questions. But if you desire not to reply I will not insist, only answer what is comfortable to you.'

'That's fine. Ask away.'

Jianyu reached down and took Julian's hand in his, clasping it tightly between both of his own.

'You were tortured in the war?' He asked after a moment.

Julian nodded silently, that much was very obvious to anyone, then remembering Jianyu couldn't see murmured, 'Yes.'

'In view of your health why did you decide to make this visit.'

'Oh! I've always wanted to see this part of the world. Always fascinated me... the Far East. And I guess it might be my last chance.' The lie came easy, rehearsed often in his head.

There was a long silent pause while Jianyu seemed to reflect on his reply and Julian was suddenly very conscious of the firm grip of the old man on his hand. He knew it was a lie. Somehow he knew.

'You have a wife? Charlie's mother? In England perhaps?'

'Indeed. Been happily married for nearly twenty years.'

Jianyu stayed silent, reflecting, aware of Charlie's warning not to ask too many questions. But it was gnawing at him, the doubt, the possibility, something he had to find out.

But if it was him, if it was possible that after twenty years he had returned, how could he not recognise the man who tended him, questioned him. Surely he himself had not changed so much in that time. Had he not been blind his own eyes would have told him the truth he thought, he would surely recognise his onetime friend. But the voice, it had come to him suddenly, the memory of the young Englishman from the lodge, Myitsu's lover, Sandar's father.

If it were him, why? Why with a wife in England and a son at his side would he seek to make this last pilgrimage to his past. Neither his wife nor his son would surely approve of such a quest if they knew of his lover, the woman who once shared both his bed and his life. Perhaps he had kept it a secret, a shameful interlude in a young man's brief visit to a foreign country that he would try to put behind him once back in the country of his birth.

'And you Jianyu? Are you married?' Julian had found the long silence disturbing. Wondering just what the old man was thinking. But Jianyu ignored the question.

'And what are your impressions of the country so far Mr.....Mr...I'm sorry I do not know your family name.' He asked.

Julian stared at the men whose blind eyes seemed to be watching him intently, aware of something, something he couldn't quite grasp. A connection perhaps.

'Drake. My name's Drake.'

In a faint whisper Jianyu found himself repeating the words, a whisper that the Englishman could only just hear.

'Julian Drake, Julian Drake.'

And he withdrew his hands from Julian's and clasped them tightly in front of him and bowed a little.

'Sir, I will return tomorrow with some medicine that should help you recover from your long journey and give you strength for the coming days. I'm afraid that is all I can offer you.' He bowed once more before turning and with hands outstretched sought for the door.

'Jianyu!' Called out Julian as he was about to disappear into the darkness of the corridor, 'Thank you, Jianyu. I feel better now...much better.'

Jianyu stopped in the doorway briefly, turning his head and nodding towards the figure on the bed before making his way carefully down the stairs to where Charlie and Sandar waited, unaware of their connection, step brother and sister.

He heard their voices as he descended, talking animatedly, sharing. And he paused on the stairs as it came to him that Sandar had practically no friends of her own age except Zara, Mr. Patel's daughter, certainly no men friends, for the men of the town were a rough and uneducated lot, unaware of life outside the town and the valley. Even the girls of Sandar's age were simple minded. Mostly without any schooling they lived in a perpetual search for a husband who could provide for them, however modestly. Nothing else was of any note or importance.

It was good to hear her talking freely with the young Englishman, a pleasure denied to her up to now. Jianyu wondered if they could become friends as well as half siblings should the truth be declared. A brother, even a half brother and an Englishman could be good for the girl he thought.

It was not in the old Chinaman's nature to worry too much about the future, but his thoughts had been often about Myitsu and the sadness that seemed to affect her recently. He also wondered about Sandar, what could her future hold here in this backwater. He felt acutely his responsibility towards the two women. And then there were the rubies, the hidden treasure, what role would it play in these uncertain times.

He continued down the stairs to the reception where the Thakin Bo had resumed his interrupted sleep behind the counter, and passed outside.

'Is it always this hot?' Charlie was saying, 'I'd have thought at night it would have cooled off a bit, but I think it's as hot now as during the day.'

'Now is the hottest time of the year for us, but this year it's exceptional. The monsoon is late and it won't get cooler until it arrives. You should stay indoors between mid-day and five o' clock, you must feel it more than us.'

The two young people were looking at each other, and had been since Jianyu had left them alone.

They were easy, comfortable, slipping effortlessly into a dialogue where one might imagine they had known each other for a long time. Charlie was intrigued by the girl, her strange and for him exotic beauty, her obvious intelligence, but above all by the feeling that here was someone different to any girl he had known in England. A girl who had grown up in a country far from his own. A girl with a strange language, an unknown religion, a different culture, and a different view of the world.

And for Sandar, Charlie was like a sudden break in the clouds that lets an intense beam of sunlight illuminating a dull, grey, and familiar landscape. Here was the outside world that had come to her with its mysteries, its strangeness, its promises. Suddenly Mogok, the town, the valley, the lodge, the mine itself with its dark and violent past seemed small, petty, trivial.

Charlie himself was so different to the men she had known however briefly. She felt immediately that she could trust him. His face was open, honest, and he looked at her without dissimulation; he liked her she could tell. And she liked too his quick mind, the warmth in his voice, and the humour that was never far below the surface.

They both turned, almost reluctantly towards Jianyu as he appeared in the doorway, even blind he could sense he was breaking an intimacy.

'What's the verdict Mr. Jianyu?' Charlie asked, standing up and helping the old man down the steps and guiding him to the bench.

'Your father is very tired Charlie. Above all he needs to rest for at least five days. I will return tomorrow with some medicines for him that will help his recovery. As for his underlying condition there is little I can do for a cure. However I can give him something that will reduce his blood pressure and slow his heartbeat, this will minimise the risk to the embolism.'

Charlie reached out and took Jianyu's hand.

'I can't thank you enough Sir, you've taken a great weight off my mind, you and miss Sandar that is.' He turned and smiled at her, again their eyes locking on each other, as if unwilling to look away.

Chapter Thirty Six

Charlie lay in the stifling claustrophobic darkness of his room unable to sleep, although frustratingly he could hear from the next room his father snoring gently. It was not just the heat that kept him awake and restless, but the kaleidoscope of new and novel impressions that filled his head. The girl, the strange Chinese man, the dilapidated hotel in the place that seemed lost in another time another world, and the glimpse he had seen on the way into the town on the bus of the remains of the mine, wrecked and destroyed, but still dominating the valley with the dark silhouette of the broken wheel. He now knew without doubt that it was here the answer to his father's past; the stories and secrets as yet untold, and about be revealed. In a way he felt fear, fear of something unknown that awaited, but there was excitement too, and then there was the girl.

He would ask her tomorrow when she came with Jianyu to bring medicines. Ask her some of the questions, discretely and carefully that might lead to information about the mine, its history, what had happened during the war. Perhaps he would show her the photograph, and maybe she would recognise the place, the people. Already he looked forward impatiently towards the morrow, and seeing her again.

The bed was damp with his sweat under him and eventually he stood up, stripped off his pyjamas and dried his body with a small towel he had brought with him. Outside the open window the moon was setting, the town in darkness save for one or two streetlights far away. No breeze stirred the air in the room or outside and he lay down naked on the narrow bed and waited for sleep, thinking of the girl.

District Inspector Zeya was already in a foul mood when he opened his office in a small recently built building on the Mandalay Road at the entrance to the Mogok. Like most of the town's inhabitants he had slept badly because of the heat, and he knew even before stepping inside that it would be even hotter in the airless interior. He was supposed to have an air conditioning unit, promised five years ago on completion of the place, but it had never materialised in spite of his numerous letters and phone calls to the regional headquarters in Mandalay. No money was always the excuse, certainly nothing for a forgotten outpost like Mogok.

He wedged the door open with a lump of concrete left over from the construction of the building, pushing against it angrily with his foot. He hated that lump of concrete, for it seemed to symbolise the whole situation he found himself in. Unchanging, left over from another time, useless except for the most trivial and pointless tasks, and he kicked at it again in pointless irritation.

As always at that time of the day he asked himself how he would pass the time. Write a report about something that when received in Mandalay would be filled away unread? Find somebody to arrest on a made up charge? Inspect a couple of shops for something they might be selling without proper paperwork? It was all impossible in that heat. He would certainly not stir from the office after twelve. He would send his deputy Tin Shwe home at lunchtime so could take a nap in his chair with his feet up on the desk.

He knew now he had made a mistake all those years ago just after the war. He could have stayed on in Mandalay or even Rangoon, he was well known and respected in the movement, and his old associate Thakin Aung San, gave him the choice of several positions before he was deposed himself. But Zeya had his reasons for returning to Mogok, he had unfinished business there, and the modest position of District Inspector seemed perfect for his plan.

The war had changed and matured Zeya. His experiences with the government in exile, the now discredited communist party, and the British administrators before independence, had all resulted in a certain loss of youthful idealism. The lies and deceits of the politicians of all colours had forced the young Zeya to confront the uncomfortable fact that politics was after all a pragmatic exercise, unconnected with truth, service, comradeship, but driven instead by the hunger for power by the leaders. Not the desire to serve, but the desire to be served. Having come to this conclusion, and it came to him in the months following the Japanese defeat, he was left somewhat adrift, and eventually followed the familiar and well-trodden path to self-interest. He would abandon the cause that was once his guide, and concentrate on his own advancement, in the financial sense.

He had never forgotten the rubies of Mogok, the treasure he had once handled every day and passed on to his colonial masters. He thought about it a great deal, counting in his vivid and fevered imagination the amount of money that had passed through his hands during the time he had worked for the mine with its British boss and international shareholders. And then trying to guess how much had been squirrelled away, hidden or stolen, in the dying days of the mine as the Japanese approached.

He knew it was there, all the facts pointed towards it. The rumours rife at the time suggested over two months production had not left Mogok when the Japanese came. And they had not stayed long in the town, making only the most superficial search of the remains of the mine and the town. If they had found anything the townsfolk would have known it. It was still there, somewhere, waiting to be discovered.

And then there was the girl Myitsu, still living in the old lodge with a daughter but without a man. He thought she must know something, but she played dumb, pretending total ignorance. She had money from somewhere, that much was sure, and the only source of money in Mogok was rubies. Although he had never been able to prove anything he believed she had from time to time sold the red gems to a dealer in the town, an Indian by the name of Singh, a distant relative of Mr. Patel, once the mine's bookkeeper. He had searched his premises on several occasions without finding anything, and had left with dire warnings of what would happen should he be found to be trading in the stones. But money could buy silence he knew too well, and rubies produced money, a lot of money.

He thought about Myitsu a great deal, and not just in connection with the missing gems, although in his mind they were inextricably linked to the girl. He remembered how he had been attracted to her all those years ago when he had first seen the girl-child dancing in a tiny village just outside Mandalay. Already she enjoyed a certain regional fame and the young and impressionable student was fascinated by the aura that surrounded her. Deeply engaged in the independence movement and the communist party he had sought her out, determined to enlist her in the struggle, to have her beside him as a comrade and perhaps later something more. In his naive ignorance he interpreted his feelings as a political aim, rather than a romantic desire, and justified his actions as necessary for the end result.

But now, after more than twenty years he was able to accept that it was the woman he desired, not as a tool, but as a lover or even a wife.

She had rejected him when he first arrived back in Mogok after the war, but she was still young then, still under the impression that the father of her child would return to her. In the succeeding years he had tried and tested her fidelity to the vanished Englishman, and she had remained steadfast in her loyalty; foolishly, unreasonably, and deaf to his approaches. But recently he had sensed a weakening in her faith, a lessening in her vitality surely caused by the realisation that the dream of her one-time lover was just that, a dream. And she was now reluctantly waking up to a new reality, the Englishman's absence, and his own presence. He would wait a little, he had patience, but he knew that his time was coming, she would accept him, for there was no one else.

The unwelcome sound of his telephone ringing interrupted his thoughts, and he hoped that whatever it heralded would not entail a journey away from the police station. He recognised immediately the voice of Thakin Bo with some surprise as it was early in the day and the man usually never stirred before the sun was half way to its zenith.

He listened silently as the man gabbled out a story of two foreigners arriving at his hotel without a guide or even any papers showing they had permission to travel to Mogok unsupervised. He had reluctantly allowed them to stay in order that he could inform the authorities while they were safely located in his hotel, otherwise they might have simply disappeared he suggested, hinting of sinister motives.

Zeya grunted a few words to him and put down the phone. He would have to walk down to the hotel and find out what the strangers were dong in Mogok. They were probably just a couple of tourists who had wandered off from an official party and wanted to see for themselves the real Burma, not the sanitised version the official guides presented. He would have to send them back to Mandalay, requisition a car and driver, perhaps even go himself. The journey in the present heat would be insupportable. He picked up his uniform cap from the desk where it had lain untouched for several weeks, wiped his sweating brow, and jammed it firmly on his head before stepping out into the mounting heat. It was nearing what the Burmese call the Evil Time, when nothing moved in the blinding heat except tailless vultures floating high above the town on motionless wings, and black columns of ants snaking across the empty road, their motives sinister and unfathomable.

Zeya arrived at the hotel a few moments before Sandar and Jianyu and was studying the hotel's register when they walked into the reception. He was immediately curious as to their presence there, a curiosity that became a suspicion when he learnt they were also there to see the two foreigners, and had, what's more, already met with them the previous evening. Thakin Bo's hurried explanation of the indisposition of one of the men and his desire to see a doctor did nothing to allay Zeya's suspicions.

He had never liked Jianyu, although he had known about him all his life. He couldn't see why he lived there in the jungle outside town as it was commonly known that he was a man of some intelligence and learning and could have bettered himself with a little effort. He had stayed in Mogok during the war and had made himself popular amongst the townsfolk by treating the many who were injured in the fighting. By some means he had become close to Myitsu and her daughter, and always accompanied them on their infrequent visits to town. Zeya was suspicious of the intimacy shared by the three, afraid that the Chinese man might become a confidant, trusted with secrets kept from himself.

He had considered many times the idea of removing Jianyu using a trumped up charge, a word with the district magistrate who visited Mogok only when absolutely necessary would have put the man in prison for the rest of his life. But he never quite dared because Jianyu was so well respected in the town as a healer, and his friendship with Myitsu was a consideration he could not ignore.

Zeya decided quickly that he would ignore their presence for the moment.

'Go to the men and bring them down, tell them that I wish to talk with them.' He demanded Thakin Bo, pretending a confidence he did not quite feel. Until he knew exactly who the foreigners were he would be circumspect in his approach, for who could know if they might be influential and important people?

Charlie appeared a few minutes later, unshaven and with wet hair. He smiled at Sandar and Jianyu.

'Sorry! I wasn't expecting you so early. Didn't sleep too well with the heat.'

Sandar nodded towards Zeya.

'Charlie, I think the policeman here wants a word with you.'

Charlie's heart sank; he had hoped to remain out of the eyes of the authorities for at least a few days. They had been warned in both Rangoon and Mandalay that they were not permitted to travel anywhere without an official guide, and immediate expulsion would be the result of any transgression.

'Where is the other man?' Asked Zeya in his most abrupt and uncompromising tone.

Charlie was surprised to hear the man speak good English, and explained that his father was recovering from their long journey and needed bed rest.

'I will need to see him, but perhaps not today. Your situation is most irregular here, you have no guide or permission to be here I understand.'

'Well, yes... I know. But we didn't think it necessary...we'll not be staying long...just looking around, visiting.'

Charlie was wondering if this was the time to offer a financial inducement to the officer, but hesitated in front of the others. He had been told that everyone could be bribed in Burma, that it was accepted practise.

'Why have you come here? We do not cater for tourists in the town, unless part of an official group.'

'Just a spur of the moment decision really.' Said Charlie, waving his hands about vaguely, 'Went to the bus station in Mandalay and picked one at random...crazy really I guess, especially with my Dad not being too well.'

'Your passports?'

'Had to leave them with immigration in Rangoon when we arrived.'

'I will see both you and your father tomorrow at the police station to take a statement, at say eleven o clock. Bring any paper work you have with you, also any cameras, photography is forbidden in the town. And do not leave the town until the situation has been clarified.'

After Zeya had gone, to return to his office a little worried and perplexed, Charlie reached out and took Jianyu's hand.

'So sorry we weren't ready for you Sir, but I woke my dad and he'll be ready for you now I guess. Shall I help you upstairs?'

Jianyu clasped Charlie's hand affectionately.

'No need young man, I can remember. My eyes might be useless but I find other senses can sometimes make up for my loss. You can talk to Sandar while you wait, I'm sure there is much you want to discuss.' And he paused meaningfully, before continuing, 'Sandar, please pass me my bag, I will be about half an hour with the gentleman.'

Sandar handed over the leather bag she had been carrying, then watched closely as the old man made his way carefully up the stairs. She turned to Charlie.

'How is your father today?'

'Well, better I think. Said he slept well, was thinking about getting up and about today, he's very anxious to be out and about as soon as he can manage. Shall we sit outside.'

They took up the same places they had left the previous night and for a moment stayed silent, content just to look at each other.

'What will you do today?' Asked Sandar eventually.

'Depends a bit on how Dad feels. If he's up to it we'd like to explore the town a bit. Not sure what there is to visit here...perhaps you could suggest something?'

Sandar laughed. 'Oh there's nothing much here to see. One small old temple in the town, a bigger one outside, a market, a few shops, and of course the ruins of the old mine you've probably noticed already.'

'Ah yes, the mine, I've heard a bit about it, used to be quite famous I believe, rubies wasn't it?'

'Yes, rubies mainly, and they still dig for them around the town, but the mine was destroyed in the war so it's just small scale now. But Charlie, please, if anyone offers to sell you any don't buy. The government has strictly forbidden foreigners to buy except from authorised dealers in Rangoon and Mandalay, anyone caught buying unofficially gets a long prison sentence, even foreigners. And even to be caught in possession risks prison. You would not like the prisons in Burma Charlie.

'Oh, no risk of that. We've not any spare cash for that sort of thing. But I'd like to go and see what's left of the mine. What happened to the people who worked there in the war, the Europeans I mean?'

He was surprised how easily he had managed to turn the conversation towards what he needed to know.

Sandar paused as if to reflect before answering.

'The manager and his wife were killed in an air raid.'

'And that was all the Europeans there were? Not many to run an important mine.'

'There was an English engineer there, but he just disappeared.' She said quietly.

For a moment Charlie couldn't speak, unaware he was staring intently at the girl opposite him.

'Charlie...what is it?' She asked nervously under his fixed gaze.

'Nothing...sorry...just thinking.'

'What Charlie?'

Charlie reached his decision suddenly, feeling it must be the right moment, unable to resist the temptation.

'Sandar, I've not been perfectly frank with you. I hope you will excuse me.'

'What is it Charlie?'

'It's why we are here...my dad and I. We're looking for something.'

'Here? Here in Mogok? What can you look for? There's nothing here!'

Charlie reached into the pocket of his jacket and pulled out the photograph.

'Sandar, can I show you this, and can you tell me anything about it? Like where it is taken, who the people are.'

He pushed the small print across the table towards her. She took it and turned it around. Charlie heard a sharp intake of breath.

Sandar stared, unable to understand what she was seeing, it was the same picture as the one on the wall at the lodge, the picture she had known all her life, exactly the same except unfaded and obviously copied from a page in a book.

Charlie was staring at her, aware.

'You know something.' He breathed.

Sandar nodded slightly, unable to speak.

'What? What do you know?'

'Why are you here Charlie? Where did you get this?'

'I copied it from a book. A book written by one of the men in the picture. A book about Burma.'

'But why Charlie? Why do you come here with this picture? What are you looking for?'

'Sandar, it's my father in the photo. The young man standing behind the others. Taken here in Mogok in nineteen forty one or two.'

In a sudden movement she was on her feet, as if ready to flee. Her hand covered her mouth, stifling a silent cry, a cry of despair that showed only in her eyes.

'Sandar! What is it? What's the matter.'

She stared at him in horror, as if he had become a snake or some other repulsive creature. Her mind tried and failed to grasp the full significance of his words except for the one terrible fact Charlie had related so casually. Her father...her mother's lover...the man she had waited for the past twenty years, faithful, true, adoring...had married another women and fathered a child with her. Now he could never come back to her. She was betrayed. The dream was shattered, the spell broken, and it was for the girl standing there by the concrete table in the brittle heat as if the world itself had tilted on its axis, everything familiar had gone away leaving a black and empty void where even the echoes had died.

They both became aware that Jianyu was standing in the doorway, holding the arm of a thin and rather gaunt middle aged European in a light tropical suit. He was smiling at the two young people.

'Good morning miss Sandar, good morning Charlie.' And Sandar stared for the first time at the man from the photo, her father.

She glanced at him for only a fraction of a second, a heartbeat, before looking away quickly. Her eyes danced from Charlie to Jianyu.

'Jianyu, we must go. I must go to Mother.' She stepped away from the table and took Jianyu's arm and relieving him of his bag.

'I'm sorry Charlie.' She murmured, not looking him in the eye and leading Jianyu away. Charlie stood up, calling after her.

'Sandar, can we meet again...please. I need to know about the picture.'

Neither Sandar not Jianyu turned or made any reply, passing down the nearly empty street, her arm in his, walking quickly as if fleeing.

From the window of the hotel reception Thakin Bo watched their hurried departure and wondered. There was something strange happening and it disturbed him to think his hotel was involved, he would inform Zeya he decided, as the policemen has requested.

'I want to know everything.' He had insisted earlier, 'Where they go, who they meet, what they do...everything. Understand?'

Thakin Bo understood perfectly and went over to his desk and picked up the phone.

Chapter Thirty Seven

'Daughter we must talk before we see your mother.' Most men of over seventy would have been out of breath as Sandar led Jianyu along the main street. She was walking unusually fast, looking straight ahead and ignoring the brassy sun and the thirty-five degrees of heat that beat down on the town from a pale opal sky. But Jianyu, although shorter than Sandar maintained effortlessly her pace, his arm linked with hers and striding confidently as if he could see the road in front of them.

'What did the young man tell you?' He continued, 'did he reveal that you are brother and sister? That you share the same father?'

Sandar ignored the question, not so much concerned with her own relationship as with the effect of such news on her mother.

'Sandar, we must reflect. This is both wonderful and terrible news. I recognised your father's voice the moment he spoke, but I cannot understand why he did not recognise me.'

Sandar turned briefly towards him, as if evaluating his appearance. It was true she thought that as long as she had known him he hadn't changed. Still short but strong, his hair cropped close, his face unlined and young. Only the greying of his hair and the white scales covering his eyes betrayed the passage of the years.

'Perhaps it is not true. You could be mistaken Father, there is something I cannot understand here. What do they want? Why are they here?'

'If you had not run away like that I would have talked to them both, the truth would have come out. Perhaps they are looking for your mother.'

'I don't want to be near that man, I won't let him near mother, he disgusts me. It's what they always said about the British men who came here, they take a woman, use her, and then discard her. How can I look upon that man as a father?'

'And Charlie?'

Sandar stopped suddenly, turning to face Jianyu.

'I don't know anymore. I'm so confused. I thought I liked him, and he liked me. But I can't accept the son of that man as a friend let alone a brother. I want them to go away.'

They stood still and silent in the centre of the street, their shadows a black pool about their feet as the terrible sun rose towards its zenith over Burma. High, very high above the town two solitary vultures hung almost stationary in the air thermals rising from the baked earth, then sensing an almost imperceptible change, they turned together as if upon a signal, and glided away towards the mountains far to the south where unnoticed by the people of Mogok, black and heavy clouds were at last gathering about the peaks.

Charlie and Julian watched the two figures disappearing down the main street and turning into the road leading to the east.

'Is there something I'm missing here?' Julian asked, a slight frown on his pale face. 'We were getting on well, the doc and I, persuaded me to come downstairs...He's a remarkable man don't you think?'

Charlie also had the impression he was missing something; something very important that had slipped past him un-noticed. She had been shocked to learn that Julian was his father, that he had lived here before, but what could have made her react like that he wondered. Obviously it was something bad, she had immediately broken off contact and left.

'Dad, she knows it is you in the photo. I had to tell her. But as soon as I did it was like a bombshell to her, a shock for some reason.'

As soon as he had spoken the words the same thought came to both men. They turned to stare at each other.

'How old do you think she is Dad?' Charlie asked eventually, his voice tight, strained.

'About twenty I'd guess.' He said, as much to himself as his son. 'Difficult to tell, they age quicker here than at home, could be a lot younger...but she's tall.'

'And mixed race...'

'And mixed race, as you say Charlie.'

The idea hung in the air, unspoken, enormous.

Charlie turned to look after the two figures but they were gone, only two black dogs stood irresolutely in the empty street, staring at each other, too hot to fight or even bark.

'Dad...do you think...?

'Charlie I don't know, I just can't tell. But that's why we're here isn't it.'

For some unknown reason Myitsu had felt better that morning when she took breakfast in the kitchen with Sandar and Jianyu just as the sun was rising. The bleak depression had gone and the after effects of the pipe she had taken before sleeping still gave her a feeling of quietness and tranquility.

Sandar had told her briefly about the two Europeans in the hotel and that Jianyu had promised to return with her that morning. Sandar thought it a little strange that she had shown little interest in knowing about them, imagining that she would have been curious to find out more about them.

'I will go to the temple when you return.' Myitsu told Jianyu, 'If you are not too tired.'

'If it is as hot as yesterday you should wait until the evening, daughter, it will be too much for you. I myself have never experienced such heat.'

Myitsu laughed, a rare and welcome reaction lately, never missing an opportunity to tease the old man about his age.

'Then indeed it must be an event of great rarity honoured father, several hundred years perhaps.'

Jianyu frowned in mock severity.

'Have a care my children, when the rains come we will pay dearly with great discomfort, I have a feeling that...'

'Rain! Discomfort! Why father I will dance in the rain with joy when they come.' Interrupted Sandar laughing. 'I have forgotten how it feels to be cool and comfortable.'

Jianyu had stood up and gone over to the window to look out at the lightening sky.

'Still no sign.' He murmured to himself. ' But there is a strangeness in the world.'

After Sandar and Jianyu had left for the town Myitsu went out onto the veranda and lay down in the hammock, reaching up to pull on the rope to make it swing slightly. She closed her eyes and slipped into the post opium state of half- dream half-consciousness.

The two Europeans in the town floated into her thoughts and she wondered vaguely what brought them to Mogok. Perhaps the mine, perhaps one day the mine would re-open. Several times men from the government in Rangoon had appeared to spend a day examining the remains of the buildings and material, but anything of value had been stripped long ago and although promises were made by petty officials that work would soon start on its rebuilding, nothing ever transpired. The state was too bankrupt, turbulent, and isolationist to find investment for such a risky project.

Almost reluctantly her thoughts turned to Julian. Before she could think of him only with pleasure. The happiness they had found together, their complete compatibility, the joy of their physical union. But lately the sadness had invaded her thoughts of him, the feeling of loss, hopelessness, and solitude. She must try to think less about him she resolved, try to concentrate on her daughter and her adopted father, for who could tell how much longer the old Chinaman would be with them.

Sandar appeared walking rapidly through the broken gates and along the overgrown path towards the lodge. She was alone.

'Father has gone to his house.' She called as she mounted the steps to the door. 'I must shower...so hot...so hot.' And without going to the veranda to greet her mother she went quickly up the stairs to her room.

'And the Europeans? Did you meet them?' Myitsu called after her. But from above only the sound of a slamming door came as reply.

In her room Sandar stripped off her clothes, then wrapping a length of pale blue silk about her body, threw herself face down on her bed and shut tightly her eyes.

They had not come directly to the house, they had not asked about her mother, and the older man had perhaps pretended not to know his old friend. It could only be they had no wish to make contact.

Then if it was not for her mother they had come, what was the reason? Why make such a journey with a man in fragile health to a place so remote, so devoid of interest to the usual tourist. And then she thought about the mine, and the rubies. Her mother had told her of the gems he had given her to hide, both the little jar kept hidden in the house and the strongbox whose location she had been shown as a young girl.

She sat up suddenly; convinced she had found the answer. It must be the rubies that had lured then back, the possibility that they were still hidden after all the years, waiting, like her mother.

Similar thoughts had come to Jianyu. Sandar had left him at the end of the short trail to his little hut in the jungle, he had no need of help to find his home from there, so familiar was the ground, and he wished to be alone to think. It was better that Sandar and My-itsu were left alone too, he thought, at least until things were decided, like what to tell Myitsu.

He made himself herb tea, moving surely and deftly about his tiny kitchen, and took it outside, to sit on the floor, legs crossed in the lotus position, and reflect upon the situation.

His priorities were simple, and had been for twenty years, to protect the two people he loved. Protect from not just physical harm, but mental suffering. He had no illusions about the effect it might have on Myitsu to find out the father's situation, she had lived for his return since the day he had left and disappeared into the mountains in the old car.

Rumours abounded after the war when Jock's old car was found burnt out by the trail only a few miles from Mogok. Julian had been killed in an ambush by the Japanese or perhaps natives, he had wandered into the jungle and died of starvation, he had been captured and killed by the Japanese, had escaped and returned to England with a fortune in rubies hidden somewhere about him. These were only a few of the stories repeated and elaborated on by the gossips of Mogok.

What disturbed Jianyu most was the remembrance of his friend. The Julian he had come to like and admire did not fit the idea of a man who would forget so easily and callously the woman he loved. For the old Chinaman knew, absolutely and completely, that the young Englishman had been deeply in love with Myitsu.

It had never been talked about, but Jianyu had often seen them together, noticed the way the man's eyes were constantly drawn to the young woman, the warmth of his smile when he looked at her, the way his hand discreetly sought out hers at any opportunity, they way he might mention her in conversation, always with respect, almost awe in his voice.

Jianyu himself had always thought his friend was dead, although never letting the women know this. It was inconceivable that he could have reached safety. Jianyu had journeyed himself through the mountains and jungles of the north himself and knew the dangers he would have faced; hunger and thirst, sickness, dangerous animals, unfriendly natives, and the Japanese who were swarming over the country at that time.

He and Julian would have to talk again, just the two of them. But Sandar did not wish to see the men again, and that presented the problem of how to get to town and find the hotel on his own. He had never tried before, but surely it must be possible, he remembered well the road and once in the town he could ask someone for help. He would wait until sunset and hope it might cool down a little, he decided, there was a little money somewhere in his hut, he would use that if necessary to purchase a guide.

Chapter Thirty Eight

Mogok's police inspector arrived back at his office extremely hot, worried, and ill tempered. He found his assistant, Aarav waiting for him and seated in Zeya's own chair with his feet up upon the desk.

Aarav was a small sallow complexioned man with prominent yellow teeth that he was constantly picking at with broken matches or whatever suitable implement came to hand. He oiled his hair excessively and was followed around by an odour of stale coconut and sweat. He held little respect for his boss, being several years his senior, and resenting that Zeya had been appointed by the authorities in Mandalay to his position from outside town.

Reluctantly he stood up to allow Zeya repossess his chair.

'They've been on the phone, just missed them.'

'Who?' Queried Zeya, annoyed that Aarav should have been there to take a call meant for himself.

'Mandalay, the commissionaire, said it was urgent, wanted to speak to you.'

Zeya reached out to pick up the phone.

'No need to call him back, he said not to, told me what to tell you.'

Zeya's annoyance increased. He hated the idea that Aarav should know his business before himself, that he should have actually talked, perhaps even chatted with his superior behind his back.

'Well, what did he want?'

Aarav removed a matchstick from the top pocket of his uniform jacket and began picking at his teeth.

'They're looking for a couple of Europeans who've gone missing. Disappeared without a guide or papers. All they know is that they were asking in their hotel about how to get to Mogok. Wants you to find them if they're here and send them back, with an escort.'

Aarav stopped picking his teeth but kept the matchstick between his lips, rolling it back and forth as he studied Zeya.

'They're here, at the hotel aren't they?' He said.

Zeya wondered briefly how he knew, then realised in a small place like Mogok any stranger would be immediately noticed and the news quickly spread.

'I've just been to interview them.' He felt obliged to justify his absence from the office.

'Sending them back then? I'll take them if you like. Not been to Mandalay for ages...apparently it's going to rain there.'

'Who said?'

'The commissionaire, said there had been scores of deaths in the town from the heat, but they hoped for rain anytime now.'

Zeya seethed with impotent fury. Not only had his assistant spoken to his superior, but they had actually passed time discussing the weather. It was intolerable he thought, demeaning his authority.

'Get down to the hotel.' He snarled, 'Check up on what they do, follow them if necessary.'

Aarav leisurely replaced the matchstick in his pocket, slipped his cap on his head, and with a last sulky glance at Zeya stepped out into the street.

The news that the authorities already knew about the men was unwelcome. It made him look incompetent, he should have informed them of their presence before. Now he had little time to organise their removal. He had no desire to undertake the journey himself by car or bus in the present heat, but he didn't like the idea of sending Aarav to Mandalay where he might meet his superiors, telling them things about Mogok and Zeya he wished to keep to himself.

Then he remembered the appointment he had made for them the next day. He could wait until then before deciding, if necessary keeping them locked up until he organised transport. It was, he decided, too hot to do anything at the moment, he could rest in his office. Let Aarav look after the foreigners.

The sun was setting as Jianyu arrived at the hotel, setting in a sky that bled streamers of crimson cloud against a background of violet, purple, and grey that shifted and changed. As it dipped behind the mountains it sent brilliant beams of yellow light across the valley. The air was very still, heavy with moisture, an almost palpable thickness making it difficult to breathe.

Zara, Mr. Patel's daughter whom he had met by accident in his way into town, accompanied him. She insisted that her father would come to accompany him on his way back when he was finished.

'I should be no more than one hour.' Jianyu told her, clasping tightly her hands as they stood in the hotel reception. 'Tell you father that his old friend would greatly appreciate his company for a short walk.'

'Oh! You cannot walk Jianyu in this heat, I will tell him to bring the car if god wills it to start.'

Aarav and Thakin Bo were seated by a low table in the reception playing Lattougkhon, two bottles of beer in front of them. They watched suspiciously as Jianyu passed by them unseeing, carefully felt his way up the stairs and knocked on Julian's door.

Charlie opened it, both surprised and pleased to see Jianyu, and taking his arm led him into the small room where Julian was seated on the bed, a glass of water in his hand.

'Doctor! Or Mr. Jianyu if you prefer, we're happy to see you although I hope you didn't come out especially to visit myself. I have been taking the medicine you brought this morning and am feeling a little better.' Julian called out to him.

Downstairs Aarav looked across at Thakin Bo.

'Call Zeya.' He ordered. 'Tell him... I want to hear what they talk about.' And he stood up and crept quietly up the stairs to stand by Julian's door, his ear pressed against it.

Jianyu finished a short examination of Julian's condition, taking his pulse, and assessing his temperature with a hand on his forehead. Charlie pulled a chair up close to the bed so he could sit, then went and stood on the opposite side. Julian smiled at Jianyu.

'You didn't need to come really. In this heat too, I don't know how you people survive in it.'

Jianyu reached out and found Julian's hand.

'And yet there was a time when you were used to it, was there not Julian.'

The two Englishmen looked at each other. Then Charlie spoke, as much to his father as Jianyu.

'I think it's time we came clean, about our visit here. You seem to know already that my father was here during the war, Sandar told you I guess.' He said quietly.

'I knew already.' Replied Jianyu, 'I recognised your voice Julian, as soon as I heard it.'

The room was very quiet as the men digested this information.

'But Julian, what I didn't understand was how you could not recognise your old friend, or perhaps you did not want to.'

Julian moved uncomfortably on the bed, suddenly afraid of what was missing and about to be revealed. Before he could say anything Charlie spoke.

'Sir, there's something you don't know, we haven't told you yet. My father lost his memory, totally and completely, during the war as a result of his treatment by the Japanese while a prisoner. He has no recollection of anything before his liberation in June nineteen forty five. That's the reason we are here, to find out his past, who exactly he is.'

Julian was nodding slightly as Charlie spoke, his eyes fixed on Jianyu, bright with hope.

'What can you tell me Jianyu, I feel something, like a connection, a memory I can't quite recall...were we friends?'

The old Chinaman didn't move for some time, then suddenly struggled to his feet, lent over Julian and embraced him. When he stood up again there were tears in his blind eyes.

'You were my friend Julian, for sure. And I hope that I was yours. There is much to tell.'

Again he reached out and embraced Julian.

'What can I tell you my friend, where do I start to reveal a life. You told me much of the time before you came here you know, and I have forgotten nothing. It was a life I envied, admired; your country, your education, your profession, I was greedy for everything you could tell me.'

'I dreamed of this.' Murmured Julian, his voice tight with emotion. 'Dreamed I could one day sit down with someone and find out who I was.'

Charlie moved forward, leaning over the bed.

'Jianyu, first of all, can you tell us about Sandar? Who is she? She seems to be connected...'

Jianyu turned toward the voice.

'Sandar is your sister Charlie, daughter of Myitsu and your father.'

Julian was frowning, as if trying to remember.

'Myitsu...my wife? I was married?'

'Not married my friend, not in any formal way, but you were together for over two years.'

'And she had my child?'

'After you had gone. Some months after, you never knew, she never told you.'

'So that's why Sandar reacted like that...pure shock I guess,' said Charlie, 'but I would have thought she would have been happy to meet her dad and brother.'

'Unfortunately my friends it is not so simple.'

Both men stared at Jianyu, sensing something.

'What is it, why would she not be happy to meet us?' Charlie asked quietly.

Jianyu sighed before continuing.

'Here is the problem. A problem that is not just a problem but also a remarkable story, a situation almost beyond belief but nevertheless real and true. Before you left Julian, and you did *have* to leave, you promised Myitsu you would return. It was a promise you intended to keep I know, and a promise she believed implicitly, perhaps naively but with all her heart. And now, twenty years later, she still believes. She has waited all those years for you, faithful and true.'

He paused to allow his listeners time to realise the implications.

'Still?' Said Charlie incredulously. 'Still? How can she?'

'Oh young man, you have no idea of the strength, the power of her love...and the fidelity. She believes, and taught Sandar to believe too. And now perhaps you can understand how terrible it was to find you here, in this hotel, not one mile from your lover, your daughter, and your home. Apparently just visiting like any other tourist, forgetting your past, your life, your love. And perhaps worst of all to find you married and here with your son. Nothing could have been more cruel to those women, more terrible.'

Julian's face showed shock, dismay.

'I should never have come.' He breathed. 'I never knew, had no idea...my god what must they think of me.'

'Poor Sandar,' said Charlie shaking his head, 'what a terrible shock for her. What on earth can we do now? She must have told her mother.'

'Not yet I think.' Said Jianyu. 'Myitsu is not well, a sort of depression she has suffered from for some time now. We thought it better not to tell her for the moment.'

'Then I'll have to go and explain...tell her I didn't know...try and make her understand.' Said Julian.

'But my friend we must tread softly here. As I told you Myitsu is unwell, this will all come as a great shock to her, the end of her dreams, the thing that has kept her alive for twenty years as she brought up your daughter and survived here all alone. I tried in the beginning to dissuade her, to show her gently how impossible it was that you could return. But she clung to it with unshakeable faith, wonderful but terrible. And now you come, married to another woman and accompanied by your son.'

'What's to do then? I wish now I had never come here...what a mess it's made of things. Should we just disappear before she finds out? Let her keep her dream? But Sandar knows, and eventually she will tell her mother. The genie is out of the bottle now.' Julian was staring into space, his face strained, suddenly aged.

'But I can't ignore that I've just found I've a half sister as well as a step mum,' added Charlie, 'we can't just turn our backs and walk away.'

Charlie's thoughts strayed often to the girl. He could hardly believe that he had met her only the day before, and briefly at that. She now seemed to intrude on his thoughts constantly and he wanted desperately to see her again, to explain, and to comfort her in her obvious distress.

'It's too late to do anything today.' Said Julian, sounding tired. 'I suggest we sleep on it and get together tomorrow. Jianyu, do you think you could persuade Sandar to come and see us, we can start with her and see what she thinks about telling her mother.'

Jianyu nodded. 'I am sure she will come, I will tell her enough to excite her curiosity. Shall we say towards the end of the afternoon? Perhaps it will be less hot by then, I feel a change in the air.'

After Jianyu had left accompanied by a solicitous Mr. Patel, Julian and Charlie sat in an uncomfortable silence, broken after several minutes by Julian, speaking quietly, almost as if to himself.

'It's my mess Charlie, it's up to me to sort it. I realise now it was a mistake coming here.'

'Dad, you had to find out, try at least. Don't you remember how you felt...not knowing anything?'

'I've felt other things you know Charlie since we arrived here. I've not remembered anything, but I've felt something, well, two things actually. One is good, a feeling of happiness, like finding Jianyu, finding that I had a friend, hearing I had a daughter, and even this Myitsu. I must have loved her once Charlie, believe me please, I'd never have fathered a child on a woman I didn't care for...'

'I know that Dad.'

'But there's something bad here too. Something that makes me afraid. And it makes me question if I really want to find out more and remember maybe things that are best left alone and forgotten...'

'Like what they, the Japs, did to you. Dad, I understand, it's been locked away for a reason, and we can only guess what happened. But surely now you need the full truth, the good and the bad.'

'If it was just a matter of listening to people telling me about my past it would be fine...but what if my memory does come back, everything...like the doctor said it could. If I remember things I've shut away because they are too terrible, too unsupportable to recall. It might be like living them over again, and perhaps never being able to put them away for the rest of my life. Charlie, I'm not a very brave man, I'm just scared, you understand.'

Charlie was moved to reach out to his stepfather and take his hand.

'Not true Dad, that's rubbish.'

Julian smiled at him and squeezed the hand holding his.

'But it's like I said Charlie, it's only me who can sort this out. And the best thing is for me to go and see this Myitsu tomorrow, try to explain how things are, and then we take our leave. You can always write to Sandar if you want to stay in touch. I feel it would be more appropriate that I don't keep any contact...I'm thinking about your mother Charlie, how she'd feel.' It was the

first time they had mentioned her since their arrival in
Burma.

Chapter Thirty Nine

A claustrophobic blanket of low dark grey cloud hung over the town and the valley the next day. Dawn had come late as the sun failed to appear but the heat was unabated, seeming even more unbearable in the heavy gloom. The people moved lethargically about their routine tasks, opening shops, preparing the market, looking up warily at the motionless sky. Weeks without rain had almost dried up the lake in the centre of the town, leaving only a small pool of stagnant green water that even the dogs wouldn't touch.

Sandar arrived at the hotel that morning and found the two men waiting for her at the table where they had sat before. They both stood up to greet her formally but her expression of cold disdain discouraged any attempt to shake hands, and she ignored Charlie's invitation to sit down.

'Jianyu asked me to come, he said it was important, otherwise I didn't want to see you again.' She announced, her face expressionless, as if making an effort to hide feelings too deep and disturbing to show.

Julian leaned against the table, half sitting.

'I know Sandar, I'm glad you came, and I understand how you must feel...' Replied Julian.

'Oh those are easy words to say, and do you expect me to believe...believe that you are glad to see me when you have ignored us for twenty years or more...that you can imagine how I feel...how my mother would feel if she knew your false heart, that you had fooled her into believing your promises. Ah! You must have laughed at her, the simple Burmese country girl you seduced and abandoned. She has told me...told me of her love, her happiness when you were with her, and she believed. Believed because her heart was pure and could not comprehend your mind, so different from hers.'

'Sandar that's not true, I would never treat a woman in that way...'

'But you did, didn't you!' Sandar cried out, her strange, beautiful eyes filling with tears, 'you deserted her, and the child you had made with her. I grew up without a real father, just with stories, memories, promises... and now I see they were all false. Nothing is left for me, and if my mother learns of you it will kill her.'

'But Sandar, there's things you don't know.' Interrupted Charlie, seeing his father was quite unable to reply to her accusations. 'There is a reason why we are here now, why my father couldn't come before, why you never heard from him.'

'A reason! I know the reason...he forgot. He just forgot his little adventure in the colonies, the little girl he had there.'

'Yes Sandar!' Julian almost shouted, 'I forgot, I forgot everything. Your mother, Mogok, Burma, my past...everything. It all went.'

Sandar was very still for a moment, sensing something outside her knowledge of the situation, staring at her father, accusing, questioning.

'What...what does this mean? How can a man forget such things?'

'Sandar, I cannot tell everything because it is lost to me. But I only know that I was a prisoner of the Japanese for several years, and though I don't remember I must have been badly treated...'

'He was tortured Sandar.' Interrupted Charlie. 'Very badly.'

'All I can remember is from when I was liberated at the end of the war. Everything before that has gone. Absolutely everything. I'd even forgotten my name.'

Sandar swayed, her eyes still fixed on her father, and sat down suddenly on the concrete bench.

'So you understand Sandar, I couldn't come back before, I didn't know about...' he waved his hands vaguely towards the street, the town, the grey and gloomy valley, 'about this, you, your mother, everything.'

'Then how, and why are you here now?' Sandar said in a quiet voice, 'What do you want here?'

'Charlie did it.' Said Julian, 'He found the picture, and managed to trace the location.'

'And the Reverend Sprout filled in a few more details,' said Charlie, 'and told me about your mother.'

Sandar looked from Julian to Charlie. 'But you have a wife now, Charlie's mother, she is in England? You will go back to her?'

Julian sat down, close to the girl, who turned away from him.

'Sandar, I'm so sad it's worked out like this, but please try to understand I knew nothing about your mother and you. It had gone, completely. Back in England I fell in love with the woman who looked after me, and she's been good to me, a good wife, and she doesn't deserve to be abandoned...not now...not after all this time. When I decided to come here to look for my past I thought it would be just finding out things, listening to people's memories, like reading a book. I didn't know what waited for me here, all these feelings...it's like another world I've fallen into, strange, alien, and sometimes menacing.'

'You think I am strange...alien?' She turned sharply towards him. 'Your daughter! Your wife! Is that what we are to you, aliens?'

She made as if to stand up but Julian quickly put a hand on her shoulder to restrain her.

'No...Of course not, not you...the situation.'

As if the touch of his hand had triggered some-thing inside her, broken a barrier Sandar covered her face with her hands, her shoulders shaking, weeping silently.

Charlie moved towards her, moved by her emo-tion, and placed his hand gently on her other shoulder. After a moment, as if of its own volition her head in-clined until her cheek rested upon his hand.

'Sandar, please, don't think badly about us. We never wanted to hurt anyone. Dad's a good man...really...kind and totally honest. We'll try to put things right.'

Sandar was lost in a whirlpool of conflicting emo-tions. Her previous hatred of the two Englishmen fought with the unexpected and unknown feeling of warmth she suddenly felt. This was her brother's hand against her cheek, a brother she had never suspected existed. And that was her father's hand, strangely comforting, on her slim shoulder. She felt now the loneliness, the isolation of their existence in the big house in the jungle, living for a dream that had now come true but in a way that made their lives meaningless.

The young woman believed implicitly in fate. This was what was meant to be, what was written in the book of her life. There was no point in fighting against it. These two men had appeared to play their parts at their ordained time and place, they had overturned the exist-ing order of things, rearranged her life, her thoughts, her emotions.

Under the feelings of loss and the realisation of her father's life with and love for a woman not her mother, lay a feeling of warmth. Something strange for her, a feeling of attachment, the need to join her life to theirs, to belong, even to love.

Already she felt a growing concern for this man her father, his obvious physical weakness and fragility, his gentle compassion. She looked up through her tears at him and in the blurred outline of his face she saw herself. His eyes looked into her soul and she opened her heart to him, for she felt suddenly what it meant to have a father.

Then Charlie was offering her a white handkerchief to wipe away her tears and she turned to smile at him, her brother.

'Sandar, I must go to see your mother. I have to explain face to face. And then I think we must leave, Mogok, Burma, all this. It's for the best.' Said Julian. 'Charlie, we have to see that policeman at eleven. It'll be too hot after that to go and see Myitsu, we'll have to leave it until it cools down a bit. Sandar, can you come and show us the way there, but I'd like to see your mother alone first and without your telling her anything about us.'

'Dad, if we're leaving tomorrow maybe we don't need to see the police, or maybe I can go alone, I don't see any point in dragging you there in this heat.'

Zeya was annoyed when he saw that the young Englishman had come alone, arriving at his office just before the appointed time. The father had not looked so ill yesterday as to prevent his attendance, but Zeya pretended that it was of little consequence, a minor detail in his supposedly busy schedule. He motioned Charlie to sit opposite him and pretended to be busy shuffling some papers around on his desk before looking up at the young man.

'Did you bring the documents I asked for yesterday?' He began sternly, fixing Charlie with what he hoped was an intimidating glare. 'Your presence here is very irregular you understand. Wandering tourists are not welcome in Myanmar as you must know...the security situation makes it too dangerous for them.'

'We are aware of that,' said Charlie, 'and we've decided to leave tomorrow, on the bus to Mandalay. We're sorry if we have caused any problems.'

For a moment Zeya was lost. They were leaving, without as far as he could see having done anything or seen anything. It seemed strangely pointless. To give himself time he began to shuffle his papers as if looking for something important.

'I see.' He murmured after a long pause, picking up a sheet of paper and pretending to scrutinise it closely. Then, deciding on a different approach he smiled at Charlie.

'Well, I hope your visit here was satisfactory however brief. Perhaps you will return someday, under more regular conditions of course, foreigners are always welcome in Myanmar, even ex-colonisers.' He smiled even more broadly, anxious to show a more friendly aspect.

'I doubt we'll be coming back,' said Charlie, 'Our business is finished here, or will be today.'

The word 'business' caused a minor shock to Zeya. What possible business could there be for foreigners in Mogok apart from the old mine he wondered? The answer was obvious, there was none. He desperately wanted to ask, to find out, but obviously they would never tell him. They had come here in secret, without government knowledge or permission, it could only be to do with the mine he reasoned.

Not knowing quite how to continue he asked, 'did your visit satisfy your curiosity, I'm afraid it's a dull town, not much of interest you must have discovered.'?

'On the contrary,' Charlie continued, 'It's been an amazing experience. We came to find out something, and that's what we have done. Not quite the way we imagined, and not all that we hoped for, but enough to make our visit quite memorable.'

'Find out?' Zeya said, his voice betraying his shock. 'May I ask what you found in this poor forgotten town?'

'Oh, nothing of interest to anyone else,' Charlie replied, 'Just personal things, from long ago.'

Zeya could think of no way of continuing his questioning without arousing suspicion in the mind of the young man. He'd play dumb, try to find out more in his own way.'

'In that case I need not detain you any further. I will be at the bus stop tomorrow to ensure your safe departure. It will be an uncomfortably hot journey I fear, but then who knows, perhaps the monsoon will finally arrive. You may go now.' Zeya dismissed him without looking up from his desk, taking up another paper at random and beginning to scribble furiously on it with the blunt stub of a pencil. Charlie stood up and left without a word, glad to be free of the man's presence, feeling something vaguely threatening behind the official facade.

Back at the hotel Sandar had stayed with her father, anxious to spend as much time with him as possible. She was torn in two by her emotions, wanting on one hand to embrace and accept the new relationship, but on the other deeply afraid of the effect of his presence on her mother. She wanted to know so much, about his life before Burma, his own family, the events leading up to his disappearance, but of all this he could tell her nothing. It was both frustrating and disturbing. He told her what he could remember; the voyage back home, the time in the nursing home and meeting his wife, their life together.

'And Charlie?' She asked, 'When did you have Charlie?'

Julian looked at her with surprise. She hadn't realised, of course, Charlie had never referred to him as stepfather, so she'd assumed he was his parent.

'Sandar, Charlie is not my son, I mean by blood. He's my stepson. My wife was married before, her husband killed early on in the war, Charlie was his son. Of course it doesn't make any difference in practice, I'm the only Dad he's known, just as he's a real son to me. But he was two years old or more when I met his mother.'

The implications took more than a few moments to sink in for Sandar. She had liked Charlie from the beginning, and felt a growing affection for him that she had put down to sibling feelings. But now, those feelings took on another dimension, strange and exciting, something quite outside her experience.

'So Charlie is not blood brother to me.' She said, feeling slightly embarrassed, 'Not like real brother.'

'I'm sure he would love to be your real brother.' Said Julian, 'You can still keep in contact with him, write to him, it's what he'd like.'

They were in Julian's room, having been driven indoors by the mounting heat, although there seemed to be little difference between the outside and the inside. Julian had asked for and eventually been provided with an ancient electric fan that he had installed on the window in an attempt to stir the air. The thing had managed to turn slowly at first, but then gave up all movement and merely vibrated gently giving off a smell of burning rubber. Julian had quickly turned it off.

The father and daughter were unaware that Aarav stood the other side of the door to the room, his ear pressed against it, trying to make what he could of the conversation within.

'What will you say to my mother?'

Julian made vague gestures with both hands, shrugging his shoulders.

'The truth I suppose, what else can I tell her. She must be an extraordinary woman, quite extraordinary.'

'She will be...I don't know how to say it...but I fear it will destroy her.' Sandar said gently.

'I hope not Sandar, I wouldn't want to hurt her...and I just wish now I hadn't come here, stirring up the past, opening old wounds.'

'But I think I understand now father...may I call you father?'

'I hoped you would Sandar, very much.'

'I understand your need to find out.'

Julian reached out and took the girl's hand in his.

'I came looking for something, something that was lost all those years ago when the Japanese came. Something very precious to me, in fact something everyone finds precious.'

'And now, you have found at least something, is it precious to you father?'

'You...your mother...my friend Jianyu...of course it is precious. But it's another world, a world I cannot live in and can't remember.'

'Perhaps you could try?'

'I hoped Sandar, I hoped that when I came here it would come back to me, my previous life. But there's nothing...I feel a complete stranger here. And now I think I can accept that, and return home to the only life I have, the one I know.'

'I wish you could stay...but I know it's impossible. You can't abandon Charlie's mother. But I hope you don't forget us here.'

'I will take what I can back with me, the memory of you all, your image, my daughter that I never knew.'

Suddenly there were tears in his eyes and he embraced Sandar, pulling her close to him, kissing her forehead. Slowly she returned his embrace, her arms around him, a man she had not known until two days ago who was now her father. The man she had thought never to encounter.

Chapter Forty

Aarav arrived back at the police station just as Charlie was leaving, brushing past him with a suspicious glance as he entered the office.

'I told you to stay and watch,' Zeya snarled at him, 'what are you doing back here?' Aarav gathered himself, sweating and out of breath from the brisk walk from the hotel. He had information that his superior knew nothing about, the secret of the Englishmen's visit to the town, and he relished the feeing of superiority it gave him. He sat on the edge of the desk much to Zeya's annoyance, and whipped the sweat from his face.

'I heard them talking...just now.'

Zeya sat back in his chair and stared at his deputy.

'And?'

'I found out why they're here.'

Zeya experienced a feeling of sick hatred for the man, wondering if he had really discovered what he himself had been unable to find out.

'Oh! And why is that...they're leaving tomorrow you know. I've arranged it.'

Aarav retrieved a matchstick from his pocket and began picking at his teeth with it.

'I listened at the old man's door, while he was talking to that girl. Heard it all.'

Zeya sighed, aware of the man's limited knowledge of English. He was probably making something up, trying to impress, or maybe simply bored with waiting around at the hotel.

'Well? What did you hear? What did they talk about?'

Aarav looked around, as if afraid to be overheard, and lent over the desk towards his boss.

'The old man said they came here looking for something precious...his very words...something precious. I know what that means.'

Zeya raised his eyebrows, startled in spite of his skepticism. Aarav nodded enthusiastically.

'Yes...that's what he told her...and then he said something like it was lost when the Japanese came.' And he stared at Zeya, a triumphant smile on his face.

Zeya swallowed nervously, if this was true it could change everything.

'Is that it?' He managed to say without seeming too impressed.

'Not quite...I couldn't make out exactly what he said next but I definitely heard him say he'd take back what he could with him...back to Europe I guess.'

He stood up, folding his arms and looking complacently at Zeya.

'What about that? You know what they're talking about don't you?'

Zeya said nothing, shocked by the revelations, unwilling to share with his deputy the obvious conclusion they had both come to.

'Can't you guess?' He goaded Zeya. 'It's obvious isn't it. The stories are true...about the rubies that were hidden from the Japs. They've heard about them somehow, and come to find them. And it looks like they have. And now you say they're off home tomorrow. What are you going to do about it?'

Zeya, unable to sit still, stood up and began to pace the room.

'I don't see how.'

'How what?'

'How they'd know about the rubies, even if the stories were true. It's a lifetime ago now, why would they wait over twenty years to come and get them?'

'I don't know...but I know what I heard... why don't you arrest them on suspicion. Make them talk. It's illegal for foreigners to have rubies mined here. Life in prison might make them think about it. Or they could just disappear.'

Zeya's mind had been following the same ideas. But to have them arrested and then sent down to Mandalay would involve the authorities there, and even the British Consul, there would be nothing in it for him but extra paper work. Making them disappear was a real alternative, he remembered the American journalist who had talked to some dissidents a couple of years ago, the government had claimed to know nothing of his whereabouts or fate when he disappeared, but Zeya knew he'd been taken by the secret police up north to a place far from Rangoon or Mandalay, interrogated for a few weeks, then shot. The man in charge of the disappearance, an old colleague of Zeya had been congratulated by his superiors on his action and discretion. Nobody cared if foreign governments protested, Myanmar was now a country without friends. It was a country ruled by a military clique supported by a vast secret police force. Nobody talked politics, nobody complained, and nobody spoke to foreigners about the situation.

Zeya was too nervous to sit idle now, pacing the floor under the skeptical stare of Aarav.

'Get back to the hotel...no...stay here, I'd better go. I'll have to find out what's going on before they disappear. If Mandalay call don't tell them anything...at least don't say anything about what you heard...just say I'm organising their return tomorrow by bus, they can pick them up at the bus station.'

He seized his cap from the desk, jammed it firmly on his sweating head, and set out for the hotel, determined to verify the truth of his deputy's statements. He half believed it could only be a mistake, the man's grasp of spoken English was limited, and his written English non-existent. It would turn out to be a stupid misunderstanding he thought.

He arrived at the hotel panting with heat and drenched in sweat to find the man Charlie with Sandar waiting in the reception for Julian. They looked curiously at Zeya, his usual cool and composed appearance replaced by a strange and perspiring agitation.

'Did you forget something?' Queried Charlie after a moments silence, 'Forget to ask me something?'

Zeya produced a stained rag from his pocket and mopped his face.

'I decided I must interview your father after all. I've come here to advise him...'

'Then you are in luck inspector.' Julian spoke from the top of the stairs. 'We were just about to go out. What is this advice that would seem to be so urgent?'

Zeya looked up at the figure coming slowly down the stairs. For a moment he was simply confused, not able to process what he was seeing, then refusing to accept what was plain. The light was not good, the single bulb glowing faintly over the stairs unable to relieve the gloom of the room, but Zeya was in no doubt that the man coming towards him was the engineer from the mine, Myitsu's lover and Sandar's father. Older, frailer, marked and lined, but unquestionably the same man. A man returned from the dead. Then he remembered the name, the name he'd seen on the hotel register but failed to recognise. Julian Drake reached the bottom of the stairs and held out a hand to him.

No words came to Zeya as he automatically took the hand, dry and cool, and shook it briefly.

'You look hot inspector, I hope it's worth your coming here whatever I can tell you.'

The spectre from the past pretended not to recognise him Zeya thought, pretended not to know the man who had worked for him and alongside him for two years. Jock's assistant, the man who knew everything about the mine, and perhaps the man who had knowledge of the missing rubies. Zeya's mind reeled, trying to grasp the implications. The whole situation seemed impossible, bizarre, inexplicable.

He played for time by wiping his face vigorously with the rag, avoiding eye contact with the Englishman who stood waiting patiently in front of him, a slightly amused expression on his face.

They haven't changed thought Zeya, still the same arrogance and sense of superiority, half hidden under a false smile, and he remembered suddenly how he had hated working for them, a hatred forgotten in the passing years but lying dormant, and now awoken.

'I omitted to inform your son of something when I interviewed him this morning.' He said, resisting the urge to blurt out his knowledge of the man's identity. Julian inclined his head, still smiling.

'Something that might prevent unforeseen trouble for you and your friends.'

'Oh! That does sound a bit ominous, what possible trouble could we have?' Said Julian.

'I omitted to inform you of the very severe penalties we have in Myanmar for trading in precious stones. Foreigners and even ordinary citizens are not permitted to buy, sell, or trade in any way with them.'

Julian and Charlie stared uncomprehending at the man.

'Err, not sure we quite understand why you should think we might want to trade precious gems inspector.' Said Julian quietly. 'They're of no interest to us. None at all.'

Zeya was again left without an immediate response to the Englishman's admission. It had been made without hesitation or embarrassment, almost as if it had been true. Zeya felt his lips curling into a half smile.

'I hope so Mr. Drake, it would be most unfortunate if I was obliged to arrest you and your friends on such a short visit, you have hardly had time to look around I should imagine. Not that there is much to see here, but then you know that don't you sir, you know that very well.'

Then pushing his now soaking handkerchief back in his pocket he turned and left the room.

Charlie and Julian looked at each other, both thinking the same thought, the policeman had recognised him, somehow he must have known Julian from before the war.

'He used to work at the mine Mother told me.' Sandar said, 'Then he disappeared just before the japs invaded, came back after the war and independence as District Inspector. He used to bother us, always turning up uninvited asking questions, neither Mother or Jianyu like him, Jianyu even thinks he's dangerous.'

There was suddenly a stirring of the air, not a breeze and not a sound, but a change in pressure, very subtle, followed several moments later by a very faint and distant rumble. The air shook around them, and they hurried to the door and looked out over the town towards where the mountains would normally have been visible. There was a black curtain drawn across the valley, cutting off the view of the ranges to the south, and seeming to swallow the land behind.

'At last, the monsoon is coming.' Sandar said. 'If we are going to my home to see mother we should hurry, who knows when it will arrive here.'

In his hut in the forest Jianyu had also felt the strange movement of the air and heard the distant thunder. It reminded him, as it always did, of the sounds of the Japanese artillery as they approached Mogok. It was a sound he dreaded, conjuring up the half repressed memories of the huge and murderous battles he had experienced as a soldier of the Komitung.

That terrible day, the same day that his young English friend had driven away to try to escape through the mountains, Jianyu had taken most of his few possessions and hidden them in the jungle where no Japanese patrols would find them. He had made a cache of food and water some distance from the road, deciding to lie low for as long as was necessary. He had no fears of being able to survive indefinitely in the jungle, knowing every plant, fruit, and root, but he had no desire to meet the Japanese who had already exterminated millions of his countrymen in the cities of north and east China.

Now he stood outside his hut and stared blindly up towards the sky. This was not a normal monsoon he thought, never had it begun like this. The air seemed different, electric, and he could feel the hair on his head and arms prickling. He breathed deeply, smelling the usual scents of the jungle; the rich musty smell of rotting vegetation, flowers that bloomed just for one day, but also a new smell.

'There's rain nearby,' he murmured to himself, 'not far, it will soon come.'

Chapter Forty One

Myitsu had abandoned her bed, the heat and humidity too much for her to support staying inside the house. She stood on the veranda, a length of pale yellow silk wrapped around her body, waiting for Sandar's return from the town. Nothing moved in the overgrown garden below her, not a leaf flickered, not a grass stem swayed, the air was still and hot, heavy with moisture, waiting.

She had felt the movement of the air when she first came outside, and knew instinctively it signalled a change. Change was coming, she had felt it when she awoke in the morning and found the world cloaked in unnatural gloom, the sun extinguished, the air thick. She had gone to the spirit house by the gate and found the offerings of the night before untouched. She stood in the semi-darkness her head bowed, her hands together, and prayed. Around her she sensed the Nats of the forest, the spirits who had kept her safe and well since she had prostrated herself at the foot of the ban-yan tree the day Boy had been killed all those years ago. She sensed their eyes upon her, their presence close. They had come for some reason she could not guess, but she was not afraid.

She was leaning on a post of the veranda, one arm around it, very slim and almost invisible when she saw him. He had appeared suddenly, as if transported there from another dimension, another time, and was standing immobile by the broken gate, staring at the house. For a moment she was sure she was dreaming, so often had this very scene figured in her fantasies. Her fertile mind, so able to invent had pictured this daily for the last twenty years but now it was before her she could not grasp the reality, she smiled, simply happy to live within her dream for a moment. He was there, of course, had he not promised?

Julian stood looking up at his old home not seeing the woman in the shadows. At first he felt nothing, it was an old and rundown house in the jungle. The paint was peeling, the garden was a jungle, the windows were blank and dark. It looked as if nobody had lived there for many years. Was this the home of Myitsu, was it where *he* had lived and loved in the forgotten time? Could it be true that she still waited for him here? He took a step forward towards the house and heard her voice.

Through the unnatural mid afternoon semi-darkness she could clearly see and recognise him. As if he had never left he stood very still by the gate looking up at her, and her great joy forced the cry through her lips.

'Youlian.'

Startled he looked at where her pale figure stood by the post at the furthest end of the veranda. For a moment neither of them moved, and the sound of her voice was lost in the great silence that covered the darkening world. Then she was gone, flying across the veranda, through the dining room where the old furniture stood in silent witness to the new drama, and out from the front door, down the five steps to rush across the drive to where he stood, as still and cold as a statue.

She did not embrace him, throw herself into his arms, or cover the beloved face with kisses. At his feet she threw herself, as when he had left her, making obeisance, her hands impudently touching his feet, daring. And he heard her muffled voice.

'Darlin'...my darlin'...I wait for you. Now you come.'

Appalled and moved Julian reached down to lift her. Slipping his hands under her arms he drew her effortlessly to her feet and looked into the face of his one time lover, the mother of his child.

He saw a Burmese woman looking up at him, no longer young, her face painted exotically with tanaka paste, huge almond shaped brown eyes, a pouting sensual mouth, high cheekbones; the whole strange, alien, unknown. He felt her arms go round him, her body, so slight and frail pressing urgently against him, her hands small and soft stroking his hair, touching his face as if seeking assurance of its reality.

'Myitsu?' He said tentatively. 'Myitsu.'

She stretched up seeking his lips and he felt the softness of her mouth covering his. He could not respond.

'Your Myitsu.' She whispered as she pulled away a little, contemplating him with her head on one side.

'Am I much changed my darlin'? So old now, not girl anymore.'

'I am changed too.' He said simply. 'Older, but perhaps not wiser.'

'I knew you would come.' She said, as if not hearing him. 'I knew you would keep promise you made.'

'I'm glad I came Myitsu, but it's so long ago now, I don't remember...'

But there were voices inside his head now, voices he didn't know, indistinct and distant at first then becoming stronger, nearer. The voice of a boy calling him, a slight lisp, 'Papa...Papa...'. A man's rough voice, a broad Scottish accent, 'It's theft Julian, aye, and on a massive scale...'. A voice with an Indian accent, 'This car very old, sir. Very old indeed..'. And a multitude of other voices in languages he didn't know, calling, shouting, arguing, a tower of Babel, sound overlaying sound, until they ceased, and a single voice crept insidiously into his brain. A soft voice, syrup sweet, wheedling, questioning, 'I wish you would just tell me Julian, and then we can stop...'

He thought he cried out, and the voice stopped. He was sitting on the ground by the gate, the woman was kneeling next to him, her slim arms around him, whispering...

'It's all right now darlin', it's all right. You safe home now, safe with your Myitsu.'

For she had known instinctively with a woman's intuition that he bore a burden, that her man had returned to her damaged by something, someone. The years of waiting, the daily agony of not knowing, the doubts that had at times gnawed at the edges of her conviction, were forgotten in a wave of pity for the man.

She helped him to his feet and led him to the lodge, slowly climbing the five steps to the door with her arm around his waist and his hand gripping her shoulder. There he paused for a moment, peering into the gloom of the hallway as if fearing to enter. She took him by the hand and pulled him gently into the home he had left so long ago, the unremembered place.

Seated in the living room on the faded sofa brought from London by some servant of the Empire of Victoria she fussed about him. A glass of coolish lemonade was placed in his hand, the top buttons of his shirt unfastened, a damp cloth wiped gently his face.

'So hot Youlian, you not used to hot anymore. Must take care, not go out in afternoon. And no hat...where your hat darlin'?' Julian had always worn a pale straw trilby before, and she imagined it must still be with him, forgotten at the hotel perhaps.

Unable to process the magnitude of the event that had suddenly occurred she confined herself to the trivia she could understand. The questions, the many questions she was happy to leave for the moment. He was back, her man, her lover, the father of her daughter. It was all that mattered.

Julian stared around him, no longer even trying to remember. The sound of the last voice had shocked him deeply. He knew now there were things he could not bring back, things that were too terrible to expose to the bright and brittle light of consciousness. He shied away from the memory of that voice, knowing the horror it presaged for him, the forgotten time that must be left forgotten.

A great lethargy had come over him. He knew he had to talk, explain, excuse, but the strength was not there, neither moral nor physical. Although the woman was a stranger to him he was comforted by her attention, her familiarity that was almost maternal. There was no false modesty or shyness when she touched him, as if touching something of her own, something she possessed, and he found himself smiling up at her as she fussed around him.

The time would come, he told himself, later he would talk to her, for now he must rest, and suddenly he shivered, feeling a strange coldness in his limbs.

Charlie and Sandar had stayed with Jianyu in his hut leaving Julian to make his own way up to the lodge. He had insisted that they give him time alone with Myitsu. None of them could guess how she would react and they sat in silence on the floor wondering what was happening in the house at the end of the track.

The gloom had deepened during the course of the day, the sky lowering until the clouds touched the tops of the trees around the clearing. The first muted roll of thunder from far away caused them to look up at each other.

'It is coming.' Jianyu said simply. He stood up in the door of his hut feeling, scenting the air. 'There must be rain in the mountains already. Much rain I think.'

Sandar appeared beside him. 'It's not like before is it? Not like other years.'

Jianyu felt for her hand and took it in both of his.

'Daughter, it is like nothing I have known, a strangeness I do not like. We must be prepared.'

Sandar turned to look at him, a small but solid form next to her. A person she had known and loved all her life. A man she had called Father, but could no longer now that the other man had come.

'Prepare? What can we prepare Jianyu?'

'I do not know daughter, perhaps only ourselves.'

He turned away from the door and began to feel his way about the hut.

'But it might be prudent to raise what we can off the floor, much rain will fall.'

The three of them began to pile his few possessions on top of a teak writing table Myitsu had given to him many years ago as the sounds of thunder became louder and nearer, almost a continuous sound now, shaking the air, making the bamboo walls of the place tremble as I afraid of the coming storm.

Chapter Forty Two

In the mountains to the south and west of Mogok it was raining. Raining like no one had ever seen before. The hill tribe people cowered in their fragile lodges peering out at the deluge as their world dissolved into water. Many of their homes were unable to resist the weight of water running from their roofs and around their walls and collapsed, burying the   families within. Even on the slopes the water was soon ankle deep, pouring down towards the valleys and the many streams that became torrents. The stream that fed the swimming pool above the lodge began to rise, threatening to overflow the pool. A mile or more above the pool a huge and ancient Tamarind tree over hung the stream and as the water scoured its roots, it began to lean.

In the lodge, Myitsu had lit two candles in the room where Julian lay on the sofa before the windows that opened out onto the veranda. She sat next to him, holding his limp hand, her eyes never leaving his face. She tried to read into those lines his past, tried to guess what might have marked him so.

She had begun to feel something different about her man, a distance, almost a barrier. But she reasoned it must be shyness, he had always been a little shy with her when at first they had lived in this same house as master and servant. Now after all the years he must be shy again, it was normal in a man, but to regain him, to warm him and bring him into her circle of love would be a pleasant task. She remembered vividly all the things he liked in her. Every little compliment he had ever paid her, every gesture of love and desire were stored away in her memory like precious gems. She lent over him and kissed his still and empty face.

Julian had the impression of being at the confluence of two worlds, the world he remembered; England, Lydia, Charlie, a world familiar and simple, and the unremembered world of mystery, passion, strangeness and terror. This room where he lay was the meeting place where the worlds collided, each lying claim to him. He thought he had chosen, that he could reject one world and immerse himself in the other...returning to England, his wife, the life that was left to him. But now he was unsure. This new woman had accepted him, and although he remembered nothing of her he felt something, a subconscious attraction, a warmth, the faint stirrings of desire for a connection.

But not just the woman, the place too was calling to him. He wanted to know again what he had once known and lost. The familiarity of this house, the language long forgotten, the friends he must have once enjoyed, and of course his youth and health. The siren song filled the air that fluttered with the distant thunder, could he leave it all behind again? Forget again?

The woman stood up suddenly as if remembering something and went over to a cupboard in a corner of the room. She reached inside and withdrew something. Julian watched as she returned to him, kneeling before him and presenting him.

'Look Youlian, darlin', look. I keep safe for you.' And she handed him a violin, its wood and veneer bright and polished. 'Look after for you...no one ever play since you.'

Julian took it in his hands, momentary baffled, then realising that once he must have known how to play.

Myitsu stared at him, an expectant smile.

Julian ran his hands over the instrument, hoping to feel something, a familiarity perhaps, but there was nothing, just the touch of warm smooth wood, strength combined with fragility. Experimentally he put the instrument to his shoulder, his chin resting on the body. Myitsu nodded encouragingly and handed him the bow.

His fingers took up position on the strings and he laid the bow across them looking into her eyes, and as he looked her face changed.

He was looking not at a strange exotic woman, her face daubed weirdly with white patterns, but at a young girl, her features still soft and half defined, the skin smooth and unlined, her eyes bright with happiness and expectancy. A child awaiting a present.

'You remember Yulian, you remember how you play for me. Remember how I dance for you?'

Julian, the violin still silent at his shoulder, nodded slightly. He could not bring himself to say, to tell her it meant nothing to him. To destroy her dreams would be to destroy her. A girl, a woman who had lived with his image and memory filling every moment of her lonely life would not survive such a deception.

He laid down the violin.

'Maybe later darling.' The word and the lie came naturally to his lips.

'Yes, you tired...not like heat I remember. Later can play.'

Julian was tired, the short walk from the cross roads to the lodge in the forty degrees of heat had been his limit. But it was not just tiredness that he felt;   there was a tightness in his chest making breathing difficult. He knew he needed to lie down, rest a while. Perhaps he could sleep and when he awoke it would be to his old familiar world and not this baffling world of the un-remembered.

'Myitsu, I need to lie down and rest a while, do you mind?'

She frowned, suddenly concerned.

'Of course darlin', our room, same same like before, come, I help you.' And she slipped her arm through his and helped him to his feet.

The stairs took a long time, Julian leaning heavily on the slim woman who held him. Then they were in the room they had once shared. Hardly noticing his surroundings Julian collapsed onto their wide low bed, his face ghostly white, moist with sweat. His eyes closed and he slipped into unconsciousness, unaware of her undressing him, sponging his body with damp cloths, covering him with a light silk sheet.

Finally she sat next to him, holding his hand, her eyes fixed upon his face in adoration.

Clustered tightly under the shelter of a single waxed-paper umbrella, Charlie, Sandar, and Jianyu arrived at the lodge as the first heavy drops of warm rain began to fall. Sandar called out to her mother from the hall but received no reply. They looked briefly into the sitting room and the kitchen but found nobody.

'Where are they Sandar?' Charlie asked in a whisper, beginning to worry.

'Wait here, I'll look upstairs. They must be there.'

Silently Sandar mounted the stairs to the room where she guessed her mother and father would be. The door was closed, and after a moments hesitation Sandar tapped very lightly on it with her finger. At first she thought there would be no answer or reply, but then the door opened just a little. Her mother stood almost blocking entrance to the room.

'Mother, what's happening? Is the Englishman there?'

Her mother nodded, her expression dreamy, her eyes unfocused on her daughter but past her, into the distance.

'Has he told you mother? Told you who he is?'

Still gazing into a far away place Myitsu replied.

'I knew Daughter, of course I knew, when I first saw him by the gate, I knew he had come back to me.'

Sandar moved to look into the room, her mother making no effort to allow her access. She saw the shape of him on the bed, still, silent, covered by a thin sheet. She turned to her mother questioningly.

'Mother?'

'He is tired. Not used to the heat. It was always thus. He didn't even wear his hat.'

'He sleeps?' Sandar whispered.

'He must rest.' She said simply, and gently closed the door. Sandar remained staring at the dark wood surface of the door a few inches from her face and wondered.

Inside the room Myitsu regained her place on the bed, taking up the limp hand from where it lay, pressing it gently against her lips.

'Not go away my darlin', stay here safe with me. Soon be cooler, rain come, change...everythin' change now.'

Sandar returned downstairs to Charlie's questioning looks.

'He's there? With her?' He asked.

'He is resting.' She said simply. 'Give them time.'

'Has he told her, told her who he is? Why he's here?'

'She knows. She recognised him.'

'And?'

'Charlie, I don't know. I don't know what is happening.'

'Your father is very ill Charlie, it is best that he rests if Myitsu says so.' Said Jianyu. 'This heat and his condition are dangerous for his health.'

They moved into the dining room and sat at the polished mahogany table while Sandar disappeared into the kitchen to make tea while they waited.

Charlie stared around at the room lit by a couple of candles, the worn and neglected furniture, the handful of pictures on the walls...photographs turning from black and white to sepia with the passage of time, and on the table in front of him a violin and bow.

'Did he play do you know?' He asked Jianyu.

'He played well Charlie, very well. I could sometimes hear him from my home at night when all was quiet. The jungle itself seemed to be listening when he played. And Myitsu loved to hear him.

She was a dancer when they met you know, a very good traditional Burmese dancer, as beautiful as the dawn and admired everywhere she performed. But she was young, very young with little knowledge of the world, and she fell under the influence of that man Zeya, when he worked for the mine. He filled her head with his political nonsense, made her his follower and actually persuaded her to leave her work as a dancer and take employment with your father, so she might spy on him and find information concerning the mine and the rubies. Of course she never actually fulfilled his wishes, recognising immediately that your father was a good man, and she had no desire to trick or betray him. But I think more than that the two young people were immediately attracted to each other. Please don't think that your father didn't love Myitsu, Charlie, she was everything to him, he would have died to keep her safe.'

'And these rubies Jianyu, what's the story behind them?'

'Only my mother knows the whole story,' it was Sandar who spoke, entering with the tea service on a brass tray. 'And she doesn't like to talk about that time. Terrible things happened here.'

'I think you should tell Charlie, Sandar. He has a right to know.'

Sandar turned to look at Jianyu curiously. She was unaware of how much he knew about the treasure of the mine, he had never talked of it either to her or her mother. She was aware of the close relationship between the two but knew also of the danger inherent in any talk of hidden gems.

'Before the Japanese arrived, when it was obvious they would occupy the country, the mine stopped sending the rubies down to Mandalay as it was too dangerous. They kept them at the mine until the last moment, the last day. The boss of the mine wanted to stay, but told my father to take the gems and try to escape with them or hide them somewhere. The boss was killed, or died the same day, and my father had to try and escape. He left my mother here because anyone found in contact with the British was murdered.'

'And the rubies? What happened to them?' Asked Charlie. 'And what happened to my dad, does anyone know?'

Jianyu replied, 'we assumed he was captured and maybe killed by the Japanese, and never knew if he was alive or dead until you both arrived here. A month or so later I found the car he had used to try to escape a few miles up the road towards the mountains, burnt out and riddled with bullet holes. I didn't tell Myitsu.'

'A story out of a book!' Exclaimed Charlie, 'So what happened to the rubies?'

Sandar and Jianyu looked at each other, before Sandar spoke.

Some of them are here, my mother kept a small number to sell to live off, that's how we have survived all these years.'

'And the rest? What happened to the others?'

Sandar looked down, not meeting his eyes.

'Hidden.' She said simply, thinking it better not to reveal where the box with the rest was hidden.'

After a long pause Charlie spoke.

'Well, the rubies are not the problem now, we have to think of our parents.' It seemed strange to him to refer to them in that way, especially with the feelings he was experiencing towards Sandar.

He watched as she poured the tea for them, her face illuminated on one side by the faint light from the window, and the other by the yellow glow of the lamp she had placed upon the table, and thought he had never seen such perfection of features. Now he had grown used to the strange patterns of Thanaka on her skin, her different mode of dress, the straight long lustrous hair that fell almost to her slim waist, her character of fierce independence, he found himself fascinated by her. He studied her when she was unaware, drinking in the smoothness of her skin, the arch of her thin eyebrows, the rich promise of her generous mouth with small and very white teeth. Her every movement was with a languid grace, unhurried as if choreographed. Her body moved sinuously, sensually under the thin silk of her longi, the form disguised but subtly suggested. Charlie wondered what her mother looked like. If she had been half as beautiful as Sandar it was not surprising his father had fallen for her.

She looked up and caught him watching her. For a moment she held his gaze, her cool grey-green eyes locked on him, watching, calculating, perhaps wondering. It was Charlie who in the end looked away, feeling his face reddening.

Outside the sounds of the rain redoubled and they all looked towards the window. It was not like rain that fell, more like a huge waterfall that covered the land. Nothing was visible beyond a few yards from the house, only the faint hint of the gates now flanking a small river that ran between them and disappearing into the grey-black curtain that had fallen around the lodge. Beyond the thunder and the roar of rain were the many sounds of water running off the roof, down ancient drainpipes, cascading from sagging gutters.

Sandar disappeared into the kitchen, returning a moment later with a small wooden box inscribed and decorated with Chinese symbols and pictograms. She placed it on the middle of the table and sat down.

Charlie stared at it, the looked up at her.

'What is it?'

Sandar smiled towards Jianyu who was also smiling.

'An old saltcellar. I gave it to Myitsu many years ago, she did not have one.' Said Jianyu.

Charlie reached across and opened the lid. Inside there was indeed coarse salt, nearly filling the box.

Then Sandar reached over, took it from him and inverted it over the table. The salt spilled out making a small pile of white crystals. She deftly spread the pile, exposing darker lumps amongst the salt. She picked one out and gave it to Charlie, a ruby, as big as a pigeon's egg, dusted with salt, glowing red through the white. He wiped it with his fingers and held it up to the lamplight.

'My god! It must be worth a fortune.' He said, 'And how many are there in here?'

'Not many, not compared with the strong box. This was meant just for us to live on, there are some bigger than that one and a lot much smaller.'

A brilliant flash of lightning that seemed to ground in the garden just outside the window with a crash that shook the house made them blind and deaf for a moment, neither hearing nor seeing the man who had appeared in the doorway.

It was Sandar who first noticed him, and she half rose, her hand reaching out towards the gems on the table as in a futile gesture to cover them.

Charlie turned, seeing her eyes fixed on something behind him and saw the Police chief standing in the doorway. His hair was plastered to his scull, water ran from his drenched clothes making small pools at his feet, and he held a gun in his hand pointing directly at Sandar. Behind him, just visible in the gloom was his deputy.

Chapter Forty Three

'I see my warning was not listened to, or perhaps not understood.' He spoke in English, his eyes fixed on the gems spread out on the table, although addressing Charlie. 'Aarav, step forward, I want you to witness what we have here.' His deputy sidled into the room, a rifle tucked under his arm and went over to the table. He reached out and picked up a large ruby, and holding it close to the lamp peered closely at it.

'Rubies!' He exclaimed in an awed voice, 'Many, many of them.'

'Where did you obtain these stones?' Asked Zeya, stepping closer to the table, his gun still trained upon Sandar.

'They are my mother's. They belong to her, given to her by my father many years ago.'

'Oh! How romantic he must have been.' Zeya said, 'and how generous. How very generous. But then it is easy to be generous with something that is not your own, something stolen.'

'My father did not steal them, he was given them to look after.'

'Of course, I understand that. And now he has returned to claim them.'

Sandar shook her head in denial as Charlie spoke.

'That's rubbish. We don't know anything about rubies, and it's certainly not what we came here for.'

Zeya reached out and gently stirred the salt and rubies spread out on the table with the barrel of the gun.

'I cannot believe you Mr. Drake,' he said quietly, 'why else would you both be here? I know exactly who your father is, he might pretend not to know me but I know him very well. I know that he stole these rubies from the mine when the Japanese came.'

'You don't know anything about...about what happened at that time...'

'I know enough Mr. Drake, enough to put all of you in prison. The rubies are here, in front of my eyes. You are here without permission or papers, hoping to secretly smuggle them out of the country. No further proof is needed.'

Jianyu, who had neither spoken nor moved since Zeya had appeared, raised a hand as if in protest.

'Zeya, you are mistaken in this matter, there are things of which you know nothing, they are not here for the rubies.'

Zeya didn't reply, instead turning towards Sandar.

'And where are the rest?'

In the room upstairs Julian stirred and opened his eyes. Myitsu's face hovered over him, all he could see. He was aware of the sounds of the storm, the rain on the roof, water running everywhere, the almost continuous rumble of thunder, and her voice, speaking to him, but in words he could not understand. He tried to sit up, but found himself too weak and fell back upon the pillow.

'Rest my darlin', just rest. I look after you now. Stay here and rest, this your home again.'

'Home?' He felt the confusion coming over him again, 'Home? This is my home?' He stared around at the room, dark, indistinct, but lit from time to time by the flicker of lightning.

'This is your home, darlin', I keep for you, wait for you, like you tell me.'

'I told you? What...what did I tell you?'

She recoiled a fraction away from him, studying his face, her head on one side.

'You forget Yulian? No, not forget I think...you say me that you come back, come home, Myitsu must wait. You make promise...remember now?'

Julian remembered nothing, but under the intense gaze of those eyes that seemed to reach deep into his soul he nodded silently.

'Yes, Youlian remember now. Now you come back to me you never leave Myitsu alone again. Very hard for Myitsu to wait long time, no news. Sometime I think I die before you come back, but cannot, cannot die without you.'

Julian was moved to take her hand, bring it to his lips. Myitsu fell forward onto his chest, pressing her face to his body, kissing his exposed skin, overcome with emotion.

Her heart was full, replete with a happiness she had never felt before or could not remember. Relief, that the years of waiting had ended, joy in the presence of her man, anticipation of his staying at her side for the future that now stretched before them both, united, never to be apart again.

He felt the weight of her slight body upon his and automatically his arms went around her, holding her, unable to deny anything. It wasn't her fault, she had kept the faith, kept her promise to wait for him, yet he had defaulted, unconsciously, but totally. He had not returned to her after the war, he had married another woman and made his life on the other side of the world, a complete betrayal. And he wondered how he could ever make amends.

'You not leave Myitsu again my Youlian? You never leave me alone again please?' Her voice was soft, hardly audible above the sounds of the storm, the voice of a child.

He felt he was standing on the edge of a precipice, a great chasm before him, and although he re-

membered nothing he could feel something of that forgotten time, an innocence, a passion, something very
precious, a jewel of untold value.

'I promise darling. I promise I'll never leave.' And
he stepped willingly into the void.

Chapter Forty Four

Sandar stared stubbornly at Zeya as he repeated the question.

'Where are the others hidden Sandar? This is but a fraction of what was stolen.' She remained silent.

'Well, as you don't seem to know, or are not willing to divulge I should perhaps ask your mother, and maybe your English father, the jewel thief, if they could help with my enquiries. Where are they now?'

'Upstairs, he's not well, he's resting. My mother is looking after him.'

'Shall I get them?' Asked Aarav

Zeya said nothing for a moment, but looked out of the window to where the dark afternoon was drawing into an even darker evening.

'He's not well you say. I understand that, he's not young either. Fragile health...this I understand. What I don't understand is why you would put him in a prison here, where as you might be aware, conditions are exceptionally difficult. To be honest I don't think your father would survive more than a couple of days in such a place, even young and healthy people often don't live more than a few weeks. And Sandar, as a young and attractive woman I think you might find it particularly unpleasant, the warders in those places are simple brutes, recruited from the worst elements of society. It really is in your own interest as well as that of all of you here to cooperate with me, the authority, to recover these assets. Assets that are legally the property of the Myanmar Government and people.'

It was Jianyu who spoke after a long silence.

'What is it you want Zeya, what deal do you want to make. What does Sandar and her family get in exchange for the rubies?'

Zeya turned towards the blind man whose eyes seemed fixed on some point in the far distance, his face expressionless.

'In consideration of my long friendship with Myitsu I am prepared to make concessions in this matter. If the rubies are recovered, all of them, not just that miserable collection on the table there, I will give free passage out of the country to Mr. Drake and his son. They will leave as soon as practical, not by Mandalay, but by the crossing to China at Chinshwe, doubtless Chairman Mao will repatriate them eventually. They will speak to no one in Myanmar or outside once they have left. Should they talk about this, even in the far future, you three will be imprisoned.'

'But my father can't possibly travel.' Sandar spoke, 'The journey to Chinshwe will be too much for him, he's very weak.'

'That's a chance you'll have to take.' Said Zeya dismissively, 'It's a better chance than prison I believe.'

'And do you honestly think we believe you'll hand the rubies over once we're gone?' Exploded Charlie, shocked at what he could see as a means for Zeya to obtain a fortune in gems. The deputy would obviously be paid off with a share, or perhaps eliminated.

'That, Mr. Drake, is no concern of yours. Myanmar will no longer be your business once you pass the frontier.'

Jianyu turned to Sandar who was still standing irresolutely by the table.

'Daughter, you must speak to your mother, only she can decide what is to be done. A decision must be made, a hard decision, but it is for her to make it, her alone.'

Jianyu was well aware of what he had revealed. That he knew the existence of the gems, that they were hidden. But he realised that the gems were lost, their value to Myitsu and Sandar had disappeared except as a trade off for freedom. The Englishmen would have to leave, and perhaps it was for the best. What Julian had told Myitsu he had no idea, but it was now irrelevant, he would be leaving her behind once again, but at least they would be free.

Over the valley and the mountains the rain continued, its force unabated. The day was drawing to an unnatural end, the light dimming, diffuse, except where sudden and violent lightening caused brief glimpses of a changed landscape. The roads had long disappeared, becoming rivers of red and brown baring flotsam and jetsam, the lake in the middle of Mogok had filled and surpassed its original bed, overflowing into the lower parts of the town, drowning the miserable dwellings that huddled about its previous shore. The old mine workings had filled up and the wheelhouse now stood in several feet of water. And still the rain fell.

Sandar stood in the doorway of her mother's room, watching the two figures on the bed that had not moved since she entered the room. Her tentative knock had not been answered, and she had quietly opened the door reluctant to disturb the occupants.

Sandar dreaded what was to come. She had no idea how she could make the news of her father's forced departure any less of a shock to the woman who had waited so long for him. The very idea seemed unthinkable, obscene, intolerable.

She moved silently to stand over them. Her mother lay in Julian's arms, her head on his chest, one hand frozen in the act of caressing his face. All the years they had waited for him now seemed to have led to this, and she felt, knew, for the first time the love between her two parents. Before it had been just words, ideas, memories, but this was real, the moment they were reunited, made whole again. For she realised now that in all those years of waiting her mother had been incomplete, part of her missing, the man she had given herself to; her body, her mind, her hopes, her life. She reached down and gently shook her mothers shoulder.

Myitsu opened her eyes, instantly looking at the man beside her. Then she turned to Sandar.

'He sleeps.'

'He is tired, weak I think.'

'Tomorrow we must go to the temple to give thanks daughter. Have you attended to the Nats?'

'The storm is too bad, the Nats must wait.'

'Do not forget, they must be thanked too. What time is it? I feel it night, did I sleep so long?'

'Not night Mother, not yet, but the storm makes it dark.'

Myitsu sat up, careful not to wake Julian, attempting to arrange her hair with her hands.

'Strange. I feel a strangeness about. Not night you say?'

'Not yet four in the afternoon mother.'

'Fetch me my comb and brush Daughter, he must not see me like this.'

Sandar retrieved the items from the table by the window, and Myitsu went and sat in front of her dressing table.

'You knew him then?' She asked, handing them to her mother.

Myitsu began brushing her long black hair.

'Of course, I saw him by the gates, waiting. Perhaps afraid to enter. Perhaps he thought I would not know him.'

'Perhaps.'

'He's not changed. I'd know him anywhere...how could I forget?'

Sandar gently took the brush from her mother and standing behind her began to brush her hair.

'Mother, we must talk. There are things you must know.'

'What things daughter?'

The two women watched each other in the reflection of the mirror. Just behind them was the form of the man asleep on the bed.

'Zeya is here. With his deputy.'

'What does he want with us? I never trusted that man. Be careful of him.'

'He wants the rubies Mother, all of them. But there's something else too.'

It was nearly an hour later before Sandar returned downstairs. The four men were still seated around the table, Aarav had gathered up the rubies that were on the table and replaced them back in the box, without the salt this time.

'She has told me that you can take the rubies.' She said simply, her voice hardly audible above the roar of the rain. She stood very straight, her face expressionless, unnaturally pale, as if just escaped from some event too terrible to relate.

Zeya and Aarav looked up at her expectantly.

'And? Where are they?' Zeya demanded.

'Under the floor of the hut by the swimming pool in the forest, in a wooden strong-box.'

'All of them? Don't lie to me now, are all of the rubies there?'

'All, all are there, all the treasure of the mine.'

'The swimming pool? You know this place?' Interrupted Aarav.

'I went there once, somewhere up in the forest. Not far from here, next to the stream.' Said Zeya.

Both men looked at each other, then over to the window that showed outside the torrential rain, the deluge that had been falling over Mogok for the last few hours.

'The streams are flooding everywhere, there's already parts of the town underwater.' Said Zeya to no one in particular. 'Sandar, how much higher than the water level were they put?'

'I don't know, not much I think, quite close to the stream.'

Zeya stood up.

'Aarav, stay here, watch those two and the rubies. Sandar, you're going to take me there. There's no time to loose.'

'Now? In this...' And she waved towards the window, 'I don't know if I can find it like this.'

Charlie stood up to protest.

'You're crazy, you can't take her out in this...' But Zeya had seized Sandar by one arm and was pulling her towards the door.

'Leave her!' Charlie shouted as he lunged towards Zeya in an attempt to make him release her.

He neither felt nor heard the blow that Aarav delivered to the back of his head with the butt of his rifle, but slumped insensible to the floor. Sandar cried out, trying to pull away from the policeman, and managed to free herself for a moment, going down on her knees at Charlie's side, before he seized her once more, this time by her long hair and dragging her screaming and struggling out of the door and into the storm.

Jianyu had also stood up, his head turning right and left as he tried to understand what had happened. Both his hands were raised in the classic self-defence posture, the palms flat and at right angles to each other, his knees were bent and flexing like taught springs. Aarav stared him and moved warily a couple of paces away.

'Keep still old man, I can shoot you anytime I want. If you could see you would find my rifle pointed at your head, I could not miss.'

Jianyu relaxed, dropping his arms but remaining standing.

'The Englishman, is he unconscious or dead?' He said quietly, aware there was no sound from Charlie.

'Who cares? It's unimportant, if he's not dead now he soon will be.'

Jianyu looked down, trying to hear any sounds of breathing from the body on the floor, but heard nothing.

'Let me attend to him. Zeya would not want him dead, there would be repercussions.'

Aarav thought for a moment. He had no sure idea of Zeya's plans; perhaps he should make sure the Englishman was still alive when he returned.

'He's in front of you, you can check on him if you want.'

Jianyu went down on his knees and felt for the body. He gently examined his head, feeling for where the blood was oozing from, taking his pulse at the neck, listening to his breathing with his ear close to Charlie's mouth.

'Well?' Demanded Aarav, suddenly nervous that he might have killed the man.

Jianyu guessed that Charlie's injury as far as he could tell was not serious; in fact he thought he might be feigning unconsciousness.

'He's been badly hurt. He could die.'

'Who cares?' Said Aarav with more bravura than conviction, and retreated across the kitchen to stare morosely out into the storm.

Jianyu lent over Charlie, his mouth close to his ear, whispering.

'Charlie, they mean to kill us all, I know. I must get this man close, close enough to touch. Help me.'

A few moments later Charlie groaned loudly. Jianyu called over to the deputy.

'He's coming round. Quickly, help me, he must sit up.'

Aarav turned to them, staring suspiciously at the two men on the floor.

'Why? Let him lie if he's coming round.'

'He's bleeding from his head, we have to elevate him or he could die from blood loss.'

The deputy put down his rifle, leaning it against the wall, but withdrawing his revolver from its holster before he approached the two men. He knelt down next to them, the gun pointed at Jianyu.

'Put your arm under his shoulders, help me lift.'

Aarav did as asked with his left arm, still keeping the gun pointed at Jianyu. As if seeking support the Chinaman reached out casually feeling for the deputy's shoulder. The simple touch upon it told him all he needed to know, the position of the man's head and neck. He knew exactly where to strike.

The blow, delivered with Jianyu's full force to Aarav's neck paralysed the man instantly, severing the spinal cord, and smashing the third and fourth vertebra. However the final muscle spasm of the dying man fired the gun, throwing Jianyu backwards across the floor.

Chapter Forty Five

'Are you awake my darlin'? You have slept well, the storm will soon be past.'

Julian opened his eyes and the room swam before him. He wondered if he was drunk, if the drink the woman had given him earlier was alcoholic. It was not an unpleasant sensation, a little like being on a boat in a rough sea except he couldn't find the strength to stand or even sit up. Myitsu was standing at the end of the bed watching him.

'I'm awake. At least I think I am. Unless it's all a dream.'

'Then it is a dream for us both my Youlian.'

They stared at each other in silence.

'What's happening please? Is Charlie there? I should see him.'

'Charlie? There is no Charlie here my love.'

'No, my son, Charlie. He was with me, I remember.'

He tried again to lift himself up from the pillows without success. Myitsu watched without moving to help him, then when he was still again came and sat on the bed next to him.

'They've gone Youlian my love. All gone.'

She began to stroke his head, her hand soft, gentle.

'Gone? Gone where? Who's gone? My son?'

Myitsu stopped stroking him and looked toward the window and Julian noticed her eyes, strangely bright, the whites bloodshot.

'Sandar is there. She's gone to save us. Don't worry darlin', nothing bad will happen.'

'Save us? Save us from what?'

Julian felt again that reality was slipping away. Nothing made sense anymore. Charlie must be near, he'd never leave him alone, and there was something he had to tell the woman, something important, but he couldn't remember what it might be.

'I'm so tired Myitsu, why am I so tired?'

'The heat my love, you're not used to it. You didn't wear your hat either, the hat you always wear. But don't worry darlin', you can rest now. You are home with me, I can look after you.'

'I'm cold, my feet, I can't feel them...so cold. Where are my clothes?'

The woman took his hands in hers, rubbing and chaffing them.

At the touch he felt relief, there was nothing he needed to do after all, everything was going to be all right. A great feeling of happiness came over him.

'Thank you Myitsu. I feel better now. Happy.'

Myitsu brought both his hands to her mouth and kissed them.

'They wanted to take you away from me again you know.' She said quietly, very matter of fact. 'They would have made you disappear again, perhaps forever. But I stopped them, stopped them taking you. They can have the rubies, the rubies instead of you. Sandar is taking them to them now, we don't need them anymore. I kept them for you, all those years I kept them safe, and they brought you back in the end Youlian, back here to me, and your home.'

'Home? To my home?' Said Julian faintly.

'Yes...home. To home and to me.'

'I...I have to go I think...can't remember...'

'No my darlin', never. You never leave me again. Stay here happy with me...for ever.'

'For ever?' His voice a whisper as his eyes closed. Then he suddenly remembered, everything.

Slipping into the final darkness he remembered the first time he saw her as she danced on that night so long ago, Boy at his side laughing, the wail of the strange music, the smells of the market, the taste of spices on his tongue, the feeling of youth in his body with his life all before him, new, exciting, without end. And he heard her voice as a whisper in the night. 'Yes my darlin', for ever,' before a great silence fell upon his world.

Chapter Forty Six

Sandar had never walked though the forest in the monsoon rains before. The track from the end of the garden that was sparingly used in normal times was now almost totally obliterated. The branches and leafs of the plants hung low, heavy with water, the ground underneath her feet soft and slippery, here and there becoming the bed of a small stream. The light was almost gone as they walked through the grey twilight that hid everything further than a few feet behind a shifting veil of rain. She walked hunched up, trying to keep the rain from her eyes as she sought the signs of the trail.

Zeya walked a few steps behind her, his gun now holstered, watching the slim form of the girl as she moved slowly through the forest. The events of the past day seemed unreal to him. Suddenly it seemed that the uncountable wealth of the treasure of the mine, dreamt about for so long would be his. He tried without success to suspend his belief, afraid something might happen to snatch it away, but he knew now that fate had dealt him an unbeatable hand, he could almost feel the gems in his hands.

How many times in the past, working for the British boss, his owners and shareholders had he felt the terrible, intoxicating power of the stones. How bitter it had been to hold in his hand stones worth a king's ransom and later return to his miserable room alone, with just a bed and a table and a small plastic chair. How wrong it had felt, but how powerless he had been to change anything.

Now his heart beat fast, not just with the scramble through the rain soaked forest, but with the excitement of what was to come. Riches, power, acceptance by the people who had marginalised him. He could have anything, anything at all. But he would have to be careful; he would have to buy silence where necessary, he would have to eliminate everyone who knew anything about the events of this strange day.

But the girl, what could he do with her. In his novel state of euphoria he could imagine her accepting him, even wanting him. How could she resist the power he would have and could share? He would offer her a gift no woman could refuse, unlimited wealth, a house and home of her own, even a sort of respectability. He studied her as she moved before him, her drenched longi clung to her slim body, almost transparent and revealing every curve. She would be his he decided, soon. He would dispose of the others, leaving her alone, totally dependant upon him, and willing to show her gratitude for her salvation.

Drunk on dreams and desire he moved closer to her, his hand reaching out to touch what his eyes feasted upon, but she stopped suddenly. The swimming pool lay before them.

The level had risen, but not by too much. They could make out on the opposite side the remains of the hut still standing, but with its roof sagging under a weight of vegetation. Its base was only a few inches from the edge of the pool.

Then Zeya was at her side, shouting to make himself heard over the noise of the rushing water and the rain.

'Well...where is it then?'

Sandar pointed. 'In the hut over there, under the floor, in a box she told me.'

Zeya peered across the pool, its surface an indistinct boundary between water and air.

'Come on then...show me.'

Sandar hesitated, something telling her to stay on this side of the pool.

'I can't, it's deep, I can't swim.'

Zeya, impatient, stepped down the bank and into the pool. With a glance around at the girl he began to wade across, his eyes fixed on the ruin that contained his future, his dream.

Upstream from the swimming pool where the old tamarind tree lay blocking the watercourse a dam had formed. Vegetation brought down by the enlarged stream had added to the blockage building it higher and higher until a deep long lake formed in the chasm where once a small stream had run. The tree was old, immense, densely branched, but rotten in its core. The pressure on the branch that held it to the side of the gorge built steadily all afternoon as the waters rose, until the inevitable moment came when the wood ceded, splintered, and broke. Like an immense door or lock gate the whole dam pivoted open, and a wall of water was released, sweeping all before it as it tumbled down towards the valley and the town.

Sandar standing irresolutely by the edge of the pool saw Zeya emerge from the hut where he had disappeared a few minutes previously. He carried in his arms a plain wooden box, he carried it lightly, although it had in fact a considerable weight. His face bore an expression of triumph, even ecstasy, and his eyes were fixed on the girl who waited on the other side of the pool.

'I have them.' He shouted, his voice, high pitched, scarcely carrying to her above the noise of the water. 'I have the rubies. I have seen them.'

He entered the pool, lifting the box high above the surface of the water, but half way across he stopped. Staring at the girl a few feet away from him he opened the lid, as if to display the contents.

'It can be yours Sandar.' He screamed the words, 'It can all be yours.'

The ground and the waters of the pool shook, trembled briefly, and then the wall of water burst over the pool. Zeya had time to look around and see his death bearing down upon him before the water buried him, then picked him up, twisted him around in a mad vortex of swirling debris, before carrying him away. He emerged just once before being carried over the edge of the pool, still clutching the box, his eyes wide in disbelief, the box already empty.

Charlie knelt by Jianyu's side trying to stem the flow of blood from the hole in his shoulder with his own shirt he had ripped into pieces. But no matter how hard he pressed upon the wound the cloth came away sodden with blood after only a few seconds. Jianyu's eyes were closed, and he had made no sound since taking the bullet, but then suddenly he groaned, shuddered, and opened his eyes.

'Take it easy, you've been shot...I can't stop the bleeding.'

Jianyu attempted to look down at where Charlie was pressing the cloth to his chest and muttered something in Chinese.

'Bring Myitsu.' He gasped, 'She knows.'

Charlie scrambled to his feet. She knows, he thought, knows what, about medicine perhaps, first aid perhaps, and he shouted her name as he ran up the stairs.

At the top of the stairs there were four doors, three of them open and instinctively Charlie chose the closed one. Without knocking he burst inside, calling, shouting her name.

He stopped, staring at the scene inside. His eyes took in the elegant room, well furnished with quality and taste. There was still a little light from the large bay window, but a three branched candelabrum was lit on the low bedside table.

Myitsu and his father lay entwined on the bed. Her head nestled on his shoulder, her arm around him, while both his arms were wrapped tightly around the slim body that lay half upon him and half at his side. They were quite still.

Charlie tip-toed to the edge of the bed and looked down upon them.

'Dad. Dad.' He spoke quietly, as if afraid to awaken them. But he already knew, knew without observing the stillness of the bodies, the pallor of his fathers face.

He reached down to lay a hand upon his father's where it held the woman. Already cold, unfeeling, gone.

How long he stood there he never knew, but then suddenly Jianyu was at his side, struggling to hold himself upright with a hand clasped to his wound.

Without a word he staggered around the bed to where the table stood. He squatted down next to it and began to examine with deft fingers the articles scattered about its surface; the pipe, the little box that had contained her opium and was now empty, the spirit lamp, the matches. He picked up the little box, probing inside with a finger, then suddenly still.

'What is it, what has she done?' Charlie whispered.

Jianyu turned to look up at him with blind eyes.

'Forgive her Charlie. Forgive them both.'

From far away, across the rain soaked jungle, they heard the rumble of the breaking dam.

Chapter Forty Seven

'Strangest dam story I've ever come across.' Her Majesty's Honorary Consul for mid Burma, or Myanmar as it was now called was seated at a table outside a small cafe not too far from his office in Theik Pan street Mandalay. His office, a large cluttered room, served as both his place of business as well as the consulate, the only concession to the latter being a "*full ceremonial gilded flagpole*" leaning up in the corner, and a faded Foreign Office-issue framed photo of the Queen hanging on the wall. 'And I've heard a few in the years I've been here.' He added.

He was a corpulent man, unsuited one might imagine to life in the tropics, sweating heavily and lean-ing back in a small plastic chair while fanning himself with a worn straw hat. On the other side of the table where two bottles of cold beer were standing in small pools of condensation was the journalist, newly arrived from Bangkok, and charged with reporting on the after effects of the flooding that had struck the country a few months ago. The Honorary Consul, he hoped, would be able to provide him with enough materiel to write an art-icle or two without the necessity of him having to actu-ally go out into the country and search for himself. The unprecedented rains at the beginning of the monsoon season had seriously disrupted the transport system of the country, cutting off large areas, destroying bridges and roads, and making any travel hazardous.

'Been here long then?' The journalist enquired, wondering what could possibly attract someone enough to stay in a country with such a climate, such poverty, and such a repressive regime. As a journalist he knew he would have to be careful, the military government had little time for his profession. He could be expelled on the slightest whim of the authorities, and he had heard of other journalists simply disappearing, questions to the authorities from employers and families unanswered and ignored.

'Too long I guess, nearly twenty years. Can't say I really like it here, but it sort of grows on you.' He said morosely, peering into the neck of his bottle of beer into which a large black fly had just disappeared. 'But married a local gal, couple of kids, they'd never settle back home. Stuck here I guess.'

'And you say it was just after the floods it started, what exactly did happen?'

The waiter appeared with two glasses, but the consul waved him away.

'Probably filthy, you're better drinking from the bottle.' And he took a long slow drink from his, watching with eyes crossed the fly that was now floating inside.

'Started with the phone call, three days after the storm. Absolute chaos here you can't imagine. Lots of local flooding, but nothing compared to the north and east. Death toll into hundreds I shouldn't be surprised. Had this party of university academics from home on a sponsored study tour of some bloody holy site...got caught up in the storm, lost their transport, their guides, my god what a panic...bunch of old women, should never have been allowed out here. Anyway I was rushed off me feet sorting them out when this telephone call comes through, terrible line, could hardly hear a thing. English voice, telling me his father has died, asking what should he do. Well he sounded like he was a thousand miles away so I asked him where he was, and he tells me he's in Mogok. That's M...o...g...o...k.' The journalist had discretely taken out notebook and pencil, he raised his eyes questioningly towards the consul.

'Yes, didn't mean much to me either, might have heard the name but no idea where it was. Had to borrow an atlas from the police to look it up. Anyway, I asked him why he didn't ask his guide, knowing nobody's allowed to wander around here without one, and he tells me he hasn't got one. Thought I'd missheard, so surprised. So I asked him what the hell he was doing without one, and the blighter tells me he was just visiting. By now I'm getting funny feeling about this, and I ask him what his father died of, and he tells me it was a long term illness that suddenly took him. Then while I'm digesting this he asks me about taking his dad's ashes back home, if there were problems with customs here and in UK. I mean what did he take me for, how the hell would I know? The people who come here from home don't up and die very often, in fact it's a first for me. Then, without giving me time to reply he asked me if I can get a passport for his sister, so she can leave with him. Now I start to wonder if he's off his head, drunk or drugged or something, and I point out that she would have given up her passport on arrival in Rangoon, and they'd give it back when she left.' He stared hard at the journalist hoping he was sharing his outrage.

'Quite, I never like doing that myself, but what can you do?'

The consul took another draft from his bottle, apparently forgetting the fly still swimming valiantly around inside it. Putting it down he reached over and grasped the journalist's arm.

'Then just as I thought it couldn't get weirder he replies that she'd never been to Rangoon, or Mandalay even, and had spent her whole life here in Myanmar, she was Burmese in other words. His sister was Burmese. Then he points out, like some sort of sea lawyer that because her father was English, and she was born in a British colony or possession, she had the right to a British passport.'

He let go of the journalist's arm and sat back in his chair allowing him to absorb the enormity of the event.

'Well, like I said, the line was terrible and I could see there was nothing going to be settled on the phone. I had a dead Englishman and a question of nationality to sort out. I'd have to go and see for meself...wherever it was.'

'And where exactly was it?' The journalist asked when the consul showed no signs of continuing his story.

'Well, not all that far I thought at first. When I went to the police station to look at a map, they're the only people supposed to have 'em you know, it didn't look too far, up in the mountains to the north. So I got one of the cops to drive me in the car, the consulate car. And thank god I'd insisted on a Land Rover, ex-army but still a tough old tank.

Took two days. Two whole days can you believe it. Had to sleep in the car in the middle of nowhere, didn't let go of my revolver all night. The flood had carried away most of the bridges you see, and the road into the mountains had about fifty to cross. Listen...can you imagine crossing a gorge five hundred feet deep on two planks? One for each side. Well we had to do that time after time, thought we'd never make it there.' The consul passed a hand across his face as if disturbed greatly by the memory.

'But you made it in the end?' Prompted the journalist not looking up but scribbling furiously in his pad. 'And found your orphaned Englishman?'

'Straight away, absolutely no problem even though the town had been half destroyed in the floods.

Just asked the first person we saw, pointed us straight to the place.'

'A hotel?'

'Hotel! No way. That would have been too normal. No, this guy with his dead father and Burmese sister and dead mother, yes, there was a dead woman involved too, luckily Burmese not English, were residing in fine old house just outside the town. The old government lodge that they used to call bungalows in the old Empire days. Put there for visiting Europeans, government officials, tax collectors and the like. And the sister and her mother had been there since the war can you believe it, completely forgotten by the administration, both Burmese and British apparently.

Nice enough fellow he turned out to be, the son, understood immediately my problem. The two Brits had no papers of course, and neither did the sister. Nothing...not a scrap. So only their word to go on. Oh! And I forgot to mention the Chinaman.'

'The Chinaman?'

The consul lifted his bottle and drained it, the journalist noting that the fly had disappeared with the beer.

'I say, having another? Got a bloody thirst up with all this talking.'

The journalist nodded and the consul bellowed for the waiter.

'Yes, there was a shot and blind Chink being looked after by them in the house too. Shot in the shoulder, but not too badly thank god, or there might have been even more problems. Told me it was an accident, cleaning his gun. But you tell me what a blind Chink is doing with a loaded gun? Bloody ridiculous, but I didn't want to get involved with that as well.'

'The police were not informed?'

'That's another thing, the two town cops had died in the floods, only one body found apparently. So the place was sort of running itself. The local school teacher seemed to be the only one organising anything.'

'So what did you do about it? Could you get them out?'

'Now normally I'd have passed it over to the Embassy in Rangoon, told them to sort it out. But with the problems of travel and communications after the flood I could see it would drag on for months, and I guessed they didn't have money to hang around here. So had to do something, but couldn't decide what. See, the problem was the girl, I couldn't imagine the Myanmar authorities giving her an exit visa on her passport when she didn't even have one. And in any case I didn't know if she'd be let into the UK without anything to prove her story. But the young man insisted he wouldn't leave without her. You see the problem don't you?'

The journalist nodded, looking up from his pad.

'Absolutely, a tricky one for you.' He murmured.

The consul lent forward across the table, looking right and left as if afraid to be overheard.

'Now this is strictly between you and me, understand? No names no pack drill, got it?'

'Count on me.' Affirmed the journalist, hoping it was something he could use.

'I told them I'd get them out, but not overtly. I'd get a guide to take them across the border into Thailand. I knew a man and a place. Done it before a couple of times, asked by the Embassy in Rangoon, you know, intelligence types, spies in other words.' He put a finger to his lips and winked.

'Gave them a letter to Richardson, the Ambassador in Bangkok, asked him to help them out with papers. He's an old friend from way back, always flexible about rules and regulations, that's why he's so popular with the Thais.'

'So they got out OK?'

'I came back to Mandalay, organised it from here. The guide picked them up about a week after my visit and the next I heard, a couple of months later, they were safely back home.'

'The Chinaman too?'

'Christ! No! That would have been asking too much. Now this you can print if you like...I looked into the position of the lodge they were living in, and it turned out it was legally still the property of the Crown under the terms of the independence agreement. The Chink fellow didn't want to move to UK in any case so I told him he could stay there as a sort of house keeper, look after the place like. When he was up and around again of course. Said he was going to get a woman from the village to come and help. So that was sorted out.'

'And that's the end of the story? Did you hear anything after from them?'

The consul grinned, as if party to some amusing secret.

'Oh! Yes, I did. I heard from the Customs and Excise at Southampton where they arrived. Telegram asking if I knew anything about them, made the news back home apparently.'

'In what way?'

'Ha! You'd never guess. Well, going through customs they had the cask with the father and mother's ashes, they'd been cremated together, well, the customs guy asked me about them. Now British customs being what they are, nosey and suspicious, looked into the cask, poked around a bit, and found rubies. A small fortune in uncut rubies. Now apparently there's no restrictions or duty on cut or uncut gems imported into the uk, as long as they're not stolen of course. Their story, quite credible really, was that the father, who had worked in the ruby mine in Mogok before the war, had been given them by the boss for safe keeping when the Japs invaded. And his girlfriend or partner, what have you, had kept them hidden ever since. The mining company had gone out of business during the war so had no claim on them, and even the government couldn't find a reason to grab them for unpaid taxes or anything as the company had been solvent until its closure. Their little nest egg was worth at least a million they estimated, but they wanted to know from me if I thought there was any reason to dispute the story. Well, I told them it was possible, quite possible, and it was damn lucky the Myanmar authorities didn't get wind of it, because they come down hard on that sort of thing. The most extraordinary things do happen in this country you know, most extraordinary.'

'I can well believe it.' Said the journalist, putting away his note pad and wondering at the same time if he could make a credible story out of it all. It just seemed a bit too fantastic, too unlikely, but extraordinary things did happen from time to time he had to admit.

Chapter Forty Eight

'It's so long since I did this I'm not sure I can remember the words.' The Reverend Sprout admitted to his wife as she was helping him into his robes.

'Nonsense Jacob, it will all come back to you once you start.'

They were both in the vestry of St. Mary's Paddington where the minister was to join Charlie Gibson in marriage to Sandar Drake.

It was six months since the young couple returned to England on the SS Southern Cross after a long and leisurely voyage via Bangkok, Calcutta, Aden, Suez, and Marseille. The voyage had given both of them time to come to terms with the new situation in their lives. They had both lost a parent, and Sandar especially had been hard hit when that terrible day of the flood had climaxed in the horror of finding both her mother and newly found father dead, and her adopted father Jianyu wounded. After the terror of watching Zeya being swept away in the flood she had managed to struggle back to the house in a state of shock. That Zeya was gone made little impression on her, but the manner of his death, that last view of him still clutching the empty strong box, his eyes wild, unbelieving, as the waters closed over him, was burned into her memory. And the rubies were lost. Gone forever the treasure of her father, the secret of her mother.

When she had made the old Chinaman as comfortable as possible, it was in Charlie's arms she had sought refuge and solace, and they had clung together through the night of the storm until dawn and clearing skies allowed a cleansed and welcome sun to rise over the steaming mountains and the flooded town.

It was during that long and healing voyage as the ship ploughed a perfectly straight furrow across a flat blue sea that seemed to have no boundary that they grew to know each other. They talked for hours, very much apart from the other passengers even at lunch and dinner where they sat opposite each other, oblivious to the chatter around them, their eyes locked on each other, as if afraid to look away lest some spell might be broken. Then there were the nights where they would stand by the rail looking up at the velvet black sky where a thousand distant worlds were the only witnesses to their growing affection, an affection that became a love, and a love that was consummated as their ship crossed the Red Sea. Fate had thrown them together, and Sandar had always believed implicitly in fate.

The rising strains of the organ came through the door.

'Time to go.' Whispered Jacob. Maureen patted his shoulder as he made his way into the church.

'You'll do them proud Jacob, and they deserve our prayers.'

Jacob took a deep breath and walked out in front of the small congregation, where Charlie stood, nervously fiddling in his pocket, next to his best man. The organ music stopped, then started again with the wedding march, and all heads turned as Sandar appeared to a collective gasp of appreciation. At Sandar's side Lydia walked, accepting, even loving the daughter of her husband as her own.

Later, as Jacob spoke and Charlie repeated the well remembered words...*with this ring,* the three of them looked down at the simple gold ring he slid over her long slim finger. A plain gold ring with just one quite small but perfect ruby, a ruby brought to this place in the dust of her parents, a little sister to the one she wore on her other hand, her mother's ring, the treasure of the mine.

The End

ABOUT THE AUTHOR

Vernon Dewhurst is a former professional photographer having worked in London, Dublin, Paris, and the Far East. Lately he returned to University to take a BA
and began writing. He has published a book of short stories, *Strange Tales*, and a novel *Joanne*. He lives outside London with his French wife and is working on a sequel to Rubies in the Dust.

Also by Vernon Dewhurst

.

Printed in Great Britain
by Amazon

75505894R00251